THE

APOLLO

MURDERS

THE
APOLLO
MURDERS

CHRIS
HADFIELD

Quercus

First published in Great Britain in 2021 by

Quercus Editions Ltd
Carmelite House
50 Victoria Embankment
London EC4Y 0DZ

An Hachette UK company

A CIP catalogue record for this book is available
from the British Library

HB ISBN 978 1 52940 685 6
TPB ISBN 978 1 52940 682 5

10 9 8 7 6 5 4 3 2 1

Printed and bound in Great Britain by Clays Ltd, Elcograf S.p.A.

Papers used by Quercus are from well-managed forests and other responsible sources.

To Helene
who hand-built the multicolored desk on which this book was written,
as well as our entire life together

Many of these people are real. Much of this actually happened.

PROLOGUE

Chesapeake Bay, 1968

I lost my left eye on a beautiful autumn morning with not a cloud in the sky.

I was flying an F-4 Phantom, a big, heavy jet fighter nicknamed the Double Ugly, with the nose section newly modified to hold reconnaissance cameras. The nose cone was now bulbous, which meant the air flowed differently around it, so I was taking it on a test flight over the Chesapeake Bay to recalibrate the speed sensing system.

I loved flying the Phantom. Pushing forward on the throttles created an instantaneous powerful thrust into my back, and pulling back steadily on the control stick arced the jet's nose up into the eternal blue. I felt like I was piloting some great winged dinosaur, laughing with effortless grace and freedom in three dimensions.

But today I was staying down close to the water to measure exactly how fast I was going. By comparing what my cockpit dials showed with the readouts from the technicians recording my pass from the shoreline, we could update the airplane's instruments to tell the truth of the new nose shape.

I pushed the small knob under my left thumb and said into my oxygen mask, "Setting up for the final pass, 550 knots."

The lead engineer's voice crackled right back through my helmet's earpieces. "Roger, Kaz, we're ready."

I twisted my head hard to spot the line-up markers, big orange reflective triangles on posts sticking up out of the water. I rolled the Phantom to the left, pulled to turn and align with the proper ground track, and pushed the throttles forward, just short of afterburner, to set speed at 550 knots. Nine miles a minute, or almost 1,000 feet with every tick of my watch's second hand.

The shoreline trees on my right were a blur as I eased the jet lower over the bay. I needed to cross in front of the measuring cameras at exactly 50 feet above the water. A very quick glance showed my speed at 540 and my altitude at 75, so I added a titch of power and eased the stick forward a hair before leveling off. As the first marker raced up and flicked past under my nose I pushed the button, and said, "Ready."

"Roger" came back.

As I was about to mark the crossing of the second tower, I saw the seagull.

Just a white-gray speck, but dead ahead. My first instinct was to push forward on the stick so I would miss it, but at 50 feet above the water, that would be a bad idea. My fist and arm muscles clenched, freezing the stick.

The seagull saw what was about to happen and, calling on millions of years of evolved avian instinct, dove to avoid danger, but it was too late. I was moving far faster than any bird.

We hit.

The technicians in the measuring tower were so tightly focused on their sighting equipment they didn't notice. They briefly wondered why I hadn't called "Ready" a second time and then "Mark" as I crossed the third tower, but they sat back from their instruments as the lead engineer calmly transmitted, "That's the last data point, Kaz. Nice flying. See you at the debrief."

In the cockpit, the explosion was stupendous. The gull hit just ahead and left of me, shattering the acrylic plastic canopy like a grenade. The 550-mile-an-hour wind, full of seagull guts and plexiglas shards, hit my chest and face full force, slamming me back against the ejection seat, then blowing me around in my harness like a ragdoll. I couldn't see a thing, blindly easing back on the stick to get up and away from the water.

My head was ringing from what felt like a hard punch in my left eye. I blinked fast to try to clear my vision, but I still couldn't see. As the jet climbed, I pulled the throttles back to midrange to slow down, and leaned forward against my straps to get my face out of the pummeling wind, reaching up with one hand to clear the guck out of my eyes. I wiped hard, left and right, clearing my right eye enough for me to glimpse the horizon. The Phantom was rolling slowly to the right, and still climbing. I moved the control stick to level off, wiped my eyes again, and glanced down at my glove. The light brown leather was soaked in fresh, red blood.

I bet that's not all from the seagull.

I yanked off the glove to feel around my face, fighting the buffeting wind. My right eye seemed normal, but my numb left cheek felt torn, and I couldn't see anything out of my left eye, which was now hurting like hell.

My thick green rubber oxygen mask was still in place over my nose and mouth, held there by the heavy jawline clips on my helmet. But my dark green visor was gone, lost somehow in the impact and the wind. I reached back and pivoted my helmet forward, wiggling and recentering it. I needed to talk to somebody, and fast.

"Mayday, Mayday, Mayday!" I yelled, mashing down the comm button with a thumb slippery with blood. "This is Phantom 665. I've had a birdstrike. Canopy's broken." I couldn't see well enough to change the radio frequency, and hoped the crew in the observation tower was still listening. The roar in the cockpit was so loud I couldn't hear any response.

Alternately wiping the blood that kept filling my right eye socket and jamming the heel of my hand hard into my left, I found I could see enough to fly. I looked at the Chesapeake shoreline below me to get my bearings. The mouth of the Potomac was a distinctive shape under my left wing, and I used it to turn towards base, up the Maryland shore to the familiar safety of the runways at Patuxent River Naval Air Station.

The bird had hit the left side of the Phantom, so I knew some of the debris from the collision might have been sucked into that engine, damaging it. I strained to see the instruments—at least I couldn't see any yellow caution lights. *One engine's enough anyway*, I thought, and started to set up for landing.

When I leaned hard to the left, the slipstream blew across my face, keeping the blood from running into my good eye. I shouted again into my mask: "Mayday, Mayday, Mayday, Phantom 665's lining up for an emergency straight-in full stop, runway 31." Hoping someone was listening, and that other jets were getting out of my way.

As Pax River neared I pulled my hand away from my left eye and yanked the throttles to idle, to slow enough to drop the landing gear. The airspeed indicator was blurry too, but when I guessed the needle was below 250 knots I grabbed the big red gear knob and slammed it down. The Phantom made the normal clunking and shuddering vibrations as the wheels lowered and locked into place. I reached hard left and slapped the flaps and slats down.

The wind in the cockpit was still my own personal tornado. I kept leaning left, took one last swipe at my right eye to clear the blood, set the throttles about two-thirds back, jammed my palm back into my bleeding left eye socket, and lined up.

The F-4 has small bright lights by the windscreen that glow red when you're at the right angle for landing, and it also sounds a reassuring steady tone to say you're on-speed. I blessed the McDonnell Aircraft engineers for their thoughtfulness as I clumsily set up on final. My depth perception was all messed up, so I aimed about a third of the way down the runway and judged the rate of descent as best I could. The ground on either side of the runway came rushing up and slam! I was down, yanking the throttle to idle and pulling up on the handle to release the drag chute, squinting like hell to try to keep the Phantom somewhere near the middle of the runway.

I pulled the stick all the way back into my lap to help air-drag the 17-ton jet to a stop, pushing hard on the wheel brakes, trying to bring the far end of the runway into focus. It looked like it was coming up too fast, so I stood on the brakes, yanking against the leverage of the stick.

And suddenly it was over. The jet lurched to a stop, the engines were at idle, and I saw yellow fire trucks pulling onto the runway, racing towards me. Someone must have heard my radio calls. As the trucks pulled up I swapped hands on my injured eye, reached down to the throttles, raised the finger lifts and shut off both engines.

I leaned back against the ejection seat and closed my good eye. As the adrenaline left my body, excruciating pain took over, a searing fire centered in my left eye socket. The rest of me was numb, nauseous, soaking wet, totally limp.

The fire chief's ladder rattled against the side of the Phantom. And then I heard his voice next to me.

"Holy Christ," he said.

TO

THE

MOON

1

Houston, January 1973

Flat.

Flat, as far as the eye could see.

The plane had just descended below cloud and the hazy, humid South Texas air made the distances look shorter somehow. Kaz leaned forward to get a good look at his new posting. He'd been in the Boeing 727 seat for nearly four hours and his neck cracked as he craned it. Underneath him was a waterway snaking through an industrial maze of petroleum refineries and waterside cranes. His forehead touched the window as he tipped his head to track where it flowed into Galveston Bay, a glistening expanse of oily brown water that fed into the Gulf of Mexico, fuzzily visible on the horizon through the smog.

Not a garden spot.

As the plane descended towards the runway, he noticed each small correction the pilots made, silently evaluating their landing as the tires squawked onto the runway at Houston Intercontinental Airport. *Not bad.*

The Avis rental car was ready for him. He heaved his overfilled suitcase and satchel into the trunk, and carefully set his guitar on top. "I have too much gear," he muttered, but Houston was going to be home for a few months, so he'd packed what he figured he'd need.

Kaz glanced at his watch, now on Central time—midday Sunday traffic should be light—and climbed in. As he turned the key, he noticed the name of the model on the key fob. He smiled. They'd rented him a silver Plymouth Satellite.

The accident hadn't only cost Kaz an eye. Without binocular vision, he'd lost his medical as both a test pilot and an astronaut selectee who'd been assigned to fly on MOL, the military's planned Manned Orbiting Laboratory spy space station. His work and dreams had disappeared in a bloody flurry of feathers.

The Navy had sent him to postgraduate school to heal and to study space-borne electro-optics, and then used his analysis expertise inside National Security and Central Intelligence. He'd enjoyed the complexity of the work, applying his insight to help shape policy, but had watched with quiet envy as former military pilots flew on Apollo missions and walked on the Moon.

Yet Washington's ever-changing politics had now brought him here to Houston. President Richard Nixon was feeling the heat in an election year; some districts felt they'd already won the space race, and inflation and unemployment had both been rising. The Department of Defense was on Nixon's back, with uncertain direction as the Vietnam War was ending, and they were still incensed that he had canceled MOL. The National Reconnaissance Office had assured Nixon that their new Gambit-3 Key Hole satellites could take spy pictures better and more cheaply than astronauts on a space station.

But Nixon was a career politician, and easily found the advantageous middle ground: give the American public one more Moon flight, and let the Department of Defense and its vast budgetary resources pay the cost.

With DoD money behind it, Apollo 18 was redesignated as America's first all-military spaceflight, and its classified purpose was given to the

US Air Force to decide. Given his rare combination of test flying, MOL training and Washington intelligence work, the Navy sent Kaz to Texas to be the crew military liaison.

To keep an eye on things.

As he cruised south on I-45, Kaz was tempted to drive directly to NASA's Manned Spacecraft Center for a look, but instead he headed a bit farther west. Before leaving Washington, he'd made some phone calls and found a place to rent that sounded better than good, near a town called Pearland. He followed the signs towards Galveston, then turned off the big highway at the exit to FM 528.

The land was just as flat as it had seemed from the air, with mud-green cow pasture on both sides of the two-lane road, no gas stations, and no traffic. The sign for his turnoff was so small he almost missed it: Welcome to Polly Ranch Estates.

He followed the unpaved road, his tires crunching on crushed shells. There was a quick rumbling rhythm as the Plymouth crossed a cattle gate set in the road, aligned with a rusted barbed-wire fence strung left and right into the distance. Peering ahead, he saw two lone houses built on small rises in the ground, a pickup truck parked in front of the nearest one. He pulled into the other driveway, glanced in the rear-view mirror to make sure his glass eye was in straight, and opened the door. Stiff, he arched his back as he stood, stretching for a three-count. Too many years sitting on hard ejection seats.

The two houses were new, ranch-style bungalows, but with oddly high, wide garages. Kaz looked left and right—the road was arrow straight for several thousand feet. *Perfect*.

He headed for the house with the pickup, and as he took the stairs to the front door, it opened. A compact, muscular man in a faded green Ban-Lon golf shirt, blue jeans and pointed brown boots stepped out. Maybe mid-fifties, hair cut close in a graying crew cut, face seaming early with age. Had to be his new landlord, Frank Thompson, who'd said on the phone that he'd been an Avenger pilot in the Pacific theater and was now an airline captain with Continental.

"You Kaz Zemeckis?"

Kaz nodded.

"I'm Frank," he said, and held out his hand. "Welcome to Polly Ranch! You found us okay?"

Kaz shook the man's hand. "Yes, thanks. Your directions were good."

"Hold on a sec," Frank said and disappeared into his house. He came back out holding up a shiny bronze-colored key, then led the way down the steps and across the new grass between the houses. He unlocked Kaz's front door, stepped back, and held out the key to Kaz, letting him enter first.

A long, sloping ceiling joining the living room, dining area and kitchen. Saltillo tile floors, lots of windows front and back, dark paneling throughout, and a hallway leading off to the left, presumably to bedrooms. There was still a slight varnish smell in the air. It was fully furnished, perfect for his needs. Kaz liked it, and said so.

"Let's go have a look at the best room in the house," Frank said. He walked to the far end of the living room, opened an oversized wooden door and clicked on the lights.

They stepped into a full-sized hangar—50 feet wide, 60 deep, with a 14-foot ceiling. There were garage doors front and back, racks of fluorescent lights above, and a smooth-poured concrete floor. In the middle of it, spotless under the lights, was an orange-and-white, all-metal Cessna 170B, sitting lightly on its cantilever front gear and tailwheel.

"Frank, that's a beautiful plane. You sure you trust me to fly it?"

"With your background, no question. Want to take it up for a check-out now?"

The only answer to that question was yes.

After Frank pushed a button to open the garage doors, Kaz tucked his rental car into the side of the hangar, and they pushed the Cessna out and down onto the road.

They did a quick walkaround together. Kaz checked the oil, drained a bit of gas into a clear tube to check for water and carefully poured it out on a weed growing by the roadside. They climbed in and Frank talked him through the simple checklist, getting the engine started, watching pressures and temps, checking the controls. Kaz back-taxied to the far end of the road, where it led into a stand of trees. A touch of left brake and extra power and the plane snapped around smartly, lining up with the long, skinny runway.

Kaz checked the mags, and then raised his eyebrows expectantly at Frank, who nodded. Pushing the throttle smoothly all the way to the stop, Kaz checked the gauges, his feet dancing on the rudder pedals, keeping the plane exactly in the middle of the 20-foot-wide pavement. He rocked his head and upper body constantly left and right, so he could see the runway edges on both sides with his good eye. He held the control wheel full forward to raise the tail, then eased it gently back; the 170 lifted off effortlessly at 55 miles per hour. They were flying.

"Where to?" he asked, shouting slightly over the motor noise. Frank waved forward and to the right, and Kaz banked away from the two houses and headed east. He followed FM 528 back across I-45, and saw Galveston Bay for the second time that day, brown on the horizon.

"That's where you're going to be working!" Frank shouted, pointing ahead to the left. Kaz glanced through his side window, and for the first time, saw NASA's Manned Spacecraft Center—home of the Apollo program, astronaut training and Mission Control. It was far bigger than he'd expected—hundreds of acres of empty pasture stretching off to the west, and dozens of rectangular white and pale-blue buildings surrounded by parking lots, mostly empty since it was the weekend. In the middle was a long green park, crisscrossed with walking paths joining all the surrounding buildings and dotted with circular ponds.

"Looks like a college campus," he yelled at Frank.

"They designed it that way so they could give it back to Rice University when the Moon landings ended," Frank shouted back.

Not so fast, Kaz thought. If he did his job right and Apollo 18 went well, the Air Force might talk Nixon into flying Apollo 19 too.

———

Kaz pulled the throttle to idle, cut the mixture, and the Cessna's engine coughed and quit, the wooden propeller suddenly visible in front of them. The click of switches was unnaturally loud as Kaz shut off the electrics.

"Sweet plane, Frank," he said.

"You fly it better than I do. That's a skinny runway, and you made it look simple, first try. Glad she'll be getting some extra use—I'm away too much. Better for the engine."

Frank showed Kaz where the fuel tank sat against the side of the garage, and they dragged the long hose inside and topped off the wing tanks. There was a clipboard hanging on a hook just inside the door, and Kaz recorded date, flight time and fuel used. They both looked over at the silent plane, sharing an unspoken moment of appreciation for the joy of flight. Since becoming a pilot, Kaz felt he never really understood a place until he'd seen the lay of the land from the air, like a living map below him. It was as if the third dimension added a key piece, building an intuitive sense of proportion in his head.

Frank said, "I'll leave you to get settled," and headed back to his place. Kaz lowered the garage door behind him and unloaded the car.

He lugged his heavy suitcase down the L-shaped hallway and set it on the bed in the largest bedroom, pleased to see that it was king-sized. A glance to the left showed a big attached bathroom.

Feeling oddly like he had checked into a hotel, he unzipped the suitcase and started putting things away. He hung up his two suits, one gray, one black, plus a checked sport jacket, in the closet. Did the same with a half-dozen collared shirts, white and light blue, slacks, two ties. One pair of dress shoes, one pair of Adidas. Casual clothes and PT gear went into the lowboy dresser, along with socks and undershorts. Two novels and his traveling alarm clock on the bedside table. Shaving kit and eyeball care bag on the bathroom counter.

The last items in the suitcase were his faded orange US Navy flight suit and leather boots. He touched the black-and-white shoulder patch— the grinning skull and crossbones of the VF-84 Jolly Rogers, from his time flying F-4s off the USS *Independence* aircraft carrier. Just below it was sewn the much more formal crest of the USN Test Pilot School, where he had graduated top of his class. He rubbed a thumb across the gold of his naval aviator wings—a hard-earned, permanent measure of himself—then lifted the flight suit out, threaded the hanger into the arms, hung it in the closet and tucked his brown lace-up flight boots underneath.

The rattling bedside alarm woke him, his glass eye feeling gritty as he blinked at the sunrise. His first morning on the Texas Gulf Coast.

Kaz rolled out of bed and padded to the bathroom on the stone floor, cold under his bare feet. He relieved himself and then looked in the mirror, assessing what he saw. Six foot, 173 pounds (*need to buy a scale*), dark chest hair, pale skin. His parents were Lithuanian Jews who had fled the rising threat of Nazi Germany, emigrating to New York when Kaz was an infant. His face was like his dad's: broad forehead, big ears, a wide jaw leading to a slightly cleft chin. Thick dark eyebrows above pale-blue eyes, one real, one fake. The ocularist had done a nice job of matching the color. He turned his head to the right and leaned closer, pulling down slightly on the skin of his cheek. The scars were there, but mostly faded. After several surgeries (*five? six?*), the plastic surgeon had rebuilt the eye socket and cheekbone to a near-perfect match.

Good enough for government work.

He methodically went through his morning ritual, five minutes of stretching, sit-ups, back extensions and push-ups, straining his body until his muscles squawked. You get out of it what you put into it.

Feeling looser, he showered and shaved, and brushed his teeth. He rummaged in his eye bag, pulled out a small squeeze bottle and leaned back to put a few artificial tears into his fake eye. He blinked at himself rapidly, his good eye staring back with 20/12 vision.

That impressed them a long time ago during aircrew selection. *Eye like a hawk.*

2

Manned Spacecraft Center

"Houston, we have an electrical problem in the LM." Apollo Lunar Module Pilot Luke Hemming's voice was measured, calmly reporting the crisis he was observing.

"Roger, Luke, we're looking at it." The Capsule Communicator's voice, coming from Mission Control in Building 30 at the Manned Spacecraft Center, was equally calm, matching Luke's dispassionate urgency.

On the instrument panel in front of Luke, the Master Alarm light glowed bright red next to the window, where he couldn't miss it during their upcoming landing on the Moon. He pushed the red light in to extinguish it, resetting it for subsequent failures. Several multicolored lights were still illuminated on the Caution and Warning panel.

"What are you seeing, Luke?" Mission Commander Tom Hoffman leaned across to have a look, their shoulders touching in the confined cockpit.

"I think it's a bad voltage sensor," Luke said. "Volts show zero/off scale low, but amps look good." Tom peered around him at the gauges, and nodded.

The crew was hot mic, so the CAPCOM heard them. "Roger, Luke, we concur. Continue with Trans-Lunar Coast Activation."

Tom and Luke carried on bringing the lunar lander to life, taking advantage of what would be the relatively quiet three days after launch, during which they'd travel across the 240,000 miles of space between the Earth and the Moon.

Luke slid his pencil out of his shoulder pocket and made a quick note on the small notepad he'd clipped to the panel. He was tracking the failures as they accumulated; maintaining a running tally was the only way to keep it all straight in his head, especially as multiple systems failed. The Apollo 13 explosion had reinforced just how complicated the spaceship was, and how quickly things could go seriously wrong.

Tom checked his own handwritten list. "So, I see a sticky cabin dump valve, a misconfigured circuit breaker, failed biomed telemetry, and now a bad voltage sensor. I think we're still GO to continue with the full flight plan. Houston, you concur?"

"Roger, *Bulldog*, we'll watch that voltage and likely have some steps for you to take later, but you're still on track for lunar insertion and landing." Luke, a Marine Corps captain, had been the one to nickname the tough little spaceship "Bulldog" after the Marine Corps longtime mascot.

Tom and Luke finished the TLC checklist, deactivated the LM, and exited through the tunnel, closing the hatch behind them.

Michael Esdale, in his pilot seat in the Command Module, greeted them with a broad smile. He was the one who would be orbiting the Moon while Tom and Luke went down to the surface. "I'd about given up on you two," he said. "I made snacks, figuring you might be hungry after all that heavy switch throwing."

Tom squeezed past Michael into his seat on the left, while Luke settled in on Michael's right.

"How's *Pursuit* doing?" Tom asked.

"Ticking like a Timex," Michael answered. A US Navy test pilot, Michael had been the one to name the Command Module. As the world's first Black astronaut, he had decided to honor the WW2 Black fighter pilots, the Tuskegee Airmen, and their unit, the 99th Pursuit Squadron.

"These snacks are . . . simple," Luke said, popping a Ritz cracker with a square of cheese on top into his mouth.

"NASA's version of shit on a shingle," Michael said. "Maybe some Tang to wash it down?" Despite the TV ads, astronauts hadn't drunk Tang in space since Gemini in the mid-1960s. One of the early astronauts had vomited Tang during space motion sickness, and reported that it tasted even worse coming back up.

Tom pushed the transmit button. "What next, Houston?"

"Take a fifteen-minute bathroom break while we reset the sim. We'll pick up again in the Prep for Lunar Orbit Insertion."

"Sounds good," Tom replied. He pushed a small knob on his wrist-watch and the Apollo 18 crew clambered out of the Command Module simulator.

Kaz, who was watching them on the multiple consoles in the instructor station in the adjoining room, had allowed himself only a moment to think that it might have been him in that sim, prepping for Apollo 18. He'd flown with Luke and Michael, all test pilots together, out of Patuxent River; until the accident, he'd seen them nearly every day, and gone for a beer with them most nights. As he watched the experts create one malfunction after another for the crew to deal with — before the launch, it was crucial that Tom, Luke and Michael see all the possible things that could go wrong and learn how to deal with them — he felt a little rueful that he was about to throw them the biggest mission curve ball ever.

After the bathroom break he saw Michael and Luke head directly back to the sim, but Tom stopped for a quick check-in with the instructors. When he spotted Kaz, he came directly to him, a big smile on his face. "Well look who the cat dragged in! Kazimieras Zemeckis! You're even uglier than I remember."

Kaz shook his hand, smiling back. He didn't know Tom as well as the other two, but they'd been classmates in the same Test Pilot School group at Edwards Air Force Base in California's Mojave Desert. "Good to see you, Tom," he said. "You three are doing good work together."

"Yeah, we're getting there. These torturers here are making sure of that."

Kaz said, "I need to talk with you all after the sim." He paused. "Update from Washington."

Tom's forehead furrowed. He didn't like surprises, especially as the crew commander. He looked at his watch, and then nodded, curtly. "Okay. But time to head back in now. See you at the debrief."

As Kaz left the sim and walked out of Building 5, he had to stop for a moment to get his bearings. He looked at the parking lot ahead and the nine-story rectangular building on his right, and matched it with what he'd seen while flying over in the Cessna. He turned right across the open central quadrangle and headed towards the Mission Control Center.

From the outside, MCC looked like just another three-story block of stuccoed cement, with windows tinted dark against the Texas sun. He followed the path around to the entrance, where the architect had made a perfunctory effort to give the nation what they expected of their space program—angular concrete forms stuck onto the postmodern Brutalist cubes. *Government ugly.*

He reached into his sport jacket pocket to retrieve the new NASA ID badge he'd been issued that morning. A guard sitting in front of three heavy silver doors took it from him, checked the building access code and handed it back.

"Welcome to MCC," he said pleasantly, pushing a button. The clunk was loud as the nearest door unlocked. *Like a bank vault*, Kaz thought. *Let's see what valuables they're keeping inside.*

The immediate interior was as underwhelming as the exterior. Gray, fluorescent-lit corridors, functional linoleum and fading prints of the Earth and Moon in cheap black frames on the walls. Kaz followed the arrows on the small signs saying MCC. One of the two elevators had an Out of Order sign on it, so he looked around and took the stairs.

He showed his badge to another seated guard, who nodded and pointed with his thumb at the solid-looking door behind him. Kaz gave it a push, and then pushed harder at the unexpected weight. He closed it carefully behind him, trying not to make much noise. He was suddenly inside the hub of manned spaceflight, and the experts were at work.

He'd entered a room of pale-green consoles, each stacked progressively higher, like in a theater. The workstations all faced the three big screens on Kaz's left, glowing with yellow-orange hieroglyphics of numbers, acronyms and schematics. Behind each console Kaz could see a face, lit up by the displays, hazed by cigarette smoke. Each specialist was wearing a half headset, so they could hear both the radio conversation and the voices around them. Mission emblems of previous spaceflights, all the way back to Gemini 4, hung on the walls.

Kaz stood watching the Flight Control team as they communicated with the Apollo 18 crew, now back at work in Building 5. He spotted a familiar face, a fellow test pilot who raised a hand to wave Kaz over. He threaded his way up the tiered levels, trying not to disturb the concentration of the flight controllers.

Kaz ended up behind the CAPCOM console, where he shook hands with Chad Miller, the backup commander of Apollo 18.

"Welcome to Houston," Chad said softly. "You were over with the crew?"

Kaz nodded. "They're doing good."

The two men watched the room work for a minute. A cartoon-like graphic of *Pursuit* was projected on the big center screen up front. The ship was about to disappear behind the Moon, so Chad asked, "Need a coffee?" Kaz nodded, and the two quietly worked their way out of the room.

Chad Miller, like the rest of the Apollo 18 prime and backup crew-members, was a military test pilot. Clear blue eyes, sandy-brown hair, square shoulders filling his short-sleeved sky-blue polo shirt, tucked in smoothly at the narrow waist of his compact body. Gray slacks, brown belt, brown loafers. His strong hands and forearms flexed as he poured coffee into two white-enameled mugs. He wore his oversized Air Force–issued watch on his left wrist.

"Cream or sugar?"

"Black, thanks."

Chad handed him his cup and led him to a small briefing room, where he and Kaz leaned easily on the long table, catching up. They knew each other somewhat from test pilot days, but Chad had worked at Edwards and Kaz at Patuxent River, so they'd never flown together. Chad had a reputation in the small community as a superb pilot, the consummate stick-and-rudder man, with an unforgiving intolerance of incompetence in himself and others. It was a trait shared by many astronauts, and Kaz respected him for it—someone who could get shit done.

At a pause in conversation, Kaz posed the question that everyone asked the backup crew. "Think you'll fly?"

"Nah, Tom's just too damned healthy." Chad laughed. "And it looks like 18 will be the last Apollo. My last chance to walk on the Moon. I've wanted to do that ever since I was a kid."

Kaz nodded. "I know that feeling. But my days of flying any kind of high-performance machine are done—the Navy prefers a pilot with two eyes."

"Makes sense, I guess. Hopefully NASA will let you fly backseat T-38 while you're here."

Kaz agreed, then leaned to glance out the open door, making sure no one was listening in the hallway.

"You coming to the debrief after the sim?"

Chad nodded.

"There's something we've all got to talk about." Kaz paused. "The Russians have been busy."

3

East Berlin, 1957

The Russian Orthodox cathedral's vestry was cold. Father Hieromonk Ilarion shifted his weight and hitched up the shoulders of his robes to cover the back of his neck, grateful for the extra layer of long underwear he'd decided to put on that morning.

Sitting on a high stool, the weak winter light shining through the nearby stained-glass window, Father Ilarion carried on with his scrutiny of the US Army's partial listing of War Children—German orphans who had been adopted by American soldiers after World War II.

The process of obtaining this mimeographed copy of the list had frustrated even the patience of a hieromonk—over a year of navigating foreign military bureaucracy and its confidentiality concerns. Ilarion had written nine separate letters, each carefully translated for him by an English-speaking junior lector at the cathedral, and he had gone twice in person to meet with the ecumenical cleric at US Mission Berlin. A complicating factor was the Americans' unspoken embarrassment that their conquering soldiers had fathered thousands of illegitimate children in

Germany. As US-Soviet tensions in Berlin heightened, it had only gotten harder to maneuver.

Finally, the list had arrived in the post. But when he'd opened the US government envelope, his heart beating fast, he'd been disappointed to see that the personal details of the adoptive families had been blacked out. Now he sipped his tea and slowly ran his thumb down every page, taking his time, carefully considering each name, trying to pick up the trail that had gone so cold in the dozen years since 1945.

Every morning Ilarion gave thanks in his prayers for his new life as hieromonk; a simple, quiet and deeply contemplative existence that was a bulwark against his harsh childhood in war-torn Berlin and his firsthand experience of the atrocities that people could commit. Still, he felt deeply guilty about losing his brother. He had let down his dead parents by failing to take care of the little boy, and he wanted to find him, and if he needed help, to give it to him.

With his rudimentary English he was able at least to puzzle out the meaning of each column: name, sex, age, hair and eye color, date of birth if known, and date and place of adoption. Many of the children had been so young that all that was listed was a first name or no name at all. The saving grace was that before the war there hadn't been that large a Russian population living in Berlin—mostly émigrés who had fled the Communists, like his own parents. He silently thanked them for giving their sons traditional Russian names. It should be relatively easy to find a "Yuri" on a list with many boys named Hans or Wilhelm, though the names weren't grouped alphabetically, or by birth or adoption date; it was like the list had been pulled together from a random pile of adoption papers. It occurred to Father Ilarion that he had no way to tell if a page was lost or if an adoption had been missed. He sighed, and carried on.

When he found his thumb suddenly next to a row describing a boy named Yuri, it was so startling he gasped. His eyes flicked along the row, disbelieving. Might this be him?

The birthday was listed as unknown, and the boy's age estimated as seven. Date of adoption was 1947, but Ilarion couldn't tell if that meant when the boy was taken from Berlin or when the paperwork was completed. His brother had been born in 1935, so this one was too young. Still, he made a neat question mark in pencil beside the entry.

He found another Yuri, and made another mark. By the time he reached the bottom of the list, he had four possible leads, none of them perfect. Then he realized he had skipped the many children with no names listed. Slightly exasperated, he started again, this time looking at any male child orphaned in Berlin who was born around 1935. It was slower going, but after a half hour he reached the bottom again. He quickly flicked the pages, counting 23 possibles. He shook his head slightly. Not possibles. Children.

Father Ilarion took a short break to make more tea. As the kettle boiled he stretched his back, and twisted his hips to ease the pain in his shorter leg. It was how he had lost Yuri. He'd been badly injured working as a bricklayer on a building site, a trade he'd learned from his father. He hadn't been able to get word from the hospital to his little brother, and by the time he'd made it back to the basement where the brothers had been sheltering, Yuri was gone, along with the only picture they had of their mother and the locket she'd treasured. In the chaos of the war-torn city, he couldn't find him. But after years of searching through death records for any sign, he'd realized that Yuri could have been adopted, and started a whole new search. He held his hands close to the kettle, happy for the radiative warmth, then wrapped his warmed palms around his damaged thigh, which still hurt when he was cold or when the weather changed. When the kettle started whistling, he retrieved a hard biscuit from the tin on the shelf, poured the steaming water over his already used teabag, and returned to the desk.

Now to be a detective. His brother had been lost in the heart of Berlin. His date of birth of 1935 was definite, so he would have been nine, but Yuri had been small for his age, so maybe the authorities thought he was seven or eight. The other certainties: blue eyes and light-brown hair.

A thought struck him. American spellings of unfamiliar foreign names might vary, so he was going to have to recheck for Yuriy, or Juri, or anything similar. He pursed his lips at the extra work, then smiled as he thought of a quote from the endless comfort of his faith: *Until you have suffered much in your heart, you cannot learn humility.*

The monk went through the list again, prioritizing. He settled on two good matches, both Yuris with brown hair and blue eyes, seven maybes, and eleven long shots. He held the two pages with the closest matches up to his eyes, inspecting every bit of information carefully, and made a discovery. The Army functionary who had crossed out the family information had not been scrupulous. Some of the black lines were thin or wavered enough that parts of the letters were visible. Ilarion went to the window, flattened the printed sides of the two sheets against the glass and started copying everything he could discern.

He was able to make out a few more of the details about the adoptive parents, but he was going to need English-speaking help and an atlas to get any further. He went through the seven next-best prospects, and added their facts to his own list. The next step would be to ask the English-speaking junior lector to help him write to the Russian Orthodox Church in America, enclosing the list, and request that they contact the churches nearest to the boys' possible locations. There was at least a chance the local churches would know if anyone in the area had adopted a Russian-speaking German orphan. This was an opportunity to bring long-lost children into the fold, after all. To give each a link to their Russian heritage and faith. To make right the wrongs of war.

To find his brother.

4

Simferopol, Soviet Ukraine, 1973

It was not a beautiful machine.

A squatty silver bathtub, riding heavily on eight spoked wheels. Two scientific instruments mounted on the front like a cross between a ray gun and a Christmas ornament. Stereo video cameras gave it lobster eyes.

Even its name was more functional than poetic—Lunokhod. Moon Rover. Typical Ivan engineering, where practicality ruled design. Not much good for pretty, but pretty much good for strong.

Lunokhod had just landed on the Moon.

Thinking through the sequence of how to take the machine down the ramp and onto the Moon's surface, Gabdulkhai Latypov—Gabdul to his friends—rubbed the sweat off his palms onto his pants legs. He repositioned the procedures book on the console and cracked his thick knuckles. He double-checked that all status lights were green, then reached out and carefully grabbed the controller. Leaning forward, he rested both forearms on the console for stability, stared at the monitor and began.

He tipped the controller forward slightly, pushed the command button and let go. The controller sent an electrical pulse through the console to the giant satellite dish outside the building that pointed straight at the Moon. The signal traversed the 240,000 miles of empty space in 1.25 seconds and hit Lunokhod's small, pointy antenna. It sent the pulse to the rover's processor, which deciphered it and briefly powered all eight wheels.

Lunokhod jerked forward slightly, and stopped. A perfectly trained dog, far from home but still responding to its master.

The rover's twin cameras took an image of the barren landscape and sent it back across the quarter million miles to Gabdul's huge satellite dish in Simferopol, where it appeared on his fuzzy black-and-white TV monitor.

Ten seconds after he'd released the hand controller, Gabdul saw that Lunokhod had moved.

"Zhivoy!" he shouted, in triumph. It's alive! He could hear the stifled murmurs of relief and excitement from the ops crew standing behind him.

Gabdul carefully pushed the controller forward again, a longer command this time, following the practiced protocol to get the machine down onto the Moon. To get to work.

Gabdul had grown up near Simferopol, on the Crimean Peninsula. His family's Tatar heritage was obvious in his thick dark hair, his wide cheekbones and the glottal sounds of his multisyllabic name. As a teenager he'd stood outside in the Crimean dusk, watching in wonder as Sputnik had raced across the sky, visible proof of Soviet technical prowess and dominance. And when Gagarin orbited Earth four years later, Gabdul decided he was going to be a cosmonaut. Just like a million other Soviet young men.

As soon as he graduated high school, he joined the Soviet Air Forces, which would send him to technical college to study aviation engineering, and after that, he hoped, to flying school. But his origins were a constant impediment. Gabdul had thought that Stalin's deportation of 200,000 Crimean Tatars to Uzbekistan after the Great Patriotic War was old history, but the bigotry in the military still ran deep—ever deeper, he found, the closer he got to Moscow. Being an ethnic minority from the edge of the Soviet Union made him second class in a classless society.

Despite his graduating in first place, other students with last names like Ivanov and Popov got all the opportunities. Repeatedly denied pilot training, at 25 he found himself a lieutenant in the Soviet Air Forces, working as a junior technical engineer at a space communications ground station near Shchelkovo, on the distant outskirts of Moscow.

Then one day his captain spoke to him during a smoke break out in the hall.

"Gabdulkhai Gimad'ovich," he'd begun formally, as the two of them stood side by side, staring out the double-paned window at the blowing snow whipping around the hulking silhouettes of the satellite dishes. "There's a new program starting, and they need smart young electronics engineers. Hush-hush for now, but apparently it will involve a lot of extra training and travel. Are you interested?"

His captain already knew what Gabdul's answer would be.

Within weeks, he was called to the OKB-52 Machine Building Plant in Moscow, for an interview and aptitude testing. He took his place in the hallway with several other young engineers waiting for their names to be called, hiding their nervousness behind impassive faces. The interview was straightforward: questions about his career, interests, family. He made sure to mention his pride in his father's army service and his own lifelong desire to serve the Soviet space program.

The practical testing was harder, and also puzzling. They had him operate a forklift truck, driving it around a prescribed course on the factory floor as they timed him. Then they hitched a trailer to it and had him back that up, around a corner. Gabdul silently thanked his father for having imparted that skill when he was teaching him to drive, back home in Simferopol.

One of the evaluators took over as the driver, and they had Gabdul observe the forklift remotely through a TV monitor and issue instructions to the driver by radio. They repeated the test in dim lighting and then they only let Gabdul see the camera image every five seconds, covering and uncovering the screen with a clipboard. He wasn't sure what they were evaluating him on, but he tried to imagine himself as the driver and say the things that he would like to hear if he was operating the vehicle.

No one gave him any explanation, just stressed again as he was leaving that he was not to discuss the interview with anyone.

One uneasy week later, his captain came into the control room during his shift.

"Gabdulkhai Gimad'ovich!"

"Da?"

The other engineers looked up as Gabdul got to his feet.

"You are leaving us. The Soviet Air Forces, in their infinite wisdom, have decided that you have communicated with enough satellites. You will report to the Lavochkin NGO in Reutov in two days." He looked Gabdul in the eye. "They haven't told me what you will be doing, so it must be highly important. So important, in fact"—he fished around in his pants pocket and pulled out two dark-blue epaulettes with a thin light-blue stripe and three stars—"that you've been promoted to senior lieutenant!"

He stepped forward, unbuttoned Gabdul's faded epaulettes and replaced them with the stiff new ones. He stepped back, and returned Gabdul's stunned salute.

The captain broke into a broad smile. Looking around at the others, he said, "Rebyata! Sto gram!" This calls for vodka!

But at first Gabdul's new posting didn't feel important. When he got to the facility in Reutov, a senior official welcomed him and 18 other trainees by lecturing them on secrecy. Then he led them into a factory clean room, where they all donned caps and lab coats and were sent to stand next to technicians who were assembling a machine that would go to the Moon. The official waved his hand at the hulking silver thing, nearly as tall as he was, and spoke to them of its purpose, its complexity and their role as the handpicked team that would drive it.

Gabdul didn't know what to think. His dreams of flying in space were crashing down around him, lost forever, but maybe driving this beast on the Moon would be cool.

At the first smoke break, one of the trainees said out loud what several others were clearly thinking. "A toy car driver? That's not what I signed up for. I thought we were going to be cosmonauts!"

Gabdul sympathized, but also noticed he was the only Tatar in the group, and felt the significance of that.

Soon several quit in disappointment. Others failed out of the surprisingly complex, rigorous training. And Gabdul felt a growing sense of something like pride. Of all 240 million Soviet citizens, only he and this small, elite team would get to do this difficult job. The likelihood of a Soviet cosmonaut ever walking on the Moon was dwindling to near zero with the repeated failures of the heavy-lift N1 rocket. But Lunokhod was *real*, and soon to launch. Even better, the new lunar simulation field and Mission Control Center were being built in his hometown of Simferopol in the Crimea.

This was a unique challenge, and a chance to make his family proud: a Tatar, in his indigenous Crimean homeland, serving the Soviet Union's space program.

It might not be his feet that would stand on the Moon, but he, Gabdulkhai Latypov, son of Gimadutin, was about to kick up the lunar dust with wire-spoked wheels.

Gabdul had become a Moon explorer.

5

Washington, DC, 1973

Jim Schlesinger was fit to be tied, as usual.

He stood by the window of his seventh-floor office, staring angrily across the George Washington Parkway towards the Little Falls Dam on the Potomac River. As the brand-new director of the Central Intelligence Agency, he wanted change, and it was happening too slowly.

"Richardson!" he yelled, without turning from the window. He'd fired his incompetent predecessor's secretary the day he'd arrived, and now waited impatiently for her replacement. The door opened, and a tall, composed woman stepped in, notepad and pen in hand.

"Yes, sir?" After 18 years with the agency, Mona Richardson had worked her way up through many types of bosses, and was rapidly figuring out how to be effective with this one.

The DCI didn't look at her. "Look at this," he barked and pointed with his chin.

Mona joined him at the window.

"That's where they're supposed to be putting up the agency road sign," he said, staring down at the traffic. "Why is nothing happening?"

"I confirmed with Fairfax County Public Works yesterday, sir. They assured me that they had the sign printed as you requested, and that they would have it installed today. I'll follow up again."

He turned and looked at her, eyes dark under heavy brows, then shook his head. They needed a sign showing people where the nation's intelligence agency was located! "Bring me more coffee, please."

Mona nodded, quietly making her exit.

Schlesinger turned back to look outside. He reached into the pocket of his tweed jacket, found his pipe and clamped it hard between his teeth. He pulled his lighter from his other pocket and lit the pipe, puffing several times, exhaling slowly through his nose. Nixon was right, as usual. This praetorian guard of outdated, clubby, shoe-leather spies that he'd inherited was smug and self-serving. They needed weeding, and he was the man to do it.

He turned and grabbed a sheet of paper off his desk, reading down the list as he smoked.

He'd fired 837 people, mostly in the so-called Directorate of Plans— the CIA's clandestine arm. He'd terminated a dozen of its senior management personally, and had changed the name to Directorate of Operations. Cutting deadwood. Making sure these people didn't screw Nixon. And the country.

His time in the RAND Corporation and the White House budget office had shown him how technology was changing the world. The United States wasn't going to win the Cold War by using old methods. The two years he'd chaired the Atomic Energy Commission had only highlighted the power of that technology. *Mutually assured destruction?* He shook his head. MAD was right! America needed better. A CIA that pushed new tech to its limits in order to gather intelligence like no other nation could. Before it was too late.

He went back to the window, glancing up at the blue sky. *Our fighters and spy planes aren't keeping up either. We're just doing what we've always done. Someone needs to shake this place, hard. And let the hangers-on fall by the wayside.*

Mona knocked twice on the door and paused, as she'd been instructed. Hearing nothing, she entered with his fresh coffee, placing the tray silently on the desk. She snuck a glance at him, still staring out at the view. He was tall, with thick graying hair, a broad forehead and cleft chin. *A handsome man. If only he weren't such an arrogant ass.*

Schlesinger spoke without looking at her. "Get me Sam Phillips on the phone."

Twenty-three miles to the northeast, on the ninth floor of the National Security Agency, a truly ugly rectangular building on the Fort Meade Army base, General Sam Phillips studied an airplane model he kept on his office bookshelf—the P-38 Lightning. It was the fighter he'd flown over Germany in the war.

The design still amazed him. Big twin turbo-supercharged Allison V-12s cranking out 1,600 horsepower, turning in opposite directions to minimize torque. He'd loved how it had felt to push the throttles to the stops, letting those giant tractors pull him faster and faster. He'd had it up over 400 miles per hour once, out of bullets and outrunning an Me-109, racing for the safety of England.

He bent down and peered head-on at the model, and not for the first time. He shook his head slightly, marveling again at how the airplane almost disappeared from the front—what the wind saw. *No wonder she was so fast.* Beautiful, purposeful engineering. The Lockheed Skunk Works thought the same way he did. Results are what count.

He took one quick glance at the framed picture the Apollo 11 crew had signed for him of the US flag they'd planted on the Moon. Neil Armstrong had handwritten the dedication: "To General Sam Phillips, with thanks—without you, this flag would not be here." Then it was back to work.

"Phone call, General," his secretary called from the adjoining room. "CIA Director James Schlesinger, on Secure One." A beat. "Are you available?"

That's all I need. He sighed.

"Yes, put him through, please, Jan." The beige phone on his desk rang, an insistent blinking light indicating which line. He picked up the handset and pushed the button.

"Director Phillips speaking."

"Sam, we need to talk about a couple things."

"Good morning, Jim. How can I help you?"

"Help me? It's not me that needs help. It's this fiasco brewing in Russia."

Sam Phillips scanned quickly through his mind. Which fiasco? What mattered to the new CIA Director?

He guessed. "The upcoming Proton launch?"

Schlesinger exhaled loudly through his nose. "You know it. What are your SIGINT boys telling you?"

Phillips shook his head. His agency provided signals intelligence to the Department of Defense, not the CIA. He'd heard that Schlesinger wanted to gather all the country's intel organizations under the CIA's control—*his* control—including the military ones. This was a battle that eventually had to be fought. But for now, he'd offer cautious cooperation; the President had put Schlesinger there by choice. "Nothing significant since the last White House briefing with the Joint Chiefs of Staff." Mostly true.

He could feel Schlesinger's blood pressure rising over the phone.

"Your job isn't figuring out what's significant, Sam, it's gathering! Tell me the latest."

Phillips decided to flood the man with information that wasn't all that sensitive, hoping it would satisfy him.

"You know about the Soviets recently landing their rover at a location on the Moon they didn't reveal to the scientific community in advance. Well, they are also just finishing final assembly and checkout of their new space station, which they're publicly calling Salyut 2. As you know, Salyut 1 had to be deorbited when it ran out of fuel eighteen months ago. After the visiting Soyuz crew was killed due to malfunction during re-entry, they grounded their resupply fleet.

"We think Salyut 2 is actually a military spy station called Almaz. Our sources have been monitoring unusual hardware deliveries, and extra levels of security. Our best guess is that they're building an equivalent to what we intended to do with MOL—essentially a huge, manned camera. Something they can point here and there around the world and see details down to an unprecedented resolution level."

As he heard Schlesinger take a breath in order to speak, he carried on quickly.

"We won't know for certain when the launch will be until we see Almaz roll between certain buildings on its railcar at the Baikonur launch site. We have people and assets monitoring that, watching out especially for when they mate it to the Proton rocket itself. Our best guess is that launch will be in early April. So our mid-April target for Apollo 18 is looking good."

As he hoped, the info dump had been enough to pacify Schlesinger.

"Okay, Sam, the President and I want to know the moment you have visual confirmation."

Clearly he meant for General Phillips to note his familiarity with the president.

"If the Soviets get this Almaz into orbit in April, how are you going to keep what's going on at Area 51 a secret?" Schlesinger asked. "They'll see everything parked on the ramp, and more importantly, the HAVE BLUE testing."

Time for some shared responsibility, Phillips thought. "I agree, Jim. We'll need to change ops there. Use camouflage covers, dummy mock-ups, and no flying during Almaz overflights. It will interrupt our activities for about five minutes a few times per day."

Schlesinger didn't pick up the cue. There was no such thing as "we" or "our" in his mind. "You've got another option too, Sam."

Phillips heard the click of the pipe stem in Schlesinger's teeth.

"Stop them being able to look at the United States, or any of our interests, from orbit."

After he hung up, Phillips stood and thought for a full minute. Then he picked the phone back up to call Kaz Zemeckis.

6

Mission Control, Houston

Gene Kranz, buzz-cut, gruff and competent, looked around the conference room at the team gathered there. Young men, mostly, and a handful of women. He was the lead flight director assigned to Apollo 18. With launch only three months away, he'd summed up the day's work by telling them that he was pleased there had been no major screwups during the six-hour simulation, either by the all-rookie crew or the Mission Control team. Gene had been a flight director since the first Gemini mission, and after six Apollo Moon landings, he treated this one as almost routine, even though he knew that almost anything could go wrong.

"Any questions?" he asked.

Kaz raised his hand. "Flight, could I have a word with you and the crew after debrief is done?"

Gene made eye contact with each of his console engineers. No question marks on any of the faces. "Sure, I think that's now. Thanks. Everyone else, you're cleared to go." The room emptied like a class dismissed, leaving only Tom, Luke and Michael, the prime crew, and

Chad, the backup commander. They and Gene Kranz all looked at Kaz expectantly as he walked to the blackboard at the front of the room and picked up a piece of chalk.

"You all know that the Russians just landed a rover on the Moon, right?" Kaz said. "Well, they're about to launch a thing called Almaz, a space station designed exclusively for spying, like MOL was supposed to be." He turned and wrote "ALMAZ" in block letters.

"According to our best intel, Almaz's camera will be powerful enough to easily see things down to the size of a small car." He let the national security implications of that sink in for a few seconds. They were all military men, including Gene, who'd flown fighters in Korea. They knew of the secret testing going on out of sight at remote airfields like Edwards in California and Area 51 in Nevada.

"Our sources say it looks like they'll be ready to launch Almaz in early April, unmanned. Once they've made sure it's fully operational, they'll send cosmonauts up on a Soyuz to crew it, and then they'll start taking pictures." Kaz paused to let that sink in before drawing the line to their own mission.

"The Joint Chiefs, with the approval of the president, want to use Apollo 18 to take a close look at Almaz in Earth orbit before the Soviet crew gets there. The Air Force just let NASA know on Friday, and I've been sent down here to brief you ASAP."

Tom said, "Wait—are we still going to the Moon?" He sounded rattled.

"Yes." Kaz turned to the chalkboard and drew a large circle. "Earth," he said, pointing. Then he drew a shape that looked like an off-kilter hula hoop surrounding it. He pointed at the spot where the hoop's curve was highest.

"The Soviets are launching Almaz from here, in Baikonur, fifty-two degrees north of the equator." He traced the curve with his finger, showing where it descended behind the globe and reappeared in the south. "Apollo 18 has to match that orbit, so after launch, you'll need to steer up the Florida coast."

"Can't do it," Gene said immediately. "If we don't launch the Saturn V straight east out of Canaveral, we don't get the added speed of the Earth's spin, Kaz. Eighteen's too heavy. We're just making it as it is."

"Agreed." Kaz quickly sketched the Saturn V rocket, Apollo Command Module and Lunar Module, stacked for launch. "To lighten the load, we need to take everything off the mission that isn't absolutely needed."

He drew an X on the LM. "That means no experiments on this mission and minimal time for *Bulldog* on the lunar surface." Another X on *Bulldog*'s exterior. "We won't be carrying a rover." Kaz looked at each of them, then drew Xs on the Command Module and the rocket. "Bare minimum gear in *Pursuit*, and a stripped-down Saturn V too. We'll need to be creative, and Washington is looking to you for more ideas. Our best estimates show we can just make it."

Michael said, "Let me get this straight. We launch up the east coast, and instead of heading to the Moon, we stay in Earth orbit long enough to go find this"—he glanced at the blackboard—"Almaz." He looked back at Kaz. "We hang around taking pictures or whatever, and then we're GO for TLI?" Trans-Lunar Injection—firing the rocket motor that accelerated them to escape velocity out of Earth orbit, headed for the Moon.

"That's right," Kaz confirmed.

Luke Hemming spoke, his voice incredulous. "With no experiments to run and no rover, what are Tom and I doing on the Moon?"

"I was just about to get to that," Kaz said. "With the added time and fuel needed to intercept Almaz, they've stripped your time on the Moon to deal with only the highest military priorities. And those just changed."

"Christ!" Tom muttered, thinking of the new pressure his crew was going to be under for the next three months, made even more intense by the inevitable new layers of secrecy.

"The Soviets landed their rover in a crater called Le Monnier, on the edge of Mare Serenitatis." Kaz drew a second circle to represent the Moon, and two smaller circles to the upper right, labeling them "Serenitatis" and "Le Monnier." "It's about a hundred miles north of where

Apollo 17 landed—and it's not where the Soviets said they were going to land. The DoD wants you to go find out why the Russians are there."

He looked directly at Tom and Luke. "So, gentlemen, you are headed to Mare Serenitatis. The Sea of Serenity."

Luke rolled his eyes. "Idiots!" he muttered.

"Okay, it boils down to two main new objectives," Gene said. "One—do a rendezvous and close approach to this Almaz, and linger there long enough to accomplish the DoD's objectives." He thought a second. "Any idea what success looks like to them, how much maneuvering will be involved and how long we've got there?"

"On the order of an hour, maybe two," Kaz said. "You'll need to burn some fuel in order to position *Pursuit* to take detailed photos. Success is a close look-see. Nothing the Soviets would see as hostile."

"Then we land in the"—Gene glanced at the blackboard—"Le Monnier crater, where we do how many EVAs?" E-V-As, or Extra Vehicular Activities.

"Our first guess is that one moonwalk is all we'll have oxygen and fuel reserves for," Kaz replied.

Gene stared into space for several seconds, calculating. They hadn't saved Apollo 13 by guessing. "We'll see about that. But for now, we plan on one EVA. What exactly does the DoD want Tom and Luke to do on the Moon?"

Kaz counted on his fingers. "A detailed survey of the area. A close-up of the Soviet rover to check out its latest sensors and discern its purpose. Retrieval of rock and dust samples, to see what is so interesting to the Russians."

"Michael can get good area imagery passing overhead," Gene said. "We'll lower his orbit as close to the surface as we can."

Michael added, "I'll need another long lens for the Hasselblad." Gene nodded.

Kaz looked around at the group, now all deep in thought, revising, replanning, updating their options. *Like five high-speed problem-solving computers.*

Tom broke the silence. "A more fundamental ops question, Kaz. Who came up with this and who's actually in charge?"

Kaz paused. Spaceflight, like test flying, relied on the crew's sense of control. Al Shepard, America's first astronaut, had set the tone when he sat atop his Mercury rocket after hours of delay and said, "Why don't you fix your little problem and light this candle?" You couldn't tell a test pilot or an astronaut that their opinion mattered less than the people pulling the strings. Or a flight director, either, especially not one as experienced as Gene Krantz.

"We want to keep Apollo 18 as close to a normal mission as possible. Training, development, launch, flight ops and return will all be run by NASA, as usual. The difference will be at the management level. In addition to your Flight Ops Department here in Houston, representatives from the Air Force, the National Security Agency and the White House will work together. They'll have their people here starting later this week, and they'll be around throughout the flight."

Chad, who had remained quiet until now, laughed out loud. Kaz knew these men's years in the military had ingrained in them a mistrust of political meddling, especially with NSA spooks involved.

Luke shook his head, summarizing it in US Marine terms. "What a clusterfuck."

Tom looked around at his crew. "This is actually going to be pretty interesting, guys. We still have the mission components we've been training for, but with added pieces that make perfect sense for us as military astronauts. A chance to do some stuff that no other Apollo crew has done—rendezvous with a non-cooperative foreign target in Earth orbit, and run what is essentially a military reconnaissance op on the Moon."

Chad piped up. "It's going to require some really efficient flying. Previous missions' fuel reserve margins are going to have to be shaved all the way down the line." He looked pointedly at Michael, *Pursuit*'s pilot, and Michael nodded soberly.

"So, Kaz, what exactly is your role in this?" Gene asked.

"They sent me down here as liaison—to translate what Washington wants for you, and to tell Washington what you can deliver. My aim is to free you guys up to concentrate on training while I run interference with management."

Luke was the one who laughed aloud this time. "Mismanagement."

Gene spoke again. "So you need to be in on everything for this to work, Kaz. We're going to be buried in the details, working the problem, building something that will hold together. I'm going to need you in Mission Control from here on out, attending all the sims."

Kaz nodded. "Of course, Gene. I figured as much, and that's what I told the folks in Washington would happen."

"Kaz, when you say 'Washington,' who do you mean?" Tom asked. "It's been—what, five years since your accident at Pax? Who exactly are you working for these days?"

"It's complicated. Legally, I still belong to the Navy. They paid for my graduate work at MIT after I recovered. But during my time there, the Air Force started asking me to advise directly on MOL and SIGINT issues. I ended up talking with the NSA multiple times, and have been called to brief the White House and the CIA, assessing Soviet space assets. I report directly to the Vice Chief of Naval Ops and do my best to keep my one eye focused on the big picture for him, but I spend a lot of time farmed out to other organizations."

Kaz made sure he had everyone's attention, then said, "One more thing. The official briefings with the NASA folks start here tomorrow. What I've told you now is for your ears only. Don't even tell your wives, please." The men all nodded. Of them, Gene, Tom and Michael were married.

Kaz turned to erase the blackboard, rubbing to remove all traces. So far, so good, but he knew just how complicated it was going to get. He expected Washington hadn't told them the half of it yet.

On the way out of the parking lot, Kaz realized there was nothing in the fridge back at Polly Ranch and started scouting around for restaurants.

He spotted a low red building that was so ramshackle it looked like something that had been dropped there from *The Wizard of Oz*. The parking lot was just an open area of grass, though the early-evening clientele had lined their vehicles up neatly with whoever had parked first. One of the cars was a Corvette Stingray, gold with black trim. Kaz had seen one like it in *LIFE* magazine; ever since the Mercury program, a Chevy dealer had been giving Corvettes to astronauts for one dollar each, considering it free advertising. *Must be an Apollo guy eating here*. He pulled in.

As he got out of the car, he spotted the small hand-painted sign: The Universal Joint, it read, with Best TX BBQ Since 1965 underneath.

Perfect.

The entrance was guarded by hip-height swinging doors in the shape of cowgirls, upholstered in red Naugahyde with heavy thumbtacks as sequins. He pushed the girls open and stepped into the low-lit, rough-hewn room. He walked carefully across the uneven flooring and took a seat on a red Naugahyde stool at the long wooden bar. "Eli's Coming" by Three Dog Night was playing loudly on the jukebox, just getting to the big choral crescendo. Kaz caught the eye of the ponytailed bartender, pointed at the Budweiser sign and held up a finger. She nodded, reached into a red cooler and pried off the cap as she brought it to him. She smiled briefly as she handed him a well-worn plasticized menu.

A door behind the bar opened directly to the outside, and Kaz realized the kitchen was just a charcoal barbecue on the back porch. He glanced at the menu and decided on the Universal TX BBQ Cheeseburger, with the works. *Eat what they do best*. He caught the waitress's eye, held the menu up and pointed, just as the jukebox changed to "A Horse with No Name." His order taken care of, Kaz took a long drink of the cold beer, happy for the quieter harmonies.

The wooden walls of the U-Joint were plastered with recent local history, a disordered collage of space mission pictures, astronaut crew photos, real estate advertising and Air Force recruiting signs from nearby Ellington Field. A helmeted mannequin in a Reno Air Races flight suit hung dustily from the ceiling. A group of after-work NASA engineers were playing pool at the lone table, lit by a low-hanging light promoting Coors beer. Small square-topped tables filled the place, four cheap chairs at each, almost all occupied. The Naugahyde cowgirls kept swinging. *The working spaceman's local*, Kaz thought.

"Coffee, please, Janie."

Kaz turned in the direction of the voice to find a short, black-haired man in black-framed glasses leaning on the bar on his blind side.

He noted that Ponytail's name was Janie. *Good to know.*

"This seat taken?" the man asked.

"All yours."

He nodded, and slid up onto the stool.

Janie set a steaming coffee in an enameled ivory mug in front of him. "Black, right, Doc?"

"You bet." He took an appreciative sip, then joined Kaz in surveying the room.

"Quite the place," Kaz offered.

The man looked at him closely for a moment. "You Kazimieras Zemeckis?"

Startled, Kaz nodded. "Have we met?"

The man's face creased in an apologetic smile. "Sorry, I'm JW McKinley, one of the NASA flight docs here. HQ medical sent us your Navy file over the weekend, and when I noticed the glass eye, I just figured."

Kaz said, "My Lithuanian maiden aunts and the IRS call me Kazimieras. Everyone else calls me Kaz."

"Glad to meet you, Kaz. I go by JW, or J-Dub if you're in a hurry."

As they toasted their new acquaintance, Kaz watched the way the doctor's shoulders rolled with thick muscle under his button-down shirt.

"You lift?"

"Just enough to keep from getting too fat. The men in my family are all built like fire hydrants." He paused as Rod Stewart started singing

"Maggie May," then said, "That birdstrike that took your eye must have been something else."

"It turned out poorly for the seagull."

The usual deflection didn't work with the doctor. Under JW's friendly questioning, Kaz found himself talking about the accident in a way he never had, confiding personal details about how the surgeries had felt and all the weirdnesses of getting a glass eye.

"You have a good bar-side manner, Doctor," he said at last. "Your turn—tell me about yourself."

JW smiled at him. "Not much to tell. I'm a Midwest kinda guy, the Air Force paid my way through medical school, I did some trauma work, and I've been a flight surgeon with NASA for the past four years."

"What school?"

"Stanford."

That was as good as it got.

"And the trauma work?"

"I spent eighteen months at the Cleveland Clinic, responding all over the state via helicopter."

Kaz gave a low whistle. "I'll bet you've seen some hairy stuff."

"Yeah, I sure have. Motor vehicle, burns, shootings. Even drownings on Lake Erie."

"What brought you to Houston?"

"I like space." JW smiled again. "Apollo's been an amazing four years."

Kaz turned his head at a sudden loud burst of laughter. He saw a short, tanned, balding man, a gap between his front teeth, holding court at a table by the wall.

JW followed his gaze. "That's Pete Conrad, Apollo 12 commander and moonwalker. He's Navy too. You know him?"

"I think I saw his Corvette outside. He left for NASA while I was still in flight school. I've never met him, but I always felt like I was following in his footsteps, only ten years after. Until the seagull, that is."

"He ejected from a T-38 last year," JW said. "Nighttime, weather here went bad, lost a generator, ran out of gas trying to get to Bergstrom.

His parachute set him down a hundred yards from the base ops building, and he didn't have a scratch."

"Better to be lucky than good. Or in Pete's case, both."

JW shot a discreet glance at Kaz's glass eye. "So how'd you end up in beautiful Houston-by-the-sea?"

"After the accident, the Navy thought maybe they would keep me flying in transports, but I said screw that and asked to go back to school." Kaz shrugged. "They sent me to MIT, then I did some time in Washington, and now I'm here to work with the 18 crew."

"What did you study at MIT?"

"I already had a master's in aerospace systems from the Navy PG school at Monterey. I really liked the science of sensors and electro-optics, so that's what I did at the Lincoln Lab in Boston."

"Wait—you have a doctorate from MIT?"

Kaz shrugged.

"And you said Washington too. Doing what?"

"The specifics are classified, but I ended up at the National Security Agency." Kaz drained his beer. "Turns out the NSA Director flew P-38s in the war and headed NASA's lunar landing program all through the 1960s. He's the one who took an interest in my work."

JW stared. "Holy cow! You're talking about Sam Phillips. He's a legend! You work directly for him?"

Kaz grinned and nodded. "But don't let that get around. Here I'm just another one-eyed ex-astronaut trying to help Apollo 18 get to the Moon."

His cheeseburger arrived, and he realized how hungry he was. But before he took a bite, he asked, "You eating?"

"Nah, I need to get home. Ferne's holding dinner for me. She'll have already fed our two little ones." JW drank the last of his coffee and slid down off the stool. "Nice to meet you, Dr. Zemeckis."

Kaz laughed and picked up his burger. "You too."

7

Lunar Receiving Laboratory, Houston

Kaz felt foolish. He'd asked for an 08:00 meeting with the NASA experts on what the Soviets might be looking for on the Moon, but now he couldn't find the building.

He glanced at his watch. *You've got six minutes.*

He drove up a divided straightaway inside the Manned Spacecraft Center for the second time, craning his neck to find the right building number. He finally spotted a large number 37 in shadow under an overhang. Then he realized he'd missed the parking lot, and had to circle the block to find the entrance. He quickly squeezed the Satellite into a spot between two aging VW Beetles—*scientists prefer Volkswagens?*—grabbed his bag and jogged to the entrance.

He saw people going into a conference room just off the main foyer and glanced at the government-issue wall clock, black hands on a round white face. NASA was big on keeping accurate time. With two minutes to spare, he followed them in and headed for the front of the room, setting his bag on the long veneer table around which the scientists had gathered. He took his notebook out of his back pocket, quickly reviewing the things he was hoping to find out, then raised a hand to get everyone's attention. The room quieted.

"Good morning, everyone. My name's Kaz Zemeckis." He omitted mentioning his military rank, knowing it sometimes rubbed scientists the wrong way. "I'm a former MOL astronaut, recently assigned as crew-government liaison for Apollo 18. I appreciate you all meeting with me."

He glanced around the room, making eye contact. *More facial hair than normal. And more women.* He spotted Chad Miller and nodded; part of the backup commander's job was to go to briefings Tom Hoffman didn't have time for.

"There are lots of details still to come, many of which are classified, but I wanted to start the Apollo 18 revised science discussion with you. I need to get smarter about moonrocks, and I hear this is the right place for that."

There were polite chuckles and nods around the table. The Lunar Receiving Laboratory had been purpose-built to quarantine returning astronauts in case they brought back an interplanetary plague from the Moon. When the first three Apollo crews all stayed healthy—it turned out that, as suspected, the Moon had no life, not even single-celled bacteria—the quarantine period was canceled. But Building 37 was also designed to house the moonrocks and dirt—*don't say dirt, they call it regolith*, Kaz corrected himself. Somewhere inside this building were racks full of bits of the Moon, 842 pounds in total, protected like the Crown Jewels. Actually, pound for pound, the moonrocks had cost more.

Kaz summarized the updated timeline of Apollo 18 for the group, and described the revised landing location, without specifying why it had changed. The lack of surprise on their faces told him that word had already gotten around. MSC was a small community, and the lunar scientists an even tighter subculture within it. They all knew that shifting political agendas were part of the deal.

"So," Kaz said, "what have we learned recently, from orbital photos, the Apollo returns here in this building or the Soviet robotic return samples, that would make you want to go have a close look at a place on the Moon where we've never set foot?"

The room contemplated the question. The Russians had successfully brought back small samples of lunar regolith on their unmanned Luna 16 and Luna 20 missions. Less than a pound in total, but they'd drilled over a foot deep to get it. Despite some published academic papers, no one knew for sure what the Soviets had found.

A tall woman with unruly long black hair raised her hand. "Astronaut Zemeckis, if I may?"

"Kaz, please."

She smiled slightly. "I'm Dr. Laura Woodsworth, one of the cosmochemists here in the lab."

Kaz nodded. She was slender and tanned, wearing a sleeveless floral print dress, with a small crucifix on a gold chain around her neck.

"We've learned more about the Moon in the past forty months than in the previous forty thousand years. Radiometric dating of the samples the missions brought back has shown us that the Moon is over four billion years old—quite close to the age of the Earth. Also, the Moon's regolith is not like Earth dust, which has been weathered by rain and wind. Instead, it's more like broken bits of glass, the result of billions of years of meteorite impact fragments."

Chad spoke up. "It's nasty stuff, Kaz, like loose sandpaper grit. Hard on machinery and spacesuits. The guys have dust stuck to their suits when they come back into the LM that makes them cough after they take their helmets off."

Kaz glanced down the table at him, wondering why Chad felt he needed to interject, but Laura nodded. "By looking at the chemistry of the rocks and dust, we're getting an idea that the interior of the Moon is more like Earth than we thought. A central heavy core, solidified magma surrounding that, and a crust on top. The crust is the gray color you see when you look up at the Moon."

Kaz felt a little like she was treating him as a know-nothing, but was also glad for the refresher. And this was a good way to build rapport with the scientists.

"One other thing before I get to your question," Laura said. "The Man in the Moon—the darker shapes you see—those are ancient lava flows. The light gray rock of the crust is anorthosite, and the darker areas are basalt. Also, the Moon is tidally locked. Do you know what that means?"

That Kaz didn't know. He shook his head.

"It means that the same side of the Moon always faces us. Only twenty-four humans—all Apollo astronauts—have seen the other side."

"Why always the same side?" Kaz asked.

"The Earth's gravity pulls hard enough on the Moon that it bulges a little towards us, like a stone tide going up and down. That internal friction, over time, slowed the Moon's spin, until eventually it got to perfect balance. Presto—we only see the one side."

Kaz held up his hands, slowly turning an imaginary Moon. "So what causes the lunar phases?"

"The Moon orbits around the Earth every 27.3 days. Depending on where the Moon is in its slow orbit, you might see it lit from the side— a crescent—or not at all."

"So, if the Moon spins just once every 27 days or so," Kaz said, "then an astronaut on the surface would be in sunlight for two weeks, and then darkness for two weeks?"

Laura beamed at him. "Yes!"

"How hot and cold does it get, then?"

"About two hundred and sixty degrees Fahrenheit at lunar noon, and minus two hundred and eighty at midnight."

Kaz whistled. "Good to know."

A man in a Hawaiian shirt and Elvis Presley sideburns, the look spoiled slightly by premature balding, spoke up. "Hi, Kaz, I'm Don Baldwin, the department head here. I've been thinking about your question about what we've learned recently. There's a couple things." He ran a hand over his head, front to back, flattening down his remaining hair.

"Some of the more recent asteroid impacts blasted pretty deep holes that haven't been covered by dust yet. They'd be a good place to study the underlying rock, to a depth we haven't been able to drill. We'll need to dig into our photo library at your revised coordinates to see if there are any new craters nearby."

Baldwin paused a moment to look hard at Kaz. His unspoken message was clear. His people hadn't chosen the location, but they'd make the best of it.

"There's another thing we're interested in. Laura, there"—Baldwin nodded at her—"spotted something surprising recently. Laura, why don't you tell him about it?"

She looked at Kaz. "A weird anomaly caught my eye as I was studying some high-res images of the surface, like a dark spot on the film. I had to double-check with a magnifying glass to be sure what I was seeing. But I found a hole in the Moon."

"What?"

"It looks to be a good size, maybe a hundred yards across." Laura flipped through her folder on the table. "I have a picture with me."

She passed an eight-by-ten black-and-white photo down the table to Kaz. He studied the glossy page with his good eye.

It looked like . . . a hole. Almost perfectly round, with the bottom partially lit by the angle of the sunshine. Like something had drilled a skylight.

Kaz looked up in puzzlement. "What made this?"

Laura deferred to her boss.

"We don't know for sure," Baldwin said. "If it was on Earth, our best guess would be a collapsed lava tube, where flowing magma bored a tunnel that later caved in. But how that could happen on the Moon is beyond us. We're forming theories."

Kaz peered closer. "How deep do you think it is?"

Laura answered this one. "We need more photos to be sure, but knowing the angle of the Sun at that time of the lunar day, our guess is, pretty deep—like a hundred yards."

Kaz looked at the hole with new respect.

"If you jumped in, with the Moon's low gravity, you'd slowly fall for eleven seconds. But you'd hit the bottom at forty miles per hour." She smiled. "I did the math."

Chad spoke again. "Yeah, I know I'm just the backup, but let's not try that. Hard on the suit."

Kaz handed the photo back to her. "So, you'd all like to see a cross-section of bedrock in a recent impact crater, and learn more about this hole. Are there more of them?"

"Probably," Baldwin said. "We're going back through all the photos. It took Laura's sharp eyes to spot this one, but now we know what we're looking for."

"Anything else?" Kaz asked.

A bespectacled younger man with shoulder-length hair and a wispy, drooping mustache spoke up. "What about KREEP?"

Kaz looked at him. "What's creep?"

"It's spelled K-R-E-E-P. K for potassium. REE for rare earth elements, and P for phosphorous." He shot Kaz a look, who nodded to show he knew what rare earth elements were. "They aren't actually all that rare, it's just that it's hard to find them in concentration anywhere. They're sort of evenly spread in the Earth's crust, due to their chemical nature. But on the Moon, we think they ended up solidifying into a rich layer just below the crust. Lots of the moonrocks in this building have KREEP basalts in them."

Kaz pondered. "Okay, but why is finding KREEP on the Moon important?"

"Theoretically, the same process that concentrated the KREEP should also sometimes enrich it with uranium and thorium. It may be feasible to mine radioactive elements on the Moon, which means we could power a Moon colony there."

Kaz was careful to keep his excitement to himself. Uranium on the Moon? Is that what the Soviet robot prospectors had found? Could this be the reason they had landed Lunokhod where they did? Finding out what the Soviets were looking for would be key in deciding exactly what the Apollo 18 crew was going to do on the Moon.

Kaz said, "Anything else I should know?"

Don Baldwin surveyed his team. "I think that's it, Lieutenant Commander." The dig was subtle, but the man was telling Kaz he'd done his homework and recognized the military component to all this.

Kaz didn't rise to the bait. "Well thanks, then, everyone. That was extremely informative. Chad and I will update the crew, and I'll be following up with you as we finalize mission planning."

Kaz caught up with Laura as they left the conference room.

"Think you'll find more holes?" he asked.

Laura turned to look at him, her gaze shifting from his right eye to his left and back again. "I expect so. If it happened once, then it can happen again. Pretty exciting to be in on discovering something totally new."

"I look forward to hearing what you find. I'm not in the MSC directory yet, so how about I give you my number?"

"Sure."

Kaz pulled out his notepad, copied his new number onto a blank page and carefully tore it out for her.

"At the rate we're looking," she said, "we should know within a couple days."

When she made no move to give him her number in return, Kaz took a chance.

"If you ever want to go flying, I have access to a little plane just west of here. Nice on a sunny day."

Laura looked at him, considering. "That sounds like fun," she said at last. "I'll give you a call on both."

He nodded. "Talk to you then."

Laura smiled at him, then turned and headed down the corridor. Kaz watched her as she strode purposefully away, her thick black hair swaying.

Kaz considered his actions; he wasn't usually so impulsive. He'd been engaged when the accident had happened, but the relationship hadn't survived his recovery, or rather the dark few months when he couldn't see a future path. He'd been careful about romantic entanglements ever since.

But there was something about Laura that he liked.

8

Lubyanka, Moscow

Espionage, like chess, is a game of patience and focus. Carefully move the pieces to ever-stronger positions, endure the setbacks, wait for the opportunities provided by the opponent and then—pounce.

Vitaly Kalugin, a long-term player at the spy game, sat down at his desk, preparing to start his day. Unlike the three men he shared the office with, Vitaly liked a neat desk. Next to his pen stand he kept a low wooden tray for incoming correspondence. He always made sure his outgoing tray was filled with the telexes and reports that he'd read and notated before he went home every night, to be sent on by the office runners to the next names on the lengthy distribution lists. The KGB was the single security agency for the entire Soviet Union, handling both domestic and foreign intelligence and counter-intelligence, while combating dissent and anti-Soviet activities. It made for a lot of reading every day.

He kept his beige phone on his left, where he could hold it and talk while writing with his right hand. An emptied ashtray was on the far right, his matches and cigarettes still in his jacket pocket. Vitaly unlocked his desk, set his lunch box into its deepest drawer, next to the half-empty bottle of Moskovskaya vodka. Irina always sent him to work with piro-zhki stuffed with meat and vegetables, a block of pale Russian cheese and pickled cucumbers or tomatoes. He got a hot lunch at the office stolovaya, but he liked to eat, and the extra food carried him through the long days.

The vodka was reserved for when there was something to celebrate, which there hadn't been for a while.

From the center drawer he retrieved a green baize-covered note-book and set it squarely in front of himself. In his filing cabinet against the wall there were dozens of identical notebooks, KGB-issue, each neatly hand-lettered on the spine with start and end dates. He flipped the current book open to a fresh page, tidily wrote the date in the top right corner, and then flipped back to his previous day's notes, quickly scanning to refresh his memory on the most current issues. He'd set water to boiling and got himself a cup of tea with two sugars, grabbed two pieces of dried cinnamon raisin toast from the communal tin, bal-anced them on the saucer and re-sat to begin working through his new stack of mail.

The KGB translation service was slow, but thorough. They provided a running supply of foreign periodicals and trade journals, and Vitaly was on the internal subscription for several. By the time they were delivered to his desk they were normally a few months out of date, but for his strategic purposes that was fine. They also made interesting read-ing, providing insight into not just what the enemy was doing, but how they explained it to themselves.

He pulled the next mimeographed, stapled bundle from his inbox and saw that it was *Stars and Stripes*, the long-running American mil-itary newspaper. His eyes darted around the paper quickly, hunting for patterns.

The front page was dominated by Vietnam War peace negotiations and US presidential election news. Nothing useful there. Vitaly licked his thumb and forefinger and turned the page, careful not to smudge the cheap ink. A photograph on page two caught his attention. It showed three men in different uniforms standing next to a model of a tall white rocket. The headline read

Military Astronauts — Moonbound!

The United States Air Force and the National Aeronautics and Space Administration today jointly named USAF Lieutenant Colonel Thomas H. Hoffman, USN Lieutenant Michael H. Esdale, and USMC Captain Lucas B. Hemming as the crew for Apollo 18, the last scheduled lunar landing mission.

Hoffman, commander, and Hemming, lunar module pilot, will explore the lunar surface, while Esdale, Command Module pilot, conducts extensive scientific experiments in lunar orbit. Esdale, who has a PhD degree in chemistry, will be the fourth holder of a doctorate to voyage to the Moon. He will also be the first Black astronaut.

Apollo 18 is scheduled for launch in April 1973. Final choice of the landing site has not yet been made. The 12-day mission will continue the emphasis on both lunar surface and lunar orbital science. Lunar surface stay time will be up to 68 hours, and three exploration periods of up to 7 hours each are possible. An Apollo Lunar Surface Experiments Package will be deployed. Mapping of the Moon and several scientific experiments will be continued from lunar orbit. Esdale will leave the spacecraft to retrieve film from cameras in the service module during the trip back to Earth.

Backup crewmen are USAF Major Chad Y. Miller, USN Lieutenant Robert L. Crippen and USMC Captain Robert F. Overmyer.

Vitaly traced the name as he reread it, his brain spinning. *My source is assigned to an Apollo spaceflight!* Kalugin had put the pieces in place more than a decade ago, but to see this news in print was somehow shocking. He took a sip of tea to hide his emotions from his three office mates, his brain racing.

Vitaly Sergeievich Kalugin's source! This was a wild dream he hadn't allowed himself to count on, even when the MOL program had been announced. The insight that they now could get into the actual hardware and operations of the US space program would be unprecedented. And this assignment also meant that his source would rise faster through the officer ranks in their military—several early astronauts were now generals. He'd also be front-of-line for future US spaceflights, including the reusable Space Shuttle their president had recently announced and the Skylab space station.

For the long game, this was a *superb* development. He leaned down to pull his desk drawer open and grabbed the bottle of vodka.

9

Ellington Field, Houston

Kaz and Chad stood next to each other at Ellington Field, the US Air Force base five miles north of the Manned Spacecraft Center. Ellington had been a military airfield since 1917 and was one of the reasons MSC was located in Houston.

Both of the men were wearing sunglasses and heavy black ear protectors against the blowing grit and noise. "What a crazy flying machine!" Kaz yelled. Chad nodded and gave him a thumbs-up. It was Chad's turn to fly the Lunar Landing Training Vehicle next.

It was a Rube Goldberg contraption that someone had once said looked like a flying bedstead. The nickname had stuck. The Bedstead had a jet engine that pointed straight up, and hydrogen peroxide thrusters mounted at all angles on an ungainly aluminum frame. The pilot's seat was open to the air, stuck incongruously on one end like a crane operator's shack. The vehicle had been designed and built in a hurry to train Apollo astronauts on how to land on the Moon, and it looked it. Hovering 200 feet in the air, held up by the raw power of the downwards-thrusting turbojet, Tom Hoffman was practicing land-ings, the peroxide jets puffing bursts of smoke to the sides.

Like a nervous dragon, Kaz thought.

They watched as Tom followed the checklist profile, slowing for-ward speed as he descended, then settling the machine gently on its four insect legs, jets puffing rapidly, exactly in the center of the painted target X on the tarmac. This was as close to simulating the Moon's one-sixth gravity as the NASA engineers and trainers could get.

Tom lifted off again, moving a few hundred yards away, setting up for another practice run. An Air National Guard F-101 Voodoo inter-ceptor jet noisily took off on the nearby main runway. Both men's eyes turned to follow it. Pilots like airplanes.

Chad yelled an explanation at Kaz, who had never seen the training vehicle in action. "Tom's setting the main engine to hold up five-sixths of the weight now. Then he flies it using just the peroxide thrusters, which gives it the same feel as the LM on the Moon. It's got close to the same hand controllers as the LM, and the styrofoam walls block Tom's view, like the real thing does."

Kaz leaned towards Chad. "How many crashes have they had? Three?"

"Yeah, but no one was hurt—she's got a good bang seat. You proba-bly heard it's zero-zero."

Kaz nodded.

The ejection seat had been designed to save the pilot even if he pulled the handle at zero altitude and zero airspeed. Most seats in jet fighters needed forward speed and enough height to allow the para-chute to properly inflate.

Tom landed again, bouncing slightly but right on target, and they could see his hands going through the extra motions needed to shut it down. The groundcrew, wearing heavy white protective gear, moved in to safe the systems. They waved the fuel bowser truck in close and reeled out its hose to refuel. A red USAF fire engine waited 100 feet away, just in case.

Chad and Kaz took off their ear protectors, glad the noise had stopped. Chad popped his finger in his mouth and then held it up, testing the wind. "Still pretty light. Should be good for my flights too."

Tom walked towards them, his white helmet under his arm. He'd taken off his olive-green torso harness, which clipped solidly into the ejection seat; he was wearing the same all-white flight suit as Chad, made of thick Nomex in case the LLTV caught fire. He'd peeled back his white hood, extra fire protection for the back of his neck. Underneath, he was wearing all-cotton long underwear. It was hot, but a worthwhile precaution. Launch was under 10 weeks away, and even a minor injury could ground him.

They all shook hands.

"Not bad for an old guy, Tom," Chad teased, some edge in his voice. He was a year younger, and his Air Force career had followed Tom's throughout.

"I bounced that last landing a bit," Tom said.

"What's it fly like?" Kaz asked.

"Like you're balancing on top of a broomstick." Tom laughed. "Sort of like a helicopter, but no rotor to give all the cross-coupling and inertial effects. It's actually fairly stable. Until it isn't. In Lunar Sim Mode the jet engine pivots on gimbals, which helps fight wind gusts and keep the thrust vector pure vertical. It gets pretty twitchy. From what the other Apollo guys have said, the real LM is gonna be way smoother." He looked at Chad and smiled. "I'll tell you about it when I get back."

Chad reached into his leg pocket and took out his thin light-brown leather flying gloves. "Yeah, well, now it's the better pilot's turn." He winked at both men, picked up his helmet bag and walked confidently towards the contraption.

"Happy landings," Tom said to his back. For a moment, they both watched Chad, donning his green harness at the base of the yellow ladder.

Tom turned to Kaz. "So. What do you think?"

Kaz guessed what he meant. "I've known both your crewmembers for a long time. Michael comes across a little too informal sometimes, but he knows *Pursuit* inside out. He'll do fine. Luke is super-sharp and will serve you well in *Bulldog*, and outside walking with you on the Moon. Looks to me like everyone's coming along well."

Tom nodded, and held his gaze. He waited a beat. "But?"

They were watching Chad strap himself into the ejection seat.

"But . . . we're still not sure exactly when the Russians are going to launch Almaz, though it's still looking like early April. And we're not sure how high they're going to orbit it, but our best guess is that it'll be low for better camera resolution, and the stripped-down Saturn V can put you there, regardless. Also, we're not at all sure what their Lunokhod rover is doing in the Sea of Serenity. Our intel is lousy inside Moscow Mission Control, but we do know they've added even more layers of security. Which makes us think it's not just another lunar science mission."

Kaz glanced back at Chad, who was working through the steps of bringing the Bedstead back to life. "And we're not sure how long we can keep this quiet. So far the press hasn't caught on that there's anything different about this Apollo mission. But there are lots of people in the know—engineers, scientists, technicians. Heck, even the cleaning staff in the Vehicle Assembly Building must be able to see that you don't have a rover attached this time. Eventually your ugly face will be on the cover of *Newsweek* with a 'Secret Military Apollo Mission' caption. And then the Soviets will be hyper-alert."

Tom thought about it and said, "Add that to the training jerk-around that intercepting Almaz has caused, plus all the last-minute changes with the Moon landing site." He looked at Kaz, his face serious. "I'm not happy about it."

Kaz nodded, commiserating. "Are you getting heat from the Air Force too?" Kaz was well aware that the Pentagon had its own agenda, bolstered by an unassailable sense of self-importance. And, unlike with typical Apollo crews, they felt they could reach out directly to the former MOL astronauts.

"I'm getting phone calls every few days from Washington," Tom admitted. "But our crew secretary is the most polite stonewaller you've ever met. Al has drilled that into all his staff, and it works."

Al was Al Shepard, Chief of the Astronaut Office. One of the original Mercury 7 astronauts, the first American to fly in space, and a man who had walked on the Moon as commander of Apollo 14. He understood external pressures on flight crews like nobody else, and he ran things like the famous Navy Rear Admiral he was.

Kaz persisted. "What's Washington calling you about?"

"Oh, a mix of things. This is a real recruiting moment for the Air Force, especially with the mess in Vietnam. They want me to be the poster boy for their 'Tame the Wild Blue Yonder' advertising campaign." He smiled. "Al's helping me stiff-arm them, so they'll just have to take what they can get from NASA PR." He shook his head slightly. "They're also asking me what I'm going to do afterwards, maybe make me the commandant of the Air Force Academy, or the Test Pilot School at Edwards, though they'd have to promote me. But the truth is, I'd like to stay here if we can swing it. The kids are liking school, and Margaret likes Houston way better than the desert at Edwards. Maybe I'll leave the Air Force and hire on directly with NASA, work on Skylab and the Space Shuttle." He smiled. "Hell, if this flight goes okay, maybe even fly in space again, as a civilian next time."

Kaz nodded. He'd do the same thing in Tom's shoes.

Both men winced at a sudden roar from the Bedstead, and stuck their ear protectors on as Chad brought the jet engine back to life.

10

Manned Spacecraft Center

"Hi, Lieutenant Commander Zemeckis, it's Dr. Woodsworth."

Kaz had been deep in study of Lunar Lander systems, getting ready to support the crew during an upcoming sim, and had picked up his desk phone distractedly when it rang, still staring at the page.

Dr. Woodsworth? Hey, she actually called!

"Good morning, Dr. Woodsworth. Did you find any more holes in the Moon?"

"As a matter of fact, I did. Four so far! Everybody's pretty excited over here in the lab. I thought it might be worth showing you the pictures."

He glanced at his watch. "How about over lunch? Building 3 cafeteria, say, noon?"

Kaz grabbed a tray and walked along the steam line, choosing as he went. He had to admit that looking down at the NASA logo printed on his tray—the famous blue ball with a stylized spacecraft and orbit—gave him a ridiculous level of pleasure that he was actually here in Houston.

As he was paying the cashier, he scanned the tables. Laura, in her white silk blouse and pleated pale-blue skirt, was easy to spot among the male engineers.

"Good to see you, Laura," he said as he unloaded his lunch on the table she'd chosen by the window and set his tray on an empty chair. "Thanks for making time on short notice."

"A girl's gotta eat," she said.

She handed him the folder of pictures she'd brought, and picked up her sandwich.

He scanned them one by one. "The holes look so similar."

"Yes, that's a surprise to us as well. They all seem to be made the same way, but we haven't figured out how." She pointed to the one he was studying. "Notice that there's no ejecta around the hole, so they weren't made by impact."

Kaz spooned a mouthful of his soup, nodding. "Do you have a map that shows exactly where these are?"

"I thought you'd never ask." From the 3-ring binder next to her she unclipped a printed page, spun it around and set it beside the photos.

"The green triangles are the Apollo landing sites. The red ones are the Russian Luna landers. The yellows are where our unmanned Surveyor probes are." She touched a red fingernail to each. "And the black hand-drawn squares are the locations of the holes."

One of them was not too far from where Apollo 17 had landed. "Is that as close to the 17 site as it looks? Did the crew see anything?"

"It's many tens of miles from the farthest point the crew reached in the rover. Too bad we hadn't spotted these before they went."

She took a bite while she waited for Kaz to ask the obvious question.

"How close is it to where 18 is scheduled to land?"

"Close enough that Tom and Luke could maybe check it out if we give them enough time on the surface." She looked up at him. "Are we going to give them enough time?"

Kaz looked around pointedly at the lunchtime crowd. "That's up to the DoD to disclose, if and when they decide to. Sorry."

Laura stared at him for several seconds, and then shrugged. "We can wait." Then she smiled. "We're geologists."

Kaz decided it was time to change the subject. "What brought you to NASA?"

For a moment she hesitated, then met his eye. "I want to be an astronaut. And this place is astronaut mecca." She paused for a moment, clearly considering what more she would say. "I was still an undergrad when Kennedy made his Moon speech. I knew that girls weren't allowed to be fighter pilots, but I figured that other skills would be needed on the Moon too. While there are still no women in the astronaut corps, the fact that Dr. Schmitt flew on Apollo 17 shows I'm at least half-right."

Kaz knew that Schmitt, a geologist, had been selected in a new category of scientist-astronaut in 1965. He listened to the undercurrent of fierceness in her voice as she continued.

"Valentina Tereshkova flew in space solo for three days a decade ago. She showed that women can perform as well as men. The 1964 Civil Rights Act gives us legal protection against sex discrimination, so eventually NASA is going to be recruiting female astronauts. I intend to be one of them." She smiled then, and raised her eyebrows at him. "Well, you asked!"

Kaz knew what she was feeling. He'd been driven by the desire to fly in space ever since Gagarin and Al Shepard had opened the door in 1961. It was the main reason he'd gone to Test Pilot School, and only the accident had stopped his trajectory. But Laura was the first woman he'd met who felt as passionately as he did about the idea, or at least the first who'd told him about it.

He said, "It's been over a year since Nixon announced the new Space Shuttle. I understand it'll have a crew of seven, and I think I remember him saying 'men *and women* with work to do in space' in his speech.

Bound to take longer than they're predicting, but I bet that's your chance. And I'd vote for you."

"I'll take all the help I can get," she said, and laughed.

"Jack Schmitt had to learn to pilot NASA jets before they'd let him fly on Apollo," Kaz added. "And it looks like the Shuttle is going to be more of a pilot's machine than Apollo capsules ever were. Have you done much flying?"

Laura looked rueful. "Not yet. I got some scholarships, but I still had to pay my own way through nine years at UCLA. I've started flying lessons here, but they're expensive. And with all the Apollo missions back to back, there hasn't been much time."

"Don't forget I asked you to go flying. The house I'm renting comes with a little Cessna trainer in the garage, which my landlord is happy for me to fly. The street at the end of my driveway doubles as the runway. I'd be glad to take you up."

Laura's gaze involuntarily flicked from his good eye to his glass one and back. She realized what she was doing, and looked down.

"Let's tackle this issue of me only having one eye," he said, not wanting to embarrass her, but also wanting it out of the way. "I've been flying with the Navy since college, fighters and test, and NASA's letting me into the back seat of the T-38s sometimes. You can trust me to fly a Cessna. We can go over all the basics you're getting in flight school."

Laura looked intently at him, then she nodded. "That's really kind of you. I'd love to."

Kaz checked his watch and glanced out the window. The weather was still good. No time like the present. "Sunset's a little after six these days. Got time for a flight right after work? Leave here, maybe, 4:30?"

"Today?" Laura said, but it didn't take her long to decide. "Where do you and the Cessna live?"

He had just turned the plane around in the hangar entrance when he spotted a white VW convertible Bug slowing to cross the cattle gate.

Wiping his hands on a rag, he watched as it shifted quickly up through all four gears on the straightaway, and then braked hard and turned smartly into his driveway. He waved at Laura to park to one side, pantomiming how the plane was going to roll out.

He smiled. *Scientists do love Volkswagens!*

As he watched her climb out of the car, Kaz saw that Laura had knocked off work early too, as she was now wearing bell-bottom jeans. He suddenly realized he was nervous, and that it had been a while since he'd felt that way.

"Found you!" she said. "I've never been out this way before."

"Glad you did." He glanced at his watch. "We have about an hour until sunset, so let's get flying. No lights on the runway here," he said, waving at the road, "so we need to land before it gets too dark."

"It's a taildragger," Laura said, as they walked around the plane, which was resting on its tailwheel with the nose sticking up into the air. "I've only ever flown planes with nose wheels."

"These have some advantages—the tailwheel acts like an anchor to keep you straight, especially landing on grass, and you don't carry the extra weight of a big, heavy wheel up front. Though you need to use your feet more on the rudder pedals."

They climbed in their respective side doors, and Kaz showed her where the release was to slide the seat forward. He was conscious of every movement of his hands as he helped her retrieve and attach the dangling shoulder strap, happy to be so close to her in the cockpit. He verbalized everything he was doing as he coasted down the driveway, started the engine, checked key instruments and lined up for takeoff.

He looked at her as she reached to touch the oil pressure and temperature instruments with her fingertip.

"Ready to go?"

She looked around the instrument panel methodically, finding and focusing on the airspeed, altitude and tachometer. "All set!"

Kaz nodded, then smoothly pushed the throttle all the way in and they began to roll. As the tires left the pavement, he glanced across at her. Her face was alive with delight, eyes darting around the instruments and outside as the ground fell away.

The early-evening air was smooth, and he turned towards MSC, leveled off and talked Laura through the basics of piloting the Cessna. Then he let go, saying, "You have control."

She sat rigidly erect, focusing straight ahead. Kaz had her do some gentle turns, and her posture relaxed slightly. He pointed out the Spacecraft Center, and then Seabrook and Kemah as they crossed the Galveston Bay shoreline.

"Want to do something fun and beautiful?"

She looked wide-eyed. "Sure."

"I have the aircraft." Kaz lowered the nose to pick up speed, and then smoothly pulled hard up and to the right until they were looking down the wing at the water, with airspeed slowed to bare flying speed. The plane's nose gently followed the arc back down, and he reversed and did the same thing in the other direction. The contrast between the noisy rush of the dive and pull-up accentuated the ensuing grace and quiet as they floated over the top. He did one more turn to the right, Laura looking straight down out her side window at the dark waters of the bay.

She turned to him. "That's wonderful! Like a falling leaf!"

He nodded. "It's called a chandelle. Really reminds you that you're flying."

He leveled off and let go of the controls. "All yours again. Let's reverse and head back."

As she turned west, Kaz lowered the windscreen visors against the sun on the horizon. The basic aerobatics had made him extra-aware of his senses, as they always did, releasing a liberating feeling of three-dimensional freedom. He leaned to point at MSC with his chin, his shoulder touching hers in the small cockpit.

"Nobody down there got to experience that."

She followed his gaze, and didn't lean away. "We're lucky. Thanks for asking me to go flying with you."

"Hey, you're the one flying!"

11

Simferopol, Soviet Ukraine

In the time of primordial hell, an ancient star, burning hotter and hotter as it ran out of fuel, suddenly exploded in a blinding, cataclysmic supernova. This enormous burst of energy was unleashed as a shockwave, rippling out into the galaxy now called the Milky Way. The unfathomably powerful waves pulsed through primal clouds of hydrogen and helium, scattering and pushing them together like flotsam on an interstellar ocean.

For the next 100 million years, these clouds were pulled into ever-bigger clumps by their tiny forces of gravity—an agonizingly slow ballet of gentle drifting and spinning and gathering into denser regions. The near-endless molecules of hydrogen and helium, colliding with higher and higher force, began to heat up and glow in what was becoming a central protostar. And somewhere around 4.6 billion years ago, the pressures and temperatures got to a critical level; atoms were crushed in on themselves, binding energies were released, and thermonuclear fusion suddenly began.

Let there be light.

What that brand-new Sun illuminated was a huge, swirling flat disk of the rubble of space—gas and dust and rocky remnants of previous stellar explosions—all orbiting and collecting ever faster in the blackness. Far from the Sun, the low temperatures allowed volatile compounds to stay frozen, as ice. They collided endlessly and joined into ever-increasing lumps, gradually coalescing into the gas giant planets: Jupiter, Saturn, Uranus and Neptune.

Closer to the Sun, though, the radiant heat turned the icy lumps into comets with tails, vaporizing the frozen gases. Countless rocks remained, crashing into each other, building larger and larger proto-planets. Some asteroids were a dense mix of rocks and metal, while others, from farther out, were lumpy balls of rubble held together by frozen water. One by one, over millions of years, they looped and collided, settling into the winners of this stellar game of billiards—the inner rocky planets Mercury, Venus, Mars and Earth.

But the massive gravitational pull of the two biggest planets, Jupiter and Saturn, caused resonance and disruption. They yanked rocks from the asteroid belt and the farthest regions of the outer Kuiper Belt, some the size of the inner planets, and slung them in unstable orbits towards the Sun. The resulting collisions were hugely powerful.

Earth was just a semi-molten ball of spinning rock, repeatedly bombarded by asteroids, ever growing in size. Over time the onslaught lessened, as the debris diminished. But the biggest was saved for last.

On a normal day in the young planet's life, 4.5 billion years ago, it was struck like never before. A planet the size of Mars, traveling at 9,000 miles per hour, slammed into the Earth.

The rock and ice of this attacker were violently plunged deep into the Earth's mantle, forever merging the two planets into one. It spun the Earth like a top, leaving it whipping around so fast that each day was just five hours long. The flying debris of the impact splashed high into near space, then fell back again as a rain of molten rock over the whole surface. But the inertia of the impactor was so high that great globs of itself, and of the Earth, were thrown all the way into orbit. A ring of debris, orbiting the planet, rapidly collected into one molten ball 2,000 miles across, glowing in the night sky.

The Earth now had a Moon.

And inside that Moon, an untold wealth of minerals rose, sank and churned as it cooled.

"What's that?" Gabdul's navigator tapped Lunokhod's navigation camera screen with a fingertip. "There, to the left."

They both leaned close to the frozen image on the small black-and-white screen. Gabdul had commanded Lunokhod to stop.

He moved his head back and forth, trying to decipher the grainy image. "It looks like a rock and its shadow."

The navigator grunted. "I agree." He glanced at the rest of the science team, who nodded. "Give me a minute to replot you a course, and let's go have a look."

For moving around the surface they relied on three low-res TV cameras, but Lunokhod also had four high-resolution cams and one ultraviolet photometer, a photodetector, an X-ray spectrometer and radiation detectors. It even had a penetrometer to slam into the ground to measure for hardness.

It might be fun to bash this rock!

The navigator flicked through his well-worn orbital images of the area, including some brand-new photographs taken by Apollo 15 and 17, gleaned from an international planetary exploration conference in Moscow a few weeks earlier; an American scientist had unwittingly given the images and a Defense Mapping Agency lunar topographic chart to a senior Lunokhod engineer. The new detail was superb, and added to the navigator's confidence in telling Gabdul where to steer. He quickly laid out the route to get to a good science-gathering position near the rock, and then turned it into a sequence of operator commands.

Gabdul rehearsed the movements briefly, nodded to himself, positioned the hand controller to the side and pushed the command button. After six seconds he released, and they all stared at the monitor, waiting for the image to refresh.

The dark rock was now centered in the field of view. After the navigator nodded to him, Gabdul drove straight ahead, then checked the image
again. He repeated the maneuver three times, until the rock was in perfect position at the bottom of the high-mounted navigation camera screen,
then sent the command to switch to the lower panoramic cameras.

The team was used to the long pause between each command and
the return image. It was part of their regular rhythm, a time to discuss
what they were seeing, like dissecting the magic trick before the magi-
cian pulled the rabbit out of the hat. They hashed over why the rock was
a different color than the surrounding regolith. Perhaps it had been
dropped there somehow.

The assistant navigator laughed. "Maybe it's an alien turd!" The
group chuckled, and then the new view appeared.

The two lower cameras, set apart like human eyes, gave a stereoscopic
sense of depth. Looking closely, the navigator rejudged the distance
and gave another command. Gabdul carefully moved the joystick, and
Lunokhod rolled forward another meter and a half.

When the image updated, the navigator grunted, "Perfect!" He sat
back, his job complete.

The science team swung into action. They recorded the imagery
from the cameras onto videotape, and captured the data flowing
down from the photometers on paper strip charts. So far no surprises:
a rock, like many others.

Next, they sent commands to the RIFMA-M X-ray spectrometer,
mounted low, like an insect's mandibles, under Lunokhod's front end.
Its door pivoted open, uncovering small samples of radioactive tungsten
and zirconium that unleashed an invisible cone of alpha and beta par-
ticles onto the Moon's surface. The focused spotlight excited mineral
elements in the rock, causing each atom to release fluorescent X-rays.
The return sensor sent these complex electronic signals across the void
to the team in Simferopol, who saw them as distinct frequency lines on
an oscilloscope. They ran a hard copy of the data so they could look
closely at the rock's unique signature. They saw mostly magnesium,

aluminum, silicon, some others—the proportions were a bit odd, but it was similar enough to other rocks.

Gabdul shrugged. "How about the magnetometer?" he asked, and got the thumbs-up.

At his command, a long, spindly pole that stuck out the top of Lunokhod slowly pivoted down until it was just a few inches above the rock, the small cross-shaped device on its end detecting the strength and direction of any local magnetic field. Again, none of the readings were out of the ordinary.

The lead scientist rubbed her hands together, readying for the next test. She truly loved this. It was the ultimate fieldwork, learning about a piece of the Moon that no human eyes had ever seen before today, the kind of pure exploration she'd been fantasizing about ever since she began her geology studies at Moscow University. So many papers were going to be written about what her team was discovering, and she would be co-author on them all. She'd get to attend international conferences, maybe even travel to America.

She kept her voice calm, as expected by the team. "Let's see what the Geiger counter can show us."

She watched as the heavy Geiger counter pivoted into position above the rock. *We couldn't have done this on Venus*, she thought. Only the Moon's one-sixth gravity allowed the weight of the sensor to be supported by such a delicate pole.

They maneuvered it incrementally closer, until she called, "That's enough! Let's power it up."

Her technician sent the command, all eyes fixed on the gauge as they waited the 10 seconds for a return signal.

Nothing. No radioactivity.

She frowned. "That's wrong. There's guaranteed to be background radiation at least. Send the command again."

This time the signal got through. The needle jumped to near full scale on the gauge. Her eyes widened. "Bozha moy!" she exclaimed. A rush of excitement coursed through her whole body. "It's radioactive!"

12

Ellington Field, Houston

"Is my hysterical palm tree ready?"

The ops desk clerk looked up at Tom Hoffman's grinning face. As a fighter pilot, Tom had long held helicopters in low-level contempt. To him, only the fact that he was going to walk on the Moon, and in order to do that he needed to practice landings in this backup training machine, made becoming a part-time helo pilot tolerable.

"Sure is, Tom." The ops clerk handed him the thick Bell 47G aircraft sign-out book: its daily certification of flight readiness. Tom scanned the completed maintenance actions, saw nothing new and scrawled his signature against the date. Then he retrieved his helmet and gloves from the counter, and stepped out onto the flight ramp at Ellington Field.

The sky was dotted with puffy cumulus clouds, winds were out of the south, and the March sun was surprisingly hot. The fishbowl—the enclosed full-bubble plexiglas canopy of the helo—was going to be scorching. Tom was glad he'd stopped for an extra drink at the water fountain.

The aircraft tech rolled a large red fire extinguisher close to the

helicopter, a safety measure at every engine start. Tom dropped his
helmet on the right seat, donned his gloves and did a quick walkaround.
In the distance, he could see Luke taking his turn in the Bedstead, and
he decided he'd fly over there and watch for a bit.

Tom climbed into the left seat, strapped into the four-point harness,
put on his helmet and plugged in his comm cord. He pulled the
checklist out of his leg pocket and quickly ran through the pre-start.
He circled a raised finger at the groundcrew, started the engine and
then checked all systems. Satisfied, he gave a salute, and watched the
tech roll the fire extinguisher clear.

Tom took one last close look around the instrument panel—he still
found flying helicopters unnatural and liked to be extra careful—then
radioed Ellington Ground for taxi clearance. With that, he began the
pilot's dance that makes helicopters fly.

In his left hand was the throttle. When he twisted it, like you would
a motorcycle grip, the engine revved up. The Bell 47G only had 175
horsepower; with that little motor driving the two big spinning rotor
blades overhead, it was all too easy to demand too much and over-torque
the mechanical system.

The throttle was mounted on the end of a short pole, hinged at the
far end. When he raised his hand, it changed the angle that the rotor
blades above his head were biting into the air, making them lift harder.
It was a simple, intuitive design—pull up, go up; push down, go down.
Because it moved both rotor blades together, it was called the collective.
Tom raised and lowered it once with the motor at idle, to make sure it
was moving freely.

In his right hand, Tom held what looked and felt like the control
stick in an airplane. Moving it around changed the angle of the rotor
blades individually, to allow him to tip the helicopter forward and back,
and to roll it left and right. Since the stick cycled each rotor blade
through a full circle, it was called the cyclic. When he'd first seen the
word, he'd pronounced it wrong, and had to learn to say it correctly.
Sigh-click.

By pushing on the rudder pedals at his feet, he operated the small propeller mounted on the end of the long tail boom. It provided enough sideways force to counteract the spin of the main rotors, and let him fly in a straight line.

Tom took one last look around to make sure no one was near, and started raising the collective while twisting the throttle for more power. As the rotor blades lifted the helicopter's skids off the pavement, he pushed with his left foot to keep from turning. His right hand moved the cyclic constantly, to keep perfectly level. It had taken a lot of practice with a patient instructor to learn how to hover, but now, with concentration, Tom was good at it.

He moved the helicopter clear of the ramp and switched radio frequencies. "Ellington Tower, this is NASA 948. I'd like to head over to observe the LLTV, and then work east of the field for thirty minutes or so."

"Copy, 948, cleared as requested, no traffic in the pattern."

Tom clicked his mic button twice in acknowledgment, turned right and made a beeline straight at Luke, who was just lifting off in the LLTV, setting up for another practice lunar landing.

"Luke, Tom here in the fishbowl. Okay if I stay off to the side and watch?"

"Sure, Tom. I'm going to be doing normal patterns."

Tom maneuvered downwind so that his rotor wash wouldn't disrupt Luke's air. As Luke went through the landing profile, Tom mirrored the actions in his helo. On the real Moon landing, it would be him flying the LM, with Luke on his right, assisting.

Luke touched down smoothly.

Tom pushed his comm switch. "Not bad, for a Marine."

"Thanks, Boss."

"If you need any senior officer advice, just call. I'm headed east."

"Roger that. Happy motoring."

Tom chuckled. Just before he accelerated away towards Galveston Bay, he spotted Kaz standing where he had a good view of Luke's training session. Tom nodded to him, and got a thumbs-up in response.

Under him now were hundreds of acres of cow pasture just east of Ellington Field. A good place to fly and not bother anybody, apart from some Texas longhorns. He climbed to 1,000 feet, bouncing in turbulence as the heat of the day roiled up the air, conscious of the sweat trickling down his sides. In the real LM, the guidance computers would automatically bring him close to the Moon's surface. He'd take manual control 500 feet up, at 40 miles per hour, and 2,000 feet back from the landing site. They called it Low Gate, and he maneuvered the helo to set those conditions. Looking ahead, he chose a lone cow in an open area as his planned landing site.

The helicopter was shaking quite a bit now in the unsteady air, and Tom fought it to get the parameters set right. He pulled slightly on the collective to slow his descent, and eased back on the cyclic to set 40 miles per hour forward speed. His feet were playing the rudder pedals constantly to keep him pointed straight at the cow. He cross-checked speed and altitude, and spoke aloud the words he or Luke would say.

"Houston, *Bulldog*, 500 feet, down at"—he checked his vertical speed again—"15." He released slightly on the collective to descend and eased forward on the cyclic, eyes now fixed on the cow, 2,000 feet ahead.

There was a sudden, surprisingly violent jolt of turbulence, like he'd hit an air pocket, and Tom felt the helicopter rapidly fall. "Damn!" This was messing up his approach—there wouldn't be any downdrafts on the Moon. He pushed forward aggressively on the cyclic to hold forward speed.

It was the instinctive move of a high-time jet pilot, but entirely the wrong thing to do in a helicopter, a rookie mistake.

The linkage that connected Tom's right hand to the spinning rotor blade was complicated. The cyclic stick was attached to a series of hinges and pushrods, running down under his feet, up behind his back and out through the top of the fishbowl. It connected above the motor to a horn that protruded from the spinning main drive shaft, which was attached, via pitch control rods, up to the rotors. As Tom pushed on the cyclic, it pushed up on the horn, tipping the base mechanism to change the angle of the rotors.

But what Tom thought was turbulence had actually been a pitch rod holding nut, improperly tightened, working itself loose. The vibration and centrifugal forces had combined to undo the nut faster and faster, until it had come off completely, instantaneously disconnecting the pitch rod from that blade. With no more control, the rotor blade had gone flat, suddenly dropping the amount of lift it was providing to zero.

Tom's helicopter was now held aloft by just one of the spinning blades.

As Tom pushed forward hard on the cyclic and pulled on the collective, the remaining blade dug in hard, creating bone-shaking vibration, but also far too much force on the airframe. The torque brought the nose down faster than the big blades could follow as the long tail boom pivoted rapidly up. In an instant, the whirling blades struck the tail, their tips going 650 feet per second, slamming into the drive shaft of the tail rotor. It couldn't stand the impact and sheared off.

Tom felt the helicopter start to spin. The little Franklin engine kept churning out full horsepower as Tom maxed the throttle, torquing against the still-turning blades, spinning the fuselage up faster and faster. But the Bell 47G suddenly had no lift, and no directional control. It fell from 500 feet like a whirling one-ton stone. Tom's hands were still on the controls, demanding more lift, his feet on the pedals trying to counter the spin, as the broken remains of his helicopter slammed into the empty, hard pastureland. At impact, it was going 200 miles per hour, straight down.

He'd been flying for only 11 minutes, and the helicopter's two bulbous gas tanks were near full. The crash broke them free of their mounts, spraying the 80/87 aviation fuel over the hot motor in a mist. The mist instantly caught fire, and it spread to the ruptured tanks.

Tom was still strapped into his seat, his body already badly broken by the force of the impact, when the helicopter exploded into flame.

13

Ellington Field

Luke was the first to see the plume of heavy black smoke rising from the direction Tom had flown. But by the time he got on the radio to report it, the senior tower controller was already on the phone with the Ellington crash response team, and his deputy was calling Harris County Fire.

The rural crash site made access difficult. The base's responders drove to the eastern end of the airfield, unlocked a large gate and bumped cross-country towards the smoke. The Harris County fire trucks, sirens wailing, tacked towards the crash along graveled oil well access routes. Both teams had to cut barbed-wire cattle fences to get close. The Ellington crew arrived first, but it had taken them 14 minutes. By then the fuel had mostly burned off and the cattle had scattered to the field's edge, where they stood aligned, looking on, puzzled and alarmed.

Tom's helicopter had hit the ground upright, but the force of the impact had collapsed the landing skid on one side, so the aircraft was tipped on an angle. The rotors had broken at their central shaft, and now lay in a big inverted V across the wreckage. The tail boom was a twisted mess, like an electricity tower that had crumpled and fallen over.

Orange flame still licked around the charred central block of the engine and transmission. The heat had torched the surrounding grassland, and the Ellington firefighters sprayed the site with water from their truck, then crept closer. One of the Ellington crew jumped out to use a portable extinguisher on the remaining flames, and then the fire crew chief and his senior medic approached the cockpit.

Tom's body was still slumped in place, held by the Nomex shoulder belts. His fire-retardant flight suit was only charred, and his blackened helmet was still on his head. The crew chief moved closer. What he saw inside the helmet made him quickly turn away.

The Harris County fire crew rolled up just as the Ellington medic was checking Tom's body for vital signs. She looked up and shook her head at both crews. With no one to rescue, the urgent pace slowed and the two fire chiefs refocused their attention on maintaining the crash site for the accident investigators and awaiting the county coroner.

After calling the fire crews, the tower controller had next called NASA Ops, and the ops chief had scrambled a pickup truck with airframe techs to head to the scene. Luke had quickly landed the LLTV and come to stand, stunned, beside Kaz, each of them hoping for the best and fearing the worst. Kaz flagged down the NASA pickup on the way past, and he and Luke clambered into the back.

Luke looked ahead at the diminishing black plume, and then at Kaz. Holding on as the truck bounced over the uneven ground, Kaz yelled over the noise, "What did you see?"

"Only the smoke."

Kaz nodded. They were both test pilots. Fatal crashes were a frequent part of the profession, which made understanding why one happened all-important. It also gave them something to focus on, which helped them deal with the personal tragedy and grief. "No use speculating until we know more," Kaz said. "Hopefully Tom's there to tell us."

"Shit, Kaz, we're only a month from launch."

Kaz somberly held up crossed fingers.

The lack of action at the crash site told them the story before they'd even parked. The Ellington fire chief walked over to their truck, his face grave.

"The pilot was killed, I'm sorry to say. Because we're off the base and on county land, I need you to stay clear until the police get here." They heard a siren in the far distance. "That'll be them now."

Kaz, as senior rank present, turned to the NASA ops chief. "We need to get word right away to the Astronaut Office Chief, Center Director, Air Force Liaison Office, NASA HQ." He glanced at Luke and briefly held his gaze. "And Tom's family. Can I use your radio?"

They gathered in the Astronaut Office conference room, on the third floor of Building 4 at the Spacecraft Center. Every available astronaut was there, whether NASA or MOL, along with Gene Kranz and Dr. McKinley. Since Kaz had been at the crash site, Al Shepard asked him to speak first.

He took a deep breath. "As you've all heard, Tom Hoffman was killed this morning in a solo helo crash just east of Ellington. Luke and I were at the crash site twenty minutes after it happened, and could see no obvious cause.

"Luke is Tom's designated Casualty Assistance Calls Officer, so he's gone to the Hoffman house to stay with Margaret. I asked Doc McKinley to be here to speak to us, as he's just been out to the site and talked with the county coroner." Kaz nodded at JW.

"The coroner's report will take a day or two, but there's no doubt it was the impact that killed him. His back and neck were both broken, and it happened quick." JW looked around, making eye contact. "There was a subsequent fire, but Tom was already gone."

Several heads nodded. Death was new to no one in the room, and they all preferred to hear that it happened fast. They feared fire. When the Apollo 1 crew had burned to death in a plugs-out simulation six years previously, it had shaken everyone to the core.

Gene Kranz spoke up. "Gentlemen, this is a horrible day. We need to figure out why one of our training helicopters killed Tom, but we also have a launch scheduled for April 16. It's a miserable thing, and I hate it, but the brutal truth is that this is why we have backup crews."

He looked around the room for Al Shepard. "Management is extra-complex for Apollo 18, but we need a decision ASAP as to how the crews are going to be changed. As soon as that happens, we need to be ready to sprint."

Shepard nodded, and Kranz drove his point home. "We need to get the new crew assigned, and then this whole center needs to work day and night to turn them into the team that will leave Earth for the Moon in thirty-one days."

As the meeting broke up, Al Shepard gathered six of the astronauts in his office. After he closed the door, he said, "Guys, we have a lot to do, but let's have thirty seconds of silence to honor Tom Hoffman."

Some bowed their heads in prayer, and others stared into the distance. Kaz found himself painfully thinking about telling Tom that his face would be on a magazine cover. Not now, it wouldn't.

Shepard raised his head. "Thanks, fellas," he said, as they all turned to face him. He started to count points off on his fingers. "We've already kicked off the accident investigation, and we'll need an astronaut on that. I'm designating you, Bean"—Al Bean, a moonwalker on Apollo 12, nodded—"as you were in on Cernan's investigation." Astronaut Gene Cernan had survived a helicopter crash two years previously while flying too low at Cape Canaveral. Bean had helped dig out the cause of the accident while maintaining Cernan's astronaut career. Shepard had appreciated it.

He touched a second finger. "Luke's with Tom's family, but as of today I need him to focus on nothing but Apollo 18, so, Kaz, I'm asking you to take over as CACO."

Kaz said, "Will do."

A third finger. "Gene was right. We need a new crew roster for 18, and we need it now. We've done the same thing after other training crashes, and after the Apollo 1 fire, and when TK was grounded for 13."

Astronaut TK Mattingly had been inadvertently exposed to the measles three days before launch, and his place on Apollo 13 had been taken at the last minute by his backup, Jack Swigert.

"The MOL astronauts don't really work for me," Shepard said, "but I'm sure Washington and the Air Force are going to listen to what I recommend." He looked first at Chad Miller and then at Michael Esdale. "This close to launch, it's gonna be easier on everyone if we don't do a full crew swap. So my call is that Luke and Michael are still the crew, and the commander of Apollo 18 will now be Chad."

Chad's face remained impassive, but Kaz could see the rush of excitement in his eyes. All the new commander said to Shepard was "Thanks, Al."

"At my direction, the training team is already revamping the flow from here to launch," Shepard said, "to make sure Chad, Luke and Michael get exactly what they need. The helos will be grounded for a while, but otherwise we'll carry on with training and sims. The crew goes to the Cape on April 26, so that gives us"—all 13 eyes turned to look at the wall calendar—"ten days here at MSC." He looked at each man individually. "Any questions?"

They were military men. A death had occurred, they had acknowledged the loss, and now they had their new orders. They all shook their heads.

"All right then," Shepard said. "Let's get Apollo 18 ready to fly."

14

Timber Cove, Houston

"How do you want to handle this, Kaz?"

JW was in the passenger seat of the Satellite, thumbing through the folder of papers that Tom Hoffman had filed with the Astronaut Office in case of death.

Kaz took a deep breath and exhaled slowly. "I'll take the lead. We need to free up Luke to get back to work, make sure that Margaret is coping as well as can be expected—a big reason I asked you to come with me—and answer any questions she has about what happened and what's going on."

JW nodded, still scanning through the folder. "I've met Margaret a few times, and seen her boy and girl once when they came to the clinic." He looked across at Kaz, his face grim. "A lousy day."

Kaz turned off NASA Road 1 onto Kirby, and arced right on Old Kirby Road. The astronauts all tended to live in the three new water-front neighborhoods that had been developed when the Spacecraft Center was built. The Hoffmans had chosen Timber Cove, and their snug cinderblock bungalow fronted on Taylor Lake. Kaz parked at the side of the road under some live oak trees, noting Luke's car in the driveway behind Margaret's station wagon.

They rang the doorbell, and Luke answered. The house was quiet and dimly lit. He led them into the living room, where the large bay window faced the brown bayou waters of the lake. The furnishings reflected the life the Air Force had given Tom: mismatched but comfortable sofa and chairs, a blond chestnut side table and folding screen from a tour in Okinawa, walls hung with smiling pictures of flying and family. A large mahogany stereo hi-fi and TV was against the paneled wall. Sitting on it was a wedding photo of Margaret in white and Tom in ROTC blues, the two of them young and laughing, ducking under an arch of raised swords.

Margaret was seated on the sofa, staring across the lake. Her eyes were red, but she wasn't crying now. She had her arms around her two children, who were tucked as close as they could get to her. The elder child, a girl, was crying quietly. The little boy was asleep. Margaret didn't seem to notice Kaz and JW come in.

Luke silently waved them into the kitchen.

He refilled the kettle. "I had Michael Esdale's wife, Dorothy, get the kids from school; she's standing by to come back as soon as Margaret's ready. I've been answering the phone and the door—all neighbors offering help. Word travels fast. Margaret's held together pretty well. I didn't tell her any specifics. Just that his helo had crashed, and he didn't make it." He got two mugs out of the paneled cupboard, and set a Nescafé freeze-dried coffee jar next to them. "Help yourself."

JW spooned out the crystals and when the kettle boiled, he poured, handing a mug to Kaz.

"Al doesn't want to shake up the whole crew," Kaz said after a small silence. "Chad's your new commander."

Luke nodded. "It makes sense. Minimizes the impact on the mission." He looked bleakly at the two men. "But he ain't no Tom Hoffman."

Kaz nodded. "They asked me to take over as CACO so you can get back to training." He paused. "You okay with that? Do you think Margaret will be?"

Luke shrugged. "When Tom asked me to be CACO, we never thought . . ." His voice broke. He turned away, and took two deep breaths. Then he said, "Right. If we're still going to the Moon, I'll need to get back to work. Let's go tell Margaret."

The March weather had turned to match the mood of the day, with low gray clouds moving in from the Gulf of Mexico. By dinnertime, it was raining steadily, with occasional downpours as waves of thicker clouds passed overhead. The fat raindrops made a continuous metallic din on the tin roof of the U-Joint, a background hum to the after-work wake that had gathered to honor Tom Hoffman.

The NASA Manned Spacecraft Center was a type of factory. It took in the strange raw materials of human dreams, ingenuity and tenacity, ran them through a labor-intensive assembly line of development, testing and training, and spat out astronauts and their support teams, ready for spaceflight. Regular as clockwork, best in the world.

When an accident happened, the assembly line slammed to a stop. It took internal inspections and tests to get the machinery running again, and while that was happening, the factory workers, with all their skills and creativity, were at loose ends.

The U-Joint's wet grass parking lot was filled with cars. Inside, there was a natural pecking order: Apollo space fliers sat at the tables, and junior engineers took the standing room out of respect for the astronauts' willingness to take risks.

The Apollo 18 crew, Chad, Luke and Michael, sat at their own table, the fourth chair empty. The three of them hadn't paid for any of their drinks; Janie just kept bringing them, all on the house.

Chad leaned towards the other two, elbows on the table, chin on his crossed hands. Despite the horrific circumstances, today was the start of his command, and he and these men were about to do something intensely dangerous and demanding together. He allowed himself a small smile and, attempting the first step towards a new relationship, said, "When did I first meet you two assholes, anyway?"

Michael let himself chuckle. "Pax River. Luke and I were still at Test Pilot School, and you and Tom were the Air Force hotshots who'd just been selected for the MOL program. You'd come to brief our class."

Luke looked up from the beer rings he'd been contemplating. "I think, to be accurate, we met at the Green Door." It was the Navy's equivalent of the U-Joint, a country bar in Southern Maryland, a favorite of the test pilots there. "Quite a legendary night, if I recall."

"Yeah, you're right. I remember now." Chad's tight smile faded. "Tom was there that night, with us—and he always will be."

The swinging doors banged open as Kaz and JW came in out of the rain, soaked, stomping their feet.

Chad waved a hand and pointed to the empty spot at the table. JW looked at Kaz questioningly, who by way of answer grabbed a chair off the stack by the jukebox and carried it over his head. Janie spotted them while bringing another round for the table, and stopped to add two whiskies, a beer and a coffee to her tray.

Luke spoke first after they got settled. "How are things with Margaret?"

"About what you'd expect. Dorothy's with her now." Kaz sipped his beer, looking around. "A good crowd."

Chad nodded. "Time to say something." He pushed his chair back and climbed up onto it, glass in hand. The room quickly hushed, all eyes turning to the lone figure on his chair. Someone turned down the sad song on the jukebox.

"Everyone charge their glasses, because today we lost one of our own." Chad turned his head slowly. "Look around. The walls of this place are covered with our history, and our heroes. Some made it to space, some even walked on the Moon. And many died trying. Spaceflight is hard, and it demands our best. Sometimes, even that isn't good enough. This morning we lost a friend, a test pilot, a husband and father, and a damned fine astronaut on his way to the Moon."

JW caught Chad's eye. He was still carrying Tom's folder, and he pulled a glossy eight-by-ten NASA portrait out of it and passed it up to Chad.

Chad held the photo above his head for all to see, saying, "Let's honor Tom Hoffman." He climbed down from his perch and headed for the wall reserved for the astronauts who had died. He found a space and carefully fixed the picture in place, stealing a couple of thumbtacks from the other photos. He raised his glass to Tom's portrait and said, quietly, "The Apollo 18 crew resolves that we will do our damnedest to make you proud."

He turned back to the crowd. "Ladies and gentlemen, we drink to a man gone too soon. So his loss will not be in vain, let's also drink to my crew's success on Apollo 18." He paused. "To Tom Hoffman!"

The room erupted in a toast that echoed from person to person.

Chad was too far away to notice the small tics of reaction on the faces of his two crew at his use of the word "my."

There was a moment of quiet, and to lighten the mood, Luke shouted, "Tom loved a good party, and now that he's on the wall, he won't miss this one. Drink up, everybody!"

The jukebox started back up, the pulsing keyboard of "Crocodile Rock" joining the rising voices of the crowd and the steady percussion of the rain on the roof.

Kaz spotted Laura through the smoke and crowd, grabbed his beer and made his way to her. She smiled when she saw him, and then caught herself. "I'm so sorry for the loss of your friend, Kaz."

"Thanks," he said. "It's a terrible thing. Can I get you a drink?"

She held up her nearly full mug by way of answer.

He touched her mug with his. "To Tom." They both drank.

"I never properly thanked you for taking me flying," she said. "I know it's normal for you, but it was a rare treat for me." She looked around sheepishly at the scientists in her group. "I've been boring everyone with the details, until today that is."

"You helped me remember my own joy in it."

"I'm glad," she said. She stared at her beer for a moment, then met his eye. "Do you think Tom's death will delay the mission?"

Kaz realized that most of the people in the room must be wondering the same thing. "No—we're going to get the crew trained with their new commander in time." He glanced towards the crew's table, where Chad was now sitting alone, staring at the wall where he'd just stuck up Tom's photo. Kaz realized that it was the first time he'd ever seen Chad lost in thought.

I don't blame him. It must really be sinking in.

He looked around for Luke and Michael, and found them at the center of a group of veteran astronauts, all drinking with purpose.

Laura frowned. "How do you do that?"

Kaz looked at her, puzzled. "Do what?"

"Recover so fast. Even in the Lunar Lab we've been zombies all day. It's why we came here tonight, in fact."

Kaz looked away. "It's hard for everyone," he said. He looked squarely back at Laura. "The speeches have been made, and you don't really want that beer. How about we leave?"

She glanced at her friends, then nodded. Kaz asked, "You have your Bug here?"

"Yes. Top's up, fortunately."

"Meet you at my place?"

Laura looked at him for a couple of seconds, then said, "Sure, why not?"

Both of them got drenched running from their cars into the house, and they sat on the couch with towels around their shoulders. Kaz opened a Chianti, rich and warm against the damp.

Laura took a sip, and sighed. Then asked, "So what's the answer to my question?"

Kaz had been thinking about it. "Truth is, we get used to the idea somehow." He looked out at the wet night, rain pouring down the window. "When my first good friend died on squadron, I couldn't accept it. He was a better pilot than I was, superb hands and feet, and more experienced. But on that one flight he came straight down out of low cloud at high speed and hit the water. There was nothing left."

He paused. "It made me mad. I wanted something to blame, *needed* something. So I dug hard into the details—recreating the accident, reviewing the plane maintenance records, looking at fleet reports for similar events. I developed a few probable theories. But eventually I realized that sometimes there's no answer. Flying high-performance machines is a dangerous profession, and occasionally it kills people."

He tipped his head to one side. "The grief is still there. I'll miss him forever—he should be here now, sharing in this life, a friend to laugh with into old age. It's unfair. Worse—it's random."

He took a mouthful of Chianti, swallowing slowly. "When the next friend died, the hole it caused inside me felt the same, but it seemed a little easier to bear. I'd learned the things I could do in response, and those I couldn't. When Tom crashed this morning, I felt that same, irretrievable loss, and a wave of anger that maybe I'd missed taking some action that could have prevented it. I feel the need to find out what happened so we don't repeat it, and the need to take care of his family."

He turned to look at her. "The wound is just as bad, but it's like I've developed a form of scar tissue so I can deal with it. I'll miss each of those guys for my whole life. But I'm still here. If it was me who had bought it, I'd expect them to stay focused; stay busy living too."

Laura raised her wineglass. "Here's to your friends, Kaz, the good men no longer here with you. Especially Tom." They touched glasses and drank them empty.

Then Kaz reflexively did another thing that helped him cope with loss: he pulled out his Gretsch archtop acoustic, a guitar he'd bought used in college and had dragged everywhere the Navy sent him.

They sat on the couch in the semi-darkness as he finger-picked his way through several of his favorites, singing softly, Laura joining in where she knew the words. He tried to avoid the sad ones, yet it felt like every song had certain lyrics that were magnified by Tom's death.

When he finished "Fire and Rain," James Taylor's soulful words echoing in the room, he looked at Laura in the half-light, leaned to pull her close and kissed her.

15

Washington, DC

When the 727's wheels thudded onto the concrete runway at Washington National, Kaz was already tired. It was noon in DC, but it had been a predawn departure from Polly Ranch, and the Eastern flight had been noisy and full, making it impossible for him to catch more sleep. Even his good eye felt gritty.

Now a Checker cab carried him across the 14th Street bridge into south DC, past the Jefferson Memorial and the Navy Yard, and then out into Maryland towards Baltimore. As the cab wound through the forest of the Patuxent Research Refuge, Kaz wondered, not for the first time, why Phillips had called for a face-to-face. The only change to the situation was Tom's death, three days previously. Adding a new commander to the mix made a big difference for the NASA trainers, but he didn't think it was something the NSA head should worry about. Unless there was something he didn't know.

He corrected himself: Sam Phillips was always dealing with things Kaz didn't know. The man faced a daily onslaught of intelligence from multiple sources and ever-changing advances in technology; the way the SIGINT was gathered could be just as important as the information itself. Then the head of the NSA had to sort the wheat from the chaff, feeding the key information, conclusions and recommendations up the chain to the military, who passed it via the Joint Chiefs to the President and other federal agencies.

Like the CIA.

Kaz squinted out the taxi window at the blur of trees. He'd heard about the CIA's new bull-in-a-china-shop boss, James Schlesinger. Could that be why he'd been summoned—in response to pressure from Nixon and his man at the CIA to take extra tactical advantage of Apollo 18's military agenda?

"C'mon in, Kaz!"

General Phillips, smiling warmly, stepped around his desk to greet him and they shook hands. Phillips's lean, pleasant face matched his tall, spare frame. The chest pocket of his short-sleeved white dress shirt had a notepad and a pen in it. His narrow brown tie, held with a clip, was tied in a neat Windsor knot. Pleated worsted pants were cinched high with a thin brown leather belt that matched his shiny brown shoes. A thoughtful military man in civilian clothing.

Jan appeared, unasked, carrying a tray with two coffees. Kaz thanked her and reached for his, grateful for caffeine. Phillips grabbed the other mug and led him to his small meeting table, where they sat. A green file folder, with TOP SECRET in red letters on its front, was already in the center of the table.

"How are you liking Texas?" Phillips asked.

"It's flat, hot and wet," Kaz said, smiling. "But I've been doing some flying, and it's been great to reconnect with Luke and Michael."

Phillips leaned to the left and called through the open door. "Jan, is Mo here yet?"

Kaz's mind raced ahead. "Mo" would be the overall military boss for Apollo 18—Admiral Maurice Weisner, the Vice Chief of Naval Operations.

"I'm just getting him a coffee now, General," Jan called back.

There was a knock on the frame of the door. "Permission to come aboard, Sam?"

Mo Weisner entered, smiling, cradling a coffee. Kaz stood to shake hands with the Admiral as Phillips waved him to the empty seat at the table. Weisner had been a junior officer in World War II whose ship had been sunk by Japanese torpedoes; he had lost 200 crewmates. After he'd retrained as a pilot, he'd torpedoed and sunk a Japanese destroyer escort, and gone on to command three squadrons. His gold naval wings, Distinguished Flying Crosses and other ribbons were neatly pinned above his name tag on his short-sleeved uniform shirt.

He sat and turned his heavy-lidded gaze on Kaz. "Good flight in?" The broad vowels of his Tennessee childhood made "in" a two-syllable word.

Kaz nodded. "Yes, sir, the Eastern breakfast flight." He held up his mug. "My fourth cup."

"I've read the prelim report of the crash," Weisner said, small talk over. He trained his intense brown eyes on Kaz. "They say no obvious cause. I heard you were there. Was it mechanical or did Tom make a mistake?"

"Weather was good, no other planes around, no sign of a birdstrike. My best guess is something failed in the machine. The accident board is sifting through the evidence."

Phillips and Weisner both nodded. As fixed-wing pilots, neither of them trusted helicopters.

"How's Miller doing?" Phillips asked.

"As you know, sir, he's been training alongside the crew in case something like this happened. He stepped right in and he knows his stuff," Kaz said.

"Sure, but are they gonna make it work?" Weisner asked. He'd led men in wartime. It was the key question.

"Tom was a special guy and he'd grown close to Luke and Michael. But Chad's up for it. Apollo 18 will be ready for launch."

Launch—the day the newly formed crew would leave Earth to do whatever these two senior officers decided.

Weisner glanced at Phillips, who said, "We've got some new intel about Almaz. We think they've significantly upgraded the optics." He lifted the pale-green folder and passed it to Kaz.

Inside was a collection of photographs, some with arrows and notes on them in silver and black ink. Kaz picked the first one up and tipped it into the strong light coming from the window. His dissertation at MIT had included an analysis of Soviet space assets, and his memory was clear on early designs for their space station.

"They've changed the mold line," he said, tracing his finger along the new shape of the spaceship's hull. One by one, he examined the remaining photos, looking closely at the print that showed the most magnification. "The optical window is different and the radiator arrangement has been shifted."

He looked up. "I agree with you, General. They've put a whole new capability in there." He thought a moment. "Do we have any ground-based intel on how good it might be?"

The senior men glanced at each other and, again, it was Phillips who spoke. "The CIA's been hearing some things that indicate the Soviets have used different parts suppliers and have also sent new scientific personnel to the assembly plant in Moscow."

Weisner continued. "Our best guess is they've made a significant improvement over the original design."

Kaz nodded, visualizing the components of the various systems. "The raw size of the optics in Almaz will outmatch their unmanned spy satellites, no question." He glanced back at the photographs. "That change in its outer shape means they could have put in reflective optics, using the whole interior diameter for focal length." He ran the numbers in his head. "Which means they could see things down to the sub-meter level. Maybe down to a little over a foot."

He looked up at Phillips and Weisner. "This version of Almaz could spot the two of you walking down the street and tell who's who."

"That's what my analysts have been telling me," Phillips said. "That kind of capability means we have to rethink our deployed assets all over the world, from what's on our ships' decks to our remote base activities to parking the President's car. Almaz is going to make us change and curtail what we're doing. We may have to start performing our critical ops at night, which will increase difficulty and decrease our chances of success."

Weisner said, "As you know, we've got some cutting-edge stuff going on in the high desert that's going to radically change warfare. But only if we can test and prove it in secrecy. You've been a test pilot, Kaz. You know what first flights are like in newly developed aircraft. There's no way we can do those in darkness."

Kaz set down the photos, no longer focusing on the technical details. He could feel where the conversation was heading.

"When does Almaz launch?" he asked.

Phillips said, "We've been watching their normal Proton preparations. Our best guess is in about two weeks. Somewhere in the first week of April."

"Then they'll need time to get Almaz checked out in orbit," Kaz said. "A camera that sophisticated will be too complex to load, point and operate remotely from the ground, so to get the capacity they want, they'll need to launch a crew on a Soyuz to rendezvous with the station and get the system working. The pictures will all be on wide-format film, which they'll need to deorbit in canisters or keep on board until the crew returns, maybe after a month or two."

He looked at the NSA chief. "Have you seen any indication of Soyuz crew launch prep?"

Phillips shook his head. "Not yet, no. We're still confident Apollo 18 is going to launch before the first Soyuz crew heads for Almaz."

"So as you've already figured out, that's our window," Weisner said, "when Almaz is parked in orbit, waiting for its crew." He looked hard at Kaz and added the key word. "Defenseless."

Kaz returned his stare. What these men were implying was clear, and stunning.

"So we won't just be taking close-ups of Almaz anymore."

Both senior officers shook their heads.

"You're ordering the crew of Apollo 18 to disable a Soviet spaceship?"

They nodded.

A chill ran up his spine. Kaz said, "So for the first time in history the United States is going to take hostile military action in space."

16

MSC Headquarters, Houston

"We're going to do *what?*" Luke sounded both angry and incredulous.

Kaz had phoned ahead for an urgent meeting of the key players before he'd left Washington. The three crewmembers, along with Al Shepard and Gene Kranz, had gathered in Gene's office. The door was closed.

He'd brought the top-secret file back to Houston with him, and the men in the room were examining the new pictures of Almaz.

"This comes right from the Joint Chiefs, with the approval of the White House. Apollo 18 has been tasked to disable Almaz before its crew arrives."

Luke picked up one of the photos and stared at it. "How the hell are we gonna do that?"

"Good question. The NSA ops team had a few suggestions for vulnerable points we could get to with a cutting tool—antenna cables, radiator cooling lines, solar panel cables, docking targets, fuel lines. But this means we need to maneuver very close, and be ready for a space-walk when we get there."

Chad blew out sharply through his nose. "Does Washington under-stand what they're asking? This is going to be extremely dangerous."

"Yeah, I said the same thing, and the response is that they want 'all possible effort.'" Kaz mimed the quotation marks for emphasis. "The new CIA chief, Schlesinger, has made it highest priority, and he has the President's ear."

Gene Kranz was already thinking of the practicalities. "We've got some small bolt cutters in the spacewalk inventory, but we might need to get a bigger set on board. We can't cut anything that's got current running through it, but we could cut comms or cooling lines. Maybe fuel, depending."

They all considered that.

Michael asked the next obvious question. "Who's gonna go outside?"

Gene thought out loud. "The existing plan for you, Michael, to do the spacewalk on the way back from the Moon to retrieve *Pursuit's* external film canisters was already tight for weight margins. We'll likely have to trade that to get this done."

Michael shook his head. "But I'm going to have my hands full flying *Pursuit* close enough to Almaz to pull this off. I can't do the spacewalk at the same time." They all saw him realize what he'd just said: he was losing his spacewalk.

Gene nodded. "Agreed. That leaves Luke or Chad. I don't think we have the CO2 scrubbing reserves to send you both out, and Michael's going to need help maneuvering that close to another ship." He looked at both men, his mind ticking through the trade-offs.

Al Shepard spoke. "It needs to be Luke. Michael's the Command Module pilot, and Chad, as mission commander, needs to be inside honchoing all the moving parts."

Luke kept such a tight grip on his expression, Kaz couldn't tell what he was thinking. If it had been him, he would have been equal parts daunted and thrilled.

Chad stared at Al, his jaw clenched. "I don't like this. This is a third change of plan, and we've got less than four weeks until launch! We have no good way to simulate maneuvering so close to Almaz, and very little time to write and practice new procedures. This is a recipe to screw up before we even leave Earth orbit!"

Al nodded, his face serious. "You're right. And you may fail to disable that Soviet spy ship no matter what you do. But the reality is that this sort of op is why we *had* a MOL program, and you three were chosen specifically as a military crew to carry out military tasking. These orders are coming from the Joint Chiefs and the White House."

He looked at each man in turn. "This is now top priority. The least we're going to come away with is clear, close-up pictures of this thing. And with a little luck, Luke will hurt Almaz badly enough that we can protect America's secrets for a while yet."

Gene added, "We have procedures for fast rendezvous with non-cooperative targets from multiple Gemini flights, and we did maneuvering and orbital spacewalk tests during Apollo 9. The simulation hardware is still stored onsite, so we can put together enough reality to do some training. It won't be pretty, but I think we can be ready."

Kaz thought he better point out a fundamental concern. "These photos we're looking at here are top secret. We need the changes in training to be kept quiet, and a total media blackout during Almaz ops."

Gene said, "Right, I'll keep the team size to a minimum, and allow no TV coverage or visitors." He thought further. "There'll be people in Florida gathering to watch the launch, but I think it's best to black out the whole flight after that, not just the Almaz maneuver. NASA PR and the Air Force rep can deflect questions for us, citing national security if they have to."

Chad still looked like he'd eaten something sour. "We'll do it. But when we get there, I'm gonna have Michael keep *Pursuit* at a safe distance until we figure out what's actually possible. And if it turns out we can't do it, everybody will just have to be happy with more pretty pictures to add to Kaz's file."

He was the first to stand as the meeting broke up, and Luke and Michael followed him out the door.

17

Ellington Field, Houston

Apollo 18 was L minus 18 — 18 days from launch. Time to move operations from Texas to Florida, and the astronauts were flying themselves there.

Chad, strapped to his ejection seat in a blue and white NASA T-38 jet, leaned to the left to catch the eye of his groundcrew chief, and raised his right hand high above the cockpit, spinning his finger. Michael and Luke, in their own jets, saw the motion and did the same.

The groundcrew had parked air blowers, called "huffers," beside each of the three T-38s, and had connected the huffers' long hoses to the jets through doors in the planes' bellies. At the hand signal, they switched the huffers to max output, forcing air under high pressure into the T-38 engines, spinning the turbines like pinwheels. Once each engine got turning fast enough, the pilots brought their throttles to idle, letting jet fuel spray into the combustion chambers. Spark plugs flashed and the fuel/air mixture exploded into life, driving the turbines harder, sucking more air into the front intake of the motors. The groundcrew disconnected the huffers, and the engines wound up to working speed.

Kaz was in Chad's back seat, taking advantage of the ride to the Cape, and watched as the instrument panel came to life. Dr. McKinley, as the crew flight surgeon, was with Luke, and Michael's back seat carried an Air Force photographer—who already had his camera out, taking pictures of the start procedure.

Chad looked across at the other two pilots, and got a thumbs-up from each. He hit his mic: "Ellington Ground, this is NASA 18, flight of three, ready for taxi." Luke and Michael flicked their mic buttons briefly, and Kaz heard the two quick chirps in his helmet, confirming everyone was on frequency.

"Good morning, NASA 18 flight, altimeter is 30.12, set squawk 1818, cleared taxi for 35 Left. Have a great spaceflight."

"Copy 30.12, 35 Left, 1818 set. Will do, thanks."

All three pilots reached both hands up and motioned outwards with their thumbs, signaling the crew chiefs to pull the chocks clear of the main wheels. Once safely beyond the wingtip, the crewmen stood at attention and saluted. The pilots saluted back, pushed the throttles up and taxied clear.

Luke followed Chad, with Michael behind him, all offset slightly to avoid each other's jet engine blast. They left the ramp, turning right in close sequence, and headed along the taxiway to runway 35 Left.

Kaz stayed quiet, observing. Some pilots liked to chat, but Chad was all business. As they reached the wide pavement by the end of the runway, the other two jets pulled alongside. Kaz looked across at JW. Even under the helmet, oxygen mask and sunglasses, he could see the doctor's broad smile and knew what he was thinking: this crew was going to the Moon, and he was in the thick of it.

Chad leaned to check with Luke and Michael and saw them nod. Takeoff checks complete, everyone ready.

"Ellington Tower, NASA 18 flight of three, ready for takeoff 35 Left."

"Roger, NASA 18 flight, winds 350 at 11, cleared takeoff. Godspeed."

Chad clicked his mic button twice, closed his canopy and led the trio onto the runway, Luke lining up on his right wing, Michael on his left, both raising a thumb when in position.

Chad made a wind-up motion with his finger, and they moved their throttles ahead into a detent, giving full thrust just short of afterburner. He glanced left and right, then raised his chin and dropped it. At the signal, all three pilots released the toe brakes and jammed their throttles fully forward to the hard stop. Max thrust for takeoff.

The J85 engines responded instantly. Sparks flew, and like a giant blowtorch, the raw fuel ignited in the afterburners, yellow-gold flame visibly erupting out the exhaust at the rear. Now pushing with 6,000 pounds of thrust, the jets began to accelerate down the runway.

Chad pulled his throttles back a little bit to give the other two pilots some extra margin to hold position on his wings. As the airspeed indicator wound quickly up through 140 knots, he eased back on the stick, and the nose pivoted up. Kaz glanced out to see Michael and Luke doing the same. At 160 knots, the jets' thin, short wings were generating enough lift to raise the planes' main wheels off the runway. Chad paused a couple seconds, then raised the gear and flap handles. Staring intently to hold formation, the other pilots found the knobs blindly in their cockpits and did the same. All eyes watched the other airplanes' wheels fold up cleanly out of sight, the covering doors briskly snapping closed.

The transition was complete: the T-38s were no longer compromised beasts of the ground, but clean birds of the air, accelerating up into their natural environment.

The crews settled comfortably into position, tightly and naturally holding formation, a triangle of roaring metal climbing into the south Houston sky, pointed a little bit south of east. Headed to Cape Canaveral — and launch.

They leveled off at 37,000 feet, the sparkling blue waters of the Gulf of Mexico far below them, and Luke and Michael had drifted their jets out to loose formation. The T-38 had no autopilot, and the constant corrections needed to hold heading, altitude and airspeed were tiring. Soon Chad asked, "You want to fly, Kaz?"

"Glad to." Kaz lightly rested his hands on the stick and throttle, and glanced at the navigation chart on his knee for orientation.

"Great, thanks. You have control."

"I have it." Verbal confirmation was standard practice after several airplanes had gone out of control because each pilot thought the other was flying. Kaz shook the stick very slightly as a secondary confirmation, feeling the T-38 twitch in response.

Conversation in a two-seat jet is surreal and fragmented, yet strangely intimate, even with the background din of rushing air and noisy turbojet engines and having to keep a constant ear to the steady patter of Air Traffic Control. Both people face forward, so you can't see when the other is talking; the words just suddenly sound inside your helmet, almost as if they were your own thoughts.

Kaz had been thinking about the flying, and also about Laura, when Chad's voice snapped him out of his reverie. "Kazimieras Zemeckis — it's an unusual name. Where's your family from?"

"Lithuania. It's a Litvak name — Lithuanian Jewish. I was born in Vilnius just as the war started, and my family fled, managing to get one of the last passages to New York." A short pause, as they both listened to the muffled sounds of flight. Then Kaz added, "Good thing they did. By 1942, the Nazis had killed almost the whole community, seventy-five thousand Litvaks."

"So, you're a Jew?"

"Yes, but non-practicing." Why was Chad asking about this? He tried to lighten the mood. "My mother still hopes I'll find a nice Jewish girl to straighten me out."

Air Traffic Control called with a frequency change, transferring them from Houston to New Orleans as they worked their way eastward. The morning sun was bright in Kaz's eye, and he had his dark visor rotated down into place.

"Any other Jews in the program?"

Kaz was startled. Religion was not a normal topic of conversation among astronauts. Yes, the Apollo 8 crew had read from Genesis on Christmas Eve, during their return flight from the Moon, and Buzz Aldrin had taken Communion while on the surface. But this was a weird thing to ask in the cockpit.

"Uh, not that I know of."

Kaz knew that Chad had been raised in the Midwest, but where was this coming from?

"The Soviets have one," Chad said. "Boris Volynov. He got yanked from his first flight on Voskhod in '64, but eventually flew in '69."

Kaz shook his head. Why was that important? And why would Chad have noted it in the first place?

"Huh," he replied. "I didn't know that."

Chad continued. "Have you ever been blocked for an opportunity because you're Jewish?"

"Nah," Kaz said, now determined to lighten this up. "I just tried to come first at everything so no one could say no to me. And here I am today, riding with an Apollo commander on his way to launch!"

Chad grunted, and went silent.

Kaz made a note to check whether Chad had made similar off-color comments to Luke or Michael. The man was a great pilot, but maybe more of a redneck than Kaz had thought.

The long silty tendrils of the Mississippi Delta were passing off to their left, a web of sandbars like a chicken's claw reaching out into the Gulf of Mexico. Kaz turned slightly over the southern tip, heading 100 degrees, following the jet route. Michael's voice broke in. "Hey, Boss, the photog wants some formation shots with New Orleans in the background. Okay if you two close up, and we'll move around for good angles?"

"Sure," Chad said, and Luke brought his T-38 into tight formation. Kaz watched as Michael's jet moved around, getting pictures from several perspectives. They were halfway across the gulf when the photographer decided he had enough.

Chad took control back from Kaz as they entered an area of wispy cirrus cloud that was getting thicker, telling the other two pilots to move into closer formation.

As they crossed the Florida coast, Chad selected NASA Ops on the radio, turned down the squelch and called ahead. "This is NASA 18 flight, a hundred and twenty miles back. We should be there in fifteen minutes."

The responding voice was scratchy with static. "Good morning, 18 flight, we're ready for you, weather's good, plan on landing 31."

"Wilco, thanks." Chad switched back to Air Traffic Control, and asked to begin descent. Florida rolled quickly by underneath, the crew focusing on holding formation as they went in and out of cloud, the jets extra-sensitive at just barely under the speed of sound. As they crossed over Orlando, they switched back to Ops frequency.

"NASA, 18 flight, be there in five. We'd like a couple passes of the pad for photos, and then we'll come into the break for 31."

"Roger, 18 flight, no traffic, cleared as requested."

Chad pushed the jets lower as Merritt Island and the oversized buildings of the Kennedy Space Center came into view. Kaz peered ahead to the coastline, and spotted the massive white and black Saturn V rocket next to the orange framework gantry of its launch tower.

Michael moved his jet slightly away to give the photographer a good angle as they raced past the launch pad a couple hundred feet above the 500-foot tower. They made a wide dumbbell left turn over the Atlantic shore, coming down the coast for a second pass.

With all three jets now almost out of gas, Chad continued down the coast, turning to line up with runway 31. He waved Michael to the far side, moving the jets into echelon right, positioned like the last three fingers of his right hand. They flashed in close formation across the shore, down low and fast over the runway, and Chad broke hard up and left over the small crowd of NASA support crew and media waiting for them. Luke counted "thousand one" and yanked his jet left to follow, Michael doing the same in perfect sequence. They each slowed and dropped gear and flap as they headed downwind, and landed on the 10,000-foot runway, one behind the other.

Chad slowed to taxi speed so the others could catch up, and the three of them rolled in unison up to the waiting groundcrew. They turned in, parked neatly lined abreast and, at a nod from Chad, chopped throttles to Off together. The engines wound down quickly as they opened their canopies, and it was abruptly quiet. They started pulling off gloves and helmets, welcoming the salty Florida breeze on their faces.

They were here, and their rocketship was ready for them on the pad, pointed at the sky.

18

Baikonur, Kazakh Soviet Socialist Republic

The Syr Darya river winds for 1,400 miles, from its source high in the Kyrgyz Tian Shan, Mountains of Heaven, across the flat southern steppes of Kazakhstan, until it finally empties into the broad Aral Sea. The ice-fed headwaters gleam a surreal pale blue, carrying the reflective, finely ground silt of glaciers; the ancient Persians called it the True Pearl River. But by the time it twists down through the towns, reservoirs and endless agricultural irrigation schemes, its waters thicken to an opaque, oily brown. A nondescript-colored snake of a river bringing muddy water to soothe the thirst of the nomadic two-humped Bactrian camels.

The spring thaws and ice jams regularly cause it to overflow its banks, spreading its silt up across the surrounding gray land, turning the soil a fertile, rich brown. Kazakh farmers work its shores, growing crops and grazing their sheep, cattle and horses. Their word for the river's fertile soil was the name given to the town at a long, sweeping bend in the river.

Baikonur. The rich, brown earth.

It wasn't just the river that had flowed from the east. The invasion and conquest of the region by Genghis Khan's Golden Horde was still visible in the high cheekbones, black hair and epicanthic eyelids of the Kazakh farmers. When the Tashkent railway opened in 1906, it brought a wave of different invaders, from the northwest: the round-eyed, pale-skinned ethnic Russians.

In 1955, the vast flatness of this southern land caught the eye of the Soviet space program; Chief Designer Sergey Korolyov ordered the construction of the Baikonur Cosmodrome. A new word, invented for a whole new idea. Not just an aerodrome, but a *cosmodrome*: a gateway to the cosmos.

Sputnik roared off the Baikonur launch pad and into orbit just two years later, its yellow rocket flame reflecting in the waters of the Syr Daria. Four years after that, Vostok 1 carried Yuri Gagarin around the world in 108 minutes.

But a dozen years had passed since that triumphant day—years where the Soviet domination of the cosmos had waned, and decisive leadership from the distant city of Moscow had faded. Even the first spacewalk in orbit, by cosmonaut Alexei Leonov, was soon eclipsed by the Americans who walked on the Moon.

Vladimir Chelomei, the current Chief Designer and the Director of Spacecraft Factory OKB-52, stared for a moment down his long, sharply pointed nose at his leather dress shoes and took a hard pull on his cigarette, welcoming the acrid smoke deep into his lungs. "Desyat lyet," he muttered to himself. Ten years. *And Korolyov's been dead for seven of them.* Chelomei shook his head slowly. But now Korolyov's mantle was his to take, once the Almaz military space station launched.

He and his team had first conceived of the rocket needed to lift it in the early 1960s. It would be the Soviet answer to Apollo's Saturn V, a way to win the space race and ensure that a Russian was the first man on the Moon. Gagarin had been the first to space, after all, and a Soviet man should have been the one to make the first footprints on the Moon.

But politicians aren't engineers. They'd bet on a different rocketship, Vasily Mishin's ridiculous N1, with its 42 rocket motors. Of course it had failed, during four agonizingly wasteful attempts in a row. It had even destroyed its entire Baikonur launch pad! Chelomei had tried everything within his power to change his nation's course, all the way to appealing to Khrushchev himself. But Mishin's political connections had prevailed.

Misplaced arrogance had cost Russia the Moon.

Not this time, Chelomei thought. They would win this second space race, not just for science, but also for something much easier to understand: the national security of the Motherland itself.

Almaz. A powerful Soviet orbiting spy telescope, to be operated by cosmonauts.

Chelomei was standing beside the rocket that would carry his spacecraft into orbit. It was 60 meters long, the enormous size seemingly amplified by the fact that it was lying on its side on railcars. As he waited for the Baikonur launch-pad train to start moving, he paced slowly past the six huge exhaust nozzles and down the length of the behemoth.

The UR-500K monster rocket they'd dubbed the Proton was a proven beast of a machine. *His* rocket. He stopped walking and looked to the left and then the right, taking in the sight. The Proton was still hollow and light, the huge fuel tanks kept empty until it was vertical on the launch pad, ready to receive the full load of volatile hydrazine. Chelomei knew every millimeter of it; he'd been key to the thousands of decisions that had brought it into existence. He and his engineers had solved one problem after another, even how to design it so it would fit on its railcars, able to squeeze through the railway tunnels between the factory in Moscow and the launch pad in Baikonur.

He exhaled loudly through his nose and walked towards Proton's pointed tip, to look at the real purpose of all this engineering: Almaz. His baby, no matter the long gestation period, was in position at last, attached with explosive bolts to the third stage of the rocket that would push it to orbital speed. He glanced to his left. All of this complex plumbing would be garbage then, the first and second stages tumbling to crash onto the empty Kazakh/Altai steppes, the third stage falling into the Pacific Ocean.

His eyes followed to the right, along the smooth shape of Almaz's protective shroud, sculpted down to the pointed metal tip that would be forced up through the air. The shroud wasn't just to help with the aerodynamics, though, but to disguise the shape of Almaz so it wouldn't give away its many secrets to curious launch guests and media cameras. Or the American satellites spying from above.

A klaxon sounded, interrupting his thoughts. He heard shouts of readiness from the workers along the rocket, and the deep rumble of the green and yellow diesel electric locomotive filled the hall. The giant sliding door just beyond the nozzles of the rocket began to move sideways on its tracks. He walked quickly towards the opening, ready to see the spectacle of his rocketship moving out into Baikonur's late March sunshine.

The phone rang on General Sam Phillips's desk. He leaned forward and saw one of the three secure lines flashing. He picked up the receiver and pushed the button.

"Phillips here."

"Sam, it's John McLucas. Got some good news." McLucas was head of the National Reconnaissance Office. "Looks like the Russkies have rolled their latest Proton out to the launch pad at Baikonur. We got lucky on timing with the KH-9 satellite we launched and caught them raising the rocket to vertical at the pad. We're pretty sure it's the launch you and Schlesinger were asking about."

Phillips glanced quickly at his desk calendar, counted days and nodded in satisfaction. The timing for Apollo 18 still made sense.

GO *for launch.*

They were a strange little group.

Three men, a woman and a boy dozed on the bench seats of two battered vehicles. Another man was awake, outside leaning on the rusting square front bumper of his olive-green ZIL-157 truck, staring at the sky. Occasionally he would glance at his aged watch and raise a pair of powerful binoculars, peering intently at the western horizon.

A good time to rest. The hard work would start soon.

His six-wheeled truck had a heavy winch mounted on the bumper, and strapped into the covered rear flatbed was an assortment of acetylene tanks, torches, cutting tools, hammers and wrenches.

The second vehicle was a four-wheel-drive UAZ-452 camper van, called a "bukhanka" for its homely resemblance to a loaf of bread. It had basic cooking facilities and fold-down cots, plus a heater for the cold nights. The early April days were only occasionally getting above freezing, and everyone was bulkily bundled in many layers of woolen clothing as they dozed, their heavy rubber boots lined with thick valenki felt.

The man on watch took a long, deep drag on his cigarette, welcoming the searing heat into his lungs. His name was Chot, and he was descended from the original inhabitants of these northern foothills of the Himalayas. The borders of four countries met just to the south of where the trucks were parked, and his features reflected the history of them all: Mongolia, China, Kazakhstan and the Soviet Union. His nationality was Soviet, but he was proudly Altaian.

He checked the time. "Oi!" he called, loudly. Chot's wife, son and brothers began to stir. Two p.m. in Baikonur. Time for a rocket launch.

The flight path of every Soviet rocketship on its way to space, ever since Sputnik, had passed directly over the Altai Oblast. As the rockets had gotten bigger, the Moscow designers had added multiple stages — sections that would boost the rocket in height and speed, and then, empty of fuel, separate and fall to Earth. Hulking cylinders of pressure tanks, engine bells, electronics and metal, tumbling violently to the ground on a regular basis. The Soviets knew roughly where the impacts would occur, and warned the villages directly under the predicted flight path to evacuate as needed. In reality, the Soviets played the odds, counting on the sparse population and political unimportance of the region to make any collateral damage of low concern. When there was a rocket failure, and the fuel-rich impact explosions led to loss of life, Moscow would pay recompense to the families and ensure there was no publicity. Cheap insurance to allow the space program to function.

Chot fixed his binoculars on the horizon. Having seen many launches, he knew exactly where to look. Sometimes the sun and cloud would align so that he could see the flame and smoke of the rocket itself, especially the larger ones. Today was the biggest: a Proton. He'd looked at the upper clouds and surface winds the night before, estimating from experience how they would affect the trajectory. The rocket's second stage would fall close to where he had positioned his family. If he had guessed wrong, some other group would find and claim the wreckage. He hoped he was right—the metal was worth a lot, and they needed the money.

There!

Through the binoculars he could see the actual smoke trail; squinting, he thought he could just make out the brightness of the flame. *Good.* No delays today. He checked his watch again, and went over the timing. The second stage would separate after about five minutes, and its fall to Earth would take another nine or so. In fourteen minutes, they'd know.

"Start the engines!" he called to his brothers, still staring hard through the binoculars to track the change in smoke that signified rocket staging. It was his job to spot the falling rocket body, and then there would be a race to get to the impact site. Whoever got there first had salvage rights. Just in case, each truck also carried a rifle.

He saw the smoke change, and knew his prize was now on its way. Letting the faint smoke of the third stage of the rocket drift out of sight to the east, he concentrated on where the falling section must be. Sometimes it would glint in the light as it tumbled down. He adjusted the binoculars slightly, hoping for a glimpse.

Was that a flash? He wasn't certain, but it was right where it was supposed to be. Chot could feel his heart racing. The rest of his family was staring upwards as well, everyone straining to see it first.

His young son had the sharpest eyes, and called out in his high voice, "I see it!" The boy pointed up and slightly south of where they were.

"Keep your eyes on it!" Chot ordered.

There was an odd roar of wind noise, a streak of something moving fast, and then an echoing thump of impact—a cloud of frozen dirt thrown up by the impact. "We're close!" he yelled, marking the direction. He jumped into the passenger seat of the ZIL, pointing out the direction for his brother.

I hope there's fire. They could use the smoke as a beacon.

And there it was! A small dark plume as the last of the hypergolic fuel burned itself out, released to the air by the impact. His brother saw it and pushed the truck to its limits, bouncing heavily over the rough ground, leaving the smaller van behind.

Chot scanned left and right, and saw no one else. *A great day!* His experience and cunning would provide for his family.

They came around a copse of evergreens to see the wreckage itself, largely intact on a long, sloping hillside, the smoke fading. No one else was here. The salvage was theirs!

His brother swung around and braked to a stop, carefully upwind to avoid the noxious fumes, and shut the truck off. In the distance they could see the bukhanka following their track. The hunt was over. Now they could get down to the business of stripping the carcass.

Chot looked to the sky. He didn't know where the rocket was going or what it was carrying, or even if there were people aboard, and in truth he didn't care. He was just happy that the Soviet Union had a space program.

It fed his family.

19

The Beach House, Cape Canaveral, Florida

"Pull!"

Kaz had already cocked the trap mechanism, rotating it back against the heavy spring. Hearing the yell, he yanked smoothly down on the nylon cord. An orange clay disk spun out of the track at the tip, arcing smoothly up and across in front of the beach house.

Blam!

The harsh, spitting sound of the 12-gauge shotgun echoed loudly off the clapboard and out across the beach, fading into the breaking surf of the Atlantic Ocean. The flying clay disk instantly disintegrated into shards. Hitting such a moving target took complete concentration, and was a fun distraction for three men about to undertake an unprecedented military mission in space.

"That's four dead pigeons out of five. Beat that!" Luke said, turning on the wooden deck to challenge Michael and Chad, lounging in their deck chairs. The grinding sound of the blender carried out onto the deck. JW was in the kitchen making margaritas.

Michael drained his beer and stood up, taking the gun and earmuffs from Luke. He yelled to Kaz. "You okay for five more?"

"All set!" Kaz, in the shade by the corner of the building, saluted him with his half-empty beer.

Michael put on the earmuffs, adjusting them around his sunglasses. He loaded two new shells into the shotgun barrels, braced his left foot, cocked and raised the gun to his shoulder and yelled, "Pull!"

The disc flew, and Michael tracked it with the long barrel, matching and leading its motion. He pulled the trigger, the recoil slamming the gun hard into his shoulder and cheek. The orange disk continued on its flight, falling and shattering amongst the saw palmetto.

"Uh-oh — bird away!" Luke called.

"I'm just getting sighted in." Michael repositioned and yelled "Pull!" again. He hit the next two, ending up with three out of five. "Looks like a silver medal for me," he said ruefully. "Your turn, Boss."

Chad moved his eyes lazily from one to the other. "You boys forget that I grew up on a farm. Varmint shooting was part of the job description." He set down the margarita JW had just handed him, and held a hand out for the gun. "Give me that."

As Chad loaded, JW walked down the porch stairs towards Kaz. He handed him a margarita, and toasted him with his iced tea.

Chad leaned over the railing. "You boys ready down there?"

"All set, Commander!" Kaz called.

Chad yelled, "Pull!" and pivoted, squeezing smoothly on the trigger, shattering the clay pigeon. Five tries, five hits.

He turned with a smirk. "And that, boys, is how it's done."

Luke and Michael raised their glasses in defeat as Chad put the shotgun back into its case and settled again into his chair. Kaz called up from below. "Sun's setting in an hour or so. Anyone up for a beach walk with me and JW?"

Chad waved his hand. "I'm easy here. You boys go right on ahead."

———

The narrow sandy path led 200 feet through the scrubby palmetto and sea oats before opening to the wide, pale sand of Neptune Beach on the Atlantic coast. The area had been home to a small seaside cottage community in the 1950s, but when the Air Force and NASA had started to expand space operations for Project Apollo, they'd acquired the land and torn down the small store, gas station and all but one of the scattered weatherboard houses. A far-thinking government official had spotted its solid foundations and new construction and decided to spare it from the bulldozers. NASA had christened the cottage the Astronaut Training and Rehabilitation Building to satisfy the fiduciary oversight of the Inspector General, but everyone knew it as the Beach House—a private place for crews to relax in the days leading up to launch. A rare island of no responsibility to counteract the mounting tension and extreme unspoken risk.

Kaz was glad Chad had decided not to come on the walk. He was still a little unsettled by the conversation they'd had on the trip from Houston, and was happy for some time with him out of earshot. As they all stopped to stare out to sea, he asked, as casually as he could, "So how's everybody getting along?"

Luke and Michael exchanged a glance, and Michael shrugged. "Things are different without Tom," he said, "but we're sorting it out."

Luke added, "Chad flies as well as he shoots."

Kaz said, "But he's not Tom, and he had to step in only three weeks before launch. It's got to be a lot to deal with."

Luke picked up a sand dollar and skipped it into the waves. "Well, he's got more of a temper on him than Tom did."

Michael nodded. "Yeah, he does. Plus, you can take the boy out of Wisconsin . . ."

"Anything Doc and I should know about?"

Michael glanced back at the beach house in the distance. "It's just that they've got their share of rednecks and tobacco chewers out there. Sometimes some of that attitude sneaks through."

"Chad keeps it in check for the most part," Luke said, leaning down for another sand dollar. He turned to Kaz. "It's not a popularity contest. Some of the early astronauts were right assholes to work with, but they knew how to get shit done. Michael and I have thick skins and a job to do."

Kaz turned to Michael. "Is there anything more than that? It would be good to know before you're all in space."

Michael shook his head. After a small silence, he said, "I'd prefer if he didn't call me 'boy' quite so much. But it's just how he was raised. We'll get through it."

Luke nodded. "We'll do fine." He looked out at the ocean. "But it sure would have been good to fly with Tom."

20

Ellington Field, Houston

As was often the case, the accident investigator was an unwelcome man.

When Tom Hoffman had crashed, NASA had immediately appointed an investigation board headed by the Chief of the Astronaut Office, Alan Shepard. The seven-member panel had moved quickly to cordon off and photograph the crash site, gathering and protecting all potential evidence. They were given unfettered access to Hoffman's Air Force and NASA medical records, as well as the coroner's report. They seized the maintenance history and daily sign-out log of the crashed helicopter, plus the Ellington Tower flight logs and audiotape of radio communications. The fuel truck had been impounded and sampled so they could check for possible contamination. The Houston Air Traffic Control Center provided radar tracking information of the helicopter's transponder, giving them exact speed and altitude. They consulted the Ellington Meteorological Office's record of the weather conditions, including temperature and wind, critical factors in rotary wing flight.

Once the body had been removed from the crash site, NASA maintenance techs had catalogued and retrieved all debris. The high vertical impact speed had kept the pieces of the helicopter in a surprisingly small area. The subsequent fire had reduced much of it to ash and rubble, including the light sheet-metal cabin and bubble canopy, but the seats, the tail rotor frame and the central heavy metal of the engine and transmission were relatively intact.

Piece by piece, the bits of wreckage were methodically photographed, tagged, loaded into a van and then laid out in a spotlessly cleaned and roped-off section of a secondary maintenance hangar. A silhouette of the helicopter was painted on the floor, and as each piece was identified, it was meticulously placed in its proper location.

Yet despite their methodical work, the NASA accident board had been unable to determine the root cause. The helo techs at Ellington Field had analyzed each charred piece but had found no obvious reason for the crash. A healthy pilot and a flightworthy aircraft had inexplicably fallen from the sky.

Al Shepard was frustrated with the inconclusive result. While the Apollo program was ending, Skylab and the Space Shuttle were starting. He needed any dirty laundry to be kept in-house in case a public hue and cry about cowboy astronaut antics or slipshod maintenance processes caused the already shrinking space budget to shrink further. He also owed an answer to Tom's family; he didn't want them to live with the ignominy of "probable pilot error" for the rest of their lives. But his team had found no smoking gun amidst the wreckage.

Shepard needed to get it resolved. As much as he disliked widening the circle, he called his ex-Navy contacts at the National Transportation Safety Board, and they sent their most seasoned investigator—a former Air Force Master Sergeant and senior instructor at the USAF Inspection and Safety Center, with a specialty in helicopters. A native Houstonian.

Miguel Fernandez stood between the two painted outlines, surveying the twisted, blackened metal. Extra lights had been erected on portable stands, and they starkly highlighted the angular debris, casting harsh shadows.

Looks like a dragonfly that fell into in a campfire, he thought.

Fernandez had flown in from Kirtland Air Force Base in Albuquerque the evening before, taking advantage of the travel to spend the night at his mom's place. His NASA guest pass had been waiting for him when he drove up to the Ellington hangar that morning. The reception at the ops desk had been cool, as it usually was in such circumstances. If Fernandez found something they'd missed, they were going to look bad. The duty officer had escorted him to the debris site, fetched him the coffee he'd requested, and left him on his own.

He sighed, and sipped the thick black liquid from the styrofoam cup. No one ever wanted to stick around and watch him work.

Fernandez had read the board's preliminary notes during the flight to Houston, thinking about the possible causes the investigators might have missed. He walked slowly amongst the wreckage, occasionally squatting, looking for signs that might prove any of his theories. After that first quick survey, he drained the last of the bitter coffee and retrieved his clipboard, pen and rubber gloves from his satchel. The many crashes he'd investigated had required him to develop a way to keep everything straight while missing nothing. He deliberately cleared his head of the morning's distractions and started focusing on the details.

After 45 minutes of stopping, bending, picking up parts in his gloved hand and peering at them through his high-powered reading glasses, he stepped out of the painted area at the tail boom. Fernandez was pretty sure he'd found the cause.

He tucked his clipboard back in his satchel, took his gloves off and carried his coffee cup back to the ops desk for a refill.

The duty officer looked hard at him, trying to determine if he'd discovered anything. "How's it going?" he finally asked.

"Nothing conclusive yet." Fernandez decided to reduce the hostility. "Your boys did a really nice job with the wreckage, very professional. Best I've seen anywhere." It wasn't true, but there was no harm in saying it.

A small smile appeared on the DO's face. "Thanks. I'll pass it on."

Miguel slowly walked back, sipping coffee as he mentally reviewed his inspection of each part. He set the cup on the floor and pulled the NASA board's summary notes from his bag. After he reread their recreation of the flight profile that had preceded the crash, he nodded. It all made sense.

He finished his coffee, then retrieved his Canon F-1 camera and 50 mm macro lens from his bag and also pulled out his magnifying glass and a clean pair of gloves. He slung the camera around his neck and walked to where the largest pieces sat—the engine, transmission and rotor hub. He stopped, took some establishing shots, donned his gloves and then bent down to look closely at the part he'd noticed earlier.

It was badly damaged. The force of the impact had broken the bolt and the mechanism, and the intensity of the fire, right there by the fuel tanks, had blackened and distorted the remnants. An easy thing to miss if a person hadn't seen something like it before and known to look.

He used the lens to get a magnified close-up, taking several frames from multiple angles. Then he picked up one of the pieces and took more photos. He brought the magnifying glass close, examining the shear plane of the broken bolt and the telltale marks on its remaining thread. He compared it to the remains of the matching bolt on the other side of the mechanism. He looked carefully around the nearby floor, verifying that the missing piece wasn't there somewhere.

He had a thought, and walked over to a rectangular painted area where the reconstruction team had laid out pieces of wreckage they weren't able to identify, and he sifted through each piece, just to be sure. It wasn't there, either.

The pitch-rod holding nut was missing.

Without it, the pilot wouldn't have been able to control the helicopter. As the nut loosened, the helo would have felt sloppier and vibrated more, but as soon as the nut popped off, the pilot would have lost pitch and roll control. Evidence of the rotors hitting the tail boom was obvious. The crash was inevitable.

But why had the nut come off? Critical components like this one were cinched to a specific torque and then lock-wired into place. The nut on the other side, though damaged, was still secure.

His examination with the magnifying glass had told him the answer, and the photos would verify it. The lock wire wasn't there. And the speed with which the nut had backed off revealed that it hadn't been torqued properly into place to begin with.

Fernandez looked around the tidy, professional NASA hangar, at the blue and white T-38s on stands and the technicians in white coveralls purposefully doing their maintenance work.

He saw two possible causes.

The first. Someone had skipped key steps in their procedures while installing the nut, and the confirming integrity check and sign-off had also missed it. Very unlikely. Both NASA and the Air Force used independent checks as part of standard procedure to keep just this sort of thing from happening.

The second cause. Someone had deliberately removed the lock wire and loosened the bolt. Someone with access to the helicopter after it had passed its daily inspection. Someone who was trusted inside the NASA organization.

That was much more probable — and the sabotage had led to death.

NASA had hoped he'd give them a simple answer so they could deal with it and get on with flying in space. But this was manslaughter at the very best, and homicide at the worst. Also, it crossed the jurisdictional boundaries of NASA, the Air Force and the NTSB, not to mention the local police. Once it came under the public scrutiny of a media fascinated by astronauts, it was going to get even uglier.

Fernandez had done his job and was sure of his conclusions. He mentally reviewed his reporting chain, deciding who to phone. He sure as hell wasn't going to tell anyone here. Time to hand this mess over to the powers that be.

The rest of it was above his pay grade.

21

Astronaut Crew Quarters, Kennedy Space Center

"Steak, eggs and toast? You sure about that, Boss?" Michael eyed Chad's full plate, willing himself not to picture what that food would look like if it came back up.

"I've never been motion sick in my life, and I'm not going to start today." Chad slid a sunny-side egg onto the steak, lifted both onto the buttered toast, cut a large bite and forked it all into his mouth. "Last decent meal we're gonna get for a while," he said, chewing.

Luke shrugged. "A wise old chief petty officer at sea once told me it's best to eat smooth food; makes it easier when you vomit." As Navy men, he and Michael had breakfasted on a banana each, water and coffee.

Al Shepard bemusedly watched Luke pour himself another cup. "Go easy on that, Marine. On my first flight I drank so much coffee I had to piss in my pressure suit, then lie on my back in the puddle, waiting for launch." He smiled at the memory. "A glorious first in space history."

Luke set the cup back down.

Kaz checked his watch. "About time to get dressed, fellas."

Luke and Michael pushed back from the table, then leaned into the kitchen to shake hands with the staff. Chad took one last forkful, and got up and followed them down the hall.

Al tapped Chad on the shoulder as he walked past. "Get your guys to take one last leak before they suit up."

A spaceship is, in essence, a bubble of Earth's air in the empty vacuum of space. The thin aluminum hull holds the internal pressure against the nothingness, so the crew can work comfortably wearing normal clothes, without oxygen masks. But during the riskier parts of flight, like launch and landing, when a sudden jar could pop a hull seal loose, astronauts need an extra layer of protection. Ever since Al Shepard's first flight, they'd worn a pressure suit, just in case—a form-fitting personal bubble of oxygen.

Hanging on racks in the suit-up room were three Apollo pressure suits, each custom-made for the crewmember, all of them in white to reflect the Sun's intense heat. To save weight and stowage space, Chad and Luke would wear the same suits to walk on the Moon.

Michael waddled out from the washroom, wearing a urine collection condom, heavy absorbent underwear, stick-on medical sensors and a full-body cooling suit woven with water recirculating tubes. Luke came out after him.

"Hey, Michael, your ass looks big," he said.

"Have you glanced in a mirror? You look like a snake that ate a toad!"

They padded to their suit techs, waiting patiently by tables loaded with spacesuit gear. A tall rack covered in dials and knobs stood nearby, ready to test pressurization and communication.

As the tallest of the three, Michael had the hardest time getting into his suit, a one-piece garment that opened from the back with a heavy zipper. He bent his head and narrowed his shoulders, squeezing in until his hands and feet found the arm and leg holes, finally stretching to full height as his head popped through the neck ring and his feet slid into the built-in booties.

He glanced at Chad and Luke, who were still squirming into their suits. "Every time I do that I feel like a baby climbing back into the womb."

Luke chuckled. "Freud would have a field day with you."

Michael pulled hard on a long, webbed tab between his legs, tugging the stiff zipper all the way around until it was sealed. His tech guided a black and white cloth cap over his head, and Michael pulled the chinstrap tight, getting the ear cups snug. He grabbed the flexible twin mic booms and bent them into place by the corners of his mouth; once he had his helmet on, there'd be no way to adjust them.

The tech raised his eyebrows. "Ready for air?"

Michael nodded, already overheating in the sealed rubber suit. The tech clipped a hose into a matching valve on Michael's chest and threw a switch on the control panel, and Michael could feel cool, dry air blowing through the suit, up and out around his neck.

"That's better," he said. He put his Omega Speedmaster watch on his wrist and pulled on thin white cotton gloves.

The tech held up a thick black rubber glove, and Michael pointed his fingers and thumb together to slide his hand inside. The tech expertly clicked the glove's pressure ring into place against the matching blue ring on the suit's left cuff, and then did the same with the glove and red ring on the right.

"Are they color-coded so we know our right from our left?" Michael asked. It was an old joke, but the tech laughed, cutting the guy some slack since he was about to go ride the world's biggest rocket.

Michael glanced at the wall clock. "Time to start breathing oxygen?"

The tech nodded and lifted Michael's helmet from the table. It looked like an inverted fishbowl with cloth stuck down one side. Michael took it from him and wiggled it over his head, the cloth section to the back, careful not to let the metal locking ring scrape the skin off his nose. He'd done that once in training, and now knew better.

The tech disconnected Michael's cooling airflow, locked the helmet latches in place and then hooked up recirculating oxygen and water lines. Michael was now relying on a machine to breathe, and would be until they landed back in the ocean at the end of the mission, over a week later.

The endless training and practice were over. Shit was getting real. He, Michael Henry Esdale, an unlikely little kid from South Chicago named for his two grandfathers, was about to get into a rocketship and blast off the face of the Earth. So many times he'd been told no in his life, a Black man trying to succeed in the white man's realm. It had been years of slogging to always be the best, to leave no doubt, and even then some people told him he was only here because of race politics. That he hadn't earned his opportunities, but had been handed them as some sort of favor. Michael shook his head to clear the thought. He'd earned his ticket, and it was him who was going to fly that thing.

The pure oxygen tasted dry and clean, and Michael felt his head clearing as his body absorbed the gas. Over the next few hours, the nitrogen in his blood would be gradually replaced by oxygen; that way, when he got to orbit and popped his helmet off in the low-pressure all-oxygen atmosphere, his blood nitrogen wouldn't suddenly bubble and give him the bends. As scuba divers knew, bubbles in the blood were bad, causing huge pain in the joints, and potentially death.

There were brown leather La-Z-Boy recliner chairs for each crewmember, and Michael settled into his while the tech cranked up the suit pressure, checking for leaks. As the suit stiffened, the neck ring of his helmet was pushed up to his mouth. It was uncomfortable, but workable; this is what it would be like during an emergency deorbit and splashdown. Michael moved his arms and flexed his fingers, picturing how he would reach switches against the hard resistance of the suit. The tech looked intently back and forth at the pressure gauges and a stopwatch, and eventually nodded in satisfaction. He twisted a large knob counterclockwise, and Michael gratefully felt the suit soften and his neck ring lower to its normal height. Suit check complete, he pulled out his launch emergencies checklist, flipping through it with his black-gloved hands.

Luke's voice carried to Michael through the communications lines. "Find anything new in there?"

Michael looked over, slightly sheepish. "Never too late to review."

In truth, Luke was happy to see it. Michael had the lion's share of the piloting to do after launch. They'd be heading immediately for Almaz, and Chad would be busy getting Luke and his suit and gear ready for the spacewalk. This was the first spaceflight for all of them and the pressure was intense to do things right.

Chad's voice cut in. "How are you boys doing?"

Luke leaned forward and twisted his suit so he could see Chad in his recliner. "No leaks, Boss." As the technician put the last of Luke's checklists and safety equipment into his suit's pockets, he added, "We must be getting close."

"Same here, Chad," Michael said, raising a thumb. "My suit fits like a glove."

"Especially the gloves," Luke joked.

The suit techs stepped back next to the consoles, their work complete. JW donned a headset and made one last assessment of medical status with each crewmember, while a NASA photographer walked around and took a few photos.

Al Shepard's voice came over the comms. "You gentlemen ready to go see your spaceship?"

Three hands immediately came up, thumbs raised.

"Right. Time to go get us a launch."

The ride to the pad was nine miles through palmetto scrub and a cluster of oversized rocket assembly buildings. As the van lumbered smoothly along the coral pavement, Chad spotted a bald eagle through his window. It swooped low along the road, spread its wings wide and landed in a large nest, high in a longleaf pine.

Like home, he thought. He'd loved watching birds on the farm, envying their effortless grace in flight. It was part of the reason he'd joined the Air Force; that and to prove himself, to make his parents proud. And now he was on his way to take his place among the greats. He looked down at his white pressure suit, a satisfied smile curling his lips. *I'm going to leave my footprints on the Moon.*

Al Shepard's voice broke in on his thoughts.

"Gentlemen, if I may." Al raised his hand to get everyone's attention. "It's time for the Astronaut's Prayer."

Chad had never heard of this, and from the expressions on his crewmembers' faces, they hadn't either.

His expression serious, Al looked each one of them intently in the eye, and then bowed his head. "Lord, please don't let these men fuck up." He raised his head, smirking, and they all joined him on the "Amen."

It was a joke, but it was also sincere.

The van slowed to a stop next to the Launch Control Center, a long, four-story white building. Al got up and shook hands with Chad and the other crew, wishing them luck, as did JW and Kaz, and then they all climbed out. They'd watch the launch through the fourth-floor windows of the LCC and then fly immediately back to Texas on a NASA Gulfstream jet to be in Mission Control in time for the rendezvous with Almaz. Chad was happy to see them go. It was his show now.

As the van pulled back out onto the road, the suit tech waved his hand to get their attention, and pointed forward. He knew what the view was about to be and wanted to be sure these men didn't miss it.

The van rounded the curve, and suddenly Chad could see the launch pad. Still three miles away, yet clearly visible high above the flood plain, the Saturn V rocket was like some ancient Egyptian monument to the gods, standing proudly next to Launch Pad 39A's gantry tower, gleaming white in the morning sunshine.

Their rocket. *His* rocket.

"Look at that!" Michael said in wonder, his voice muffled by the helmet.

The reality of it struck Chad like a face slap. No more simulations. It was time to show the world who he was.

The van rolled through the open gates at the base of the pad, and the driver downshifted to climb the long, sloping grade up to the rocket. The launch area was crisscrossed with train tracks and metal plates, and the van vibrated as it drove over them. The driver swung wide, stopped and then backed close to the tall gantry. He set the brake, climbed down, walked around and opened the wide rear door, facing the elevator that would take the crew up to the capsule atop the rocket.

Michael clambered out first, and the driver held out his hand.

"Boarding pass?" he demanded sternly. His face broke into a wide grin at the look on Michael's face, and he reached forward to shake his gloved hand. "Have a great flight, sir!"

He repeated the gag for Luke, who laughed obligingly. Chad stepped down, shook the man's hand and then leaned back so he could stare upwards along the full length of the Saturn V. The monstrous rocket was crackling and venting with the super-chilled oxygen being pumped into its tanks. An enormous, brooding dragon, about to belch fire and hurl itself up off the pad, into the blue of the Florida sky.

A white-suited tech was patiently holding the elevator door open. Chad tore his gaze away from the spectacle, trying to fix the image permanently into his memory, and led his crew into the elevator.

The Saturn V stood 363 feet, as tall as a 34-story building. The elevator was designed for freight, with just a framework of metal in place of walls, and the crew watched the rocket flash by as they climbed.

The thick first stage was 33 feet across—so big it couldn't fit on any road or railcar, and had been brought to KSC from the factory in New Orleans by barge, a thousand-mile trip that had taken 10 days. It was now filled with nearly 5 million pounds of oxygen and kerosene; once the engines lit, it would burn through the fuel at 15 tons a second.

The white skin of the rocket looked rough, as it was covered by a thin coating of ice. The chilled liquid oxygen inside it made the whole rocket cold, and when the humid Florida air condensed on the skin, it froze.

A *tall cold one*, Luke thought.

The ice would shatter and fall off as the engines lit.

The elevator clattered them up quickly past the black-and-white checkerboard pattern of the wide metal sleeve that protected the five second-stage motors and joined the two rocket segments together. The first stage was going to push with 160 million horsepower, and this hoop of metal had to be strong enough to handle the force and vibration.

As they passed the 20-story mark, the width of the rocket narrowed to the third stage, its hydrogen and oxygen tanks feeding a single engine that would push them out of Earth orbit to the Moon. Like the second stage, it had been built in California; both had traveled to the launch pad by ship through the Panama Canal.

Luke leaned forward and looked down. *Whoa!* He felt unexpected vertigo. The elevator was slowing as they reached the Command Module level, and he lifted his eyes towards the beach house to settle his gyros. He could see the thin strip of sand just beyond it, pale brown against the Atlantic waves.

The doors opened with a clang. Chad picked up his ventilator pack and strode off first. Michael followed, then Luke, walking along an outer railing and through a gantry door, then out to the final swing arm that led to their spaceship.

Michael leaned his helmet close to Luke's and yelled, "Like a gangplank!"

Chad had already started down the long, thin walkway of the swing arm. It was 320 feet above the launch pad, a latticework of orange-painted metal, with open sides and top. The metal grid of the floor was covered with rubber mats to block the dizzying view.

Luke yelled back, "You're next, Michael—now or never!"

At the far end of the walkway was a small, tent-like enclosure nestled against the sloping side of the spaceship. It was covered in white fabric, and, with NASA's typical artistic flair, it was called the White Room. It was just big enough for the suit techs to get one crewmember ready at a time. When Chad disappeared inside, Michael began walking.

He stayed solidly in the middle to avoid getting buffeted into the siderails by the wind. Like most pilots, he hated heights when he didn't have wings to support him. He kept his gaze focused on the White Room door at the end, and felt irrationally safer when it opened and he was able to step inside. Chad was already swinging himself into the capsule's darkened interior.

Luke took a few paces out onto the gantry and looked around while he waited his turn. His eyes followed the long crushed-gravel trail of the giant tracked crawler that had slowly carried the rocket-ship to the pad. At the far end were the Vehicle Assembly Building and the Launch Control Center; he peered at them, imagining the hundreds of engineers and technicians at their consoles, staring back at him through its windows.

He swung his gaze to the left, and could pick out the flag and crowds at the NASA Press Site. Squinting, he could just see the low, dark rect-angle of the digital countdown clock. Farther left, across the water of the Banana River, he could see glinting reflections from the thousands of cars that were parked there, the spectators jockeying for position on the beach. His parents were somewhere in that mass of people, and he raised a hand and waved to them, thinking of how they must be feeling and silently thanking them.

Movement caught his eye, and he realized the door had opened and a tech was waving at him. He hustled down the gantry.

The techs were fast and methodical as they checked Luke's suit. He handed them his ventilator and lifted his feet individually so they could slip off his protective yellow galoshes. Then he grabbed the handlebar above the hatch and swung his legs inside, fighting the bulky suit. Chad was already strapped into his seat on the left, and a tech was tightening Michael's restraint straps on the right. Since Luke would be doing the Almaz spacewalk soon after launch, he was in the center seat, nearest the hatch; it would simplify configuring his umbilical and getting himself efficiently outside. Lifting his weight, Luke slid on his back into place.

The tech leaned his face close and asked Luke to hold his breath so he could swap the hoses from the ventilator for the built-in ship lines. Luke could feel him making connections, and suddenly sound crackled in his headset. The tech leaned into Luke's sightline.

"One, two, three, how do you hear me, Luke?"

"Loud and clear, thanks."

The tech cinched down Luke's straps, double-checked that the checklists were still Velcroed and clipped in position, and gave his visor a wipe with a chamois cloth. Then he looked Luke in the eye.

"All good?"

"All set," Luke said.

As the tech retrieved the last of his equipment and gave the cabin a final once-over, Luke looked around. Lying on his back, he could turn his head left and right, its weight supported by his helmet. He listened to the low hiss of ship's oxygen flowing up and behind his head, feeling it blowing steadily down across his face to keep his visor from fogging. He glanced at Chad and then at Michael; both of them were all business, lit by the sunlight from the overhead windows as they focused on their instruments, double-checking against the checklists mounted in front of them.

Facing the crew was a complex array of over 600 switches, instruments and indicators that allowed them to control the spaceship, now as familiar to each of them as any airplane they'd ever flown. No one could reach all the switches, so they each had specific responsibilities. Squarely in front of Luke were the propulsion system, atmospheric control and the cluster of emergency lights that lit up in yellow and red to signal that something was wrong. There were still a few lights on, as the vehicle wasn't quite ready for launch, and Luke checked from memory that the pattern was correct.

He felt a tap on his helmet and leaned back to see the tech, his eyebrows raised in a polite question. Luke gave him a thumbs-up, and watched as he checked with Michael and then Chad. Then the tech waved, clambered carefully out and closed the hatch.

Luke looked at the digital mission timer squarely in front of him, counting down: two hours, ten minutes to launch.

Fifteen miles to the east, a ship called the *Kavkaz* waited patiently. She wasn't particularly big, and her hull was better suited to the landlocked Black Sea than the open waters of the Atlantic, but she was based on the classic Mayakovsky fishing trawler design and could handle the rougher seas well enough. Only 85 meters long, she had a more-than-ample 14-meter beam, and her 2,200-horsepower single-screw diesel could push her through the water at a useful but unimpressive 12.5 knots.

Kavkaz's true merit didn't rest on her hull and engine, though. It was in the gleaming white dome and multiple antenna towers mounted on her upper decks. She was a Primorye-class surveillance ship with high-speed satellite datalinks back to the Soviet Union, and she was patrolling the Florida coast just outside of the US 12-mile limit. And she had been tasked by HQ in Leningrad to observe this final Apollo launch.

The Captain was content. It was not a complex mission, and the mid-April Florida warmth was a very welcome break for his crew. They'd spent the previous two months in the North Sea, and when the orders had come to steam south, everyone had been glad. It was the twelfth Apollo launch, and they'd all been virtually identical. *Proshche parevoy repeh*, he thought. Simpler than a steamed turnip.

He'd told the chief communications officer to pipe the NASA countdown through the ship's loudspeakers, and every crewman who wasn't needed belowdecks was up on the rail, most with binoculars and cameras hanging around their necks.

The American voice echoed through the Soviet ship. "This is Apollo Saturn Launch Control. We've passed the thirty-six-minute mark in our countdown, and completed the range of safety command checks, all still going well. A short while ago Spacecraft Test Conductor Skip Chauvin asked Commander Chad Miller if the crew was comfortable up there, and Chad reported back that 'We're fine—it's a good morning.'"

The Captain, who spoke English passably, looked across the calm seas towards the Florida shore. *I agree, my fellow captain, it's a very good morning.*

The US Coast Guard cutter *Steadfast* was trailing the *Kavkaz* by a half mile, making sure they didn't stray too close. It was a cat-and-mouse game both of them had played many times before, and they were easy with it. The recently signed US-Soviet Incidents at Sea Agreement had made the rules clear for both sides: stay out of each other's way, follow the regulations and, most important of all, take no hostile-looking actions.

The Captain checked his watch: 15:00 in Moscow, 08:00 here in Florida. Just over a half hour until launch. He checked his binoculars and his camera as well. He didn't want to miss this.

The small black-and-white portable television was out of place in the Berlin cathedral. Alexander, now the senior lector for Father Ilarion, had brought it and set it up in the vestry at the monk's request. He extended the twin silver aerials, twisting and tilting them until he had a clear picture from the local station. He pushed the small buttons on top while the NASA announcer was talking, setting the volume. Alexander stepped back, and the picture faded. He grunted, readjusted the antennas and stepped back again. The picture held this time.

In truth, Alexander was excited for the chance to see the last Apollo launch, the last of America's planned manned Moon missions.

He heard the hieromonk coming down the hall and double-checked that the TV picture was still good. He'd positioned two chairs facing the screen.

"Pochti parah?" Father Ilarion asked. Is it almost time?

"Da. Minoot pietnadset." Yes—about 15 minutes.

The NASA announcer was speaking. "All still going well with the countdown at this time. The astronauts aboard the spacecraft have had a little chance to rest over the last few minutes. In the meantime, we have been performing final checks on the tracking beacons in the

Instrument Unit, which is used as the guidance system during the powered phase of flight."

"Shto skazal?" *What's he saying?*

The monk's grasp of English remained minimal. Alexander translated, summarizing as the NASA public affairs officer spoke. Ilarion leaned towards the small screen when they showed a close-up of the rocket on the pad. He frowned.

"What's that steam coming out of the ship?"

How should I know? Alexander thought with some exasperation. *Why do people think interpreters have knowledge beyond language?*

He guessed. "It's excess fuel as they fill the tanks to the brim."

Father Ilarion nodded. "What an amazing thing!"

They listened as Houston Mission Control started communications checks with the capsule. Alexander raised his hand, palm open, for silence.

"Apollo 18, this is Houston on VHF and S-band. How do you read? Over."

They both held their breath to listen for the voice crackling across the thousands of kilometers.

"Houston, Apollo 18. Have you loud and clear."

A wondering smile spread across Ilarion's face.

"This is Apollo Saturn Launch Control. We've passed the eleven-minute mark, all still GO at this time. The spacecraft is now on the full power of its fuel cells. The Commander has armed his rotational hand controller, and we have now gone to automatic on the Emergency Detection System. We're aiming for our planned liftoff at thirty-two minutes past the hour."

The voice echoed tinnily from the multiple small loudspeakers mounted on poles along the Banana River causeway. Cars were parked at all angles, thousands of them jammed together on the narrow strip between the road and the beach. With launch just 10 minutes away, the early-morning lineups at the food trucks and portable toilets had evaporated, and all faces were turning towards the launch pad, seven miles to the north. The morning sun was already hot, glaring down on the deck chairs, blankets and sunglasses of the excited crowd.

Laura sat on the back bumper of a Dodge van, holding a black coffee and rubbing the overnight grit from her eyes. She and three others from the Lunar Receiving Laboratory had made a last-minute decision to road-trip to the Cape for the launch, a monotonous, 15-hour five-state haul across I-10 and down I-75. Their NASA badges had gotten them early access to the causeway the night before, and they'd slept in the van backed right onto the beach, which meant she now had an unimpeded view straight across the water to the Saturn V.

Don Baldwin, his Hawaiian shirt adorned with rockets and clouds, sat next to her. "Got lucky on the weather."

She looked around at the blue sky and the light skiff of wind on the water, then stared across the water towards the rocket. "I'm glad we made the drive." She said it partly to convince herself; it had been an uncomfortable sleep. As the announcer called "Mark, T minus ten minutes and counting," she shook her head to clear it and sat up straighter.

The loudspeakers blared the familiar GO/NO-GO dialogue, STC querying each console in Launch Control for their readiness. Laura felt her gut clench as several of them reported problems, and then relax as they worked through them. She listened for Chad Miller to add his "GO," and then a different voice came on. "Apollo 18, this is the Launch Operations Manager. The launch team wishes you good luck and Godspeed."

She glanced at her watch, her heart starting to race. Four minutes to launch. Some of her experiments were inside that beast, and she'd helped to train the crew. She focused her camera lens on the rocketship, squeezed her finger on the shutter button and took the picture. Her thumb found the lever and advanced the film.

C'mon, baby, we scientists are ready! Time for all you engineers to do your stuff. Get that crazy monstrosity off the ground!

———

The Saturn V's F-1 engines were beasts with a power the world had never seen. Five of them waited at the bottom of the rocket, sleeping in suspended animation, their blood vessels dry, their hearts and bellies empty. Hungry and ready for the fuel and spark that would bring them to life.

Ten minutes before launch three valves had clicked open, allowing the first of the kerosene and chilled oxygen to gush down from the tanks, high above. This potential explosive power now waited to be mixed, just one valve away from exploding into the barely controlled hellfire that would push the massive weight up and away from the Earth.

Luke was aware that the pre-valves were open; he knew the entire sequence by heart. The giant dragon beneath them was awakening. He'd wondered how he would feel just before launch. *Not afraid*, he observed. *Good*. Either this thing was going to work or it wasn't. He felt . . . ready.

Movement on his right caught his eye. Michael's left knee was bobbing up and down, an unconscious release of pent-up emotion and energy. Luke was glad both of his knees were still.

He glanced at the clock. One minute to go. Sixty clicks of the second hand and the games would truly begin. He watched Chad reach and push the button to align the gyros, giving the rocket a final snapshot of orientation for accurate steering. It was the last crew step prior to launch.

Luke turned the page of his checklist and put his thumb next to the top of the table. Chad and Michael would be watching lights and instruments, but he'd be looking at height versus speed. The whole 11 minutes and 39 seconds was laid out in the table. When his thumb got to the bottom, they'd be 93 miles up, going 25,599 feet per second. 17,500 miles per hour. Five miles a second.

22

Launch Pad 39A, Kennedy Space Center

Starting the world's most powerful engine wasn't easy. It took about nine seconds to crank one up—the time an Olympic sprinter could run 100 yards. The time it takes to tie one shoe.

The most dangerous nine seconds of the whole flight.

The amount of fuel needed to push the Saturn V off the pad was staggering: 3,400 gallons every second. That required fuel pumps with their own jet engines, just to spin them fast enough. The rocketship had five of these jets pumping the kerosene and oxygen into the rocket chambers, where it would mix, explode and storm out the 12-foot-tall exhaust nozzles in a 5,800-degree, 160-million-horsepower inferno.

The crew's eyes were glued to the engine instruments as the clock counted down into single digits.

"T minus ten, nine, and we have ignition sequence start."

Four fireworks ignited inside each engine: two to spin up the fuel pump, and two to burn any flammable gases lurking in the exhaust nozzle.

"Six, five, four . . ."

Two big valves opened, and liquid oxygen poured from its high tank down through the spinning pump and into the rocket, gushing out the huge nozzle under its own weight like a frothy white waterfall. Two smaller valves clicked open, feeding oxygen and kerosene to fuel the jet engines, spinning the pumps up to high speed. The pressure in the main fuel lines suddenly jumped to 380 psi.

Conditions were set, with everything ready to ignite the rockets. Just needed some lighter fluid.

Two small discs burst under the high fuel pressure, and a slug of triethylboron/aluminum was pushed into the oxygen-rich rocket chambers. Like the ultimate spark plug, the fluids exploded on contact.

"Three, two . . ."

The middle engine lit first, followed quickly by the outer four; if all five had started at once, they would have torn the rocketship and launch pad apart. Two more big valves opened, and high-pressure kerosene poured into the growing maelstrom.

Luke felt the rippling vibration through his back and heard the deep, rumbling noise from 300 feet below. *Different than the simulator!* He glanced left to where Chad's eyes were focused. The five engine lights had gone out, confirming full thrust.

"One, zero, and liftoff, we have liftoff, at 7:32 a.m. Eastern Standard Time."

Hell, unleashed, creating 700 tons of thrust in each of the five engines—enough total power to lift more than 7 million pounds straight up. The ultimate deadlift.

The last of the ground umbilicals feeding the rocket disconnected and snapped back. The four heavy hold-down arms that had been clamping the base to the pad hissed in pneumatic relief and pivoted away.

The Saturn V was free.

Chad's eyes clicked around his instrument panel, confirming. The small, square Lift Off light was glowing, he could feel the vehicle moving, and the digital mission timer was counting upwards.

"The clock is running, Houston."

Apollo 18 had begun.

Father Ilarion's jaw had gone slack. What he was seeing on the small screen was far removed from his daily life, and yet the power and danger were palpable to him.

As the final 30 seconds before launch had ticked down, he'd grabbed Alexander's hand, squeezing hard. While the announcer's voice counted through the last 10 seconds, Ilarion's grip intensified until his entire arm was shaking, the flames from the engines filling the screen and the rocket lifting off the pad, agonizingly slowly.

"Slava Bogu!" Ilarion said in abject wonder. Praise God! His eyes remained locked on the flickering image, but he didn't understand what the NASA announcer was saying. "Is everything still all right, Alexander?"

"Yes, Father, the rocket is working perfectly. The astronauts are having the ride of their lives." He pried his hand out of the hieromonk's grip and shook his tingling fingers.

The two men watched without speaking, the blue TV light oddly illuminating the icons on the bare plaster walls as the image on the screen shrank to a wavering flame in the sky.

"Roll and pitch program, Houston."

The three crewmen were intensely hawking their instruments. The rocket had climbed clear of the launch tower and then turned to steer up the east coast; they could see the precision of it in the motion of the black-and-white ball of the artificial horizon. As Chad radioed the expected motions to Houston, Luke noticed the sunlight changing angle through the windows, confirming that the ship was guiding properly.

"Roger, 18. Thrust good on all five engines."

Hearing the voice of their CAPCOM was reassuring. It meant that a team of experts was comparing expected height and speed to what the ship was actually doing, and that they matched.

Luke traced his thumb along the table in his checklist, confirming what Houston was telling them. He tried to hold his hand steady against the deep, powerful throbs and fast, jittery shaking, but the vibrations made it hard to line up the numbers. The relentless roaring of the engines filled the cockpit with a symphonic cacophony punctuated by terse communications with the ground.

Luke leaned his head forward against the motors' thrust and caught Michael's eye. "How's that for a cat-shot?" he said, referring to the steam catapult that had once launched their jets from aircraft carriers.

Michael grinned. "Better!"

As the fuel rapidly burned and the vehicle got lighter, it accelerated faster and faster through the thinning air. Luke felt his head and arms getting pushed back as the g-force mounted. He leaned against the headrest, which was buzzing as the rocket shouldered itself through the atmosphere.

He checked his gauges. "Cabin pressure's dropping." Open valves were letting the air inside the cockpit vent as the pressure around the ship dropped with altitude. They'd let it fall all the way to 5 psi and then close the valves to hold it there, using pure oxygen for the rest of the flight. An elegant way to flush the spaceship of Florida air.

"Shake it, baby!" Michael's voice quavered slightly with the intensity of the vibration.

The air had been pushing back against their increasing speed, putting a heavier and heavier load on the structure of the ship. The engineering name for that pressure was Q, and they had just hit the speed and height where it was at maximum. Max Q. From now on, with the air getting rapidly thinner with height, the forces would drop. It was the heaviest load the rocket's structure was designed for, and Luke was glad to be safely through it. He gave Michael two thumbs up.

The CAPCOM's voice confirmed the good news: "18, you are GO for staging."

Soon the first stage of their rocket would run out of fuel and would shut down, separate and fall into the Atlantic. But for now the crew was still being crushed at nearly four times their weight, getting close to the design limit for the rocket itself. Rather than slam all five engines to a stop at once, the computer shut down the center motor to drop the forces while the remaining four burned the last of the fuel.

"Inboard cut-off," Chad reported. Luke instantly felt the load on his body lighten, like there was one less person lying on top of him. But the remaining four engines kept pushing as the ship got lighter, and the g-load rapidly climbed again.

"Christ!" he grunted. He'd pulled lots of g as a fighter pilot, but wasn't used to the relentless load of a rocket. It was getting hard to breathe against the steady weight.

"Hold on!" Chad yelled.

Wham! The crew was thrown forward against their straps as the four big engines stopped and the now-empty rocket body separated.

Slam! They were snapped back into their seats like they'd been rear-ended as the second stage lit, five new engines exploding into life.

"Holy shit!" Luke exclaimed. He'd been warned by previous crews of the violence of staging, but it was far more physical than he'd anticipated. Like crashing into a wall.

"Looks like we got all five," Michael reported. The second-stage engines had lit properly, settling in to their six-minute push to near-orbital speed.

The NASA Public Affairs announcer spoke: "Apollo 18 now forty-six nautical miles in altitude, eighty nautical miles downrange. Coming up on tower jettison."

They no longer needed the nose-mounted rocket that had been poised to yank the capsule off the Saturn V in an emergency close to the ground. A small rocket in its tip fired for a second and pulled it clear, and it tumbled, unused, into the ocean.

The flash of the tower separating reminded Luke that they were now 50 miles above the surface—the imaginary line where the US Air Force had decided Earth's atmosphere legally ended. His thumb slid past the critical altitude in his checklist. "Congratulations, fellas, welcome to space! We're officially astronauts!"

"About frickin' time," Chad muttered.

The spectacle of the launch was magnificent from the Captain's ringside seat aboard the *Kavkaz*. As the American rocket rose off the pad, his men had broken into spontaneous cheers, and then again as they heard its rumble nearly a minute later. Their binoculars and cameras pivoted as one, tracking as it climbed almost perfectly vertically and then started to pitch over and head on its way.

A frown crossed the Captain's face as he studied the rocket through his own binoculars. He'd positioned the ship almost perfectly east of the launch pad so the rocket would pass directly overhead. Instead, it was accelerating unexpectedly to the right, moving north.

The sensors mounted on the antenna towers on his ship were grabbing multiple frequencies, including transmissions from the ascending rocket. His optical sensors were also tracking the bright light of its engines. He turned to his communications officer. "Do you have a solid directional lock on the rocket's transmissions?"

"Da."

"Get me their launch azimuth."

The comms officer set to work. He rapidly plotted the angle and estimated distance to the ascending Saturn V from the ship, building a series of points on his chart. He wished they also had a radar lock on the rocket, but they were restricted from pulsing energy at it. Still, with enough plot points, he should be able to figure out where Apollo 18 was headed. He expected the resulting line to be mostly easterly, like all previous Apollo launches. But as he added pencil marks, he stared at his chart: there was no denying the data. This line was tracking northeast.

As soon as he was certain he had it right, he aligned the straight edge of his chart protractor through the points, averaging the dispersion. He smoothly drew a pencil line on the chart, angling up from the Florida coast. He extended the line, and was intrigued to see it ran almost parallel to the coast of the Carolinas.

Flipping his protractor around, he took an accurate reading of the angle as it crossed the latitude and longitude grid lines. He sat back briefly and visualized the extended line all the way to the equator. He checked his numbers, and turned to report. The calculation had taken him less than 90 seconds.

"Tell me," the Captain said.

"Apollo 18 launched out of the Kennedy Space Center inclined at fifty-two degrees, meaning it was tipped fifty-two degrees from the equator." The comms officer had worked with the Soviet satellite fleet, and knew what that meant. "The same orbital inclination as our launches from Baikonur."

The Captain nodded. "Prepare an encrypted message for immediate LF transmission to HQ in Severomorsk," he said. He dictated the message, proofread the officer's transcription and signed off for urgent transmission, warning his communications officer, "Keep this information to yourself."

He turned back to stare at the sharp trail of smoke in the sky. *Where are you going, my fellow captain? Are you truly a moonship? Or do you have some other star to guide you?*

"18, Houston. You are GO for orbit—GO for orbit."

They were 1,100 miles from Kennedy, 110 miles above the Earth, still accelerating.

"Glad to hear those words, Houston," Chad replied. The second stage had done its work perfectly, and the third stage was now in the fine-tuning phase that would deliver them to the exact altitude and speed needed for their intercept of Almaz. They'd been rocketing for over 11 minutes, and this final stage was carefully pushing them with just a little over half a g.

"Almost there, boys," Michael said, his attention focused on the digital readouts and the timer as the speed climbed to over 25,000 feet per second.

And then it was over. The third stage shut itself down exactly on time, and the smooth, easy push of its single engine was instantly gone. For the first time in their lives, the three men were weightless.

Luke burst out laughing. "We're here!" He plucked his checklist off the Velcro and floated it in front of his helmet, gently spinning it. "Would you look at that!"

Michael leaned back and peered through his overhead windows. The blackness of space and the curve of the blue North Atlantic horizon filled his view. "Mother of God!" he said.

"Work to do, boys," Chad interjected, bursting their bubble. They each turned the page in their checklists and began the urgent steps that would convert their vehicle from a rocketship to a spaceship.

"Houston, we're with you on Launch page 2-10," Chad said.

A pause. No response.

"Houston, do you read?"

The returning call was scratchy and garbled.

Michael spoke. "I think I heard him repeat that we were GO for orbit there at the end."

Chad nodded. "Agreed. It's likely just bad comms through the North Atlantic relay ship." He glanced at his flight plan. "We'll have them back through the South Pacific ship in an hour or so."

Chad turned and looked at them both.

"Step one complete, boys. Now let's go find us a spy satellite."

23

Kennedy Space Center

The white and blue NASA helicopter was waiting in a roped-off area on the lawn beside Launch Control, its blades slowly turning. Kaz paused to look up at the last of the Saturn V's dispersing smoke, then grabbed the handrail and swung into the passenger bench seat in the back, next to Al Shepard. JW was already strapped in on the far side.

"What a launch!" Kaz shouted.

JW had a huge grin on his face, and Al nodded, unclipping the headphones from the bulkhead and cinching up his lap belt for the short ride to their jet, which would take them back to Mission Control in Houston.

The whine from the engines increased and the rotors spun up. The pilot was a Vietnam vet, and expertly plucked the helo off the ground, turning and pitching to accelerate to the south, towards Patrick Air Force Base.

Kaz looked down out the side window at the roads, already jammed all the way back to the causeway with departing cars and camper vans, thinking that Laura was somewhere down there in that mess. One day maybe he'd be on the ground watching her launch into space. The image made him smile.

The helicopter rapidly covered the 25 miles across the Banana River and along the sands of Cocoa Beach. Soon the Air Force housing and broad runways of Patrick filled the windscreen. The pilot brought the helicopter in fast, flared hard and set it down as light as a feather next to the NASA Gulfstream G-II that was waiting for them. He turned and nodded, nonchalant.

"Well flown," Al Shepard said. Kaz saw the pilot's neck flush red and knew that he'd dine out on that compliment from the first American in space for the rest of his life.

As they climbed out, Al raised a finger to Kaz. "Have them hold the jet. I need to make a phone call." He turned and walked briskly towards the hangar. Kaz and JW transferred the bags and climbed the airstairs onto the G-II.

The plane filled quickly as key Apollo mission personnel arrived at Patrick. By the time Al walked back across the tarmac, his was the last empty seat, next to Kaz. As he settled in, the plane's flight engineer raised the stairs and the pilots started taxiing.

Al didn't speak as the plane climbed away from Patrick, staring out the window as they headed west across the Gulf towards Houston. Finally he turned to Kaz, looking somber.

"Tell me again what you saw that day at Tom Hoffman's crash. From the moment you got to the field that morning."

Kaz didn't ask, but guessed this had something to do with the phone call Al had just made. He kept his tone factual, trying to recall the exact timeline of the morning and who he'd seen when. He described arriving at Ellington, walking through the hangar and then hitching a ride from the ops desk to watch the LLTV fly. He was starting into what he'd observed as Tom's helicopter flew past when Al interrupted him.

"Did you notice Tom's helo on the ground as you drove out to the LLTV site?"

Kaz thought back. "Not really. It was a decent day for weather; several jets had gone flying. The ramp was, maybe, half-full."

Al nodded. "Did you see anyone out on the ramp?" Then, before Kaz could answer, he asked, "Did you go out on the ramp?"

Kaz was startled. "Me? No, I didn't go out on the ramp, and there was nothing unusual that I remember." He closed both eyes, trying to picture it. "There was a T-38 starting, with the normal two groundcrew, one out front and one by the tail." He opened his eyes. "And a fuel truck."

Al looked at him. "Fueling what?"

Kaz shook his head slightly. "I'm not sure. It was driving out towards Tom's helo, but I'm not certain which aircraft it was headed for."

Al drilled further. "Who all did you see at ops and in the hangar?"

Kaz pictured his path, step by step. "Standard gate guard, a couple of the instructor pilots. Chad was there—he'd flown the LLTV before Luke. There was some sort of tour group with a NASA security guy. Normal faces at ops and maintenance."

He shrugged. "Sorry, Boss. I don't remember anything strange." He paused, then said, "Why you asking?"

Al looked around the plane. Everyone but them was dozing after the early-morning intensity of the launch. He leaned close and briefed Kaz on the facts of what the accident investigator had found.

Kaz made a low whistle. A backed-off bolt was someone's serious fuck-up. Or worse. He stared at Al, his eyes asking the next obvious question.

Al didn't answer, just said, "I don't think there's any point in telling the crew, do you?"

Kaz nodded. "And not the family, until we confirm the cause. Likely good if Gene Kranz knows, but otherwise this can wait till they get back."

He could see Al relax slightly. He pulled down the window shade, and tipped his chair back. "Agreed. I'll tell him. Now I'm going to shut my eyes until we get to Ellington. We've got a very busy few hours coming up." His voice was flat. "Looking forward to having Almaz behind them, and firing the engine to head towards the Moon."

Kaz's fake eye's socket was stinging with fatigue and the dry airplane air. He pushed the button to recline his own chair, and tried to find a comfortable position to doze, deliberately turning his mind away from all the troubling implications.

Navy pilots need to learn to nap anywhere, anytime. Soon both men were asleep.

The telex from the *Kavkaz* made the beige desktop machine in Severomorsk, home base of the Soviet Northern Fleet, chatter noisily as it printed the one-page message. The naval communications operator waited until the noise stopped, then leaned across to scan the security clearance and destination printed across the top. His eyes widened and he flicked his gaze away, deliberately not reading the contents.

He took extra care tearing it off the printer roll, and placed it neatly into a pinkish internal mail envelope marked ОСОБОЙ ВАЖНОСТИ—TOP SECRET. He hand-carried the envelope down the hall to the office of his superior, knocked briefly on the door, then set it into the man's inbox like it was hot to the touch. Keeping his gaze averted, he retreated quickly, glad to have done his part properly. Glad it wasn't his responsibility now.

His boss yawned, reading a message from a submarine commander who was taking his vessel back to dry dock. It was essentially a list of the major systems that needed work. He sighed, thinking, *Our fish are fast, but our parts don't last.* He scrawled his signature on the forwarding envelope, addressed it to the Severomorsk Quartermaster, put the multi-page message inside and flipped it into his outbox. He added an annotation to the tracking table in his green baize notebook, and reached across to his inbox for the new arrival.

Pink folder. TOP SECRET. *Atleechna!* Something worthwhile, hopefully!

He hadn't gone into Naval Communications and qualified for the highest security rating so he could push shopping lists around like a flunky clerk in a warehouse. He unwrapped the string holding the flap closed, and slid the page out.

He read it quickly once, and then again, more carefully. He thought for a minute, and then double-checked who the Captain of the *Kavkaz* had directed it to. He flicked his notebook open to the last page, to the list of naval departments and interfaces with other government organizations.

Nodding, he swiftly made a couple of neat notations on the routing envelope highlighting the urgency, and added a subsequent destination. As he started to slide the page back inside, he stopped and rechecked the message timestamp. Frowning, he glanced at his watch, and then reached for his desk phone. He ran his finger again down the list in his book, found a number and dialed it.

This one couldn't wait for internal mail. There was a potential real-time threat to the Motherland, and it was outside of the Navy's jurisdiction.

He listened to the ringing on the other end, rereading the message, preparing exactly what he was going to say.

It took three more phone calls and a total of 36 minutes for the *Kavkaz's* message to get cleared from Severomorsk through the bureaucratic layers all the way to Vladimir Chelomei, as the Almaz Program Director. The tinny telephone speaker on his desk rattled as the *Kavkaz* Captain's words were read to him verbatim, including the timestamp. Chelomei's thoughts clicked like tumblers as he unlocked what the information meant—what the Northern Fleet communications officer had grasped a small piece of.

Those American bastards are heading for my ship!

Gene Kranz leaned back in his chair and looked at his Instrumentation and Communications officer.

"INCO, why isn't 18 hearing us?"

Gene's voice was carried via headsets to everyone in Mission Control, but because of the military nature of the mission, it was blocked from going beyond the building.

"Not certain, FLIGHT. Likely a problem with the relay ship—we haven't had to station one this far north before. They got a good tracking lock, but voice is intermittent. Should be better when we pick up the South Pacific ship at seventy-two minutes."

Gene thought about it.

"FDO, how we looking?" Gene pronounced it "fido." FDO was the Flight Dynamics Officer, in charge of tracking the vehicle's position.

"Right on the money, FLIGHT. Perfect set-up for the rendezvous."

Gene nodded. "Let's work the updated tracking and start getting preliminary numbers for the first burn." The Apollo spaceship had launched into orbit perfectly aligned with Almaz, below and behind it, catching up. It was going to take two careful engine firings to raise the orbit enough so they could fly alongside. "Meanwhile, INCO, let's look hard at onboard comms so far, make sure we're not seeing anything wrong with 18's hardware."

"Copy, FLIGHT, in work."

Gene looked at the digital clocks on the front screen and addressed the whole room.

"When we pick them up over the South Pacific, Luke will be getting his suit ready to go outside, and we'll need to verify all systems are good to support that. We'll also be fifty minutes from the first burn, so we'll need updated tracking to get the right numbers on board.

"Let's be ready, people. This is an Apollo like no other."

The technician at Motorola was an expert with a soldering iron. She'd learned her skill in her dad's garage in Phoenix, the two of them building Heathkit radios and amplifiers together, him admiring her steadiness of hand and fierce concentration as she fed in the minimum amount of metal and flux for neat electrical connections.

When Motorola had hired her, she and her father had both taken great pride in the fact that she was now being trusted to assemble Apollo communications hardware. The complexity of circuitry required methodical assembly and exact handiwork, wiring and soldering each layer into place. The necessity for perfection demanded extra levels of inspection. After she'd bent over, staring intently through her protective glasses to accomplish a task, she'd move out of the way while a supervisor verified the quality of her work. Layer by layer, one soldered connection after another, they had built the main communications blocks for the Apollo Command and Service Modules.

She wore a cotton suit over her clothes, her hair tied up inside an elastic cap, to avoid stray strands or lint getting into the circuitry. Her mouth and nose were covered by a mask so that her humid breath didn't add any moisture. The room of technicians looked somehow robotic, all individuality blurred; anonymous pale-blue figures at electronics benches, intent on their work.

As she had leaned forward to accomplish one particular join, her mask bunched slightly under her nose. She ignored it, focusing on getting the tip of the soldering iron perfectly in place to heat the adjoining exposed wires. She wrinkled her nose at the tickling sensation caused by the mask and wiggled her pursed lips side to side. But it was no use, and she sneezed. She stifled it, as she had stifled other sneezes, focused on keeping her hands steady as she fed in the solder and flux.

She finished, pulled her hands away and tipped her head to one side, examining her work. She allowed herself a small smile under the mask. It looked perfect. She rolled her chair slightly away as the inspector leaned in to double-check. Satisfied as usual, he nodded, and made a checkmark in the long list on his clipboard. She adjusted the mask slightly away from her nostrils and continued working.

Unknowing.

Her stifled sneeze had jostled her arm and created an imperfection on the underside of the join. Like a pebble, a small ball of solder had cooled separately, trapped and hidden under a thin covering strand. A little sphere of metal, held securely in place against gravity.

Pursuit was the last Apollo Command Module to fly, and not all of its equipment was as rigorously tested as the first flights had been. The qualification process had already been proven, and money was tighter than ever. The original heavy vibration testing had been reduced to an approved laboratory shake test; the solder imperfection held through it, and the transponder passed its subsequent functional check flawlessly and was carefully installed in *Pursuit*'s avionics bay.

But the combination of actual launch vibration and acceleration shook it loose. The heavy forces at Max Q stressed the thin metal covering strand, and the sudden jolt of staging broke the ball free. The second-stage engines' acceleration pushed the small drop of solder into the adjoining circuit board and held it there. A tiny bit of metal, fallen out of harm's way, held in place by the forces of the launch.

When the third-stage motor shut off, the spacecraft was suddenly weightless, orbiting around the Earth. The little metal orb drifted gently up from its resting place, becoming a tiny conductive balloon in a playground of circuitry.

Small thrusters fired to point *Pursuit* in the right direction, giving a gentle acceleration to the ship. It moved sideways, floating the metal pebble into a new part of the transponder's circuitry. As Chad pushed the comm button to talk, the circuit was activated and shorted across two wires touching the solder ball, welding it into its new resting place. The electrical short dropped the current well below normal, and the signal didn't get through. Chad's voice dead-ended inside the box.

A stifled sneeze, 19 months earlier in Phoenix, Arizona, had caused the failure of the primary voice circuitry for *Pursuit*, Apollo 18's Command Module.

The crew was just talking to themselves.

CENTRAL INTELLIGENCE AGENCY—
UNITES STATES OF AMERICA

The President's Daily Brief—Addendum
16 April 1973—08:00 EST

FOR THE PRESIDENT ONLY

PRINCIPAL DEVELOPMENTS—Addendum

NASA reports a successful launch at 07:32 EST this morning of Apollo 18, with an all-military crew reporting to Vice Chief of Naval Operations, Admiral Maurice Weisner, and the Joint Chiefs. Initial mission tasking is in support of the NSA and CIA, to photo-document and, if possible, disable the Soviet spy satellite Almaz ('Diamond'), which launched from Baikonur USSR on 3 April. Almaz has the most capable on-orbit optical spy capability of any spacecraft, Soviet or American, estimated to be able to resolve objects on the surface as small as one foot. If operational, this would have significant negative SIGINT impacts for the USA.

Almaz needs to be operated real-time by cosmonauts on board, required for film loading, un-
loading, processing and subsequent film de-orbit/
parachute return to the USSR. Almaz is as-yet unmanned and thus pre-operational, with no CIA/NSA
indications of the upcoming cosmonaut launch date.

At approximately 10:35 today Apollo 18 astronaut
Captain Lucas Hemming, USMC, will perform a solo
spacewalk to photograph and disable Almaz by cutting external cables and/or cooling/fuel lines.
Unlike all previous Apollo missions, there is a
total public blackout of communications and crew
activities during this 2-hour phase of flight, and
potentially subsequent.

Once Almaz ops are complete, Apollo 18 will fire
its engine to leave Earth orbit for the Moon at
approximately 11:30 EST. Transit to the Moon will
take 3 days. The flight profile will more closely
resemble all previous Apollo missions from that
point forward.

-Addendum End-

24

Pursuit, Earth Orbit

"Woo-hoo, sorry, guys. That one's a real stinker!"

The air pressure inside the cabin had dropped steadily, as planned, during launch, and was now holding at one-third of what it had been in Florida. The gases in everyone's guts had expanded, and all three of them were farting.

Michael winced. "Geez, Luke, keep that in your own spacesuit, would ya?"

"How's the alignment going, Michael?" Chad had jettisoned the exterior covers that protected the optical systems during launch, and Michael was sighting through the built-in cameras, carefully turning *Pursuit* to align with specific stars. When he was sure he had it exact, he entered the data into the navigation computer. They needed precise orientation for the upcoming maneuver to raise their orbit up to match Almaz.

"Looking good, Boss. The stars are right where they were in the sim."

"Well, that's a relief," Luke said. He was folding his launch seat out of the way to make room for his spacewalk. "That Saturn V sure gave us a hell of a ride!"

Michael chimed in. "I felt like a crash test dummy!"

Chad interrupted. "Boys, you got any snags we should tell Houston about?"

They both shook their heads at Chad, who was still strapped into the left seat. Making eye contact while weightless was new to them all; it was strange to have no common up or down as a reference.

Chad confirmed the S-band comm switch was in transmit/receive. He leaned to his right and watched as the radio signal strength jumped, showing communications lock with the *Rose Knot* relay ship, 106 miles below, off the Australia coast. He pushed the black transmit trigger on his rotational joystick.

"Houston, Apollo 18's back with you."

No response.

Chad rechecked his switches and leaned over to the communications sub-panel to verify that everything was set correctly. He called again, and frowned when Houston didn't respond. Michael floated over and tapped the keyboard display that showed digital uplink activity from the ship.

"Data's flowing fine, Boss."

The CAPCOM's voice broke in. "Apollo 18, it's Houston, how do you read?"

Both men exhaled in relief. "Try using your mic to answer," Chad told Michael, who pushed his trigger. "Loud and clear, Houston, how us?"

No response.

Michael pictured the communications system in his head, considering possible causes. "Data's good both ways, and we're hearing them fine. So we have a problem with voice downlink."

Chad agreed. "Houston, if you hear, we're swapping to VHF." He reached up and threw the switches to select the simpler, traditional aircraft radio system, and tried again.

"Houston, this is 18 on VHF, how do you hear?"

There was a light buzz of static in the headsets. Luke had stopped what he was doing to watch them work the problem. This had suddenly gone from annoying to serious. He said, "Can you send a null data command to let them know we're hearing them?"

"Good idea," Chad responded. He thought for a second, and then punched in five zeroes and pushed Enter. The computer rejected the command and the Operator Error light came on. He typed 11111, reselected S-band communications and waited for Houston to call again.

"Apollo 18, Houston, we see your null entry. How do you read?"

Chad pushed Enter. The Operator Error light came on again.

A smile spread on Michael's face. "You're setting up a code!"

Chad shrugged. "Let's see if they catch on." He ran his thumb down the flight plan. "We only have comms via this ship for another ninety seconds or so."

"Apollo 18, Houston. If you hear us, please retype all ones and Enter."

"Bingo!" Chad said, punching in the numbers.

The CAPCOM's voice sounded relieved. "18, we see that, thanks. All systems look good to us except downlink voice. It might be a weak transmit signal, so we'll try again on the big dish at White Sands in twenty-two minutes, and will have other ideas there. If you copy, press all zeroes and Enter."

Chad did as instructed.

"18, we see that. If you have any serious issues on board, type all ones. If nominal, type zeroes."

Chad sent five zeroes.

"Good to see, 18, thanks. Talk to you in twenty."

Chad turned to his crew.

"Looks like we're still on for now, but this is a primitive workaround. Luke, keep getting things set for the spacewalk. Michael, get out the comm system schematics. I do *not* want a simple comm problem to lose us the Moon."

Michael was by the window, his face lit by a faint glow. "I'm on it, but guys, stop for a minute and watch this. First sunrise in space."

Chad and Luke looked up through the windows to see the sunrise happening as they raced towards it at five miles a second, the faint purple glow of the night horizon quickly overtaken by the dawn.

Luke gasped as the Sun burst into view.

"That's the most beautiful thing I ever saw," Michael said reverently. "It's like someone just poured a rainbow onto the edge of the world."

"Nice," Chad said. "But it also means we've got ninety minutes. By the next sunrise, Almaz should be in our sights."

"Right," Luke said, and began gathering more gear for his spacewalk. "Where are you in EVA prep?"

"Doing good, Boss. I've got my long umbilical attached on the backpack, coiled for you to pay out as I go. Over-gloves and external visor are ready."

Luke rummaged in a narrow open locker, carefully retrieving a large, square Hasselblad camera with a stubby lens, mounted on a pistol grip. He clipped it into the frame built into the chest of his spacesuit, listening for the click, and then unclipped it and stowed it with his other gear. He reached back into the locker and pulled out yard-long orange bolt cutters. After the mission changed, he and an EVA tech had bought them at a Houston hardware store. They'd wired a small metal ring to one of the handles so Luke could make sure they didn't float away while he was outside. He tucked the tool under a bungee next to the camera.

Michael had unfolded the pull-out page with the communications system schematic from his thick reference checklist and was tracing wire lines on the diagram, looking for possible culprits. "Boss, check my thinking here. Our voice comm problem affected both of us, and only for downlink, so it's got to be a specific failure in a common location." He double-tapped a rectangle on the drawing. "My guess is inside the main USB transponder."

He flipped to a following page. "We can get at it in the avionics bay if we need to, but we'd need to tear things down some to get there."

Chad thought about it. "Let's wait and see what Houston says." He checked his watch. "Speaking of which."

Right on cue, a voice cut in on the cabin speaker. "Apollo 18, this is Houston via White Sands, how do you read?"

"Houston, I have you loud and clear." Chad paused. "How me?" The crew collectively held their breath.

"18, Houston, you're weak but readable. We're just confirming tracking now, will have the Almaz rendezvous burn pad up to you shortly."

"Copy, Houston." Weak but readable was good enough for now.

Gene Kranz wanted everyone in Mission Control to hear what he was about to say. "Everybody, listen up. This is FLIGHT. Give me a green when you're ready." He had a multicolored matrix on his console, with one small square for each officer in the room. When they each pushed the green button on their desks and Gene saw all lights turn to green on his, he knew he had everyone's undivided attention.

"INCO, talk to me. What's the workaround for 18's comm problem?" With the first maneuvering burn rapidly approaching, the room needed answers.

"FLIGHT, it's a weak signal on their return voice loop," INCO said. "Looks like a partial short somewhere, likely the connectors or inside the USB transponder box itself. For now, we'll have workable comms through the big antennas in Madrid and Canberra, as well as stateside. We'll have everything but return voice through all other sites. Once we get past the Almaz rendezvous and TLI burn, we have crew actions that should fix the problem."

Gene didn't like the word "should."

"INCO, what's your confidence in the crew repair actions?" Without there being a high probability they could fix the comm malfunction, he didn't want to fire the big engine that would take the ship out of the relative safety of Earth orbit and send them on an unstoppable three-day voyage across the void to the Moon. Counting three days there and three days back, it was basically a week of the crew's lives he'd be gambling with. He needed the communications to work.

"FLIGHT, worst case, we'll have what we just saw through White Sands—weak but readable. As we get farther from Earth it will get better, since we'll be in range of one or two of the big antennas on Earth all the time. No gaps. Also, deploying the high-gain antenna on *Pursuit* will help boost the signal."

Gene nodded. He had one more key question. "Will the Lunar Module have the same problem?"

"Nope, FLIGHT, the LM's independent."

Gene looked around the room. "We're about to talk to 18 again via Madrid, and then we have the first rendezvous burn." He paused. "Anyone have any concerns?"

Silence.

Not ideal, Gene thought. *But we've seen far worse. We found a way to get Apollo 13 safely back; we should be able to solve this little problem.*

"Good work, INCO," he said. "Everyone, let's uplink the rendezvous data ASAP. I'll be looking for a GO for the burn from each of you as soon as it's on board."

Gene raised his eyes to the front screen, watching the white projected image of the Apollo spacecraft crossing the North Atlantic west of Ireland. Just ahead of it was a red rectangle, tracing the same curved path across the globe.

What secrets do you hold, Almaz? We're about to go find out.

"Luke, you got everything stowed for the burn?"

Luke was hanging on to Chad's headrest, staring out the window at the orange dryness of the Sahara Desert. "Sure do, Boss. I'm ready to surf."

Michael leaned across to check the instruments in front of Chad. "Attitude looks good, Boss."

Chad nodded his agreement. The spacecraft had pivoted exactly in space to align with the instructions sent up from Mission Control. Next communications would be over Madagascar, but this engine firing to raise their orbit up to match Almaz was taking place in between ground sites. No one was watching except the crew.

"Michael, as soon as this burn's done, I'll get out of the left seat, and you can fly *Pursuit*."

"Roger that, I'm ready."

Their eyes were fixed on the digital counter.

"Ten seconds, Luke," Michael cautioned.

"All set, thanks." Luke had the Hasselblad in his free hand, and the electric film advance was whining and clunking as he snapped images out the window. "I can't believe this view of the Nile."

"Three, two, here we go," Chad said.

With a low rumble they could feel through the hull, the liquid hydrogen J-2 engine ignited 100 feet below their backs, instantly pushing with 200,000 pounds of thrust. Luke clattered against the aft bulkhead. "Whoa, Nellie!" he said, trying to keep the camera from banging the window.

"I told you to hold on!" Chad said.

A checklist detached itself from the Velcro with a ripping sound and sailed past Michael's head. Luke grabbed it out of the air and handed it back.

Michael said, "Temps and pressures look good, engine's gimballing fine." The single J-2 engine bell was pivoting precisely on its mount, ensuring the thrust was pushing *Pursuit* in the right direction. Through his seat, he could feel the small steering corrections and vibration. "Engine cut-off in fifteen seconds."

Chad raised his right hand and pointed to the pressure gauges. "Three, two, one." They confirmed that the timer and lights agreed.

"Good cut-off."

"Guys, as soon as you get a chance, take a look. You can see all the way from the Rift Valley to the Horn of Africa!"

Chad safed the switches, unbuckled his straps and carefully floated out of his seat. "Coming up for a look. Michael, the ship is yours."

"Aye aye, Captain! I have control." Michael floated into the left seat and loosely buckled himself in place. Their orbit was now shaped like an oval, with the high point raised to equal Almaz's altitude. They had one more engine firing over the Pacific so they'd match the Soviet ship's circular orbit exactly, and then they'd be in visual range for Michael to maneuver up close. He'd been practicing it in the sim relentlessly ever since Kaz had brought the orders from Washington, but today was the real thing. He noticed that his palms were damp and wiped them on the heavy cloth of his spacesuit, then gently held onto the hand controllers, picturing the motions he'd be making.

"Hey, Luke, what was that Astronaut's Prayer again?" he asked.

Luke laughed.

Michael exhaled to concentrate, and focused on what was coming. *Lord, please don't let me fuck this up.*

Operating the ship had kept Chad fully occupied, and the seat straps had stopped him from fully sensing weightlessness; it had seemed more like an extra-realistic sim than actual spaceflight. But as he floated out of his seat to change positions with Michael, the reality of where he was physically struck him.

Whoa! His balance system was working hard, trying to sort out what was going on. He reached for the handrail next to the window, jerkily missing it once and then grabbing hard to steady himself. A wave of dizziness went through him, momentarily blurring his vision. He closed his eyes to let it pass.

Luke was floating next to him. "You good, Boss?"

"Never better," Chad said flatly, opening his eyes and focusing on the horizon. The medicos had warned him that he might feel motion sickness, but he'd spent a decade flying and testing fighters and had dismissed their concerns. Like all military pilots, he was proud of his iron stomach.

Luke tried to distract him by pointing out the window. "I wonder if there are people on that speck?" A tiny, circular volcanic island in the South Indian Ocean was passing underneath, its shadow pushed long across the ocean by the rapidly approaching sunset. Chad slowly pivoted his whole body to look, keeping his neck rigid to stop his head from moving.

He flicked his eyes down to see. "Real garden spot," he grunted. He closed his eyes again, slowly.

As they drove into orbital darkness, the light around them swiftly changed from bright white to orange to blood red, like a fading flare was illuminating their faces.

Chad gagged, his whole body convulsing as he tried to contain it. He fumbled in his leg pocket, yanking out a sick bag just in time to get it positioned over his face as the steak and eggs shot out of his mouth like a jet. Luke grimaced and pulled himself across the hatch to the other window. He poked Michael and silently pointed with his chin.

Did they really have to make the bag transparent?

They both winced and watched in morbid fascination as Chad gagged again, the vomit ricocheting off the far end of the bag and flying weightlessly back onto Chad's face. The cabin filled with the sour smell of vomit.

Luke pulled a cotton napkin out of his shoulder pocket and silently waved it to get Chad's attention.

Chad took it from him. He squeezed the sick bag closed with one hand and mopped his face from forehead to chin with the other.

Michael tried humor. "Well, at least we can't smell Luke's farts now."

Chad took one more swipe at his face and then stuffed the cloth into the sick bag, rolling and sealing the open end with the attached red twist tie. He pulled his own napkin out of his shoulder pocket and more carefully wiped his face and hands.

"I'll get you some water," Luke said. He squeezed past Chad to flick the pressurization switch, and pulled out the water dispenser, squirting it onto Chad's napkin.

"Thanks," Chad mumbled, wiping his face once more. He held up the half-full barf bag, a disgusted expression on his face. "What do we do with this for the next week?"

"I'll chuck it when I go outside," Luke said. "Maybe I can use it to disable Almaz."

"Very funny," Chad said as he Velcroed the sick bag next to the hatch, his newly empty stomach making him feel much better. He took a deep breath and checked his watch.

"We're going to have to start cabin depress soon for the EVA." He looked at Luke.

"Let's get you dressed for battle."

"Apollo 18, Houston, back with you through Madagascar. Looks like your burn was right on the money. We're genning up prelim numbers for your second burn now."

CAPCOM paused. "If you copy, type five balls."

Michael had the digital response ready and pushed Enter.

"We see that, and all systems look good. If you have any problems, type five ones."

Maybe this isn't so bad, Gene Kranz thought, sitting in his Flight Director chair. *Might be better for everyone if they can't tell us exactly what they're doing when we're close to Almaz.*

ALMAZ

25

Rendezvous, Earth Orbit

The Apollo crew had put their gloves and helmets back on, and the suits were stiffening as the pressure inside the capsule dropped in preparation for Luke's spacewalk. Luke was watching the vomit bag inflate with the air trapped inside it, and hoped it wouldn't leak or burst before they got to hard vacuum. He asked, "How you feeling, Boss?"

"I'm fine. Michael, how'd the burn look?"

"Right on the money. We should see Almaz ahead and above us soon."

As soon as Michael caught sight of the space station, he'd manually maneuver *Pursuit* up close and try to match speeds exactly so Luke could physically reach out and touch the Soviet ship.

Tricky flying, but Michael had talked at length with astronauts who'd done the same sort of thing during the Gemini program. Wally Schirra had got to within a foot of another Gemini ship, and easily held his position there.

Luke was in front of one window and Chad at another, both peering into the blackness. The horizon was a faint purple glow arcing around the Earth.

"We're still night for a few minutes," Chad said. "I don't see the ship yet. How soon until we get comms back with Houston?"

Michael held the Flight Plan in his overinflated left glove and clumsily ran his finger down the column. "We'll have them in ten minutes or so."

Chad thought about it. "The plan is to wait for Houston's GO to open the hatch, but if we see that we're getting there early, I'll make the call."

Luke floated away from the window to give Michael a clear view and grabbed onto *Pursuit*'s hatch opening handle. "I'm ready," he said.

The wooden door of Mission Control opened abruptly, and Al Shepard strode in. Kaz caught it swinging as he and JW followed, and quietly closed it behind them. Al had phoned from ops at Ellington, and the three of them were up to speed on *Pursuit*'s communications problem. They climbed the tiered steps past the floor-level console, heading to join the officers at their assigned positions: JW to SURGEON on the second level, Kaz beside him to assist the CAPCOM, and Al up two more levels to the center back at DFO, Director of Flight Ops. They each reached into cabinet drawers under the consoles and retrieved headsets, plugging in and becoming part of what was going on.

Gene Kranz waited until all three were settled and then took a moment to summarize mission status for everyone.

"As you can see on the screen, Apollo 18 is mid-Pacific and should have just completed the second burn, making them co-altitude with Almaz. They're also suited, with Luke Hemming ready for the EVA. Cabin depress should be just about complete to vacuum, waiting for our GO to open the hatch.

"As soon as we pick them back up off California, SURGEON, I want an immediate update on Luke's suit telemetry."

He looked to the front row at the Guidance Officer. "I'll need trajectory as soon as we can get it, to make sure the second burn went well and to run the calculations for the upcoming Trans-Lunar Injection burn.

We need to get those numbers on board prior to losing uplink—timing is very tight. TLI is going to happen beyond comm range, and we need to give the crew everything they need while we have them."

Gene glanced at the digital clock at the front of the room, then said, "We'll pick them up in ten minutes, and TLI is set for thirty minutes from now. Be ready, people. This is a critical half hour."

He glanced back at Al Shepard and raised his eyebrows to see if the Chief Astronaut wanted to say anything. Al gave a curt nod of approval and raised his right hand in a thumbs-up.

"Okay, back to work, everyone. Let's do this right."

"There it is!" Michael's voice was a mixture of awe and focus. "Right on the money!"

As if a cloak had been suddenly pulled away, the rising Sun lit Almaz, centered in *Pursuit*'s windows. Chad had a stopwatch Velcroed on the window frame. He aligned a small transparent ruler with the length of Almaz, started the stopwatch and read the calculated distance to Michael.

"We're eleven hundred feet away. I'll have a closing rate for you shortly."

"Roger," Michael responded, carefully firing the maneuvering jets to hold Almaz centered in the window. "I think we're a little closer than eleven hundred, and see a healthy closing rate."

Chad watched the second hand move on the stopwatch, thinking. "Luke, we're only ten minutes or so from needing you in position. Let's get the hatch open now."

"Roger that, Boss. In work." Luke double-checked that the rotary switch was turned to Unlatch, and began pumping the handle. With each stroke, the 15 rubber rollers that held the hatch tightly in place rotated away from the structure.

Chad made another careful sighting with the ruler and checked it against the stopwatch. "Looks like eight hundred feet, and closing at"—he calculated—"five feet per second." He frowned. "I'll need a couple more range marks before you can trust my speed calls."

"Understood," Michael said. He was happy that what he was seeing looked just like the visual simulator they'd set up for him in Houston. No surprises.

"All latches retracted, the hatch is loose. Opening it now." Luke had his left hand on Michael's seat, stabilizing as he pivoted the hatch out and open on its hinges. He glanced up, relieved to see the barf bag still secure on its Velcro. As he moved, his feet rotated quickly across the cabin and accidentally kicked Chad, tumbling him.

"Watch what you're doing!" Chad grabbed on to a bulkhead rail to stabilize himself, then repositioned in front of his window.

"Sorry, Boss." Luke cautiously moved his feet back between the two seats and began pulling himself up and through the hatch.

A voice in their headsets. "Apollo 18, this is Houston, how do you read?" Michael pushed the mic trigger. "Have you loud and clear, Houston, how me?"

Static. Gene Kranz looked at CAPCOM. "Did you get that?"

"Sorry, FLIGHT, no, unreadable." He looked at the forward screen. "They're still at max antenna range. It should get better as we get closer."

"Copy." Gene queried his other consoles, relieved to hear that the trajectory looked as expected, and the maneuvering fuel burn had been lower than budgeted.

JW said, "FLIGHT, this is SURGEON. Luke's heartbeat and respiration are high. I think he's started his spacewalk."

Gene looked at his Environmental Control officer for confirmation.

"FLIGHT, telemetry shows the hatch microswitches are open, and the cabin at vacuum. I agree, the EVA has begun."

Gene nodded, and glanced at the wall clock. "CAPCOM, tell them they have our GO for EVA."

As CAPCOM's voice passed the information through their headsets, Chad snorted. "No shit, Sherlock." After the kick from Luke had spun him, he was feeling queasy again. He focused on taking another distance measurement.

"Holy crap, this is beautiful!" Luke's lower torso and legs were still inside the capsule, but his head and shoulders were outside. "First things first." He cautiously twisted and reached down to dislodge the barf bag, and then carefully threw it in a straight line backwards to their direction of flight, so it would fall into a lower orbit. "Bomb's away!" He checked that his bolt cutters had floated out clear of the hatch on their tether, confirmed that his camera was secure and reached for the nearest handrail.

"Boss, you would not believe this view! I'm ready to move out if you're set to feed me umbilical as I go."

Chad said, "Michael, I show five hundred feet and three feet per second. You agree?"

"Yep, that matches what I see."

"Okay, Luke, I'm with you. Your umbilical's clear." Chad's voice sounded strained.

Luke smoothly pulled his feet clear and out, and pivoted his suited body like an obese rock climber, walking his hands along the rails that were mounted across *Pursuit* to the adjoining Service Module. A foot restraint was installed at the far end for him to click his boots into, so that he could have both hands free.

In case the CAPCOM could hear him, Michael reported, "Houston, 18, we're at four hundred feet and closing at two and a half. Luke just got outside and is getting into the foot restraint." No response.

He looked up again at Almaz, trying to judge how fast he was drifting towards it. He glanced across at Chad.

"You got a new data point for me, Boss?"

Chad didn't respond. Then both Luke and Michael heard him retching in their headsets.

Throwing up inside a sealed spacesuit was a misery. The flown astronauts who had told them about it had described the stink, the smeared visor, the stomach acid getting into their eyes, and trying not to inhale any of the floating chunks and bile.

Michael took another hard look at Almaz, assessing his approach speed. He gave two small decelerating pulses on the hand controller, and liked what he saw.

"Luke, how you doing?"

"Michael, it is fricking gorgeous out here! But I'm having trouble swinging around to get my feet in. Can you check that my umbilical isn't snagged?"

Michael looked at Chad again, who'd made no response to Luke's call. He released the controls and twisted in his seat, reaching as far as he could, feeling for the umbilical. It was pulled taut on the hatch mechanism, and he shook it like a garden hose to try to work it clear. He felt it give, and some extra length played out through his hand.

Luke said, "That did it, thanks! I'll get my feet in now."

Michael let go and his seat straps floated him back, centering him in position. He looked once more at Chad.

"Boss, how you doing?"

"I'm okay," Chad said thickly.

"Roger, if you can get me another data point, that'd be great." He hoped the task might help Chad work through his nausea.

"Apollo 18, Houston, comm check."

"Have you loud and clear, Houston, how us?" Michael said, then focused on the Soviet ship, correcting the sideways drift that had started while he was dealing with the umbilical.

His eyes caught unexpected movement. *What the hell is that?* A solar array turning? A comm antenna tracking them, maybe?

Luke's voice was in his ears. "Man! My left foot just won't . . . uhh . . . c'mon, twist in there!" His attention was focused down, trying to get into his foot restraint.

Michael peered hard at Almaz, trying to reconcile what he was seeing. "Houston, you hearing Luke? He's almost in position. Range and closure all good." *What is that?*

———

In Mission Control, the CAPCOM looked at Gene. "FLIGHT, I didn't get that, sorry." The voice comm from *Pursuit* was fading in and out.

Kaz pushed his mic button. "FLIGHT, I think I heard Luke say something, and pretty sure that Michael said good range and closure."

Gene nodded. "Let's just watch the data. They're busy enough without us calling for voice checks."

JW spoke, slight concern in his voice. "FLIGHT, SURGEON, Luke's heart rate and respiration are spiking."

"Roger, keep a close eye, let me know if it gets beyond limits."

Luke finally had his feet anchored. "There!" he said, the word a long exhale, heard by Michael and Chad, but lost in the bad connection with Mission Control. "That sure was harder than in the sim. Leaning back now."

He looked down and checked the camera on his chest. "Hasselblad's all set. Time to get some photos." To point the camera he needed to use his whole body, concentrating on alignment as he looked up at Almaz, about 200 feet away.

The bright white reflection off Almaz's exterior radiators momentarily blinded him. He squinted and turned to the side, away from the reflection, attempting to photograph one end of the Soviet spaceship.

The shape he saw was not what he expected.

"Hey, Michael, what's that end cone thing on Almaz? It's not like we briefed. It looks like some sort of add-on." He pushed the shutter trigger on the camera and started a slow pivot to the right to get the full, planned photo survey of the exterior. "Maybe it's some sort of return capsule?"

Chad was still keeping very still, fighting his nausea. Michael's hands were busy on their joysticks, slowing *Pursuit*'s closure rate, easing the two vessels closer together. He'd been glancing at all edges of Almaz to assess speed and angles at the same time as he was trying to figure out what he'd seen at the base of the solar array.

Just then, Luke spoke rapidly, his voice loud.

"Guys! There are two spacewalkers on Almaz! Houston, Almaz is manned! It has cosmonauts aboard, and two of them are outside!"

A beat as he considered that. "It's like they've been waiting for us!"

26

Almaz, Earth Orbit

Michael's voice was urgent. "Houston, 18, are you copying Luke's calls?"

Radio silence.

Christ! What do we do now?

"Boss, are you seeing this?"

Chad turned to face Michael, his visor smeared with vomit. The sudden motion triggered his nausea again, and he bent forward, pulsing weightlessly as he retched.

Michael shook his head in frustration and stared back through his window, slowing the approach, the vehicles drifting to within 50 feet of each other.

Luke's voice came through Michael's headset. "Okay, I've got a full photo survey done. The cosmonauts seem to be staying put. Maybe they're supposed to be observing us?"

Michael watched them; their visors were turned to his ship, both holding onto an Almaz handrail. "Maybe, Luke. I'll ease a little closer and set us up to fly slowly along the full length so you can get better-resolution photos. You got enough film left?"

"Yep, plenty." He paused, looking at the cosmonauts. "I don't think I should try to disable their ship. You guys agree?"

Michael looked across at Chad, still curled up on himself. Chad raised a thumb.

"Chad agrees, and so do I. Let's just get the close-ups, and then I'll maneuver us away."

Luke adjusted zoom and focus on the lens. "Maybe they'll wave on our way by."

"Almaz, Almaz, how do you hear me?" Chelomei's voice crackled in cosmonaut Andrei Mitkov's headset.

"We hear you clearly, Comrade Director. The American ship is ten meters away and slowly closing, with the hatch open and one space-walker outside. He has a large set of what look like bolt cutters with him. They are maneuvering now, repositioning forward, towards our re-entry capsule."

Chelomei's worst suspicions were confirmed. These men had been sent to attack his ship. "Mitkov! Be ready to physically stop the American from damaging Almaz. Take action as required."

"Understood. Both of us are moving forward towards the capsule now."

Chelomei whipped his head around at the flight director and shouted, "Where's that video feed?"

"We're just getting a solid relay lock now, Comrade Director. We'll have it on the front screen in a few seconds."

As if on command, a fuzzy black-and-white image appeared next to the Earth map at the front of the room. It showed a section of Almaz's curved hull against the blackness of space, with the broad arc of the Earth below.

"Where is the American ship? We need to turn to face it!" Chelomei had a plan, but he had to get Almaz properly aligned against the aggressors.

The flight director gestured impatiently at his comm tech, who spoke to the crew. "Almaz, we need updates on the relative position of the other ship, in orbital coordinates."

Mitkov paused from moving hand-over-hand along his vessel, and released one hand to pivot his whole spacesuit and look. The other cosmonaut paused behind him.

"They are aft and below us, five meters away now, co-aligned. Their command capsule is abeam our return capsule, holding distance steady, drifting forward slowly," he reported.

"Copy." The comm tech turned and looked questioningly at the flight director, who was holding his two hands up, picturing the orientation. He twisted one wrist, deciding on the needed rotation, then spoke urgently to the officer in charge of Almaz attitude control. "Start a max pitch rate pure down, and be ready to cancel the motion and track as soon as they come into the field of view."

The console officer rapidly typed on his keyboard and then paused briefly, his finger sliding across the screen to verify accuracy. With a small flourish, he raised his hand and stabbed the transmit button.

All eyes turned to the large screen, waiting for the video to reveal the attacking American vessel, squarely in Almaz's sights.

"Shit, they're moving, Michael!" Luke's voice was urgent.

Michael had been watching the Soviet spacewalkers as they slowly clambered along Almaz's hull, and he misunderstood. "Yeah, I see them. And it looks like their suits have backpacks, so no umbilicals."

"Not them, the whole ship! I just saw the thrusters fire. It's pivoting towards us!"

Michael moved his head left and right to take in the whole vessel. The blunt end was rotating downwards. He carefully tipped his joystick forward to match the rate, and then tapped his hand controller to start moving aft along Almaz.

"I see it, and am pitching to match. Should be good for you to start on the final photo pass anytime."

Luke took one more look at the two cosmonauts moving towards him, like white birds on an elephant's back, and then focused on his camera work. "Roger. Their pointy capsule is in my field of view now, starting pictures." He pressed the shutter trigger, carefully twisting his spacesuit to hold the image centered.

The CAPCOM's voice broke in. "Apollo 18, Houston, no response necessary, but your final TLI numbers are on board. New TIG is 3:25:00, need to get Luke inside prior-to. We should have you over Cape Town during the burn." A brief pause. "You have a GO for Trans-Lunar Injection."

Chad mutely raised his thumb again.

"Roger, Houston, 18 is GO for TLI," Michael said. He glanced at the clock and realized that was just 14 minutes away. He watched Almaz moving in the window and did a quick mental calculation.

"Luke, did you copy that call? You'll need to hustle inside as soon as this sweep is done so we can get the hatch closed prior to the burn."

"Copy, wilco, no sweat." A pause, and then Luke asked, "Michael, is Almaz pitching faster now?"

"Working on it," Michael responded, staring out the window. He'd added a couple pulses to his joystick to match rates with Almaz. *What were the Soviets up to?*

Luke's voice came again, and higher pitched. "Hey, the cosmonauts are getting pretty close to me. One of them's carrying a big monkey wrench, and the other has something like a drill!"

Chad straightened himself and rasped, "I'm gonna poke my head outside." He cautiously maneuvered under the hatch opening, trying not to trigger any more motion sickness, pivoting his whole body and moving his head and shoulders out into space.

"What the fuck?" Luke sounded incredulous. "Are these assholes coming for me?"

"What's going on?" Michael could only see the wide fuselage section of Almaz in his window.

Chad called, "The lead cosmonaut has pushed off of Almaz."

He watched in disbelief as the spacewalker floated across to *Pursuit* and grabbed a handrail near Luke. He moved closer, then swung his wrench towards Luke's visor.

"Luke, watch out, on your left!" Chad yelled.

Luke, his feet locked in their restraints, deflected the blow with his suited forearm and swung back with the bolt cutters. "You bastard!" he yelled.

The cosmonaut got his arm up in time to protect his visor, and the bolt cutters bounced off.

Now the second cosmonaut made the leap and began maneuvering towards Luke from the other side. He started twisting back and forth in the foot restraints, swinging the bolt cutters in an arc to keep them both at bay, his other hand held high to ward off blows.

Michael could hear Luke's grunting and harsh exhalations. "Boss, we need to get Luke inside now!"

"Agreed! Luke, pop your feet out of the restraints and I'll haul you clear!"

Michael pushed his transmit button. "Houston, if you're hearing this, the cosmonauts are on *Pursuit* and attacking Luke!"

Chelomei was yelling. "Increase the rotation rate! We have to get that ship in front of us!"

"Yes, Comrade Director." The pointing officer sent another command, firing Almaz's thrusters yet again. He checked the updated values. "We're at max design pitch rate for the solar panels now."

All eyes turned to the front screen. Rising up from the bottom of the video image was the conical white tip of the Apollo capsule.

Chelomei pointed to the screen. "Arm the R-23!"

The mechanisms officer, sitting one row ahead, responded. "Sending the command now."

As Almaz turned, the spacewalkers came into view—three fat figures in a clumsy slow-motion dance, intent on mutual destruction. The cosmonauts held tight to *Pursuit*'s handrails with one hand, swinging their makeshift weapons with their free arms, as the astronaut, one foot still braced, brandished his bolt cutters.

Bile rose in Chelomei's throat. His ship, *his* Almaz—so capable, so much of a threat that the Americans had decided to attack it in front of his eyes! He'd known this might happen. And he'd prepared for it.

He grabbed the headset off the desk and shouted into it. "Mitkov, both of you get back to Almaz. You need to be clear of the American ship, and fast!"

The grunting of the two cosmonauts in combat transmitted steadily, blocking the incoming call from Earth.

Chelomei tried again. "Mitkov, do you hear me? Return to Almaz!"

No response. The tech repeated the Director's words multiple times, urgently trying to get through.

Finally, Mitkov replied. "Moscow, I hear you! We're returning!"

Chelomei pivoted towards the flight director. "How much time do we have?"

"About thirty seconds, Comrade Director, forty-five maximum until we're out of antenna range."

They watched the screen, the Apollo ship remaining centered as the console operator reversed the thrusters on Almaz to hold steady. An astronaut was sticking out of the American hatch, guiding the umbilical of the spacewalker, who had got both feet free and was now floating up towards Almaz. One of the cosmonauts was traversing the gap between the vessels, the other still holding on to the American ship, ready to push off.

Chelomei spoke, his command loud enough for everyone to hear it without their headsets.

"At fifteen seconds, send the signal. All rounds! Fire the R-23!"

Vladimir Chelomei had not sent a defenseless ship into space.

The Kartech R-23 cannon was a unique design.

It had originally been built as the tail gun for the supersonic Tu-22 bomber, with a single short barrel to avoid the aircraft's turbulent airflow. As its bullets fired, the expanding gas from the explosion not only pushed the projectile out of the barrel, but also rotated a four-chamber revolver mechanism that loaded the next round. At full speed, the cannon spun at 2,600 rpm, a blistering 43 rotations every second.

It was the Soviet Union's fastest-firing single-barrel cannon, small, light and purpose-built. To keep its overall length short, the chambers loaded oddly, from the front, the pointy bullets encased in cylindrical galvanized metal sleeves, like deadly silver lipsticks.

For the cannon to fit onto Almaz, though, the engineers had to make it even smaller and lighter, choosing lower-caliber 14.5 mm bullets that allowed for a slimmer barrel and revolver. The entire space gun, loaded with 32 rounds, weighed just 70 pounds. Then, to further minimize mass and complexity, they'd removed the gun's aiming mount, simply bolting the R-23 to Almaz's hull. In order to line it up with the target, they had to turn the entire 20-ton space station.

The new design's rate of fire was 1,800 rpm; that meant all 32 bullets could be expended within one second. A brief hail of hardened steel through the emptiness of space, each spinning projectile traveling at over 2,000 feet per second.

All it needed was someone to pull the trigger.

With 15 seconds left in the comm pass, the Moscow technician pushed the button on his console to initiate the fire command. The signal traveled up via relay satellite and then down to the relay ship in the North Atlantic, which sent it directly back up to the receiving antenna on Almaz. The spaceship's decommutator routed the signal through Almaz's onboard wiring and amplified it into an electrical fire signal that the R-23 could recognize. It also sent a command to the ship's thrusters to ignite the maneuvering engines to counteract the impending recoil of the gun.

When the electrical signal reached its destination, the space cannon flashed into operational life.

The firing pin slammed into the percussion primer at the base of the loaded round, causing an instant explosion, which ignited the main nitrocellulose charge. The ensuing blast hurled the bullet down the rifled barrel and spun the revolver to accept the next round. Each successive round's explosion sped up the rotation until the cannon was turning at full speed.

As the chambers rotated, the used, empty cartridges flew out in a glittering trail of tiny satellites, slowly tumbling as their orbits decayed, to fall and burn up in the atmosphere.

But the sixteenth round jammed.

The problem was the strange bullet design. To securely hold the projectile in its unusual casing, a specially built machine at the OKB-16 factory squeezed the galvanized steel from both sides, crimping it solidly in place. Round 16 had an undetected bit of a broken high-tempered steel lock washer stuck to its underside, which the machine had crimped into its casing. The round looked normal, but the primer chamber was nearly penetrated.

As the rotating drive mechanism forced the defective round into the cannon's chamber, the casing crumpled, the primer chamber burst, and the heat and friction of the collapsing tube ignited it. The main charge sympathetically exploded, and the resulting sudden burst of expanding gas shattered the fast-spinning revolver.

Instantly, pieces flew in all directions—a deadly pinwheel shedding hardened steel parts. Some flew harmlessly off into space. But several were hurled into the pressure hull of Almaz, their ragged edges cutting through the thin aluminum as if it wasn't there. The air in the ship's main cabin started spewing out through the jagged holes.

One fragment followed an especially unlucky trajectory. Mounted just inside the hull was a bundle of tubes and cables carrying cooling glycol and electrical power, routed together for easy maintenance. A finger-sized piece of broken steel ripped through the bundle, cutting power to multiple Almaz systems and splitting fluid lines that immediately began spraying liquid into the rapidly dropping pressure inside the spacecraft.

Almaz was fatally wounded, a robot whale, mortally stabbed by its own explosive harpoon.

The 15 bullets that the cannon had successfully fired formed more of a spray pattern than the engineers had expected. Twelve of them had sailed past Apollo and the spacewalkers, destined to eventually fall to Earth and vaporize in the upper atmosphere.

One round nicked the edge of Apollo's open hatch door, scoring the metal and carrying away a small piece of the rubber seal that the North American Aviation technicians had carefully fitted and glued in place around its circumference.

Another collided with Luke's oxygen and power umbilical adapter, which attached to his suit just below his chest. Traveling at 850 meters per second, it tumbled through the delicate pressure regulator, wires and valves, tearing them open.

The third bullet struck senior cosmonaut Andrei Mitkov as he was floating back to Almaz. The bullet caught his helmet as neatly as if it had been fired by a sniper, hitting him squarely above his visor, creating a punctuation mark between the middle letters of CCCP.

The 175-gram projectile, designed to penetrate metal, passed through the successive layers of fiberglass, flesh, bone and brain as if they weren't there. The exit hole out the back of Mitkov's helmet was only slightly larger than the entry hole. A small spray of gray and red followed the bullet, quickly spreading and vaporizing in the vacuum of space.

Mitkov's body spun backwards with the force of the impact, tumbling like a rag doll until it struck Almaz. His lifeless arms flew forward on impact as if giving the ship a final embrace. His ivory-colored Yastreb suit deflated against his body as he slowly bounced clear, floating silently away towards the darkness.

The remaining cosmonaut, still clinging to *Pursuit*, watched in horror.

As the rapid darkness of the orbital sunset overtook it, Almaz slowly tumbled in space. The effect of firing the gun and trying to counteract it with the automated thrusters had been only a best guess by Chelomei's engineers. In reality, the forces had combined to add one last torquing moment to the ship as it died.

Inside the punctured hull, the pressure rapidly dropped to zero. Unlike the Apollo capsule, the main section of Almaz had never been intended to function in the vacuum of space. The spraying glycol from the severed coolant line had bubbled and evaporated as if it were boiling. The film canisters, with their hard-earned, precious first images carefully exposed and recorded on the wide celluloid filmstrips, had burst open. The temperature had dropped rapidly, and the ship's automated systems failed, one by one, as they vainly tried to keep critical systems warm on battery power.

A faint, thinning trail formed behind Almaz, where the venting atmosphere had spewed small fragments and liquid as the pressure had dropped. The hull's rotation had left a curved arc in the darkness. A keen observer might have been able to follow the track back to the slowly tumbling, lifeless body of the cosmonaut.

In Moscow, everyone was quiet at their consoles. Chelomei looked around, glowering. There'd been no time for confirmation that the cannon had fired, and the next communications ship was still 40 minutes away, over the South Pacific.

Questions tore at him. Had he made the right call? The Americans had been the aggressor! It had been *they* who had deliberately intercepted *his* ship, and they had put an astronaut outside carrying bolt cutters, irrefutable proof of destructive intent.

Chelomei clenched his jaw. All he'd done was react defensively, a course of action that had been cleared in advance. He'd been right to decide to arm Almaz. He'd known just what a valuable asset it was, and that it might come under attack. Events had now proven him correct.

He glanced at the timer on the front screen: 38 minutes until they could recontact Almaz and its crew. A little over half an hour to organize his thoughts, preparing for the inevitable avalanche of questions.

He began preparing his answers. The United States of America had attacked the Soviet Union in space. It was a purposeful, dangerous new escalation of the Cold War. Only *his* forethought had allowed them to be ready, and to respond. He nodded to himself. He was in the right and had acted as a soldier should.

Let them ask questions.

But first he had to talk to the crew to find out the result of his orders. Then everyone would be able to see how Almaz, how *he*, had helped change the course of Soviet history in space.

"What's going on?" Michael yelled. Almaz had spun faster than he could keep up and was now starting to roll. He'd pulsed his thrusters to keep clear, and was eyeing the countdown clock to the TLI burn that would take them towards the Moon.

"Bastards fired a gun at us!" Chad hissed, then choked as he suppressed another wave of nausea.

"They *what*?" Michael hurriedly rescanned his gauges. "I don't think they hit anything vital. All temps and pressures look normal." He rechecked the timer. "We have to get that hatch closed. Luke, are you in?"

"Almost," Chad grunted.

Michael focused on the small DSKY screen, double-checking the numbers as he maneuvered to the right orientation for the Trans-Lunar burn. Out of the corner of his eye, he saw Chad pull Luke into the center of the capsule and then reach past him to close the hatch.

"No time for cabin repress now, guys," Michael warned. "As soon as you get the hatch secured, hang on. We're almost at burn time. Chad, I need your eyes on the gauges with me."

Chad exhaled heavily as he worked to crank the hatch handle. "How soon do we get comms back?"

Michael awkwardly peeled his flight plan checklist off the Velcro, his glove still inflated against the vacuum in the cabin. "We'll pick up South Africa one minute into the burn. Unlikely they'll hear us, though."

Chad grunted an acknowledgment and eased himself across into the right-hand seat.

Michael's eyes flicked from instrument to instrument like a hawk watching potential prey. "Ignition in forty-five seconds. Attitude looks good, temps and pressures normal."

Chad was doing the same on the other side of the cockpit. "I see good attitude, 180, 312, 0," he said, sounding hoarse but much more in control. "I confirm a burn of 10,359.6 feet per second, duration 5:51." He paused. "Ullage settling."

"TIG in ten seconds." Michael glanced to his right. Luke was floating by the window, where he could see out. "Luke, hang tight," he called and locked his gaze back onto the gauges.

"Three, two, one, here we go!"

The single J-2 rocket engine burst back into life, to push them this time all the way up to escape velocity—fast enough to leave Earth orbit and coast to the Moon.

"Steer, baby, steer," Michael muttered. Pushed back into his seat, he could feel the guidance system adjusting the motor's exhaust direction, counteracting the fuel sloshing in the tanks.

"Tank pressures look good," Chad said. "No comms yet." Sunlight was flaring in the window as they approached sunset over the Central African coast.

Michael glanced back at Luke. "Good riddance to Almaz! Can you see it in the rear-view mirror?"

Luke, pressed by the acceleration into the rear wall of *Pursuit*, didn't answer.

"Luke, what went on out there? It sounded like a frickin' rodeo!"

Still no answer.

Both Chad and Michael twisted their suits to look at Luke. Michael reached to grab one of his feet and tried to pull him forward with one hand, against the push of the engines. "His suit feels soft!" he exclaimed in alarm.

Chad grabbed for his other foot, and they urgently pulled him forward. Michael spotted the bullet's damage. "His umbilical's wrecked!"

Luke's body turned, and Michael saw that his visor was clouded by condensation. He strained to see inside. "His eyes are closed."

"Shit!" Chad said, taking command at last. "The switches are on your side—start an emergency repress! I'll watch the burn."

Michael whipped to his left and moved the valves to let oxygen pour into the cabin. He watched the cabin pressure indicator, preparing to pop Luke's helmet off the moment it rose high enough.

The needle on the gauge stayed at zero. He tapped it rapidly, hoping the mechanism was stuck.

No response.

"Boss, I think we may have a cabin leak!"

The two men looked at each other across Luke's inert body, their thoughts racing.

"It's either the hatch didn't seat or a bullet hole," Chad said. "Hatch is quicker to check." He stared at Michael through the smears of vomit on his visor. "I'll keep watching the burn. You cycle and clear the hatch."

Michael unsnapped his harness and, fighting the force of the engine, closed the oxygen switches and reached behind him to the hatch handle, cranking fast to reopen it as quickly as he could. He watched as the mechanical rollers retracted, and pushed hard on the door as soon as they released. The darkness outside in contrast to the interior lights made it hard for him to see the rubber seal.

He rapidly traced the hatch edge and found the scored metal where the bullet had grazed it. He felt sick when he saw the torn rubber.

"Chad, looks like a small section of the door seal is missing! I'll grab the patch kit—I think it'll hold."

He had to move Luke out of the way to access the aft storage cupboard, cursing under his breath as he hunted for the right container. When he found it, he tore it open, pulling out the heavy plasticine-like block inside. Pivoting back up to the hatch, he rolled the sealant into place, making it extra thick where the rubber was missing and using his gloved thumb to smear it smooth along the metal. The patch kit container bounced free and floated through the hatch, out into the darkness. *Fuck!* He checked his work.

"Okay, Chad, I've got a good glob in there. Should do it. Closing the hatch now!"

Bracing with his other hand, he got a secure grip and pivoted the hatch towards himself, carefully keeping an eye on his makeshift repair to be sure it stayed in place.

As he had the hatch nearly closed, something blocked it. He pulled harder, then leaned back slightly to see the whole circumference, wondering what was in the way.

What Michael saw, he couldn't believe.

Pinched between the swinging hatch and the structure of *Pursuit* was a gloved hand.

Someone was trying to get in.

COSMONAUT

27

Pursuit, Trans-Lunar Burn

"How's it looking?" Gene Kranz's words were clipped with urgency.

Apollo 18 had just come into range of NASA's Deep Space Network satellite dish near Johannesburg, South Africa. The downlinked data was starting to appear on the Mission Control console screens, and Gene urgently wanted to know how the Trans-Lunar Injection engine firing was going.

"Burn's underway, FLIGHT." A pause as the Flight Dynamics console operator evaluated the rows of flashing numbers he was seeing. "Everything looks right on the money."

The Environmental Control officer spoke, mild surprise in his voice. "FLIGHT, EECOM here, they're still at vacuum."

Gene thought about it. Time had been tight, and the crew would have had no real need to deal with the distraction of repressurizing until after the burn.

"Copy, EECOM." He visualized what the crew was doing, double-checking. "Confirm the hatch shows closed?"

"Roger, FLIGHT."

So crew was inside, the ship was behaving itself, and they were on their way to the Moon. *Just need to get this damned comm snag fixed.*

"CAPCOM, let them know we're here, and that we see good numbers on the burn so far."

As CAPCOM keyed his mic to speak, the EECOM said, "FLIGHT, wait!"

Gene looked over the top of his console at the officer, who had turned so he could make direct eye contact. "The switches no longer show closed. The crew is opening the hatch during the TLI burn!"

Gene looked to his left. "SURGEON, you still getting Luke's data?"

JW shook his head. "FLIGHT, his signal seems intermittent. Not sure what to make of it."

Gene frowned. Biomedical sensors were notoriously unreliable, especially since the crew didn't like everyone knowing their heartbeat and often weren't too careful about attaching the electrodes. He looked at the front screen. There were still three minutes left in the burn, and that would take them almost to the end of the communications pass. Then they'd have a 23-minute gap until they could talk to them through Australia.

"CAPCOM, let's wait until there's forty-five seconds left in this comm pass to update the crew with what we're seeing."

Kaz, standing behind the CAPCOM, looked at Gene and nodded. Let the crew work the problem, but backstop them with the latest data from Mission Control before they went silent again.

"Listen up, all consoles," Gene said, pausing until conversation quieted. "Looks like we're headed to the Moon, but with bad comms and maybe a hatch problem. We still have Lunar Module extraction and S-IVB separation to get through before we'll have good two-way communication. We need to help the crew but stay out of their way until they get through this phase."

He paused and looked around at his team.

"I want a crisp update for them in twenty minutes. All systems abnormalities, and any changes to the flight plan." He turned to his left.

"And INCO, I want my comms back ASAP. We need to get this flight back to normal."

The glove was smooth and white, the rubberized fingers bulging with pressure as the cosmonaut held on against the accelerating spaceship.

"Chad! One of the cosmonauts is trying to get in!"

"What?" Chad pivoted his suit hard to see, pushing Luke's inert form out of his way. "Shit!"

He glanced back at the engine instruments. "We've got a minute left in the burn," he said, "and we've got to get air to Luke, fast. Bring the cosmonaut inside, and let's get the oxygen flowing ASAP!"

Michael pushed the hatch open and held out his gloved hand. The cosmonaut's other arm came arcing out of the darkness and grabbed it. Straining against the rocket's acceleration, he helped the cosmonaut inch into the cramped space. Michael yanked the Soviet suit's life-support backpack in last, trailing on its hoses, then squeezed up and around the cosmonaut's feet to check that his makeshift pressure seal repair was still in place. He pulled the hatch closed and lunged for the locking handle, rapidly cycling it, counting strokes.

As soon as it was locked, he pivoted and threw open the cabin repress switches to get some life-giving oxygen flowing. Sweating heavily, he reached down and pulled himself back into his seat.

Chad's voice cut in. "Three, two, one—burn's complete."

The sudden freedom of weightlessness was like coming inside out of a gale.

Michael kept his eyes glued to the cabin pressure gauge, which was rapidly climbing towards 5 psi. "Hatch seal's holding," he reported. As soon as it passed 3, he reached under the cosmonaut to get to Luke's helmet. Chad was already there, pulling at the neck latch. As the helmet came loose, Michael guided it up and off Luke's head.

Michael yanked off his right glove and jammed a finger up under Luke's jawline, feeling for a pulse.

Nothing.

He used his thumb to peel Luke's eyelid quickly back, but saw no response. He held his palm over Luke's nose and mouth. Nothing.

Unlatching and peeling off his own helmet, he grabbed Luke's jaw with his still-gloved left hand and pushed back on the top of his head with his right; sealing his lips over Luke's cold mouth, he blew hard into his lungs. He turned, hearing the rattle of the exhale, and then filled Luke's lungs again.

No response.

Bracing Luke with one hand, he slammed his other into Luke's chest, trying shock the heart back into action. The thickness of the spacesuit absorbed much of the blow. Their suited bodies bounced off the panels in weightlessness.

"Help me!" he yelled to Chad.

The two of them took turns slamming their gloved fists into Luke's chest, as Michael repeatedly blew more oxygen into his lungs.

But Luke's skin didn't pink up and his eyelids didn't flutter. Saliva floated from his slack mouth in a sticky, weightless web.

Lunar Module Pilot Luke Hemming, Captain in the United States Marine Corps, veteran of three hours of spaceflight and one spacewalk, was dead.

Bumping against them in the confined space, the cosmonaut was moving, hands twisting to open glove locks, then reaching for the neck handle that released the white helmet, CCCP printed in large red letters across its front.

Michael gathered the floating gloves, then helped to guide the helmet clear.

The cosmonaut, who was wearing a tight brown leather headset underneath, unclipped the chinstrap and peeled it off. Longish brown hair floated free in the weightlessness.

Michael frowned. The thick hair, matted after the spacewalk, was cut square across the front, in bangs. He saw no trace of a beard or sideburns. The guarded brown eyes now looking challengingly into his were unmistakably feminine.

The cosmonaut was a woman.

"Spasiba," she said evenly, nodding slightly. "Senk you."

Chad pivoted up from the other side of the cabin. He'd taken his helmet off, and the sharp smell of vomit came with him. "A woman! Good Christ!" He gestured at the jammed cabin, loose articles floating everywhere, the extra crewmember overfilling the already cramped confines. "What are we gonna do with *her*? Shit!"

Michael tried to take stock. "Luke is dead, the TLI burn's complete so we're going to the Moon regardless, our comms are still bad, and now we have a female Commie stowaway!"

Who was watching them both warily.

"We gotta get comms back ASAP." Chad grabbed his flight plan. "Next pass is Australia in"—he checked the digital timer—"four minutes. Maybe we'll get lucky and they'll hear us this time."

Michael said, "I need to pull the Lunar Module out of the S-IVB. And we've got to figure out what to do with—her." He looked at the cosmonaut and spoke deliberately, indicating himself. "My name is Michael." He pointed to her. "What is your name?"

She held his gaze. "My nem, Svetlana." She turned and looked at Chad, expectant.

"I'm Chad." He pointed at her, frowning. "You just wait there." He opened both hands, palms towards her to signify that her whole body needed to stay put. "Michael and I have work to do."

She stared back. Chad gave her a long look. *Must be a tough chick to hang on outside during all that.* He turned to Michael.

"You get into the LM extraction checklist. Before I do anything else, I need to clean up my suit."

Michael looked at the two of them, and at Luke's inert body. "What a shitshow."

The technician at Honeysuckle Creek had been waiting for this moment. It was 2:20 a.m. on Tuesday 17 April. The temperature outside had gone down to just above freezing, an early taste of Australia's approaching winter. She'd turned the antenna system heaters on and set up the automated tracking, and now she double-checked her watch.

Apollo 18 was to be the very last of the Moon missions. She hadn't been lucky enough to work any of the previous flights, and was excited to be part of this one. Though she just had to throw a few switches and wouldn't actually talk with the astronauts, she didn't care. She held her Kodak Pocket Instamatic camera at arm's length to try to get her face and the operator's console in the picture, smiled proudly and pushed the shutter. The flash lit up the empty room. Her mum was going to be so excited to see that photograph.

Setting the small camera on the desk, she rechecked the digital timer and pressed the mic button on her headset cord.

"Houston NETWORK, this is Honeysuckle Creek, all set for the Apollo 18 pass."

The voice crackled back through her earphones.

"Roger, Honeysuckle, acquisition should be at 02:25:30 your time. Appreciate the late-night help."

The Australian technician was thrilled to know she was talking directly to Mission Control in Houston. She listened to the status report.

"FLIGHT, Honeysuckle's ready, should have signal on time."

"Copy, NETWORK, thanks."

A shiver went down the Australian technician's back. *That was Gene Kranz, the man who saved Apollo 13!*

She watched the oscilloscope on her left, waiting for the spike that would show a return from the Apollo craft as it appeared over the horizon. Exactly on time, the display jumped. She made sure her voice was calm, matching the tone from Houston.

"NETWORK, Honeysuckle, I see it on the scope now. You should have comms and data shortly."

A pause.

"Yep, thanks, we're seeing it now."

The CAPCOM's voice came into the Honeysuckle technician's headset, halfway around the world.

"Apollo 18, Houston, we're with you through Australia. How do you read?"

All she heard was a burst of random noise.

"18, Houston, we heard some static, but you're still unreadable. Should be fixed when you get rid of the S-IVB, and the high-gain antenna deploys. We're evaluating trajectory now, but you're looking good for LM extraction. If you copy, type all zeroes."

There was a pause.

"Okay, 18, we see that, thanks."

A frown creased the Honeysuckle technician's forehead. She'd been half listening to the earlier Houston conversation about a comm problem, but hadn't realized the crew couldn't talk to Earth.

"Holy dooley!" she muttered.

"18, Houston, the LM extraction maneuver start time will be 3 plus 55 plus 27, separation time 10 minutes later."

Michael glanced at the timer, double-clicked his mic button and sent all zeroes, to acknowledge. "Maneuver starts in 90 seconds, Chad."

Chad nodded, carefully wiping out his suit with biocide.

The demands of the task helped Michael focus; he needed to physically separate *Pursuit*, flip it around and mate it with the lunar lander, still housed inside the S-IVB rocket, and then extract the lander. It was a delicate sequence he'd practiced thousands of times, but never like this. He pantomimed his upcoming hand movements on the controls, deliberately ignoring Luke's feet floating next to him and the cosmonaut—Svetlana—occasionally bumping into his shoulder.

"Apollo 18, we see the S-IVB maneuver is complete. You have a GO for T&D."

Transposition and docking. Time to put all that training to work. Michael reached forward and pushed the Launch Vehicle Separation button.

Bang! The sound of pyrotechnics rang through the ship as long lengths of explosive cord cut the metal structure joining them to the rocket. Michael felt Sveltlana turning in alarm. "It's okay," he said, giving her a reassuring thumbs-up. *Do Russians even know what that means?*

Chad was watching through his overhead window. Bits of metal and cover panels were drifting slowly clear. "Looks like a clean separation."

"Okay, here we go." Michael tipped back on his joystick and *Pursuit* responded, smoothly turning through a half circle to align for docking. The curve of the world rotated into view as he worked to center the Lunar Module in his window. The ship that Luke had named *Bulldog*. He pushed the thought out of his head.

"Moving in now." He pushed forward on the other joystick, and *Pursuit's* small thrusters fired in response, small pops of noise filling the cabin like someone was tapping on the hull with a hammer.

"18, Houston, as soon as you can we'd like you to deploy the high-gain. We expect that will resolve our comm problem."

Now that *Pursuit* was clear of the rocket, there was room to pivot out the large four-dish antenna.

"Roger, in work." Chad reached forward and threw the switches as Michael stared intently out his overhead window, maneuvering *Pursuit* closer to the docking target. Small pieces of debris and ice tumbled slowly across his view.

"Lots of small bits in the way, but *Bulldog* looks clean," Michael reported. The top of the Lunar Module protruded from the rocket body, harshly lit in the direct dawn sunlight.

No answer from Houston. Chad rechecked the antenna deploy indications.

"Switching the high-gain antenna to REACQ," he said, and flipped the switch down to force the antenna into reacquisition, making it search automatically for the radio signal from Earth.

"Almost there, Chad." Michael spoke intently, focused on hitting the target dead center. He stared unblinkingly out his window, making tiny adjustments with his hand controllers as *Bulldog* filled the field of view.

There was a metallic scraping sound, and they felt a small, sudden deceleration into their seat straps. Luke and Svetlana's suited forms bumped forward in the cockpit.

"Capture, Houston!" Michael reported with satisfaction.

Three small latches on the tip of *Pursuit*'s docking probe slid into place and clicked inside *Bulldog*'s docking mechanism, the indicators on the panel going from barber pole to gray. The two ships were mechanically attached.

Michael exhaled in quiet relief. He threw the switch to retract the docking probe, to pull in and solidly lock the ships together. They could hear the low grinding of gears. All that remained was to release *Bulldog* from the rocket body, and for Michael to back away and slide it out. Houston could then fire the thrusters on the rocket and move it safely clear.

"Apollo 18, we show a successful docking. Nicely done. Please give us a voice check." No hint in the CAPCOM's tone that this voice check was critical.

Chad glanced quickly at Michael, took a deep breath and pressed his comm trigger. "Houston, Apollo 18, how do you hear?"

The relief in the CAPCOM's voice was palpable in their headsets. "We have you loud and clear now, 18! How us?"

"Loud and clear also, Houston. Glad to be talking with you again." Chad paused, his voice going flat. "As soon as we can, I need to talk privately with the Director of Flight Ops."

He glanced at Luke's body, and at the cosmonaut.

"We've got some major issues to discuss."

28

Mission Control, Houston

Kaz pushed the button marked Speaker on the beige telephone on the desk in the Director of Flight Operations observation room. He heard the buzz of the dial tone, and then tapped in the Washington number. He glanced up through the window at the operators at their consoles, and then around at the other men in the room.

The faces were tense. Deke Slayton, a Mercury astronaut and the Flight Ops Director, was seated behind the desk, visibly pained and angry at the loss of another astronaut. Al Shepard was standing, staring at the large screen at the front of Mission Control. The Manned Space-craft Center Director, Chris Kraft, stood next to him, a sheen of sweat on his broad forehead from the sprint he'd made from his office in the headquarters building.

They heard the phone ringing, and a female voice answered.

"National Security Agency, General Phillips's office."

"Hi, Jan, Kaz here in Houston, we need to talk to the General right now if possible."

"He's in a meeting. Just hold on a minute while I get him."

The voice of the CAPCOM talking with the Apollo crew came tinnily through a metal speaker on Deke's desk. They were working on opening the hatch between *Pursuit* and *Bulldog*, following the mission timeline as they awaited further instruction.

A sharp click from the speakerphone. "Kaz, Sam Phillips here. What's up?"

Kaz took a breath, quickly clarified who was in the room with him and then summarized the wild sequence of events that had just transpired in orbit.

Phillips had been the director of the Apollo program during several fatal astronaut plane crashes and the fire that had killed the Apollo 1 crew. He understood what Luke's death meant to these men.

"Deke, Al, Chris, I am so very sorry to hear this." They heard him exhale angrily through his nose. "Our intelligence let us down, badly. No one thought Almaz was manned, nor did we know it was armed. As NSA Director the failure is mine, and I am responsible for Captain Hemming's death. My deepest condolences."

Brief silence as Phillips thought further.

"We need to maintain the complete news blackout until we decide our path. I'll call the Joint Chiefs chairman now, and he's going to want an immediate briefing to the National Security Council and the President."

Al Shepard spoke. "Sam, we're working on what to do with Luke's body, and how the crew should deal with the cosmonaut. The only good news is that our spaceships are healthy, and we've got some time to regroup during the three days' coast to the Moon." He paused, glancing at Kraft and Slayton. "But we need a whole new plan for what to do when we get there."

"Yep, I hear you, Al. This will put way more fingers in the pie than anyone wanted. If you don't mind, I'm gonna need Kaz to keep us up to date and to be the one who passes sensitive direction up to the crew."

Al and Deke nodded. That made sense to them.

"Kaz, I'll need you back on the phone in a bit, to give an update at the Security Council meeting with the President."

"Understood, General. Meanwhile, I have a suggestion for what you might discuss with the Joint Chiefs."

This was why Phillips had recruited him. "Go ahead," he said.

"We badly need damage control with the Russians. For now, outside of Mission Control here, no one knows what's happened. Not even the Soviets, I'd guess, who must still be in the dark about what actually occurred, and specifically about the status of their two cosmonauts. We need to move fast to update them that one of their crew is alive, and to offer them a nuanced apology for the nightmare that happened at Almaz that offers them a potential benefit. Give them an option that they can take uphill to Brezhnev, along with the bad news."

He paused.

"We have a healthy orbiter and lander, three people alive on their way to the Moon, and the cosmonaut's and Luke's spacesuits—the crew confirmed that only the umbilical got damaged and his suit's okay. Michael Esdale can fly *Pursuit* around the Moon as planned, and Chad Miller is fully trained to fly *Bulldog* down to the surface."

Kaz made eye contact with the three men in the small room with him.

"The cosmonaut should fly in *Bulldog* with Chad, while Michael orbits in *Pursuit*. We can help the Soviets put the world's first woman on the Moon."

Time to get out of my suit, Svetlana decided.

The two astronauts had already doffed theirs, and had opened the forward hatch of their capsule. The thickset white one—*Tschad, he said he was called, and he acts like the commander*—had gone through into the connecting tunnel. The other, the Black one—*Mikhail*—was reading from a checklist and watching pressure gauges.

The third astronaut, suited with his helmet back on and strapped into the chair next to her, was dead, like Andrei was. She felt a surge of anger, but shook her head. "Pazhivyom, oovidim," she muttered. *I'm still alive, so let's see what's next.*

She unplugged the two hoses to her life-support backpack and wedged it and her helmet, gloves and comm cap behind the headrest of the Black astronaut's seat, against the underlying structure. He ignored her, focusing on activating the Lunar Module.

She was careful with her actions; on Chelomei's instructions, she and Andrei had brought weapons outside to defend the Almaz. She double-checked that hers was still safely concealed in her leg pocket. *Best keep that a secret for now.*

The Yastreb spacesuit was flexible, with an outer thermal coverall and a double inner rubber pressure liner. She slid down the long zipper, peeled back the Velcro flap and started unlacing, like undoing figure skates.

With the long laces floating free, she reached in near her belly and pulled out a rubber stub neck, held tightly closed with double-wrapped elastics. She released and unwound them, and then opened the neck, shaking it loose like the end of a large balloon. She worked her arms out of the sleeves, bent hard forward while prying the neck ring over her head, and emerged through the central opening. It reminded her of self-birth every time she did it. She pushed the upper half down around her hips and slid her legs out, turning and floating free.

She was now wearing only her byelyo—long white cotton underwear—and socks. She thought for a minute, then peeled the thermal coverall off the suit and put it on. *That feels better.* She rolled the inner pressure suit tightly so that the weapon was in the middle and tucked it beside her helmet.

Svetlana had been in space for two weeks, and had become adept in weightlessness. She pivoted smoothly, found a handhold on a support strut and floated silently next to Michael while she rolled up the cuffs on her oversized coveralls.

Michael glanced at her. "All okay?"

She nodded. "Da, okay."

———

Michael called down the tunnel to the Lunar Module. "How's it going, Chad?"

"All the latches look right, Michael. I think we're good to jettison the S-IVB."

Michael pushed the transmit button. "Houston, 18, we show good for separation."

"Roger, 18, concur, you are GO for Pyro Arm and extraction."

There was definite comfort in the familiar technical jargon and practiced actions. Michael set the switches to power the four explosive charges that would sever connection to the rocket body and push the *Bulldog* Lunar Module clear.

"Ready, Chad?"

"All set."

With Svetlana watching beside him, Michael leaned forward, flipped up the protective cover and raised the S-IVB SEP switch. There was a solid thumping sound, and they floated forward against the slight acceleration as springs and small thrusters pushed *Bulldog* free of its launch rocket. Michael stared up through his overhead window as the ships silently floated apart.

"There she goes, Houston, looks like a clean separation."

"Roger, Michael, good news. In a couple minutes we'll maneuver it clear of you."

Michael glanced at the cosmonaut and gave a quick nod, raising a thumb. She stared at him, unblinking.

I wonder if she's ever seen a Black man before.

With what sounded like forced nonchalance, the CAPCOM said, "Apollo 18, if now's a good time, the Flight Director would like to talk with you."

Chad poked his head out of the connecting tunnel to *Bulldog* and nodded at Michael to respond.

"Roger, Houston, we're listening." Michael realized that Svetlana didn't have a headset on. *Probably for the best. Who knows if she actually speaks English?*

Gene Kranz's familiar voice came into their headsets.

"Chad, Michael, I'm on a discreet comm loop, so we have some privacy. First of all, nice work on the TLI burn and S-IVB sep. Despite everything that's happened, you're on your way to the Moon.

"It's a terrible thing that we lost Luke, and my heart goes out to you both. No one here suspected there was a crew on Almaz, and we sure didn't know the ship was armed. Your reactions were a credit to the military services, and Luke will be forever honored by the Marine Corps as their first-ever combat fatality in space.

"Take any time you need to deal with it, but when you're ready, we have a few things."

Chad spoke. "Gene, we appreciate it." He looked at Michael, who shrugged. Death wasn't welcome, but it wasn't new to either man. "We're both okay with doing what needs to be done."

"Okay, thanks. As you can imagine, Washington is about to get involved, and we still have to decide what we're going to do when we get to the Moon—orbit and land, or just slingshot around and come straight back home. Those are going to be tough decisions, and Al, Deke and Kaz are working it on your behalf right now."

Chad and Michael nodded.

Gene continued. "For now, we need to decide what to do with Luke's body. The team is looking at options, but we recommend he stay sealed up in his suit for now." The message was clear: Luke's decomposing body would overwhelm the spaceship's air purifiers.

"We understand, Gene, thanks. His suit looks like it's airtight," Chad said. "I recommend we stay on the lunar orbit and landing trajectory for now, stick with the timeline. Keeps options open."

Michael glanced at him. *No way would Chad want to lose the moonwalk.*

"Agreed." Gene paused. "Is the cosmonaut listening? Does she speak English?"

"She's not on a headset, and it seems like she only knows a few words," Michael said.

Gene nodded. "For now I recommend you just treat her like a new crewmember, show her the critical safety and ops items, keep her out of trouble."

Svetlana noticed them both looking at her, and looked questioningly back.

"Makes sense, Gene," Chad said. "We'll let you know how it's going."

"Good. We're going to stay under total media blackout until told otherwise." The implied message: there was no need to limit what they said on the radio. "You two have any questions?"

Chad looked at Michael, who shook his head.

"Nope, thanks for the update."

CAPCOM spoke. "18, we're back with you, if you can pick up in 3-9 of the Flight Plan. We'd like the LM/CM Delta-P, and for you to get the cabin fan filter back on."

"Roger, Houston, in work." Michael flipped the page of the checklist and glanced at the cosmonaut. She calmly watched him, then turned to look at Chad. Michael saw her frown.

Looking over at Chad, Michael saw a faint smile on his commander's face. *What was that about?*

The phone rang on the flight director's console in Moscow. He picked it up and listened intently, making notes in his green daily logbook. He interrupted a couple of times to verify details, and then slowly set the phone down.

He turned to face Chelomei.

"Comrade Director, as you know, our ground stations have been listening for transmissions from the Apollo capsule."

Chelomei's stare burned into him. Ever since they'd sent the command to fire the gun on Almaz, they'd had no comms. It had been more than one full orbit, and neither of the relay ships had been able to get even basic telemetry data from the orbiting station. More ominously, there had been no word from the Almaz crew.

"Khvatit!" Chelomei spat. "Out with it!"

"It seems the Americans also had a comm problem, and recently got it fixed. Our interpreters are now hearing the Apollo crew clearly." He took a deep breath and then spoke in a rush. "The battle at Almaz killed one astronaut and one cosmonaut, and appears to have very badly damaged our ship. They referred to"—he checked his notes—"a 'trail of debris.'"

Chelomei's lips went thin.

"The Apollo Command Module was damaged but has been repaired, and they have fired their engine to leave Earth orbit for the Moon. They have extracted their lunar lander from the rocket body, as per normal. Somehow, after our crew's defense of Almaz, one cosmonaut was still clinging to the American ship as it turned for the Moon, and has since gotten inside."

He straightened in his chair. "Captain Andrei Mitkov is dead, Comrade, killed in battle. His body has floated free. Senior Lieutenant Svetlana Gromova is the one who is aboard the Apollo ship."

Chelomei wanted to scream. *Almaz a trail of debris. And Mitkov killed? The Americans did this!* He glared past the flight director, his thoughts reeling.

He took a lung-filling breath, held it and then forcefully exhaled, pushing it all out, clearing his mind. He pictured what was going to happen, assembling the logic. Since the Americans had not stayed in Earth orbit, they must still be intending to land on the Moon. And with only two astronauts, one would have to be in the lander, the other in the orbiting capsule.

So where would Gromova be?

What would I decide if I were the Americans? He nodded slightly. Having Gromova on the surface as an extra set of hands would be safer than a moonwalker being there solo. He thought through it again, weighing benefits, and reached the same conclusion. The Americans had to be thinking the same thing.

A Soviet on the Moon. From disaster, potential triumph!

But they were at the Americans' mercy. They couldn't even talk with Gromova unless NASA let them. Chelomei pictured the assets at his disposal, and what might be possible. He started a mental list of what was needed and who could provide it. He glanced at his watch and realized it was still evening. He grabbed the flight director console's phone and began making calls.

29

The White House

Bob Haldeman stood impatiently at the corner of the long, highly polished mahogany table in the West Wing of the White House. The hastily called National Security Council meeting was starting late. As President Nixon's fiercely loyal Chief of Staff, Haldeman was an unyielding taskmaster, and the delay made the veins in his forehead bulge below his tight crew cut.

Sam Phillips had arrived from his NSA office across town, and the Joint Chiefs Chairman and the Secretary of State were already at the table. Henry Kissinger, the head of the Council, had just taken his corner seat. CIA Chief James Schlesinger was still standing, pipe in hand, talking with Nixon. Haldeman placed a speakerphone in front of Nixon's chair to tie in to Houston and said, "Gentlemen, let's get seated, please."

Nixon looked at Haldeman, who nodded, and then walked around to sit midway up the side of the table, his chair bracketed by US and Presidential flags. He glanced at the phone on the table next to his cigar ashtray, and turned to Kissinger to begin.

"Mr. President, we have . . . a very tense situation . . . that has developed in space." Kissinger spoke like he was dictating a letter, in German-accented chunks. His gravelly voice was serious, his face impassive behind heavy-rimmed glasses.

"I will let Sam Phillips summarize what has occurred. But what we need to decide today is how to advise the Soviets, and how to turn this to our advantage."

Sam Phillips let that sink in before he spoke, and then he chronologically reviewed the events that had occurred that morning in space. As they listened, the faces of the men around the table darkened.

"The bastards!" muttered Schlesinger.

Sam continued. "I spoke with NORAD, and they're tracking multiple objects near the Almaz Space Station, confirming some sort of breakup. They estimate the lighter pieces will decay and burn up fairly quickly, and the main ship will re-enter Earth's atmosphere in about six weeks. A few dense pieces will likely make it to the surface, but the odds are they'll land in an ocean somewhere."

He made eye contact with Nixon. "Mr. President, if you concur, I'd like to get our rep in Mission Control on the line."

Nixon frowned. He hated ad hoc meetings and surprises. Haldeman and Kissinger prepared detailed daily written briefings for him, which he found much easier to deal with. But this was an unforeseen, serious event that required immediate action.

"Go ahead."

Haldeman walked around the table, reached carefully past the president and pushed the blinking button on the phone. Light static came through the speaker.

Sam Phillips said, "Kaz, I'm here with the President and National Security Council members. Can you hear us?"

"Yes, sir, loud and clear."

"I've summarized what you and I spoke about, but what we need is the latest info and recommendations from there at NASA." As he talked,

Phillips made eye contact with James Fletcher, the NASA Administrator, seated across from him.

Kaz was sitting in the Director of Flight Ops room, looking through the glass at Mission Control. *Christ, I'm talking to the President!* His heart raced, but he kept his voice calm, matching Sam's tone.

"Mr. President, this is Lieutenant Commander Kazimieras Zemeckis, MOL astronaut and military liaison to Apollo 18. As General Phillips has probably told you, both the Command Module and the Lunar Lander are healthy, and they're on their way to the Moon, arriving in orbit there in"—he glanced at the timer on the front screen—"sixty-nine hours. A little under three days.

"The crew is asking for direction on a few key issues, and NASA needs to decide a couple things soon, all at your direction, sir."

In preparing for the call, he'd tried to visualize the group he was talking to, and their concerns. "The main question is, do we land on the Moon or not? The military purpose of the landing is still strong—to determine what the Soviets have found there with their unmanned Lunokhod rover. It could have key tactical and scientific importance for America."

Nixon glanced at General Moorer, the Joint Chiefs Chairman, who nodded as Kaz continued.

"With the death of Captain Hemming, we lost the Lunar Module pilot, but Commander Miller can fly the LM to the surface and do a moonwalk solo, if needed. Lieutenant Esdale would operate the Command Module in orbit, as planned. The wild card is what to do with the cosmonaut. She apparently has no English, but the crew's been using sign language."

Kaz paused, thinking that was enough for the moment.

The men around the table were all looking in different directions, visualizing options. The CIA chief took his unlit pipe out of his mouth. "Lieutenant Commander Zemeckis, this is Jim Schlesinger. I want to hear *your* recommendation."

This is unreal, Kaz thought. *I'm just a frickin' pilot!* He took a breath.

"Sir, I think we should land and the cosmonaut should go to the surface too. We can store Captain Hemming's corpse in the cosmonaut's spacesuit like a body bag. The crew tells me she's about the same size as Luke, so she can wear his suit. She'd be more useful in the LM than orbiting with Lieutenant Esdale." He decided to be frank. "She's an unknown and a threat to the mission, whether we land or not, but this way we stick to the plan as closely as possible, and have the best chance to accomplish our key objectives."

Phillips turned to the President. "Sir, Kaz also pointed out to me that this would give us leverage to deal with the Russians. Trade their silence on what really happened at Almaz for a chance to have public American-Soviet cooperation."

Kissinger slowly nodded, then haltingly spoke. "We have been planning your summit with Brezhnev in June on preventing nuclear war. This would give us a good advantage."

Haldeman, the most political of Nixon's trusted men, looked the President in the eye and chose his words carefully. "With you having signed Title IX against sex discrimination, and the Supreme Court's Roe v. Wade decision, the women's libbers would *love* you for being the president that put a woman on the Moon." In front of this group, he didn't mention the recent worrisome developments in the Watergate investigation, but both he and Nixon recognized the looming need for increased popular support.

Kissinger's deep, reasoned voice cut in again. "I can call Dobrynin now to set up an urgent briefing with Brezhnev." Anatoly Dobrynin had been the Soviet ambassador in Washington for over a decade, and he and Kissinger met often.

Nixon looked around the room, waiting to see if anyone had anything else to add, probing his own thoughts. This was a lousy situation, but if they played it right, he might gain the kind of support he'd once felt when he congratulated Armstrong and Aldrin, live on national TV, as they stood on the Moon. They could spin the astronaut's death as something that had happened while rescuing a failing Russian spaceship; the man would be seen as a héro. They could use the fact that the Soviets had opened fire with Almaz, killing an astronaut who was merely taking pictures, as a key negotiating tool with the Politburo. And the world would know that the Russians couldn't walk on the Moon without America's help.

Win-win. He looked around to see all the men waiting for him to speak.

"Guys, let's not screw this up. We need to control the information carefully, and get Russian buy-in ASAP. I want NASA to minimize our risk by keeping the mission as short as possible to meet the military needs. But let's do it. Let's land Apollo 18, with a cosmonaut aboard, on the Moon."

That was nuts, Kaz thought, gathering his papers to walk back into Mission Control. Yawning and shaking his head to clear the exhaustion and adrenaline, he stopped to fill his coffee cup from the communal pot in the hallway, thinking about what steps this course of action required.

The crew needs an interpreter.

He climbed the steps to the Flight Director level, and walked over to Gene Kranz, catching the eye of Al Shepard behind the Flight Ops console. Kaz filled them both in on Nixon's approval. When he mentioned the interpreter, Gene said, smiling, "I'm a step ahead of you."

He raised his chin to point at the CAPCOM console, where a woman with long blond hair was standing, looking awkward. "That's Galena Northcutt. She works in the Mission Planning back room, has a math background and spoke Russian at home growing up. I've asked her to fill in until we can get someone here from the State Department."

The CAPCOM got Galena seated and showed her how to communicate with the crew. Kaz stepped around Gene's console and down one level to stand behind her. He retrieved his headset and plugged in to listen to Gene's updated briefing to the room.

"Gentlemen. And ladies." Gene glanced at Galena, the only woman there. "We've just received approval from the highest level to proceed as planned with Apollo 18. We still need to confirm with the Soviets, but the current intent is to have the cosmonaut on board"—he checked his papers for the name—"Svetlana Gromova, ride in place of Luke Hemming. I need TELMU to work suit-check and sizing, and Ops and Procedures to start revising checklists for the Commander to fly the LM without the usual help and to minimize total mission time."

TELMU was the console in charge of the spacewalking suit while on the lunar surface. The technicians nodded their heads at the Flight Director's instruction.

Gene continued. "We're fortunate to have a Russian speaker already on staff, to help CAPCOM and the crew communicate."

Galena looked around uncomfortably and waved.

"We'll gen up more translation help shortly, and the plan is undoubtedly going to shift as the Russians get involved."

He turned and looked at JW. "SURGEON, I need you to sort out a plan for Captain Hemming's body using the cosmonaut's spacesuit."

JW nodded. He'd already been looking up flesh decay rates and off-gassing concerns in a confined living area.

"That is all for now, people. Let's rethink our assumptions, given these new circumstances, and revise the plan to get the crew what they need and Apollo 18 safely to the surface of the Moon and back. CAPCOM, let's get the crew working the timeline, and offer up Miss Northcutt to help them talk to each other. Let's have Kaz talk to the crew directly on this, as he has the latest details."

The CAPCOM nodded.

"You ready?" Kaz asked Galena. Her eyes were wide, but she nodded.

Kaz pushed the transmit button. "Apollo 18, Houston, how do you hear?"

Chad's voice came back through Kaz's headset. "Loud and clear, Houston."

"18, we'd like you to keep working the timeline, but meanwhile we have someone here to translate for you. My suggestion is to get the cosmonaut on a headset, and then we can act as relay for your conversation."

"Copy, Houston, in work."

Svetlana was floating next to Michael, watching with interest as he aligned the ship and methodically recorded the star angles into the computer. It intrigued her how similar it was to the system they had on Almaz. She felt the commander tug on her sleeve.

"Put this on," he said, holding out a headset on a long white cord. She held his gaze as she took it and slipped it into place over her ear, swinging the mic boom in front of her mouth. She frowned, wondering who she would be talking to.

"Houston, the cosmonaut has a headset on and should be able to hear you now." As he spoke, Chad showed her the volume thumbwheel on the cockpit side panel. She nodded and lowered it slightly.

Kaz looked at Galena. "Just repeat what I say in Russian, okay?" She nodded, moving her thumb on the unfamiliar transmit button.

"Svetlana, this is Mission Control Houston. How do you hear me?"

Galena repeated what he'd said in Russian. "Privyet Svetlana, zdyess tsenter upravlenia polyotami ve Houstonyeh. Kak nas slooshetyeh?"

Warily, Svetlana responded, and Galena translated for the room.

"She said, 'Houston, this is Senior Lieutenant Svetlana Gromova, I hear you.'"

Kaz nodded, and continued. "Tell her your name and that you're a NASA flight controller who speaks Russian. You're here to help interpret for her with the Apollo crew and with us in Mission Control. Also tell her we're contacting her team in Moscow to enable them to talk with her as soon as possible."

Galena blinked up at him. The CAPCOM slid a piece of paper and a pen in front of her, and she scribbled the key points and then broadcast it to Svetlana.

There was a pause, and then Svetlana spoke rapidly, Galena taking notes and translating.

"She'd like to know what happened to her crewmate, and to her ship. She also wants to know what's going to happen now."

Kaz looked at Gene, and at Al Shepard. Both men shrugged, as if to say "Tell her the truth." He pushed the transmit button.

"Apollo 18, for simplicity, let's just communicate like usual and allow time for Galena here to translate as we go, sentence by sentence." He paused while Galena interpreted.

"Senior Lieutenant Gromova, this is Lieutenant Commander Kaz Zemeckis. I am sorry to have to tell you that your crewmate has died, and that your spaceship was fatally damaged. We are glad you have survived and are safely aboard Apollo. The mission is continuing to the Moon, as planned, for now. We'll get you more details soon."

Galena translated. There was a pause, then he heard Svetlana quietly say, "Spasiba."

"Thank you," Galena translated.

Gene leaned back to Al's console, shaking his head. Both of them had flown jets in the Cold War and Korea, with Communists as their sworn enemy. Gene muttered, "I never thought I'd see the day."

30

Mission Control, Houston

JW took off his headset and walked up to talk directly with the Flight Director.

Gene gave him his full attention; SURGEON didn't come talk to him often. He beckoned to Kaz and Al Shepard to join them.

"I've been looking at postmortem decay rates," JW said. "Captain Hemming's body will currently be in autolysis, or self-digestion, as his membranes and cells break down. The gas from the bacteria and decay, especially in his gut, is going to get rapidly worse. His body could bloat to double its size, and the gas will vent through his anus and esophagus. The odors of putrefaction will be extremely unpleasant." JW was matter-of-fact, but Kaz felt himself trying not to think that this was Luke he was talking about.

JW continued. "The body will also be stiffening soon, with rigor mortis starting in the neck and torso. That will last about twenty-four hours. The limbs and joints will be too rigid to transfer into the other suit within an hour or two. Oh, and the bowels will have evacuated, so there will be urine and probably feces for the crew to deal with."

Gene raised a palm, signaling JW to stop. *Doctors.* "Sounds like the timeline is critical. What do you recommend?"

"We need to get Luke's body transferred into the cosmonaut's suit and sealed up ASAP. Then they need to store it someplace, hopefully cool, to slow bacterial activity. Maybe even vent it to vacuum, if possible, to kill the bugs."

"Maybe a burial at sea?" Al Shepard suggested. "It would be honorable that Luke's resting place was the surface of the Moon. Pretty sure *Bulldog* has enough weight margin for his body. And keeping him in *Pursuit* all the way back to Earth would add a bunch of risk — atmosphere contamination and re-entry weight and balance."

Gene nodded. He thanked the doctor, then stood squarely in front of his console and addressed the room. "Folks, we need to have the crew transfer Captain Hemming's body into the cosmonaut's pressure suit before they go to sleep for the night. It's already been a long day, I know, but once rigor mortis sets in, it will be too difficult. CAPCOM, please advise the crew, with translation."

Kaz stepped back down to his console and checked that Galena was ready. He spoke: "*Pursuit*, Houston, when you have a minute." Code for *This is important*.

Michael's ears perked up, and he caught Chad's eye. "Go ahead, Houston, *Pursuit*'s listening."

Kaz described the plan, and the reasons behind it. He had Galena translate the key details, especially the planned use of the cosmonaut's spacesuit.

Svetlana's head whipped around at that, looking at her stowed suit.

"*Pursuit* copies all, thanks." Michael said, his voice somber.

Svetlana floated abruptly in front of him, frowning. She waved a finger and shook her head, saying something forcefully in Russian. The only word Michael recognized was "nyet."

Galena listened to the rapid-fire, agitated voice, and translated for all in Mission Control to hear. "The cosmonaut says she can't allow her suit to be used by anyone but her. It's custom-sized, and she'll need it for re-entry and landing. She's demanding to talk to senior management in Moscow, or she won't authorize it."

The room was briefly silent as they digested this.

Gene Kranz shook his head. "Galena, tell her that we're working on getting a link with Moscow as fast as we can, but that she is a guest on an American vessel, and operational needs outweigh her concerns. Tell her we'll have a pressure suit to protect her for re-entry. And repeat what you say in English too, so the crew knows."

Galena read up Gene's words, and Chad replied immediately. "Houston, this puts us in an ugly situation here. She's mad, and blocking us from getting at her suit. I may have to force her out of the way while Michael grabs it."

Kaz raised his hand to get Gene's attention, and got a nod.

"Chad, Kaz here. It's going to take a while for you two to get Luke out of his suit. I recommend you start on that now, and hopefully we'll hear from Moscow while you're in process. Also, she'll likely get distracted at some point, and you can just grab it." He shrugged, as Gene raised a thumb.

"Copy, Houston, concur. We'll start now."

In Moscow Mission Control, known by its Russian acronym, "TsUP," the communication technician was listening to the American chatter coming back from the Apollo ship. "She's asking them to let her talk to us, Comrade Director. Something about not allowing them to use her Yastreb suit." The tech looked puzzled, trying to piece together the one-sided conversation, unable to hear the transmissions up from Houston.

Chelomei stared at him, thinking. *Her suit? Why would they want her suit? Was something wrong with theirs?*

He blew out sharply through his nose. *Damn, I need to talk to her!* He glanced at his watch. Nearly midnight. Another night sleeping on the cot in his office.

He stood, curtly telling the flight director, "I'll be back in the morning. Send someone to fetch me immediately if you hear any other developments." He turned on his heel without waiting for an answer and strode out of TsUP, his steps echoing loudly down the tiled hallway.

He needed to accelerate diplomacy at the highest level. As soon as Moscow woke back up, he'd call his contacts in the Kremlin.

Michael was undoing the umbilical hoses from Luke's suit. "Look here," he said, pointing. Chad leaned in, and saw the ragged metal where the bullet had split the oxygen feed line and regulator.

"That's what killed him." Chad scowled at the cosmonaut, who was glaring back at him as she hung on firmly to the crew headrest, covering her rolled-up spacesuit.

"Look at that Russian bear, showing her lack of gratitude," Chad said disgustedly. "All we did was save her life after they fired on us, and killed Luke here."

Michael had undone Luke's gloves and was pulling them off the lifeless fingers. The pale skin was already starting to blotch with death.

"Help me with the helmet," Michael said as he pinched and released the latch on the neck ring. The two of them guided it clear of Luke's head, the glass of the visor still fogged.

As the helmet came away, Luke's sightless eyes appeared, wide open and bloodshot. Chad looked away, muttering "Christ!"

Michael reached in and closed Luke's eyelids. "Sorry, buddy," he said. He turned the body over, peeled back the Velcro and snaps, and unzipped the suit's long pressure seal.

He reached an arm inside around Luke's body, bending him at the waist, and started prying the upper half of the suit off his shoulders. As he forced the neck ring over the back of Luke's head, the arms slid out of the sleeves and the upper torso popped free, loosely waving in weightlessness like a released jack-in-the-box, banging into structures, filling the confined space.

"Geez, Luke, you're scaring me!" Michael forced the joke to try to settle his own nerves. Svetlana had jammed herself into the far corner, as far clear as possible, now holding her spacesuit tightly rolled under her arm.

Chad grabbed Luke's boots and tugged, moving down the tunnel towards the LM. Michael disconnected the inner plumbing and electrical leads to Luke's body, and then helped work his legs clear.

The cockpit had become a jumble of floating bodies and gear. "I'll stow the suit in the LM," Chad decided, gathering the helmet and gloves and moving down the tunnel.

Michael began removing Luke's liquid-cooled long underwear, feeling like he should apologize to his friend. *This feels too personal.* He pulled down the long front zipper and peeled the stiff, tube-filled fabric away, relieved to see that Luke's low-fiber prelaunch diet had meant he hadn't shat himself. The underwear was damp with urine, but that would dry before the cosmonaut had to put it on. *Tolerable.*

"What are you doing?" Chad had reappeared and was looking past Michael at the cosmonaut. She had partially unrolled her suit and, smiling uncertainly, held it out.

Chad frowned. "Had a change of heart, did you?"

"Maybe she understands better now that we've got Luke out of his suit," Michael said.

"Yeah, maybe." Chad reached his hand out, beckoning, and she released her suit, floating it to him. He looked at her body and then at Luke's. "Let's hope this fits."

They unrolled the suit, flipping it around, inspecting the design differences. "Looks like the Russians enter from the front, through this balloon opening," Michael said. He raised his eyebrows at Svetlana, and she nodded. They fed Luke's legs inside, working them down into place, and then pulled the suit over his arms. Chad had to pry hard to get the helmet ring over Luke's head, as the body was stiffening, but with yanking and pushing, he made it work.

Svetlana held out her helmet. Chad took it and guided it over Luke's head, nestling it into its seal. There was an obvious over-center latch sticking out the side, and he lifted and clicked it into place, tugging and twisting on the helmet to check it was secure.

He looked up at her. "Gloves?" He flexed his fingers to demonstrate. She retrieved them from under the seat, and he slid them onto Luke's limp hands and locked the mechanism.

Michael had been trying to figure out how the air seal at the front of the suit worked. "I see that we need to pinch this internal body balloon closed, but what holds it?"

"Vapross?" Svetlana asked.

"Yeah, how do you Russians do this?"

She floated across and quickly gathered the loose rubber into successive folds with one hand, squeezing excess air from the suit with the other. Two rubber ties floated free, and with practiced motions she tightly wound them around the folds, tucking the bulbous end of each tie into a matching eyelet. She tucked the double-sealed balloon end inside the fabric of the suit, next to Luke's body.

Michael nodded, impressed. "Simple design." He pulled the outer fabric covering closed and began crisscrossing the laces tightly all the way up the torso.

Chad was looking at the umbilical connections, poking with his finger. "Let's hope these one-way valves keep Luke airtight."

Svetlana had chosen her moment. While the commander had been down the tunnel and Mikhail had his back turned, she'd grabbed the weapon from her bundled suit and tucked it flush against the backpack. She'd strapped it into place, muffled inside the thermal insulation cloth to avoid the clink of metal on metal. As she replaced the pack under the seat, she double-checked that the weapon was concealed.

Lucha sinitsa ve rookak chem zhuravel ve nyeba. She wasn't sure what was going to happen, but a bird in hand was definitely better than one in the sky.

She assumed they were lying to her about talking to someone in Moscow. If that happened, fine, but why would they allow it? Capitalist

Americans, with a cosmonaut as a captive prize on their ship? They were going to make a spectacle of her, exploit the opportunity and use her as a bargaining chip. Better to be ready.

Better to be armed.

Michael guided Luke's body up the tunnel to stow it in the LM, and in the sudden lull, Chad noticed he was hungry. And thirsty. The nausea had passed, and his body was telling him it was time to eat.

He leaned back and rummaged in the food locker, looking for packages that were marked for him with an identifying small red Velcro square. He found a brownie in a vacuum-sealed pouch, and the utensils container with scissors. As he was cutting the plastic open, he saw Svetlana watching him.

He realized it must have been a while since she'd eaten. "Hungry?" He held out the brownie.

She nodded. He handed her the package and found himself another. They chewed in silence.

He dug through the packets again and came out with a long, clear bag with grainy powder inside. He grabbed the water dispenser, a pistol-like contraption mounted on a hose, turned the red butterfly valve and carefully injected water into the bag through an opening in the bottom. He shook the bag to dissolve the powder and cautiously unrolled the drinking tube, biting its end closed between sips.

He filled a second one, read the label and floated it to her. "Pineapple grapefruit drink—you'll love it."

She'd been observing, and unrolled the tube and drank.

"Here, you can fend for yourself." Chad found one of Luke's food packages and held it out to her, pointing at the color-coded Velcro patch and then at her. "You—blue. Me—red." He jerked a thumb towards the LM. "Michael, white. Ironic, eh? You get it?"

She nodded as she took the package, rubbing the blue Velcro with her thumb. "Svetlana 'bloo.' Spasiba." She pronounced the English word like it had a new taste in her mouth.

"Yeah, whatever."

She used her fingers to squeeze the last of the juice up the drinking tube, and then rolled the empty package tightly together with the brownie packet. "Kuda?" she asked.

"In there." Chad pointed at a covered opening in the starboard wall. She jammed the empty plastic in and down, compacting the volume, and then held her hand out for his.

"Sure, toots. You clean up." He floated her his empties. She stuffed them away and then looked squarely at him.

"Tooalyet?" She pointed at her midsection and made a brushing-away motion with her fingers.

"Toilet? Right, you'll be needing that by now." He thought a moment. NASA had provided a condom-like adapter for the men to piss into, filling a urine bag. For shitting they had an open-mouthed plastic bag with a sticky seal that held it in place against their naked rear ends. Toilet paper and wet wipes were in attached bags.

Chad shrugged. She'd figure it out. He opened the storage locker and got her one of each.

She turned them over in her hands, nodding as she compared them to the similar Soviet equipment. *Muzhshini!* Men!

She floated to the far corner, turned away from Chad and started to peel off her coveralls.

"Oh, hey, hey!" he objected. "I don't need to watch you crap!" He turned and faced the port wall and went back to revising the landing checklist. "Try not to stink up the place."

Svetlana paused and looked around. One astronaut was in the LM and the other was now deliberately not watching her. The control panel of switches was in front of her. She made a mental note. *An excellent way to get privacy.*

She might need it.

31

Mission Control, Houston

EECOM had been looking at the effect of the sunlight on the side of the ship in the direct glare of the Sun, and temperatures were nearing peak allowable. The standard plan to deal with it was to slowly spin the ship once every 20 minutes, like a slow-motion barbecue spit. With all the problems, they had delayed starting the spin. "FLIGHT," he said, "before the crew goes to sleep, we need to set up rotisserie mode."

Gene asked, "INCO, what'll that do to my comms?"

"FLIGHT, the Hi-Gain antenna won't track as well while we spin, so it'll drift in and out." INCO peered over his console. "We can stop and start the spin when we need to talk, if FDO agrees."

The Flight Dynamics Officer checked a data table on his screen. "It'll use a bit more propellant, but our margins are good."

The astronauts' official sleep period wasn't for several hours yet, but they'd had to get up at 3:00 a.m. for the early-morning launch. The timeline called for a 90-minute nap, and Gene knew after the craziness of the flight so far, as their adrenaline ebbed, they'd need it. A thought occurred to him, and he waved Kaz up to his console. Al Shepard came around to listen.

"How should we handle sleep now?" Gene looked at Al. "Do you think one of them needs to stay awake to keep an eye on the Russian?"

"Absolutely," Al said. "I sure don't want a Commie floating around unsupervised inside our ship."

"I suggest a new sleep rotation cycle, Gene," Kaz offered. "Chad needs to be well rested for his moonwalk. That's our top priority. I expect the cosmonaut is on Moscow time, nine hours ahead, so she'll likely be ready for some shuteye about now too."

Gene nodded. "Let's keep Chad on the planned day/night schedule and move Michael to cover while Chad sleeps."

Kaz said, "I suggest *Bulldog* as the astronaut sleep area, so they get peace and quiet. The cosmonaut can just unplug her comms and sleep in *Pursuit* with whoever's awake."

Gene pushed his mic button. "EECOM, you're approved to set up Passive Thermal Control." He looked back at Kaz. "Let the crew know the new plan."

Kaz nodded and returned to the CAPCOM console, Al and Gene watching him. As a Navy pilot, Al was always ready to take a dig at the other armed services, and Gene was Air Force. He smiled and raised an eyebrow.

"Not bad for a one-eyed sailor."

"Sleep? How the hell do they expect me to go to sleep?"

Chad had listened to Kaz's instructions and was now looking at the new pencil marks he'd made in the Flight Plan. "I'm sure it sounds nice to them, sipping their coffees there in Houston, but it's nuts! How am I going to rest easy with Luke's corpse floating next to me and *her* running around?"

Svetlana glanced at him, frowning slightly at what might have caused his obvious anger. The interpreter hadn't translated the lengthy conversation the two Americans had just had with Houston.

By now Michael was used to Chad's temper. "No choice, Boss. It just makes sense. We've got to have you in tip-top form for hopping around on the Moon, especially when you'll be babysitting her. I'll have lots of time to catch up on my beauty sleep once I get the two of you undocked."

Svetlana looked from one to the other, and back again.

Chad said, "Yeah, okay." But the anger was still clear on his face. "You need any help getting us spinning?"

Michael held his nose to talk. "This is your captain speaking. I'll be putting the plane in rockabye mode for your sleeping pleasure. Please pull down the window shades and have a good rest, travelers. When you wake up, the stewardess"—he stuck out a thumb at Svetlana—"will be ready to serve you a delicious vacuum-packed meal. Sweet dreams, and we'll be there before you know it."

Chad smiled in spite of himself. "Clown."

Michael tapped the data screen. "Maybe take extra clothes with you. It's colder in *Bulldog*."

Chad nodded and rummaged in a locker for a jacket, then floated down the tunnel to the LM.

What was that all about? Svetlana wondered. She peered down the tunnel, and back at Mikhail. He glanced at her and brought his palms together beside his head, tipping it to one side. Then he pointed at the empty crew couch.

He wants me to sleep? She glanced at her watch and did a double take. It was one in the morning. She paused to assess how her body felt, and suddenly experienced a wave of fatigue. Michael had gone back to looking at the control panel, and she stole a look at the backpack, still securely wedged and barely visible under his seat.

Maybe a quick rest wouldn't be a bad idea. *Tiki chass.* Nap time.

She floated onto the right-hand couch and loosely strapped herself in. She took one last look his way, then closed her eyes. Within seconds her thoughts took her into sleep.

Michael glanced over at her inert form, and then leaned to look down the darkened tunnel. He reached over and shut off the cabin overhead

232   CHRIS HADFIELD

lights, then punched in some hexadecimal code on his keyboard to set an alarm for 30 minutes, just in case he dozed off too.

We're on our way, and I'm flying the ship alone. But man, is this fucked up.

The inside of the lander was completely familiar to Chad after the hundreds of hours he and Luke had spent in the simulator. And yet, with weightlessness, it felt strange, like diving inside a ship underwater. With no gravity to define up and down, even this small space was disorienting. He looked around in the harsh sunlight, adjusting his mind to the weirdness. *Like a sideshow fun house.*

Michael had strapped Luke's body up against the ceiling with one of the sleep hammocks. He'd rotated the gold visor down on the helmet so Luke's face was covered. *Better that way.*

Chad fit the sunshades into place over the two large, triangular landing windows. The labels and tips of all the switches, coated with luminescent paint, glowed in the darkness. He opened a locker to retrieve the other hammock and sleeping bag, and wrapped them around himself, clipping a strap to a handrail to keep from drifting. He consciously uncoiled the muscles in his body, took a deep breath and smoothly exhaled it. He was glad the motion sickness had passed.

A thought struck him. NASA had encouraged them to bring a few small private items, and he'd had a copy made of his parents' wedding picture. He reached down inside the sleeping bag, unzipped his leg pocket and slid it carefully out.

The glowing panels illuminated the black-and-white photo softly. Chad angled it to see the faces. His father, a man he only vaguely remembered, looked at him confidently, hair freshly cut, dark suit ill-fitting, with the pants too short, obviously borrowed for the day. Money had been tight. Chad looked into his eyes. *Could you have imagined this, Father?*

As always, though, it was his mother he couldn't look away from. She'd worn her best dress, a dark print with a large bow at the neckline. She'd added a long white veil that reached all the way to her calves. He rubbed the photo with his thumb. Her highly polished black shoes gleamed over her dark stockings. She was clutching red roses, and not for the first time, Chad counted them. He could see six clearly and, with care, one more, partially covered. Seven roses, an odd number for good luck, bought by this man, for this woman, on a day filled with promise.

Chad brought the photo closer. Her expression captured him most of all.

His mother's face was round, her cheekbones high. Her wide-set eyes looked squarely at the camera. He could sense the joy of the day in the way she held her neck, so straight and proud. The veil wasn't hers, and she knew it, but the day was, and so was a future together with this man. Her broad, full-lipped mouth bore the gentlest of knowing smiles. A smile Chad could still see and feel in his memory.

He touched the likeness just below her eyes. *Were they brown, or blue like his?* He wished he could remember.

He felt against his chest for her locket, fumbling along the thin chain in the unfamiliarity of zero gravity, finding it floating up near his shoulder. He pulled it around and held it between his thumb and forefinger, turning it slowly. A simple silver pendant, engraved with a winter rose. He looked back at the newly married couple. *Did you buy this for her, Father?* It had been hers, worn against her warm skin. He touched it to his lips and tucked it back under his T-shirt.

He shook his head, sighed deeply and carefully guided the photo back down into his pocket, zipping it safely closed. He relaxed his arms and was slightly surprised to see them float up in front of him. He glanced at Luke's body, suspended above him.

Chad had always held his secrets close. It somehow thrilled him to know that no one ever suspected that he was anything but an over-achieving farm boy from Wisconsin, as all-American as you could get. Even the couple who had raised him seemed to have forgotten where he came from; they'd done their good deed and adopted a lost Russian boy from the rubble of Berlin, making amends for the wickedness of the

World War. They'd convinced themselves that he was too traumatized to remember much about the violence of his childhood before America, even though he was nine when they'd brought him home. Better to forget it, anyway, in an America that was so deeply anti-communist.

And Chad might have forgotten too, if his brother hadn't contacted him. Oleg, the brother he'd thought had died in the war, who'd left him so alone after their parents were killed. But in Chad's first year of college, Oleg had finally tracked him down. It had been a shock to hear his brother's voice again, even through an interpreter. Chad had found that his spoken Russian was rusty, but was amazed at how easily his comprehension of his mother tongue came back. His secretive nature made him careful not to let on how much he understood; Russia was the enemy, and he didn't really know his brother anymore, not really. It was smarter somehow to keep the interpreter between them. Smarter not to tell his adoptive parents, or anyone, about this connection to his past. And especially smart once his Air Force dreams started to come true and he was on track to fly in space.

And now the cosmonaut doesn't know I speak Russian. Even better, no one else does either. The power of that thought made him smile in the darkness. Pulling the cosmonaut into their ship had opened a Pandora's box of unexpected opportunity. Now that she was going to the Moon's surface with him, he just had to keep his eyes open and figure out what he could do with it.

For a tense hour or two after Luke had died, Chad had thought all his sacrifices were going to be for nothing—that the higher-ups would abort the Moon landing and order them home. His control had been dangerously thin, but now he realized that the cards were falling into place.

He had another thought, and his smile widened.

She's my wild card.

32

Lunar Surface

The rock had lain on the surface of the Moon since well before humanity had begun keeping time.

Throughout all recorded history, small meteoroids and asteroids had drifted through the solar system and smashed into the Moon, kicking up powdery dust that fell slowly in the low gravity, leaving an unblemished, dry beach surrounding this particular small, protruding, gray-brown rock.

Until recently.

In the weeks since the radioactivity had been detected—a possible nuclear power source on the Moon, a chance for the Soviets to regain the upper hand in the space race—the smooth plain had started to resemble a dirt bike rodeo.

Gabdul and his team in Simferopol had backed Lunokhod away and reapproached from all sides, photographing and analyzing this most interesting of rocks, the eight wire wheels churning the regolith. The two-week lunar night had slowed operations, as they'd closed up Lunokhod to keep it warm, but the recently risen Sun had kicked off a renewed frenzy of activity.

The rock was about the size of two fists, sticking up above the dirt. They'd started calling it "Ugol"—Russian for "ember"—glowing eternally. Careful to not disturb it, Gabdul had driven the cameras and scientific instruments as close as he safely could, peering from all angles. They had all wondered whether Ugol was just the tip of a larger boulder underneath; the Geiger counter had shown no significant radiation in the surrounding area, so maybe the lunar soil was a better insulator than they thought. But after much scientific and operational discussion, they'd decided on today's plan.

Gabdul was going to bump the rock.

Not a straightforward thing to do. No one had thought to put fenders on the rover, as the intent had been to *not* run into things. It would be a disaster to damage Lunokhod, or one of its key instruments. If Ugol was part of a deeper bedrock, banging into its unyielding surface could do permanent harm.

During the 13-day-long darkness of lunar night, the Simferopol crew had repeatedly gone out into their Moon simulation yard with the full-scale Lunokhod mock-up, working through options. Having unmoving cameras on Lunokhod made the challenge harder; getting close enough to hit the rock with the rover's heavy frame meant losing sight of it.

They'd decided to touch it firmly with one wheel. The titanium rims and stainless-steel mesh tires were tough, and if Ugol was simply resting on the surface, they should be able to dislodge it. But it was going to need delicate driving, and Lunokhod was heavy, even on the Moon.

After the lunar night had ended, they waited several more days because Gabdul insisted that the Sun be high in the sky to minimize long shadows, and so its glare wouldn't shine into the cameras.

On the simulation field, Gabdul had backed Lunokhod into position and practiced on the approach track countless times: he set the precise distance using camera views, knew to move the hand controller for exactly the right length of time and then give a full reversing input just before letting go. These maneuvers had proven to give the most impulse to the rock while minimizing the chances of damage.

It had taken patience, but today was finally the day.

Sitting at his console, Gabdul leaned forward, steadying his arm. He looked at his navigator, who nodded. The image on the screen showed they were exactly in position. Gabdul mouthed a quiet countdown. "Tree, dva, adeen, pusk!"

He smoothly moved his hand controller forward to its limit, held it firmly while counting in his head, swiftly brought it fully back into reverse and then released it. All eyes locked onto the small TV screen, waiting for the slow image refresh to show them what had happened.

The 10 seconds seemed interminable, as Gabdul muttered "Davai, davai!" under his breath—C'mon, c'mon!

The grainy screen flickered impassively to its new image. It showed nothing remarkable—just the soil beyond the stone and a bit of the horizon. But it was exactly what they'd simulated, with everything still level, nothing visibly wrong. Gabdul glanced at his systems technician, who had been worriedly scanning his updated data.

"Pa paryadkeh," he said at last. All seems in order.

Gabdul nodded, and smoothly pulled back on the controller, commanding Lunokhod to reverse enough for the cameras to reveal the result of their work. He counted rhythmically to three and released again. If all worked as in the simulation, it would show Ugol's new position; if it had moved, they should be able to detect it against the surrounding dirt.

The lead scientist had been standing back, but now she grabbed the back of Gabdul's chair and leaned in to look as the new image popped onto the monitor. She'd printed the previous screenshot, and held it up to compare the two side by side. Her eyes flicked back and forth, left and right, scanning for differences.

The new tire track was obvious. Where there had been undisturbed dust, now there was a darker waffle print, the soil kicked up from the sudden momentum reversal. Gabdul touched the edge of the stone on the paper and then the same point on the screen. "I think it moved!" he said, delighted.

The scientist leaned closer, inspecting where he'd pointed. Ugol's edge had been smooth against the dust, but now, in the bright sunlight, there was a darker stripe where they met.

"I think you're right, Gabdul. Ugol has shifted!"

She stepped back and straightened up, crossing her arms. So Ugol was *not* a solid part of a radioactive outcropping. This puzzling lump of a rock was not attached to a mother lode. She focused again on the screen, one hand on her chin, a fingertip tapping her high cheekbone. *How did you get to this place, little one? Did a heavy impact excavate you from deep in the Moon and chuck you up onto the surface? Are there more like you just below the surface?*

It was a planetary geologist's dream. *What are you, Ugol, where did you come from, and what can you teach us about the universe?*

33

Mission Control, Houston

It was shift change, and the number of people in Mission Control had doubled. Each console was overcrowded as the oncoming crew listened to the details of what had happened, making notes and asking questions, so they could seamlessly take over responsibility. An Apollo mission was like a nine-day multi-person relay race where no one could let the baton of technical information and decision-making drop.

Kaz was briefing the oncoming shift CAPCOM. The State Department Field Office had provided a Russian interpreter, who stood calmly beside them, absorbing all the new jargon.

Just before his shift went off headset, Gene Kranz spoke.

"People, that was a helluva day. You worked through many serious problems, some unprecedented in the history of manned spaceflight." He made eye contact with each console.

"We've got the tragedy to deal with, as well as the complexity of handling a new, non-English-speaking foreign crewmember. But the bottom line is we had a successful launch and have a resting crew, a healthy spaceship and a clear mission."

"The real work is just beginning. Get some sleep. See you back here in"—he checked his watch—"fifteen hours."

Kaz had given the U-Joint a long look as he drove home, but the idea of the noisy bar hadn't appealed to him, especially knowing that another astronaut from the Apollo 18 crew would soon be joining Tom on the honor wall. He'd stopped at the grocery for supplies instead. He wanted a stretch and an easy run, a quiet beer and a bite, and maybe some time with Laura. He turned up and into his Polly Ranch driveway, parked and glanced at his watch as he got out and closed the car door. She'd said she'd try to come over after the long drive back from Florida, maybe get in around eight.

Perfect.

He tossed his bag on the sofa and put the food in the fridge, wrinkling his nose at the house's stale air. *Smells like an absent bachelor's pad.* He opened the screened windows as he changed into PT gear, letting the early-evening breeze blow through.

The sun was nearing the horizon as he stepped out onto the driveway and started his 5BX stretching. The disrupted schedule at the Cape and the long periods of sitting had made him stiff. He'd learned it was best not to think about it; just put the body through the practiced 10 minutes of isometrics, work smoothly to the limits, ignore the creaks. Let his mind separate and wander.

But the day kept crowding into his mind. He pictured what the crew was doing in the capsule as he transitioned from stretching to sit-ups. He guessed they would not be sleeping easily. Chad with his quick temper not responding well to all the changes of plan, and Michael trying to be a calming influence, minding the ship and doing the right thing. Both men on edge with Luke's body hovering unavoidably and a female cosmonaut thrown into the mix.

A lot of tension on board.

He stood to do the back extensions, grimacing, then distracting himself by deliberately trying to reimagine the situation through the cosmonaut's eyes. *What had she just been through?* Her crewmate killed, Almaz wrecked and abandoned, the wild ride she must have had, holding on to the outside of a spaceship with its engine firing. *Like Slim Pickens in* Dr. Strangelove. *Craziness!*

He thought back to what he knew of women cosmonauts. He'd only heard of one, with a name that was oddly easy to remember because of its rhythm: Valentina Tereshkova. What was she—a skydiver and Air Force officer? She had made a short solo flight 10 years earlier, with the Soviets going heavy on the propaganda. But this woman—Svetlana—was likely very different. Working as part of a military spy crew, low-profile, long-duration; it would be a mistake to underestimate her.

He felt the grit of the pavement on his palms as he started into his push-ups, doing them in slow motion for maximum effect. The painful pull across his chest and in his shoulders was almost pleasant; unmistakable feedback that he was at his limit, working his muscles, feeling his own strength.

Tomorrow should be an easier day as the crew transited towards the Moon. Maybe fire the engines once to fine-tune their exact trajectory. A chance for the crew to settle in to the new reality and start focusing on replanning the upcoming landing.

A quiet day would be welcome.

He stood and easily jogged down the drive and turned onto the runway. He glanced at his watch. Forty-five minutes ought to be about right. He set a pace that he knew would get his pulse to 145 or so, and settled into the run.

He'd just cracked open a bottle of Lone Star, his hair still wet from the shower, when he heard the sound of a small engine climbing the driveway. He smiled, opened a second bottle and headed for the front door.

"I am so glad to be back," Laura said, smiling at him tiredly as she climbed out of her Beetle. She had on a new Walt Disney World T-shirt featuring Minnie Mouse posing self-consciously in a red dress, and was carrying an overnight bag. When she reached him, she took the beer and touched his bottle in a toast before taking a long, thirsty swallow.

With the sparkle returning to her eyes, she said, "If you also have food, you're the perfect man."

"How about tuna on toast with pickles?" Kaz took her bag and held the door, and she followed him into the kitchen.

"What did you think of the launch?" he asked as he made the sandwiches.

"We all said the countdown together," she told him with a grin, "and when that Saturn V blasted off—the rolling noise of it!" She shook her head, marveling. "It gave me an external heartbeat. And so bright—like seeing another sun!"

Kaz carried the sandwiches over to the table and sat down with her, delighting in her pure emotion. He'd been so wrapped up in the technical details, aware of all the dangers, and inside Launch Control, protected from the sound, that he felt he'd somehow missed what she'd seen. And a rare, shared experience. "I would have liked to have watched it with you," he said.

She looked at him, a half smile on her lips. "Well, you had important astronaut stuff to do. I was just a lunar geologist there for the fun of it." She took a big bite of her sandwich, then washed it down with the last of the beer. "You got another one of these?"

As he opened the fridge, she popped a pickle into her mouth, talking around it. "How's the mission going?"

He brought her the beer. As the lead geologist for the flight, she needed to know about Luke's death and also that a female cosmonaut was going to be landing on the Moon, but still he took a moment before he began to speak, wishing that he could sustain her feelings of wonder just a little longer.

Her eyes went round at the news. "Luke is dead, killed in space? I can't really take in how horrible that is. Are you okay?"

When Kaz shrugged and nodded, Laura said, "I guess we had this conversation the night after Tom died."

Her brow furrowed as she thought through the implications. "This means a whole new plan for surface ops." Her frown deepened. "Sounds like less science is going to get done."

Kaz nodded again. "You're right. We need to come up with a new timeline tomorrow. One that Chad can support on his own, with maybe minimal help from the cosmonaut, Svetlana."

"Well, that's something, anyway," Laura said. "The first woman on the Moon."

There was a moment's silence as they sat and pictured it, then Laura's mouth cracked open suddenly in a wide yawn. She blinked. "The day's catching up with me." She stood and carried her plate and half-finished beer to the sink. She turned to meet Kaz's eyes.

"I'm going to have a quick shower. How about you meet me when I come out?"

34

The Kremlin, Moscow

It wasn't often that Vitaly Kalugin went inside the Kremlin. Rarer still that he was called there for an urgent meeting.

The Kremlin wasn't physically far from his KGB office; just a 15-minute walk from Lubyanka, past the ornate, onion-domed St. Basil's Cathedral on the corner of Red Square and through the primary business entrance at Spasskaya Bashnya, the Savior Tower. But on this fine April morning, he made it in 12. It was an important meeting. He glanced up at the large clock on the tower: 11:40. He wouldn't be late.

Kremlin means "fortress," and its 15-foot-thick, red brick walls implacably reinforced the name. Vitaly walked up to the guard at the base of the clock tower, showed his KGB badge and was allowed to enter. He followed the footpath through the deep gate and turned right.

It always surprised him how pastoral this fortress was inside its walls. Spring flowers were in bloom, and the long grove of trees, each neatly dedicated with a small sign to a Soviet hero, was coming into early leaf. The noisy gray grind of the vast city seemed suddenly distant, and the immensity of Mother Russia herself, still thawing from winter, almost unimaginable.

Vitaly checked the time yet again as he neared Building 14, the four-story yellow-and-white-painted Presidium. *I need to calm myself!* He deliberately slowed his pace before entering through the broad wooden doors and climbing the stone steps towards the meeting room.

The files were in his briefcase, clasped firmly in his left hand.

For an enormous, paper-driven bureaucracy, word had traveled fast. The night admin team at Lubyanka had taken the phone call asking what the KGB had on a cosmonaut, Senior Lieutenant Svetlana Yevgenyevna Gromova, and on two American military astronauts, Lieutenant Michael Esdale and Major Chad Miller. The immense filing system had churned on the names, flip cards leading to file folders in labyrinthine underground storage halls. Photostats had been made, the designated case officers identified, and papers distributed. When Vitaly had arrived at his desk that morning, early as usual, the Miller file had been on top of the pile in his inbox. A red bookmark was stapled to the front with "Srochna" typed on it. Urgent.

Vitaly had read the cover note, considered his moves over his first cup of tea and then started a cascade of revealing phone calls. All leading to now.

The hallway door was open. After a small pause, he entered the conference room.

The far wall was all windows, stretching from the low bank of radiators to the ceiling, to let in the natural light. The impact was marred somewhat by the drab view of an identical room across a small inner courtyard. Spider plants sat on the radiator sill, adding a touch of natural green. A long table paralleled the window. Apart from a young pomozhnitsa placing water glasses and teacups in front of each chair, he was alone.

He resisted the urge to recheck his watch. He chose an unassuming far corner seat, set down his briefcase and went to stand by the window. The server set up a tea trolley along the wall by the door and quietly left.

Vitaly looked out at the sunshine, reviewing the details in his mind, realizing this might be a watershed day in his career. He felt his heart start to race, and he scowled. *Uspokoisya!* Quiet yourself!

He heard a rumble of deep voices in the hall, and three people came in, led by a tall, wide man in a gray suit, his hair combed straight back off a broad forehead, thick, wire-rimmed glasses magnifying his tired eyes.

Vitaly was stunned. Andropov! The head of the KGB himself. The rumor was that he was soon to become a full Politburo member. What was he doing here? On the phone they'd said there'd be senior representation at the meeting, but he'd never thought it would be Yuri Vladimirovich himself. *Bozha moy! Am I ready for this?*

Keeping his face a calm mask, he dipped his head in respect. "Dobry dyen, zasluzheni Predsedatel." Good day, honored Chairman.

Andropov peered at him through his glasses. "Kalugin, da?"

Vitaly nodded. "Da. Counterintelligence agent, Special Service II, Vitaly Dmitriyevich."

Andropov nodded. "Sadeetyes." Sit.

Vitaly sat.

The KGB Chairman took the chair at the head of the table, gesturing with his chin at the two other men. He spoke very clearly, pronouncing the names in an educated accent. "Vladimir Alexandrovich Kryuchkov. Vladimir Nikolayevich Chelomei." He rightly assumed Vitaly would know who they were.

Vitaly met the eyes of each man, and again nodded in respect. Kryuchkov was head of the KGB First Chief Directorate, responsible for all operations abroad, including Vitaly's department. Chelomei was a senior director in the Soviet space program.

Kryuchkov, as Vitaly's boss, took the lead. His round face with its high-domed forehead was marked by a squashed nose, broken badly at some point long ago.

"Vitaly Dmitriyevich, please brief us on the situation." He used the patronymic to ease the gap in seniority, which helped to put Vitaly at ease.

He took a steadying breath. These were smart, accomplished, power-ful men. *Where to start?*

He quickly summarized the events that had transpired in orbit over the past 20 hours. While he spoke he glanced at Chelomei for con-firmation that he had his facts right; the man's furrowed brow and pursed mouth gave away nothing. But he didn't contradict him, either. *So far, so good.*

Moving to more familiar ground, he gave a quick intelligence summary of the woman cosmonaut and the American astronaut, Esdale. Their records were clean, nothing suspicious in the files. No leverage there.

The three senior men listened, their faces impassive. They knew he was keeping the key information for last.

"The third person in space, American Air Force Major Chad Miller, gives us the greatest opportunity." Vitaly's heart rate slowed as he explained in detail, recounting how he'd fostered agents in the heart of the Russian Orthodox Church around the world, looking for angles and access routes to the West. He shared the details of Miller's file, starting with the boy's adoption in Berlin. Andropov nodded slowly as he heard how Vitaly had used an agent, the church interpreter, to send money to the pilot, ostensibly from his long-lost brother, eager to help with the young man's expenses when the adoptive parents, farmers apparently, had run low. And how Miller had never refused such handouts. The KGB chief looked at Kryuchkov, who nodded back.

"That gives us a position of strength. Spasiba, Vitaly Dmitriyevich. This Miller would not want the Americans to find out where that money actually came from."

Vitaly inwardly thrilled at Andropov using his name.

Andropov turned to Chelomei. "Vladimir Nikolay'ich, I know little of space. I commiserate with you on the loss of our Almaz space station, and the tragic death of cosmonaut Mitkov. These are blatant acts of American aggression, and help set our course of action." His old eyes blinked behind the thick lenses. "Nyet huda byez dobra"—there is no bad without good. "What other levers do we have here?" he asked.

"Respected Chairman, despite the tragedy of today's events, I have good news from the Soviet space program." Vladimir Chelomei's deliberately formal phrasing lent import to what he was saying.

"With what I have learned from Agent Kalugin here, and an important discovery made just yesterday by the Lunokhod team that is exploring the Moon's surface, I think we may have a rare opportunity."

Having gained the room's attention, he laid out his plan.

Kryuchkov had lifelong experience in diplomacy and subterfuge. He quickly evaluated the idea, considering the weaknesses as he rubbed his broken nose with his forefinger.

"We need communications with the cosmonaut—*private* communication. Can we get it?"

"Da, Vladimir Alexandrovich," Chelomei said. The two men worked in different fields, but were roughly equivalent in power. Chelomei had reached the same conclusion earlier that day, and had issued orders. "I've thought of a way to reach her."

Andropov stood. "I will take this to the Politburo, and to the General Secretary." As KGB chief and his longtime protégé, Andropov was Brezhnev's most trusted ally. "The Americans will be contacting us shortly, no doubt."

He looked at each of the three men.

"Let's make sure we're ready."

"Father Ilarion, I have unusual news." Alexander, the diocese interpreter, spoke quietly, knowing it was the best way to get the hieromonk's attention in the morning, after prayers and liturgy.

Ilarion was finishing his light breakfast, tapping the last crumbs of his toast off the small plate into his teacup, careful to waste nothing. "Good news, Sascha?" He looked up at the younger man curiously. "What is it?"

"The accomplishments of your brother have come to the attention of the Church in Moscow. One of my fellow interpreters there was working with the American Embassy church members, and he called me to let you know. They think it does you and your family great honor, and have been speaking with officials at the Soviet space program."

Ilarion's eyes widened.

"It seems the Church wants you to come to Moscow, and has obtained permission for you to go to Mission Control, where you will be able to talk directly with your brother while he's on the Moon. It's a rare honor indeed and will be a wonderful surprise for him."

Father Ilarion looked stunned by the prospect of a trip to Moscow and a chance to talk to his brother in space. His stroked his beard as he considered it, his eyes blinking rapidly behind his thick lenses.

"They say there is an Interflug flight from Schönefeld Airport direct to Moscow Sheremetyevo every day," Alexander urged. "The space program will cover all costs and accommodation."

The monk's face clouded. "But surely my brother won't want surprises to interrupt what he's doing. He'll be too busy."

Alexander nodded. His KGB handler had anticipated this, and provided some suggestions.

"They say that they often have family members speak directly with cosmonauts, who can be lonely so far from home. Contact with family is good for morale, for their mental calmness." He added a specific suggested phrase. "Your brother would be the most distant member of the flock you've ever had the chance to give solace to."

Father Ilarion turned his head away, eyes unfocused, trying to imagine what his brother was seeing. He nodded slowly. "You're right, Sascha. Earth must be very small for him now."

He turned back to Alexander with his brows furrowed. "But his Russian is rusty, and I have no English. I'm also not a traveler. Would you be coming with me?"

Alexander felt a rush of victory, but managed to keep his face calm, his expression helpful. "Yes, Father, the officials at Mission Control recognized the difficulty and asked that an interpreter accompany you. I'd be honored to help."

35

Mission Control, Houston

In the end, the Moscow-Houston communication had been surprisingly simple to set up.

Kaz stood at the CAPCOM console with the State Department translator next to him. The doctors confirmed that despite the staggered sleep schedule, the crew had gotten a reasonable night's rest. At least the astronauts had; the cosmonaut wasn't wired for heartbeat.

They had a mid-course correction coming up soon—a quick engine firing to change the ship's direction very slightly, based on careful tracking of *Pursuit*'s path. It saved fuel to do it early—to steer exactly towards perfectly entering orbit around the Moon.

"*Pursuit*, Houston, I have the burn numbers when you're ready."

"Roger, Kaz, I'm ready to copy." Michael had the flight plan floating in front of him, his pencil poised to write in the blank table.

"Okay, Michael, it'll be posigrade 10.5 fps, burn duration 0:02, perilune will be 53.1 . . ." Kaz went through the values carefully, the Mission Control specialists listening attentively to make sure he made no errors. When he finished, Michael read them back, verbatim.

"That all sounds good, Michael." A pause. "Is Chad listening?"

Michael glanced across at Chad, in the opposite seat. Svetlana was floating at a window, alternately looking at the Earth and the Moon.

"He's not on headset, but can be. What's up?"

Kaz answered carefully. "After the burn, we're going to patch Moscow through by phone to talk with the cosmonaut. We'll have sentence-by-sentence translation, to make sure it's all kosher, but wanted to give you a heads-up to think about it."

Michael passed the message to Chad, who frowned and donned his headset.

"Kaz, Chad here. I need this conversation to be controlled. Who's going to cut it off if we don't like how it's going?"

Kaz looked back at Gene, behind the Flight Director console. He and Gene had discussed just this.

"We agree, Chad. INCO will have his finger on the switch to stop comms at any moment. We recommend you do the same."

Chad looked at the switches on his comm panel. "Yeah, I'm gonna pull the plug on her the second I don't like what I hear."

"Sounds about right," Kaz said. "Mid-course burn is in three minutes, and we'll have someone from their Mission Control tied in shortly after that."

Chad glanced at Svetlana, who had turned to face him. "Copy."

When the KGB interpreter standing next to him relayed what Chad had just said, Chelomei grunted.

Eavesdropping on transmissions from the Apollo craft was nothing new. Since the start of the Apollo Moon landings, Russia had been listening in. The Soviet Central Committee had ordered Moscow Scientific Research Institute No. 885 to build the huge, 32-meter-wide TNA-400 satellite dish that towered over the Simferopol complex. It had required some clever reverse engineering; the Soviet technicians had experimented with the signals from the early Apollo flights, carefully demodulating the carrier and subcarrier frequencies until they could pick out voice and data, and even watch the fuzzy television images sent from the distant craft. They couldn't hear the transmissions going up to Apollo, but during the eight hours each day when the Russian side of the Earth was facing the Moon, they received everything the spaceship sent back.

It wasn't a total secret. The CIA had learned about the new antenna when an SR-71 spy plane had taken high-altitude photographs of it. The top-secret report summarized: *A 105-foot dish antenna such as this one would permit communications and telemetry reception at lunar distances. The antenna is operational.*

But Director Chelomei had just added a capability that no one at NASA or the CIA knew about. For it to work, he needed to discern some specific details during today's hastily arranged telephone link. And if both Houston and the crew were ready to pull the plug at the sound of anything they didn't like, he'd have to be subtle. He impatiently waited as they did their course correction burn.

Kaz said, "Looks like a good burn, Apollo. You're on your way."

Michael agreed as he safed the engine systems. "Copy, Kaz, thanks. And we've got all three of us on headsets now, whenever you're ready. The Commander's standing by at Panel 6."

Chad's finger and thumb were gripping the S-band transmit/receive switch.

Kaz glanced at Gene Kranz, who nodded.

"Moscow, this is Houston Mission Control, comm check."

The interpreter repeated what Kaz had said, in Russian.

An unfamiliar male voice crackled into Kaz's headset. "Zdyess Moskva, kak shlooshetye nas?"

The interpreter translated. "Moscow here, how do you hear us?"

Kaz realized he'd been holding his breath, and exhaled. "We have you loud and clear, Moscow. Stand by to speak with Apollo 18." He looked across at INCO, nodding, and got a thumbs-up.

"Apollo 18, this is Houston. Mission Control Moscow is on comms with us. Go ahead, Moscow."

Gene Kranz shook his head slowly. *Bloody Commies talking to his spaceship.*

The interpreter translated the first burst of Russian: "Senior Lieutenant Gromova, this is TsUP, how do you hear?"

Svetlana responded. "TsUP, I hear you well."

Chelomei, sitting at the flight director console in Moscow, held the phone receiver firmly. "Svetlana Yevgenyevna, this is Director Chelomei. We are very glad to hear your voice. How is your health?"

She began to respond immediately, but Chad slammed the transmit switch to receive only, holding up a hand. "You need to wait for translation." They listened as the interpreter repeated what Chelomei had said.

Chad looked hard at her. "Okay?" he queried.

"Da, okay."

He selected the switch back to transmit/receive.

"Tovarisch Director, it's an honor to speak with you. My health is fine, thank you."

The pauses for translation made the conversation awkward.

"They have found you a place to sleep on board the small vessel?" An innocuous question.

"Da. There is room in the capsule for two, comfortable, with one of them sleeping in the lander."

Come on, woman, give me more details! Chelomei urged silently.

"They alternate, and considerately leave me my own lounge chair in the capsule." She added a personal note. "I'm adjusting to the Houston time zone."

Chelomei nodded his head. *Excellent.* She was getting it.

He expressed his deep condolences on the death of her commander, Mitkov, and congratulated her on her resourcefulness and strength in getting aboard the Apollo ship.

She paused, waiting for the translation, and then thanked him, adding a question. "They used my suit to entomb the dead astronaut, and its PM-9 life-support system is now stowed. Please confirm that I'll be wearing their spacesuit from now on."

Chelomei smiled broadly. *Clever girl.* The PM-9 wasn't the life-support backpack; it was the model number of the weapon that had been on board the Almaz. She'd found a way to let them know she was secretly armed. He kept his tone matter-of-fact.

"Da, they have told us the sizing will work for you in their suit. And if you haven't heard yet, they are planning for you to wear it in the lunar lander, and to have the honor of being the first Soviet citizen to step onto the Moon."

Svetlana had suspected that was the new plan, but this was her first confirmation. She looked at Chad, who nodded, and was surprised at the surge of excitement that suddenly rushed through her. *I'm going to walk on the Moon!*

Her voice quavered. "That is wonderful, Tovarisch Director! I will do my best to make everyone proud."

Chelomei played back in his mind what they'd just said; nothing sounded suspicious, and the woman had demonstrated that she was aware of hidden meanings. Time to get Miller's attention.

"We are certain you will, Sveta. Your brother in Berlin is especially proud of you."

Chad squinted at her as the interpreter translated. *She had a brother in Berlin?* That was a strange coincidence. But why had Moscow mentioned that?

Svetlana's face revealed nothing. "I'm delighted to hear that. Please pass my best to my whole family."

Enough for now, Chelomei thought. Time for platitudes, plus one last hint.

"We will be in daily contact, Svetlana Yevgenyevna, and look forward to speaking with you. Your ears can look forward to hearing the Russian language so far from home."

"Spasiba, Tovarisch Director. Until next time."

Chelomei nodded, satisfied. "Doh sledusheva." He placed the handset in the cradle, ticking through his mental checklist. All messages sent. Time to move on to the next step.

What the hell had they meant? Chad thought. The conversation had felt fishy, somehow. *Do they know about my brother? How could they?* He stared hard at Svetlana as he stowed her headset, but she met his gaze impassively.

He thought further. *If they do, then they probably know I speak Russian.* He continued to stare at her, considering all that had been said.

But she doesn't know.

He took a deep breath and exhaled through his nose.

Good.

"Hey, Chad, I just noticed something." Michael's voice was relaxed, subdued. He'd borne the brunt of the sleep shift so they could continuously monitor the cosmonaut, and he was tired.

"What's that?" Chad was reviewing LM procedures, penciling in what he was going to do differently to land on the Moon without Luke to help.

"It says here in the flight plan that we just hit exactly halfway. Old Mother Earth and the Moon are both"—he checked the book—"107,229 miles away." He floated to the window next to Svetlana and twisted to look at one, and then the other. He made hand motions to try to explain the concept to her, defining a length, cutting it in half, and then pointing at the Moon and Earth.

She watched his hands and then looked at his face, quizzically.

"I don't think she gets it," Michael said. "What do they teach them in cosmonaut school?"

Chad kept reading, ignoring him.

Michael imitated Chad's voice. "I don't know, Michael, my guess is Soviet doctrine, invasion routes, whitewashed history and bad fashion sense. You know, Commie stuff."

He answered himself. "Thank you, Chad, for that keen insight. I think the Command Module Pilot is getting a little punchy. My turn for some sleep."

Chad looked up, hearing the last part. "You sleeping in the LM?"

Michael looked at him, bemused. "Yeah, as planned, if you're okay holding down the fort here."

Chad glanced at Svetlana and turned back to his page. "Yeah, we're set."

Michael gave Houston a heads-up so the doctors could track his rest, and then floated down the tunnel, emerging into the small cabin of the LM. He wrapped himself in the bag and hammock and glanced up in the darkness at Luke.

"I miss you, buddy," he murmured. "I'm sorry you've joined the dead." *What a long strange trip it's been.*

The night shift in TsUP, a minimal skeleton crew of two technicians and an interpreter, were listening carefully and heard Michael's call to Houston. Director Chelomei had left strict instructions to record all communications from the Apollo craft. He wanted to know who was sleeping, and when.

The interpreter translated, and the shift lead carefully wrote the Cyrillic characters next to the time in the large green ledger they had started for cosmonaut Gromova's flight to the Moon and back:

00:30 *Moscow Standard Time*   *Esdale sleeping alone in the lunar module.*
                                Miller awake in command module.
                                No word from Gromova.

Not very interesting. But hopefully useful.

36

Timber Cove, Houston

The house was a truncated A-frame bungalow with an attached garage, set on the brackish shore of Taylor Lake, 10 minutes east of the Manned Spacecraft Center. When Kaz and Al Shepard arrived, there was already an ugly brown Dodge Polara in the driveway. The double whip antennas and driver's side searchlight gave it away as an unmarked police car. The Harris County Sheriff's car, in fact.

With everything that had happened in the 36 hours since launch, Kaz had pushed the findings of the crash investigator into the back of his mind. But now that Apollo 18 was safely on its way to the Moon, he'd faced the fact that out of everyone who might have sabotaged Tom's helicopter, three of the suspects—only two of them still alive—were on board the spaceship. Al Shepard had alerted the sheriff and asked him for discretion, agreeing to help him look for evidence to quickly clear the three as potential suspects.

As Kaz pulled in and parked, two men got out of the Polara. The driver was in uniform, 30ish, with a crew cut. The passenger was a strongly built man in his 50s in a rumpled suit and tie, heavy-rimmed glasses below a combed-back wave of hair, graying at the temples.

Al walked up to him and they shook hands. "Hi, Jack, thanks for coming."

Jack Heard had been the Houston police chief for 20 years, and had recently been elected sheriff of Harris County, which included Ellington Field airport, the rural scene of the helicopter crash and this house. Chad Miller's house.

"I'm happy to serve NASA and a hero of the nation, Al," Heard said, and turned to Kaz, his sharp cop's eyes flicking across his face, missing nothing through the thick lenses. "You must be Lieutenant Commander Zemeckis. Sorry to hear about the death of your friend."

Kaz was startled. Luke's death in orbit hadn't been made public. Then he realized the sheriff meant Tom Hoffman. He said, "Thanks," and they shook hands.

Heard said, "That's Deputy Buddy Beauchamp," nodding at the uniform, who tipped his head.

Kaz led them all towards the front door, taking in the cedar shake siding and the multicolored entryway glass.

"Major Miller own this house?" Heard asked.

Al replied. "No, apparently it belongs to some dentist who rented it to Chad fully furnished."

Kaz unlocked and opened the door, turned on the light, and they stepped into another world.

The living room floor was paved with ocher tile. The walls were covered to shoulder height in gold shag carpeting. The fluorescent light fixture Kaz turned on alternated between red, yellow and blue light. The far wall was all glass, facing onto a swimming pool with Taylor Lake beyond it. A basket chair hung on a long chain from the ceiling, and a bulbous, shellacked rock chimney rose from the gas fireplace. Gaudy masks hung on the walls above the shag carpet.

"Quite the place," Sherriff Heard said. "A dentist, you say?"

Kaz had never been in Chad's house and was trying to reconcile the hippie-Playboy décor with the abrupt, judgmental military man he knew. It was a rental, but still.

There was a pool table to their left, with a low, wood-framed couch. The sheriff said, "You two have a seat while Buddy and I have a quick look around. We shouldn't be long."

Al and Kaz sat.

"I'm glad the Astronaut Clinic has their own dentists," Al said, making Kaz smile. After a moment, he asked, "You didn't see Michael out at Ellington that day, right?"

Kaz shook his head. "No, just Luke, who was flying the LLTV, and Chad, who was leaving since he'd just flown it. Michael was scheduled for a medical check that morning, so I think that pretty much clears him."

Al nodded, staring at the gargoyle masks on the wall. Both men were considering the unspoken. Motive.

Heard and his deputy came back through, heading for the open wooden staircase that led upstairs. Heard jerked his chin towards the back of the main floor, beyond the kitchen. He smiled slightly. "You might want to have a peek in the master bedroom."

Al shrugged, and they peeled themselves up and out of the low sofa. They walked past the stone counters of the kitchen, down a short hallway and through the doorless bedroom entrance.

Both men stopped. Three walls were tiled floor to ceiling with gold-tinted mirrors. The fourth wall faced the lake. It was all glass, and curtainless. Life-sized statues of topless mermaids flanked a king-sized bed that was suspended off the floor on heavy gold-colored chains. A recessed wall unit was lined with the same mirrored tile, each shelf adorned with a variety of nude female figurines.

Kaz walked past the bed to the closet. Pulling open the sliding doors, he was somewhat relieved to see familiar single-man's items on the hangers and shelves, shoes tidily aligned along the floor. There was a flight suit, along with a couple of jackets, trousers and crisply pressed shirts. He slid the doors closed and came back to Al, shaking his head. "This place would give me the creeps," he said.

They heard a voice echoing off the stone-tiled floors. "Hey, guys, c'mon back here."

They found the two cops standing at the foot of the staircase, and as soon as they reached them, the sheriff ushered them back out to Kaz's car, leaving his deputy by the front door. Heard said, "We found some things in the bedroom that Major Miller was using as his home office. Beyond the deviant dentist furniture, I mean."

He glanced back at the house. "I've called for a couple more deputies to help do a thorough search. We'll use an unmarked and guys out of uniform, to keep the profile low for as long as we can." He eyed the neighboring houses. "We can be thankful for small mercies that there's a media blackout on the mission."

He looked at Kaz. "I still need to have a quick look at the other crewmen's homes, if you can let me into them."

Kaz nodded. "Of course." He glanced at Al. "Have you briefed the sheriff on what's been going on?"

"Yeah, Jack knows about Luke, in strictest confidence." Al glanced at Beauchamp, standing mutely by the front door. "But nobody else."

"I know what you're thinking, Kaz," Heard said. "This is going to escalate. But my job is pretty clear. A civil-registered helicopter flying from a Harris County airport crashed on county land, the pilot died, and indications are that there was sabotage. So I'm investigating a murder. The fact that one suspect is dead and two others are off the planet doesn't bother me." He briefly stuck out his lower lip, considering. "In fact, it's better. I know exactly where they are, and when they'll be back."

But Kaz was thinking beyond the investigation. He was going to have to tell Sam Phillips that the man who was about to walk on the Moon, to find out what the Soviets were up to there, was now a viable suspect in a murder.

37

Mission Control, Houston

"FLIGHT, EECOM."

Gene looked over his console. "Go ahead."

"FLIGHT, my back room has been working the numbers, and we've got a revised status."

This was interesting. EECOM handled oxygen consumption. With the leak in Luke's umbilical at Almaz and the need to repair the hatch seal, Gene had been waiting to see whether and how much it would impact the planned mission.

"I'm listening, EECOM."

"Now that the tank temps have stabilized and we've got an update on current consumption with the LM hatch open, it looks like we lost considerably more O2 than we thought. It's very tight for full duration."

Oxygen wasn't just the sole gas used in the spaceships for breathing, it also fed the fuel cells to generate electricity.

"How tight?"

"It depends how much we take from the LM tanks. Assuming we're still protecting for multiple spacewalks with two crewmembers, it takes us well into the red."

Gene had already been thinking that the military would have to be happy with just one moonwalk. A short one.

"If you model for just one, five-hour lunar surface walk, how do the numbers look?"

EECOM countered with a question. "Both crewmembers working outside the whole time?" It would increase oxygen consumption.

Gene pictured Chad's and Svetlana's likely tasks on the surface. Better to assume worst case. "Yes."

EECOM had a quick side conversation with the technicians in his back room. "FLIGHT, with that revised plan, and if we start using oxygen from the *Bulldog* tanks now for cabin air, we have green margins through splashdown."

"Good to hear, EECOM, thanks."

Kaz spoke up quickly. "FLIGHT, Michael's just gone to sleep in the LM, and the repress valve in there makes a loud bang. If EECOM can wait, I recommend we delay tapping *Bulldog*'s oxygen until he wakes up."

Gene nodded. "SURGEON, how much beauty sleep will he need?"

JW answered. "My best guess is about four hours, FLIGHT."

EECOM piped in immediately. "We can wait that long."

Gene decided. "Sounds good. CAPCOM, plan to wake Lieutenant Esdale at"—he glanced at the digital timer at the front of the room—"thirty-seven hours mission elapsed time."

"Houston, 18, with a problem."

Well, that's not what I want to hear. Kaz set down his coffee next to the console ashtray. He deliberately made his voice calm to respond. As CAPCOM, he knew that the way he said things affected the psychology of both the crew on orbit and the team in Mission Control; being aware of his tone was especially important considering the parallel murder investigation. "Problems are what we're here for—go ahead, Michael."

"Hey, Kaz. Chad and I have both noticed that Luke's spacesuit is bulging. Looks like maybe his body is decomposing and the gas pressure is building up in there. We're not sure where the pressure relief valve is in the cosmonaut's spacesuit, but we sure don't want it burping nasty gases into *Bulldog*."

"Copy, agreed, checking."

Chad caught Michael's eye. "How about we ask Princess here to show us where the suit vents its overpressure?"

Michael nodded. "How good's your sign language?"

Svetlana, dozing on the right side of the cockpit, felt someone shaking her. Opening her eyes, she saw the commander pointing at the other astronaut disappearing into the tunnel to the lunar lander. He waved his hand for her to follow.

Shto? She followed the feet into the tunnel.

Michael had floated up against *Bulldog*'s ceiling next to Luke's body, and Chad moved to his designated position on the left, where he'd fly it. Svetlana took the open position on the right and looked at them questioningly.

Mikhail was speaking, moving his hands around her Yastreb space-suit. She could see that the suit had ballooned. The astronaut sud-denly opened his fingers and made a sharp hissing sound, and then raised his shoulders with a questioning look on his face. He was point-ing at the oxygen and comm connections on the suit's front. She found all the English words distracting. *What does he mean?*

The other astronaut frowned disapprovingly. He impatiently repeated the bursting motion with his hand, and made a harsh "Pssssss" sound that he tailed off.

Ah. She got it. Floating up next to the suit, she pointed to two fist-sized protruding round knobs over the left rib cage, and mimed a twisting motion with her hand. She then reached up to the helmet and touched a gray butterfly valve under the left ear. She mimicked pinching and turning it, and made the same hissing noise the astronauts had made.

Michael looked closely where she'd pointed. "I think the two chest valves are pressure regulators. They've got some Russian writing on them, and arrows to show direction of turn." He switched his inspection to the helmet. "This looks like a simple purge valve."

Chad had been silently sounding out the Cyrillic writing on the two chest valves. One said "Unscrew all the way for flight" and the other said "Screw in all the way." He spoke as if he was making an educated guess. "I bet one's for overpressure, and the other's for underpressure." There were no labels on the helmet valve. He pointed at it. "That one looks like just a manual open/close."

Michael nodded. "Makes sense."

Both men pondered the information.

"But what do we do if the stink inside starts coming out of one of these?" Michael shook his head. "Even after death we have to deal with Luke's farting."

Chad ignored the humor. He had an idea. "We've got the small tap line here in *Bulldog* we can put on the egress hatch pressure valve. We could wrap it tight with tape directly to this helmet valve, and crack them both open very slightly to suck the extra pressure out to vacuum."

Michael evaluated. "Yeah, that should work." He smiled. "It'll put us in the running for the duct tape hall of fame."

Chad donned the LM headset and pushed Transmit.

"Houston, we think we have a solution." He described what the cosmonaut had shown them, and his plan.

Kaz replied, "Roger, *Bulldog*, sounds like it might well work. Let us think about it."

Gene Kranz spoke. "EECOM, I want you to use the interpreter and get on the horn ASAP with whoever the suit specialists are in Moscow. Make sure we're understanding the valve function properly and get their input into the crew's manual vent idea."

Kaz waved the interpreter to the EECOM console. Gene spoke again.

"Meanwhile, CAPCOM, tell them to start building the setup on board. We can't wait too long."

They moved the suit cautiously, like a fragile balloon, down towards the floor of the lunar lander, strapping it into place. Chad screwed a metal tube onto the pressure valve on the square hatch while Michael peeled sections of tape off a large roll, carefully wrapping the tube to join the helmet purge valve.

Svetlana pictured the Yastreb suit schematics. *If they keep the flow rate low, it ought to work.* She looked around the cockpit. They'd been keeping her in the other part of the ship, and this was her first chance to see the lander in detail.

I'm going to land on the Moon in this!

The thought thrilled her. She'd graduated top of her class from the Moscow State Aviation Institute, and became an aerobatic instructor pilot as well as a test pilot at the Gromov School outside Moscow. Her father had been a decorated fighter pilot in the Great Patriotic War, and his influence had been key in her cosmonaut selection.

Papa will be so proud!

While the men were distracted, she looked closely at the lander's controls, picturing herself flying it. *That must be the rotational controller on the right, to turn the vehicle.* It looked like a joystick, similar to what she'd trained on in the Almaz return capsule. She looked on the left for the thrust controller, which would move the vehicle up and down and left and right. *That's it, no doubt.* It resembled a palm-sized drawer handle, mounted on a short, pivoting stick to move in all directions. She reached out to touch it.

"Hey, what are you doing! Get away from that!" Chad's face was a mask of rage. He pointed at her. "Don't touch nothin'!"

His meaning was clear, and she floated back to beyond arm's length. Both men watched her suspiciously.

No matter. I'd feel the same if these Americans were in my ship.

She continued her visual inspection. In front of both crew stations were familiar artificial horizons, the gray-and-black balls recessed into the instrument panel. They were surrounded by gauges. *Must be speed, height, systems pressures,* she reasoned. All flying machines were essentially the same; you just had to figure out how to get them started and how they wanted to kill you.

She realized that the triangular windows were mounted low, like in a helicopter, so they could look down while landing. She glanced around for seats, and couldn't even see fixtures on the floor where seats might be mounted. *We must fly this thing standing up!* A reasonable compromise for low lunar gravity, she acknowledged, but still it would be strange.

She looked at the commander. *Tschad.* He'd most likely be the one flying this lander with her. She doubted they'd trust a Black man to do it. *Mikhail. No, Michael.* She moved her lips, trying the English pronunciation.

Chad's voice came into the headsets in Mission Control. "Houston, *Bulldog,* we have the suit strapped down securely on the floor and the helmet purge sealed against the hatch line. Just let us know when we can open the valves."

Kaz glanced over at the EECOM console, where the tech and the interpreter were engrossed in a laborious technical conversation with TsUP.

"Roger, *Bulldog.* We're talking with the Moscow specialists now, and should have word shortly."

"Copy, Houston, but regardless what Moscow says, we're gonna take care of this. This suit is bulging, and we're the ones at risk here."

Kaz could hear him thinking, *You morons!*

"Roger, Chad. We'll get you that ASAP."

As soon as possible—the phrase echoed in Kaz's head. The whole idea of "possible" had changed in a hurry.

———

Five minutes later Kaz pushed the comm button. "18, Houston, Moscow has described the suit valving to us, and we're good here. You have a GO to vent Luke's suit to vacuum."

"Thanks, Kaz," Michael responded. "Here goes nothin'."

Michael cautiously turned the vent valve handle on the side of the white helmet, the large red CCCP letters at the edge of his vision. He heard a slight hissing sound as pressure equalized into the vent hose, and then quiet. He sniffed for leaks, wrinkling his nose, but smelled nothing.

He glanced at Chad. "All set, Boss?"

Svetlana was curiously observing the men messing with her old suit.

"Yep. But close it immediately if something isn't going right."

"Agreed."

Michael reached around the vent hose and began turning the knob on the Cabin Relief and Dump Valve test port. Houston had said it would take a full turn to start flow, and he carefully rotated it between his thumb and forefingers, like a safecracker. A hissing began, barely audible above the noise of *Bulldog*'s air recirculation fans. He stopped turning, and all three of them turned to watch Luke's suit.

At first, nothing. Then, gradually, like an air mattress deflating, the tension eased on the fabric, and the seams looked less distended. Michael was relieved to see the needle dropping in the pressure gauge on the suit's right wrist.

"Looks like it's working, Houston." He tapped the gauge to make sure it wasn't sticking. "As soon as the pressure gauge shows zero differential, I'll close the valves." He poked at the suit's cloth; it was no longer quite as stiff.

"Copy, Michael," he heard Kaz say. "Reminder to close the helmet valve first, then the hatch valve." That would suck any extra odors out of the vent hose and keep them from getting into the cabin.

Michael didn't want to take it too far or the suit's negative pressure relief valve would suck open and start pulling in cabin air. He increased the speed of his tapping on the pressure gauge, watching the needle slowly bounce towards zero.

"Looks like we're there." He closed the helmet valve, and then quickly reached and spun the hatch valve tightly closed.

Svetlana squeezed the suit lightly, near the elbow, where there was no internal bracing. "Prekrasna," she nodded. Excellent.

Chad spoke to Houston. "Kaz, that's complete, suit looks good now, but we're going to leave Luke connected to the hose, just in case we need to vent him again. It's Michael's turn to get some shut-eye. The cosmonaut and I are heading back into *Pursuit*."

"Copy, Chad, sounds good. Nice work, and sweet dreams, Michael."

In Moscow, Chelomei turned to his flight director.

"Listen to them for any word of Michael Esdale waking up."

The Moscow Electronics Research Institute engineers had initially told Chelomei that his request was impossible; there were too many unknowns, there wasn't time, and there was no way to test that it would work properly. But he had been unrelenting. "Just build the equipment!" he had yelled. He hated the inbuilt Soviet caution about running afoul of interdepartmental politics; it had allowed the Americans to beat them to the Moon.

The engineers in the end had hastily installed their thrown-together 13-cm S-band modulating uplink hardware alongside the huge TNA-400 antenna's listening gear. The modification would interweave TsUP's voice transmissions with the strong carrier frequency that it blasted skyward in a beam of electromagnetic energy, tightly focused towards the Moon by the towering dish antenna. It was like an invisible searchlight in the night, looking for the four small, circular receiving antennas sticking out of the aft section of *Pursuit*.

With luck, the processors inside the American ship would treat it as just another arriving signal to deal with. If the frequency and modulation matched closely enough to the American transmissions, it would pass through the filters, and the radio wave would be transformed into an electric signal that passed to a speaker—in this case the small one built into the commander's headset, over his left ear.

When the flight director reported that he was certain that the other astronaut was asleep, Chelomei pushed his mic button and spoke. Hoping it was only Commander Miller, but uncertain of who else might be listening, he chose his words carefully.

"Transmission test, transmission test, how do you hear me?" he said in a deliberately flat and bored tone, like an uninterested radio operator. He wasn't sure if the signal would be retransmitted by the spaceship back to Houston somehow, and didn't want to alert anyone.

Chad, who had been thumbing through the checklist for tomorrow's entry into lunar orbit, bolted upright, startled to hear the Russian language in his ear. It didn't repeat, and he snuck a glance at Svetlana, who was looking out the window at the growing Moon. Had he imagined it?

Chelomei repeated himself. "Transmission test, transmission test, how do you hear me?" He wondered whether Cosmonaut Gromova would also hear him, or only Miller. He checked the clock at the front of the room. Still 30 minutes of comms remaining until the Earth turned too far for his satellite dish to see the spacecraft.

Be patient, he counseled himself. *Miller needs time to decide what to do.*

Chad pictured the ship's comm system in his head, and rechecked the switch config. *What the fuck?* This wasn't just stray VHF radio delivering typical, unregulated noise from Earth; this was coming to him on their designated S-band frequency. To get through to his headset, it had to be a specifically modulated signal. The realization hit him. *Someone in Russia is calling us on purpose!*

But who? He kept his face calm, in case Svetlana looked at him.

Chelomei upped the stakes.

"Transmission test, transmission test. If you can hear me, respond with two microphone clicks."

Standing in TsUP, Chelomei listened intently. One click, by itself, could be anything; two would be deliberate. Three could make Houston wonder what was going on.

He waited.

Chad's Russian was rusty, but he was pretty sure he'd understood. Whoever was calling wanted two chirps on the mic.

A thought struck him, and he looked out the window at Earth. The Atlantic Ocean was facing him, but he could see from the western edge of Russia to the eastern edge of America. Someone in that part of the world had chosen this moment to contact him. He could just barely see where Moscow was in the darkness on the eastern side of the ball. *Had they known Michael was asleep and wouldn't be listening? Who would know that?*

He decided. Reaching for the transmit switch, he toggled it twice. Then listened.

In Houston, Kaz heard the clicks and perked up his ears since the noise of the mic always preceded a transmission from the ship. When no one spoke, he shrugged. *Just static.*

On the other side of the world, Chelomei heard the two clicks and was exultant. *I've made direct contact with the Apollo crew! They can hear me!* His eyes burned in triumph. Time to raise the stakes again.

"I hear your two clicks. And so does your brother. Don't reply. Listen for more in"—he glanced at the clock on the screen—"eighteen hours. After 16:30 Moscow time." He released the mic.

Chelomei reviewed what he'd said and nodded to himself. *That will give him food for thought.*

Chad was dumbfounded. *"And so does your brother"?*

That was the second time the Russians had mentioned him. It was obviously a threat of some kind, but what were they going to do? Chad pictured Oleg—Father Ilarion, he corrected himself—at his church in East Berlin, and looked out the window again, searching for Germany under the northern European clouds. *Why would they threaten me with my brother?*

What do they want?

The voice had said 16:30 Moscow time. Chad pictured the Earth turning, and realized the person communicating with him had to wait until the Earth spun enough to bring it back around. At least the next 18 hours would give gave him time to think.

He flicked through his flight plan and made a small mark at the designated time, noting that it was about when he was scheduled to wake from his next nap. Right, they wouldn't call while Michael was listening. That would be too hard to explain. He thought back. *They must have heard me telling Houston that Michael was going to sleep.*

He considered how to use this new information. He pictured his brother under threat, and took a long look at Svetlana, who was still engrossed with the view of the Moon. Eventually he nodded his head.

That must be it.

But what exactly do they know?

38

Into Lunar Orbit

"Good morning, *Pursuit*, this is Houston," Kaz said. "Sorry to wake some of you a little early, but it's Moon arrival day, and I have your LOI data anytime it's convenient."

LOI was Lunar Orbit Insertion, the firing of *Pursuit*'s main rocket engine to slow the ship down, allowing it to be captured by the Moon's gravity into a stable orbit.

They'd decided to have Svetlana sleep at the same time as Chad in *Bulldog*, so Michael had been solo, staring at the rapidly growing Moon and looking back at the tiny Earth, relishing having *Pursuit* to himself. The curve of the lunar surface's stark, ancient scars and deep shadows mesmerized him as they drew near, vastly more rugged and beautiful than the pictures he'd studied. It filled him with awe, knowing what they were about to do. "Morning, Kaz, the Moon is getting huge in my window. I've got my pencil poised, ready to copy."

"Roger. CM mass 62161, delta V 2911, ignition 75:49:50, burn duration 6 minutes, 2 seconds . . ."

As Michael scribbled the numbers in the table, he glanced at the clock. The burn was three hours away; just 180 minutes until they committed to staying at the Moon. Everything counting on the one engine to work perfectly.

He read the numbers carefully back to Kaz.

"That's a good copy, Michael. You'll make a fine stenographer someday."

"Roger that, Kaz. Good to have a fallback if this astronaut thing doesn't work out."

Floating in his hammock in *Bulldog*, Chad had his headset on, listening to the conversation. Svetlana was still asleep, floating below him, with Luke's body strapped to the floor.

He hadn't been able to sleep much, restless with wild dreams and uncertain thoughts. He looked at his watch, the Omega's hands glowing in the darkness, and added nine hours for Moscow time. *They're listening again now.*

It suddenly occurred to him that *he* was in control of this situation, no matter how it felt. Moscow could only transmit to them when he confirmed that Michael wasn't listening. No one would hear what they said except him. And *he* could choose when to respond with mic clicks. They wouldn't dare escalate and reveal their clandestine communications to Houston—they wanted this kept secret from the United States.

He looked down in the dimness at the sleeping cosmonaut, a blob of spit floating weightlessly from the corner of her mouth. Once she got on headset for them to head down to the surface, the game would change. He'd have to think about how to manage that. But for now, Moscow was his to manipulate.

He could hear Michael's voice calling through the tunnel. "Hey, sleepyheads, rise and shine. I've got breakfast ready, and we've got us a Moon to catch!"

As he took a bite of his cereal bar, Michael raised a topic he'd been brooding over. "What exactly are we going to do with Luke's body on the Moon?"

Chad was eating a sausage patty, and popped the last bite into his mouth. "Yeah, I have a few questions about that too."

Both he and Michael were wearing their headsets. Chad flicked the transmit switch on. "Houston, *Pursuit*."

"Go ahead, we're listening," Kaz replied.

"How are the fuel margins for carrying Luke's extra weight during landing, and where exactly do you want his body?"

"They've run the numbers here multiple times, and we're good on fuel, right through landing and abort scenarios. And the current plan is to have his body strapped down behind you, over the engine mount, for center of gravity."

Chad visualized how much space that would take up. He looked at the cosmonaut, who was sipping tea, watching them both. "When it's time to move him outside, is the woman staying inside *Bulldog*, or does Washington want her to get some surface time too?"

Kaz smiled slightly. Chad had his quirks and lived in a weird house, but he surely wasn't stupid. "Good question. We've been talking with the powers that be, and they think getting her feet onto the surface is important." It had been a heated discussion here at Mission Control, but the leverage it gave America to have enabled a Soviet to walk on the Moon was too important to pass up. Sam Phillips had said that Kissinger was insistent.

"She can help you move the body, and we're looking at regolith burial options. You'll see details of that in the new procedures. For now, though, we need you to resize Luke's suit to fit her. TELMU's standing by with expertise, and the interpreter's here. Let us know if you need help."

Chad looked at his watch again, picturing Moscow listening to what he'd said. *So far, so good.* "We have time before the LOI burn; we'll get at that as soon as she cleans up the breakfast dishes." He smiled. *This is fun.*

The inner long underwear with built-in cooling tubes fit reasonably well, Svetlana thought. The arms were a little long, but it was made of a stretchy material and clung to her everywhere else. Michael had turned his back as she changed, but the commander had blatantly watched her.

Tupitsa. He hasn't met Russian men.

The spacesuit was similar enough to the Soviet design that getting into it wasn't a problem. She thought the long pressure seal up her back was overly complicated and prone to leakage, but obviously it worked. The shoulders were a bit wide, and the two astronauts adjusted the sleeves, pulling internal tensioning strings and straps to shorten them to fit.

She'd worn many flight suits and spacesuits; they were always designed for men and fit poorly. She felt around inside: the boots were too big, the crotch was a little high, the hips a little narrow. It wasn't much worse than her Yastreb suit had been.

Michael got the interpreter to help, and walked her through the simple controls and purge on the front, the pressure gauge on her wrist and the backpack plumbing connections. She raised a hand in front of her face and wiggled the fingers, admiring the dexterity they had built into the design. *Better than our clumsy mittens.*

Michael asked her to flex her arms, moving his own to demonstrate. "Okay?"

She stretched both arms out straight, and then pulled them in to reach the controls on her chest. Her fingers slid back in the gloves, making it a bit clumsy, but she judged she could make them work. "Da, okay." Michael gave her a thumbs-up, and she returned the gesture with her gloved hand, a small smile on her face. *A trustworthy man.*

He undid the long zipper up her back, and she squirmed out of the suit, butt first, sliding her arms and legs out. As her head popped free, she caught Chad looking at her speculatively. She held his gaze for a moment, and then helped Michael bundle the suit. It reaffirmed her impression. *I need to watch out for that one.*

Both men suddenly looked slightly unfocused, and she realized they were listening to Houston. Michael handed her Luke's headset, and she slipped it back on, immediately hearing English chatter followed by the interpreter's Russian.

"Svetlana, please confirm you can hear clearly."

"Da, slushayu." *What's up now?*

She heard the CAPCOM's voice, and then the interpreter's.

"Chad, Michael, Svetlana, we're going to run through changes to tomorrow's timeline with serial translation, as all three of you will be involved. Let us know if you have any questions as we go. It's going to take a while, but I think we can get it in well before the LOI burn."

Chad's mind was racing on a parallel track, and he glanced out the window to confirm what his wristwatch had told him. Moscow was in sight, and would be listening to the crew's transmissions. He needed to clarify something.

"Hey, Kaz, just a thought, no need to translate, but in case the cosmonaut has a question, is Moscow on the phone as part of this briefing?"

Kaz waved a finger at the translator to not repeat in Russian. "No, we decided there's no need to let them listen in to our internal operations."

"Roger, makes sense, thanks." *I'm going to have to repeat the key info.* "We're ready to copy."

Kaz's voice. "Okay, great. I'm in the Lunar Surface Checklist, page 2-5. Chad, you'll be doing all the LMP actions here, with the interpreter ready for anything that only Svetlana can reach on her side of the cockpit." Kaz methodically read out the changes page by page, the interpreter repeating the gist in Russian, Chad and Michael penciling them in as he went.

"Kaz, confirm *Bulldog* undock time is 08:43?" Chad said. It was important for Moscow to know when they could call. Michael, in *Pursuit*, would be orbiting overhead every two hours; while he was behind the Moon, with his transmissions from Earth blocked, only *Bulldog* would hear Moscow.

"That's right, Chad, 08:43 central, Mission Elapsed Time of 97:12."

"Copy, thanks." They continued amending the checklist.

In TsUP, it was suppertime, but no one was eating. Chelomei was listening intently to the tone of the crew's responses and the translation by his interpreter, gathering information, trying to gauge the situation.

He nodded slowly as he heard Commander Miller clarify the time. *That is for us. Good boy.* He watched as the flight director wrote the undock time on the mission schedule sheet they had built. His trajectory team had already roughly calculated the orbiting ship's periods of communications blockage behind the Moon; they'd refine it once the decelerating burn was complete.

He thought ahead. There was key information he needed to get to the cosmonaut. And he needed to use the clergyman to apply pressure to the astronaut. But he had to be sure of the Americans' plan.

Glancing at the clock, he tried to will the voice in his ear to tell him what he needed to know. Not being able to hear what Houston was reading up to the crew was frustrating.

He heard Miller speak again, and then the translation came. "Copy, Kaz, I'll read back expected touchdown time and location."

This is it! He leaned over the console and grabbed a piece of paper and pen to ensure he copied down the key information as it was translated.

"*Bulldog* landing 11:17 Central, 99:45:40 MET, location 25.47 North, 30.56 East, next to a straight rille near the southeast rim of Le Monnier Crater."

Chelomei read the words and numbers he had written down, then pulled his notebook out of his breast pocket and quickly flipped the pages with his thumb, looking for what the technicians in Simferopol had told him over the phone. He found his page of notes and held it next to the sheet on the console.

He cross-checked the numbers. The location was identical.

The Americans were going to land Apollo 18 right beside the Lunokhod rover.

Excellent.

Pursuit's rocket engine was twice as big as it needed to be. The design had been decided well before anyone at NASA knew for sure how much thrust they'd need, and by then it was too expensive to change. But extra margin was a good thing, because if the engine failed, the crew died. It was one throw of the dice. One solitary engine to slow the spaceship into orbit around the Moon and, a few days later, to get them going fast enough again to escape for Earth.

The engine's name was beyond mundane—the Service Propulsion System. But the SPS was about to fire, and the crew was on their own.

Svetlana was staring out the window at the surface of the Moon rolling past them, 50 miles below. The Sun was setting, and she held up her hand to block it as they raced into the darkness of the Moon's shadow. The low Sun angles exaggerated the shadows of the ridges and craters, making the strange sight even more bizarre.

"Bozhe moi!" she murmured, reverently. My God. *Can this be real?*

She glanced up into the blackness of the sky, seeing for herself that Earth was no longer visible; the Moon was in the way. That also meant all radio signals were blocked.

"Three minutes until ignition," Michael said. He was loosely strapped in his seat, checklist Velcroed to the panel, eyes intent on the instruments.

"Temps and pressures look good," Chad responded from the other seat. Without Houston to help monitor, it was up to the two of them to be ready to react to everything.

One of the problems the rocket engineers had to solve had been how to get the fuel out of the tank and into the motor in weightlessness; pumps don't work without gravity holding the liquid at the pump intake. They'd decided to pressurize the tanks with helium in order to squeeze the fuel through the lines to the motor—175 pounds per square inch, pushing the fuel against the valves, waiting for ignition time to snap open.

They also had to choose fuel that could be relied upon to burn: aerozine 50, a highly flammable, fishy-smelling clear liquid. The oxygen to burn it was waiting in the other tank, in a faintly orange-brown liquid called nitrogen tetroxide. When the two liquids touched each other they instantly exploded into flame. This hypergolic reaction meant they didn't need the added weight of spark plugs and electrics. As soon as the two mixed, *BOOM*, the engine would ignite.

Michael tugged on Svetlana's pantleg and mimed holding on to something. He didn't want her to be surprised by the acceleration and come tumbling onto them. She nodded and grabbed a handhold.

Chad was watching the clock. "Thirty seconds."

Michael typed in the command to enable ignition. Both astronauts' eyes were glued to the gauges, hands clutching emergency checklists, ready to respond instantly if the engine didn't behave.

The time on the digital clock hit zero. The valves clicked open, the aerozine and nitrogen tetroxide swirled together into the combustion chamber, burst into expanding flame and raced out the exhaust nozzle.

"Ignition!" The urgency of concentration was clear in Michael's voice.

Floating beside him, Svetlana silently mouthed "Pusk," the Russian equivalent. She was holding on tightly, but the acceleration was smaller than she expected, like drifting in a gentle, unseen current. She peered out the window and saw the glow of the flame reflected off the flat surfaces of the lunar lander. "Lem," she said quietly, the sound of the word foreign in her mouth.

"Chamber pressure's ninety, looks like it's running smooth." Chad's voice was clinical.

Michael was watching the digital displays. "Data looks good. Still in the tight limits."

Flame poured out the back of the oversized bell nozzle at the back of the ship, the two fluids burning a bright orange, an engine pushing backwards on a capsule with a lander mounted on its nose, slowing gradually to orbital speed around the Moon.

The computers sensed tiny changes in movement and made precise adjustments to the gimbals on the motor, pointing it in exactly the right direction, constantly recalculating speeds. Michael checked the clock.

"Four minutes to go."

He'd spent the past year learning everything about this ship, this *Pursuit*. It was his to fly, but it all hinged on this motor. *Burn, baby, burn.*

If the SPS failed, he'd have to use the engine on the lunar lander to somehow straighten things out and get them safely headed directly back towards Earth. That's what they'd done on Apollo 13 after the oxygen tank explosion, but they'd barely made it.

Pay attention!

"I show ninety seconds, Chad."

"Agreed." Chad had relaxed. In his experience, once an engine lit it would normally keep going. They just had to be sure it shut down on time, and then he could focus on what he was really here for. Getting to the surface of the Moon. He glanced up and shook his head. *With her.*

"Five, four, three, two, one and . . . cut-off."

Michael's eyes flicked anxiously across the gauges, confirming that the engine had shut down properly. He read the digital display carefully. "Looks like small residuals, no correction needed." In the simulator, as the engine thrust tailed off, it often left some small, undesirable residual rates, and he'd had to manually null them. His fingers threw the switches to safe the system, a grin spreading across his face.

"We're here!" He held up a hand, and Chad high-fived it.

"Well, that's just our superior cunning and skill, boy," Chad said. "And now we can really get down to business."

Svetlana caught Michael's eye and held up a thumb, nodding slightly, her eyebrows raised for confirmation.

He laughed with relief. "Da, we made it. We're in orbit around the Moon!"

"Atleechna," she told him. Excellent.

Now she needed to hear from Moscow. She'd listened to the translated briefing from the Americans, but she wanted to hear it directly from her bosses. She was certain they had separate plans for her, and it was going to take all her wits to understand what they wanted without letting on to the others what the interpreted words actually meant.

But they were *here*! Somehow she'd become the first Soviet to get to the Moon, and tomorrow, she was going to step onto the lunar surface!

A rush of excitement went through her. She'd watched the near-deification of Gagarin, the way he'd become one of the legendary figures of Russian history. That was going to happen to her!

But not yet. As it had been her whole life, especially as a woman, first she had to perform. This time was perhaps the hardest of all: on a strange ship, in an unfamiliar suit, surrounded by a language she didn't understand.

What was it the first American who'd walked here below her had said? One small step?

She nodded to herself. *I can do this thing.* It was just one more step.

But first she needed to hear from Moscow.

39

Moscow

They were an odd-looking pair as they emerged into the Arrivals hall at Moscow's Sheremetyevo Airport. The bearded monk wore all black, a long, buttoned vest over his floor-length robes, simple black leather shoes visible as he walked, a black veil trailing from his tall kamilavka headdress. Laboring slightly beside him with a suitcase in each hand, the church interpreter was in a two-piece brown suit, square-toed shoes and a thigh-length tan trench coat cinched around his waist. It was always colder in Moscow than Berlin, and the April weather could still bite.

Father Ilarion had been quiet and thoughtful throughout the flight, observant of the newness of everything. Alexander had made sure to give him the window seat on the Interflug Tu-134. It had been noisy, seated just ahead of the engines, but Ilarion's face stayed glued to the round porthole window, watching East Germany give way to Poland, peering down at the Baltic Sea by Gdansk. His face filled with wonder as the view opened on the edge of the empty vastness of the Soviet Union.

When Moscow finally appeared, with the low gray shades of human history crowding on the switchback bends of the Moskva River, Alexander had leaned next to Father Ilarion to see the city, encircled by the early green of new leaves and grasses. The MKAD ring road surrounding Moscow in a near-perfect oval was a demarcation line separating natural from urban. The two men stared at the vast ranks of identical apartment blocks, the hulking cooling towers of the power plants and the concentric inner road patterns making a bullseye of Red Square and the Kremlin.

"Kremel, Sascha!" the monk had said, pointing for Alexander to see. The red of the high fortress walls stood out clearly against the dark pavement of Red Square and the glinting river. Neither man mentioned the enormous public swimming pool just to the west, built on the site where Stalin had torn down the Cathedral of Christ the Saviour—the pre-revolution home of the Orthodox Patriarchate.

No need to dwell on the past. This trip was about the future.

The driver was waiting for them in Arrivals, easily spotting the monk. He waved a hand, took the bags from Alexander and led them out to a squatty light-blue Moskvitch station wagon. He took care to set the bags down and solicitously open the rear door for the clergyman, politely lowering his head. He'd been told to make the monk feel important.

Traffic was light on the MKAD, and Father Ilarion's eyes darted in all directions, staring out the noisy little car's windows at the reality of Moscow, reading the overhead street signs as they flicked past. The driver took the Yaroslavl Highway to the right, towards the city center. In the distance, the Ostankino TV Tower dominated the skyline, its tapered silver bulges distinctive—the tallest tower in the world, a visual affirmation of Soviet pride and technical prowess.

As they neared Ostankino's base, a second tower appeared—a sweeping silver scimitar with a stylized rocket at its tip. Without being asked, the driver pulled the car into the adjoining parking lot and leaned forward to look up at the sight. "Pamyatnik pokorítelyam cosmosa," he said, simply. Monument to the conquerors of space.

"Would you like to have a look, Father?" Alexander asked.

"Da!" Ilarion craned his neck to look up through the side window. "My brother is now one of those conquerors," he said as he climbed out of the car's back seat.

The long, pyramid-like rectangular base of the monument was emblazoned with bold Soviet heroic figures in bas-relief, their muscular arms and stalwart male and female faces all pointing towards a cosmonaut in his spacesuit, climbing steps towards the heavens.

"Yuri Alekseyevich Gagarin. First man in space," Alexander said, pointing to the cosmonaut.

The monk stared at Gagarin's sculpted face, and then followed the majestic sweep of the titanium statue towards the sky. He blinked at the brightness.

"It's magnificent." He turned to look at the interpreter. "Sascha, I'm excited to talk to my brother. Do we know yet when it will happen?"

"Tomorrow, Father." Alexander explained that they needed to wait until the Moon was visible in the sky, so the signal would be able to get there and back from the Russian antennas. And tomorrow was also the day his brother would walk on the Moon. Tonight they would stay in quarters near TsUP Mission Control.

Tomorrow would be the biggest of days.

40

Office of the Chief Designer, Moscow

"Allo? Allo?"

Chelomei scowled, holding the receiver against his ear. *We can fly in space, but why can't we Soviets make phones that work?*

A series of static-filled clicks came through the line.

The information that Major Miller had transmitted down from Apollo had confirmed what he'd suspected. Somehow the Americans had precise information on the Lunokhod rover's location on the Moon, and had made it their landing target. The clear purpose of this US military lunar landing was glaringly revealed.

The question was why. They couldn't know about the lunar geology team's discoveries. They were too recent; the American ship's trajectory had to have been set several weeks in advance for crew training and launch timing. But they had intercepted Almaz with sabotage weapons in hand. Clearly this was the same thing: they wanted to see anything Lunokhod might have discovered, inspect the rover up close and then disable it. To stop Soviet progress on the Moon's surface.

The briefing he'd received on the most recent discovery significantly upped the stakes. It wasn't just lunar knowledge and Soviet
technology they could now steal. A naturally occurring radioactive
source on the Moon—if it was the right kind—meant many things,
including power, and heat. It could enable the fundamental technology that would spur lunar settlement. And the knowledge had to
remain the Soviet Union's alone.

He needed to protect what Lunokhod had found. Having a cosmonaut on the surface added tremendous leverage, and options. But he
urgently needed details from the rover operations team in Simferopol,
which is why he waited so impatiently on the phone.

Finally, a thin voice sounded in his earpiece. "Simferopol Luna Ops
Command. Allo?"

"Director Chelomei here. Who is this?"

Gabdul sat bolt upright, stammering slightly. "S-S-Senior Lieutenant
Gabdulkhai Latypov, Director. I'm the shift lead currently on console,
primary Lunokhod operator, seconded from the Soviet Air Forces." *Stop
babbling!* "And lead of the team that installed the Apollo uplink voice
capability." Credentials were important. With his technical communications background, he'd been key in making the uplink voice work.

"Latypov, good." Chelomei had heard the name during the antenna
modifications. "I have new information, and I need your team to be
ready."

He quickly summarized the Apollo landing details, leaving out the
fact that there would be a cosmonaut on the surface too. No need to
overburden the rover drivers. "They'll be on the surface within twenty-
four hours. How can Lunokhod best protect itself and what it has found?"

Gabdul was dumfounded that the director was asking his advice. His
mind whirled as he considered options.

"Comrade Director, we have made fresh tracks all around Ugol—that's
what we have named the rock. It will be obvious that we've been investigating it. Perhaps we could bury it with one of the probes? Or maybe push
it into the nearby rille? Also, we need to protect Lunokhod itself."

An idea struck him and he quickly explained it.

Chelomei considered, and decided the plan was good for a couple of reasons. "Make ready to do it, Lieutenant Latypov. TsUP will be working closely with you tomorrow while the Americans are on the surface."

As Chelomei hung up, he glanced at his watch. The American, Esdale, should be going to sleep soon. He needed to brief Miller and Gromova, but he knew from the transmissions that they weren't keeping her on headset.

He closed his eyes and rubbed his forehead with his thumb and middle finger, his head aching with all the moving pieces and the lack of sleep. He stood and left his office, headed for TsUP.

I'll sleep when this is over.

"Transmission test, transmission test, how do you hear me?"

It was after midnight, and the Moscow Mission Control team was tired. Michael Esdale was finally napping, now that he had safely gotten his craft into lunar orbit. Despite the late hour, Chelomei had insisted on patience to ensure that Esdale was truly asleep, so he could send a message that would be heard by Miller alone. Out of extra caution, he'd decided to use the same innocuous call, and repeated it in deliberately bored Russian.

"Transmission test, transmission test, how do you hear me?" He listened for any response and glanced at the timer on the front screen. Just two minutes left before the ship would disappear behind the Moon. He decided it was worth the risk to assume Major Miller was hearing him and say what needed to be said.

"Listen to me carefully. We have your brother, Ilarion, here, and want him to remain safe. You will hear his voice tomorrow. Once you are on the Moon, we will brief you and Gromova with the exact details of what is needed." Chelomei had reasoned that she would have to be listening while they were in their spacesuits.

"If you understand, click your mic twice." The clock showed one minute before they lost signal.

Long seconds ticked by. Nothing.

Finally, *click, click.*

A slow, Cheshire cat smile spread on Chelomei's face. "We hear your response, and will talk to you tomorrow." He decided to dig in the knife slightly. "Sleep well."

In Houston, Kaz frowned. *That's the second time I've heard that.* He decided to check.

"18, Houston, did you call?"

Chad responded with palpable irritation. "No, we didn't call. We're trying to stay quiet, to let Michael sleep."

"Copy, apologies." Kaz kept his tone contrite, but he looked back at Gene Kranz and shrugged. They'd both heard the clicks.

"INCO, any idea where that sound came from?" Gene asked.

The communications operator was studying his displays. "Looks like from *Pursuit*, FLIGHT. Maybe they just bumped the switch." It was lame, but he couldn't see any other explanation.

"Copy, but let's keep an ear out for any recurrence," Gene said. "We don't need any more surprises in the comm system."

Kaz nodded along with INCO, but he was bothered. Clicking the mic twice was something pilots only did on purpose. But Chad had denied it. Was Michael awake and trying to get Kaz's attention? Why would he do that? Was it the cosmonaut? Or was there something going on with Chad?

In TsUP, the interpreter had translated Miller's irritated response to Houston.

Good boy, Chelomei thought. But he was going to have to be extra careful. He didn't want to make the Americans suspicious, at least not until after he had achieved his aim.

An idea popped into his head, and he smiled, tiredly. He had a better plan for next time.

41

Mission Control, Houston

"Everyone listen up, this is the Flight Director."

Conversations ceased in Mission Control, and faces turned to look at Gene Kranz, standing behind his console.

"Another excellent day, people. We're in lunar orbit with healthy spaceships, and have the landing and moonwalk tomorrow."

His eyes sought out each console operator as he spoke: "The crew needs to get some rest now, but so do you. After you all hand over to the night shift, I want you to head home and get a well-deserved sleep. I need you at the top of your game tomorrow. Sweet dreams, and see you in the morning."

Kaz leaned back to catch JW's eye. "U-Joint for a burger, Doc?"

JW smiled. "Outstanding plan."

Kaz had already called Laura, and spotted her Beetle as he drove into the bar's parking lot. Despite Gene Kranz's urging that they all have a quiet night, the lot was filling rapidly. As he walked through the swinging doors, he saw her waving, two fresh bottles of beer and a coffee on the table in front of her.

"Well, aren't you a sight for sore eye," Kaz joked as he sat.

She laughed and handed him his beer, raising hers in a toast, then shut one of her own eyes, appraising. "You look good too, in mono or stereo."

He rubbed his head and took a long, appreciative swig. "I look like a guy who was ready for this beer."

"I ordered us burgers." She spotted JW coming through the doors and waved him over. "One for the doc too."

"And they say cosmochemists aren't empathetic."

JW sat with a tired sigh. He nodded thanks for the coffee and took a sip, cradling the mug in his hands. "We three have a big day tomorrow," he said.

Laura nodded. "Enough of you boys flying spaceships and counting heartbeats, it's time to get down to what we're really here for. Extraterrestrial geology!"

Kaz pulled his chair closer and leaned in. The total blackout on news had been holding, and he didn't want to be overheard.

"Are the two of you ready for everything that could happen tomorrow?"

Laura frowned. "What don't I know, Kaz?"

"The thing is, we're not really sure." He began listing what was on his mind. "We're hoping to land within easy walking distance of the Soviet rover, to see what's been interesting them, but it might be a hike, depending where Chad touches down. And Chad is going to have to spend extra time ensuring the cosmonaut stays safe—she's had no training for a moonwalk. The Russians have asked for some senior politico to talk to her while she's on the surface, so that will tie up comms for a while. We've set schedule aside to place Luke's body on the surface, and have tried it out in the sim here, but we're not really sure how long it will take. And a lot of what we say is going to have to be repeated via the interpreter, which will also slow things down."

He looked at JW. "What did I miss?"

The doctor set his coffee down. "You're talking best case. We're gambling that Chad will find a way to work with Svetlana under stress. He's the only one who can fly the ship, or fix things when they break."

He looked at Kaz. "And we both know Chad's a . . . perfectionist."

And maybe something a lot worse, Kaz couldn't help but think, then cautioned himself to keep his mind open. Just because the sheriff had wanted to dig deeper didn't mean he had to jump to conclusions. He turned to Laura.

"I'm sorry, but all of this will steal potential science time. We're really gonna have to prioritize. What's your best guess about the terrain Chad'll be walking across?"

Laura stared back at him for a long, sober moment as she processed yet another change in the mission. She said, "It's in the corner of an old crater called Le Monnier that got inundated with lava at some point long ago. It doesn't have too many meteor craters in it, so the lava's fairly young, and flat. There's likely an even layer of dust on everything, with scattered rocks from more recent impacts. Should be okay for both landing and walking."

She took a drink of her beer. "Our orbital photos aren't great, but the most interesting thing we've seen nearby is a rille—a long, straight arroyo in the lava plain, just to the west."

JW asked, "How did it get there?"

"Likely as the lava cooled it contracted. Like mud when it dries out, it sometimes leaves straight cracks."

Kaz had been thinking. "Any further guesses on one of your holes in the Moon being close by?"

She nodded. "Yes, we've been looking at formation models. They're not common, but there's a fair chance that there might be some. If so, they've been too small to see from orbital cameras."

He nodded. Chad had been in on those briefings, so if he encountered such a hole it wouldn't be a surprise. Maybe worth warning the cosmonaut about, though.

"How steep are the sides likely to be?" JW was picturing potential injuries.

"The rille could be quite steep, since it's more of a crack than a valley, but it's likely been drifted in along the edges with millions of years of dust and rock. But if there's a hole, it's a pure vertical drop, like a well, or a Florida sinkhole. And we have no idea how stable the edges might be. Better to stay clear."

JW looked at Kaz. "With all the items they removed to save weight, how good will our camera views be?"

Kaz shrugged. "There's just the color TV camera, deployed on the side to watch them climb down the ladder. It'll be up to Chad to move that onto a tripod once they're both outside."

Laura, imagining how little of the science she hoped for might get done, was looking for options. "How long are you going to let them stay outside?"

JW answered. "That's determined by how fast they use up their oxygen, and exhale CO_2 for the suit to scrub. We have lots of data on Chad, but none on Svetlana, and she may have to work harder since it's not her own suit. Also, she might not get her biomed sensors attached correctly, so we could be guessing a bit."

Laura frowned. That wasn't an answer. "So, how long?"

They both looked at Kaz.

"Original plan with Chad and Luke was seven and a half hours, as you know. Now it's five hours." He saw her face fall, and said, "We might extend, depending on how they're doing, but I wouldn't count on it."

Another thought had been niggling at the back of Laura's mind. "Maybe you can't tell me, Kaz, but does Chad have military objectives that the geologists haven't been told about?"

Kaz looked around, then said, "That will depend on what we see when they land. It could end up being purely geology." *Not likely, though.*

She glanced at JW, who was carefully keeping his face impassive.

"I should play poker with you two. I'd clean you out." She smiled and shook her head as Janie arrived, balancing the three plates.

42

Bulldog, Lunar Orbit

Chad had been seething since the Russian call. His anger had made him restless all night, pouring through him in waves that invaded his dreams and kept cresting, right at the edge of his control.

He was the one who had qualified to command this spaceship. Who was this Soviet trying to tell *him* what to do? And to bring his brother into it? Floating in his hammock, he wanted to scream. He'd made his own life, taken his own actions to get to where he was supposed to be. He'd been the top test pilot in the US Air Force, and now at long last he was about to walk on the Moon. The small-thinking idiocy of that smug voice echoed in his head, the man trying to direct his actions like he was a puppet. "Sleep well," the arrogant bastard had said. How dare he!

When Chad finally had slept, he'd dreamt of Berlin. And it wasn't the first time for this dream—it was one he feared.

The colors in it were oddly faded, like he was inside an old newsreel. He was running, trying to keep up with his brother, as buildings burned and collapsed around them. He could hear the cries of a woman, but couldn't tell if she was behind or ahead of them. Were they running

towards her, or away? Where was his brother leading him? The faster
they ran, the less sure the footing became. He could hear his own
labored breathing over the female cries, and feel the blood pounding
in his temples.

Suddenly they were on a narrow track, running along the surviving
ramparts of the burning buildings. It became a balancing act to keep
up, to not put a foot wrong, yet still move so fast. The world around him
receded, and the narrow ridge of masonry that now supported them was
impossibly high in the sky, starkly lit in anti-aircraft lights, with smoky
haze far below.

He *had* to keep up! Every step treacherous, he pushed himself, calling to Oleg, "Medlenneya!" — Slow down! Please let me catch up. Please
don't leave me alone. He pushed his muscles to the limit, pounding
frantically along the thin, wobbling path until, finally, it collapsed underneath him and he tumbled. Helpless. Weightless. Lost.

And, as he always did at this point in the dream, he forced his eyes
open through sheer willpower. He couldn't allow himself to hit the
ground, and he didn't. Floating there, his heart still racing, he could
feel the sweat on his forehead. His awareness had saved him, again,
pulling him out of the terror.

But this time he wasn't alone. Someone was shaking him.

"Chad, Chad."

He felt the cold of the LM's air on his damp face.

"Chad, time to wake up, man," Michael was saying. "Houston's calling. Time to go make history."

The list of actions to ready the LM for undock and landing was long. As
Chad and Svetlana ate a hurried breakfast, Michael helped them get
suited. He made sure Svetlana got her heartbeat and breathing sensors
properly stuck to her skin, and pantomimed again the key controls on
the suit. She watched him carefully, then nodded, saying "Da," clearly
familiar with the type of equipment.

While the two finished suiting up, Michael set as many switches in

Bulldog as he could—Houston had decided that he would take Luke's role in activating the LM's system up to the point where he had to close the hatch for undock. He strapped Luke's body into place over the engine housing, relieved to see that no more gases had built up in the Soviet suit.

He was trying not to worry about Chad. When he'd woken him up, Chad had been thrashing in a nightmare. As he came to consciousness, his eyes had been wild, staring in raw, scowling fury at whatever he'd been dreaming. When he finally recognized Michael, Chad had thanked him and quickly gotten down to work. But what had upset Chad so much? Michael knew very little about what made the man tick, he realized, and that worried him too. He heard Chad and Svetlana coming down the tunnel, their bulky suits scraping the sides, and made himself small against the ceiling so they could get into position.

Michael started a small stopwatch, counting down to undock, and Velcroed it on the panel in front of them. It read 30 minutes—plenty of time for him to clear out and close the hatch. He helped them don their helmets and gloves, got a thumbs-up from each and backed his way out of the LM, carefully tending his loose items and comm cable. He attached the bulky probe-and-drogue metal apparatus that would allow *Bulldog* to redock onto the hatch when they returned from the Moon. He methodically wiped the rubber seal to make sure it was clean, closed the hatch and released the manual docking latches that had kept the vehicles securely joined.

As he turned to face into the capsule, he realized he was suddenly truly alone. The Command Module, *Pursuit*, named by him, was his to fly. A grin spread on his face as he imagined what the folks in Bronzeville, South Chicago, might be thinking, how proud his family would be. All he needed to do was to get *Bulldog* safely undocked, and he, Michael Henry Esdale, would be solo master and commander of his own ship, in orbit around the Moon.

He rechecked his flight plan and began setting *Pursuit*'s switches.

"Apollo 18, Houston," Kaz's voice intervened. "I have good news before you disappear behind the Moon. You are GO for undocking.

Also, we observed your rendezvous radar test—no issues. *Bulldog*, we have not seen you reset the digital autopilot."

"Thanks, Kaz, doing that now. I show myself"—Chad checked the timer—"fourteen minutes from undock. Talk to you when I come back around."

"Roger that, *Bulldog*."

Svetlana was standing next to Chad, the two of them held lightly in place on their feet by restraint cables clipped to rings on their hips. She'd wondered how they were going to stay in position without seats, and was impressed with the simplicity of the American solution. She found herself alternately watching Chad's hands moving switches and staring through the triangular window at the Moon racing by. They were just coming into sunset, and the lengthening shadows were mesmerizing. Especially given that soon she was going to be down there, walking on the surface.

Michael called, "Chad, when you're ready, I'll start extending the probe."

Undocking was controlled from *Pursuit*. Michael would be the one to extend the docking probe, release the latches and set *Bulldog* free. It would then be up to him to fire small thrusters and move safely clear.

"I'm all set here, Michael. You can let us go."

The phrasing caught Michael's ear, and he found himself suddenly humming "Let My People Go" as he threw the probe extend switch. His mother loved Paul Robeson's deep, mournful version of the song, but he preferred Louis Armstrong's upbeat take. As the gears of the mechanism were grinding, slowly pushing *Bulldog* away, Satchmo's words were playing in his head.

> *Go down, Moses, way down in Egypt land*
> *Tell old Pharaoh to let my people go.*

The mechanical sound stopped, and Michael peered hard through the window at *Bulldog*, relieved to see it moving slightly, independent of *Pursuit*. He pushed heavily on the extend switch to be sure, and pulled on the hand controller for three seconds to back away. He released both controls and watched with satisfaction as his ship separated cleanly from the LM. *Just like in the sim.*

"*Bulldog,* you are *free.*"

"Looks like a good sep, Michael," Chad said. "Starting my yaw and pitch now." He carefully moved his right joystick to pivot *Bulldog* around so Michael could inspect the exterior.

Michael stared through the dark windows, *Pursuit's* interior light reflecting off the metal surfaces of *Bulldog.* "You look clean, Chad—all four legs extended, antennas pointing correctly."

"Good to hear. Checking the rendezvous radar now. Your transponder on?"

"Sure is. Ping away."

Chad reached down and selected Auto Track, and immediately saw the signal needle jump. He confirmed the tracking display bars were moving and the digital range was updating. They'd need that radar to find each other when *Bulldog* was returning from the lunar surface. "Good return, good tracking, showing range of point three miles." He looked out the window at *Pursuit* slowly moving away. "Matches what I see with my Mark One Eyeball."

"Agreed, Chad."

Michael looked ahead to the horizon, where the first light of sunrise was appearing. "We should have Houston back pretty soon. I'll be ready for landing landmark tracking."

Knowing exactly where to land was the most critical piece of information for the navigation computers. As *Pursuit* passed directly over the planned landing spot, one orbit before the landing, Michael would measure exact angles with a tracking telescope. The information would be added to data from the rendezvous radar and Earth antenna tracking, and fed back into the computer in *Bulldog.* That would give *Bulldog* the best possible information to begin descent.

Svetlana, looking ahead to the sunrise glowing on the Moon's far horizon, felt a bump on her arm. The astronaut had taken his gloves off and was removing his helmet. He gestured for her to do the same.

Now that undocking was done, it made sense. They could enjoy the unencumbered comfort for a while, then put them back on for landing. She watched how Chad stowed his gloves inside the helmet behind himself, bungeed to the floor, and did the same.

She stole a quick glance at his face, then stared for a moment longer when she realized he was completely focused on the instruments. He could have been any of the boys she had grown up with—the same round face, high cheekbones, deep-set eyes. *Where did your family come from, American?* She couldn't recall his family name.

Chad turned suddenly, holding her gaze. He looked pointedly at the NASA comm cap on her head and Luke's US flag on her shoulder. "Don't worry, toots," he said. "I won't forget who and what you are." She frowned, not understanding the words but not liking the tone.

Chad gave a short, derisive chuckle. "You just sit back and enjoy the ride. Watch how the best in the world do it."

He considered slipping a Russian word in to unsettle her further, but decided against it. *Cards are best kept close to the chest*, he reminded himself. And he might still need the extra leverage he gained by secretly knowing what the Russians were saying.

In Mission Control, Kaz was watching the timer count down to when *Pursuit* and *Bulldog* would pop out from behind the Moon. He glanced at the flight plan: they just had the tracking update and systems checks during this pass. When *Bulldog* went back behind the Moon, it would fire its engine to start descent. He read the expected time: touchdown at 11:17 a.m. Central. Lunchtime in Washington, 8:17 p.m. in Moscow. The Soviets would have to stay up late to talk to their cosmonaut on the surface.

It was time. "Apollo 18, Houston here, you should be seeing your home planet again now. How do you hear us?"

Michael answered first. "*Pursuit* has you loud and clear, Kaz. Happy to report we had a good undock."

"*Bulldog* has you five by five, Houston." Five out of five for strength of signal, and also for clarity of voice, Chad's standard military assessment of radio communications.

"We have you both the same. You'll be over the landing site in sixteen minutes if you want to have a good look, and *Bulldog*, we're ready to read you your DOI data." DOI was Descent Orbit Insertion—the engine burn that would lower *Bulldog* from 60 miles above the surface down to 6, setting up for the final descent.

Chad unclipped his checklist from the instrument panel and grabbed the pencil that floated with it, tethered by a string.

"*Bulldog*'s ready to copy."

Kaz carefully read the long sequence of numbers specifying time of engine firing, vehicle orientation, plus abort information. The guidance engineers in Mission Control listened critically to Chad's response, and quickly responded when he finished. "FLIGHT, CONTROL, good readback."

Gene Kranz raised his thumb at Kaz.

"Good readback, *Bulldog*. We'd like to do a comm check with the cosmonaut, when you're ready."

Chad glanced at her. "She's listening."

Kaz nodded to the interpreter and began. "Senior Lieutenant Gromova, this is Houston, how do you read?"

Svetlana's head came up as she heard the Russian in her headset. Chad showed her the switch to throw on her control panel.

"Slishu vam yasna," she responded.

Kaz nodded at the translation. "Svetlana, we hear you clearly as well. We have the interpreter standing by at all times if you have questions. And once you're out on the surface, we'll be patching you through to Moscow for an official call of congratulations."

She listened to the interpreter. "Ponyala," she answered. "Understood." She'd been a pilot her entire adult life and didn't like chattiness on the radio. Or in normal conversation, for that matter.

Chad had been looking at her as she spoke. "What an ugly language," he said, shaking his head.

She squinted, uncertain what he disapproved of. "Shto?"

He snorted and turned away. Out his window he was starting to see the familiar landmarks leading up to the landing site they'd trained for. There was a grid painted on the layers of the tempered glass so he could visually cross-check with what the computer was telling him. He lined up his head with the references and watched the craters roll past at nearly a mile per second.

"Houston, *Bulldog,* I'm seeing the reference craters on the horizon. Looks a lot like the sim."

"*Pursuit*'s seeing them as well, Kaz," Michael piped in. "Getting set here to update the computers."

"Houston copies both." Kaz looked across at JW. "Doc, you getting their heartbeats?"

JW decided it was good information for the whole room to know. "FLIGHT, SURGEON, we've got solid cardio and breathing telemetry from both crew in *Bulldog.*"

"Let me know if you see anything unexpected," Gene replied.

Might be really important today, Kaz thought.

Michael had *Pursuit*'s alignment telescope and sextant set up, ready to mark the data when he spotted the distinct features of the crater and the rille. He was hoping he might get lucky and see the Soviet rover as well. It would be critical info for Chad to use for manual landing.

As *Pursuit* flew closer, Michael took marks for the computer while looking unblinkingly through the eyepiece. When he passed overhead, he briefly saw glinting tracks in the area and a flash of silver dead center in the target zone. *Excellent!*

"Houston and *Bulldog, Pursuit* here. Landing landmark tracking complete, and happy to report that Lunokhod looks like it's right at the bullseye."

"Copy, Michael, good to hear. Hopefully won't be too long a walk for Chad."

"*Bulldog* here. I didn't spot anything through my window, but I'll set her down as close to Lunokhod as I can, next time we come around."

Svetlana was listening intently to the exchange. She could have sworn she'd heard them say "Lunokhod" twice, the familiar Russian sounds sticking out amongst the English. Could that be right? Was that their destination? Why were the Americans landing by the Soviet rover?

She scanned her memory for details of the Soviet Luna program, but she didn't remember much. Focused on her own mission, she'd paid only idle attention to robotic lunar geology research. In the translated planning meeting they'd had the night before, no one had said anything about Lunokhod. Could she have misheard?

She puzzled further. The astronaut in the suit she was now wearing had been carrying bolt cutters when he'd been outside at Almaz. That had shown hostile intent. Was this the second half of that same mission? To damage not only the Soviet orbital station, but also their vehicle on the Moon? She looked around inside the lander. Were those bolt cutters stowed in here? She couldn't see them, but with the stiffness of the suit, she couldn't turn her head properly to look everywhere.

She pictured what was going to happen after they landed. They'd said she would descend the ladder and stand on the surface while talking to someone in Moscow. But what would she do if Lunokhod was in sight and the astronaut started heading towards it?

Chad glanced at her and frowned. *Why are you looking so intent all of a sudden?* He saw her notice his scrutiny and immediately relax her face into its usual impassive mask.

He played back the past minute in his head. *Did you understand what we just said?* Maybe she spoke English after all, and was just playing dumb. He went through the instructions he'd received about the Soviet rover, then turned back to look through his window at the Moon's surface below, picturing exactly how it would go.

He was fine, he decided; she couldn't know his intentions. Even if she realized what was happening, she was weaker—there was no way she was going to stop him.

If there was a battle on the Moon, he would win.

It was a long, gradual descent begun in the shadowed silence of the far side of the Moon, the engine slowing *Bulldog* down, the gentle force of it pushing up through Chad's and Svetlana's feet.

Without Luke to assist, Houston had suggested that Chad relay his progress to Michael overhead so someone could double-check every needed action and help with emergencies.

Chad's voice was clipped and clinical. "H-dot's a little high. We're about 2 percent low on fuel."

Michael thought about it. "Yeah, I undocked you when we were a tad high, so that descent speed makes sense, and matches the burn rate."

"Concur."

"How does nav and guidance look?"

"PGNS and AGS compare." Chad pronounced the navigation acronyms "pings" and "ags."

"Copy. Looking good, Chad."

On *Bulldog's* instrument panel, two small lights stopped glowing.

"I see the Altitude and Velocity lights are out now, showing a 3,400 delta-H. What do you think?"

Michael was following along in his checklist. "Sounds like the landing radar's got a good lock on height. I think you can accept the updated 3,400-foot difference it's giving you."

"Agreed. Accept. It's going in." Chad pushed the keyboard button.

This is happening! I'm going to land on the Moon!

Chad heard static in his headset, and then Kaz's voice from Mission Control, 250,000 miles away.

"*Bulldog*, Houston. You're GO at five, and your fuel quantity looks good here."

Five minutes since they'd started descent. Kaz checked the clock. Seven minutes to go.

In the front row of consoles, the engineers were having an urgent discussion with the experts in their back room over signs of a steadily building navigation error. The Flight Dynamics Officer spoke his concern. "FLIGHT, FDO. Tracking shows they're going to land 3,000 feet south of track."

Damn! Gene Kranz cursed. *We can't afford to be that far off!* "CAPCOM, give them a heads-up they'll need to steer that out manually."

Kaz agreed. "*Bulldog*, guidance is taking you half a mile left into the foothills."

Chad had been looking ahead at the planned landmarks and had noticed the trend as well. "Yeah, the mountains aren't quite where I expected. I'll redesignate."

In training he had repeatedly flown a robotic camera over a 15-by-15-foot model of the Moon, built by the US Geological Survey. It was a relief how familiar the actual view out the window looked. Carefully rotating his hand controller, he set the roll angle that would align the window marks with the correct reference craters. He watched to confirm the computer had accepted the update, and snapped his eyes back outside.

Show the world how to fly this thing!

Kaz was watching the downlinked data closely, picturing what Luke would have been telling Chad. "*Bulldog*, we see the update, and show 5,000 feet, engine at 41." A mile above the surface, engine at 41 percent power.

"Copy."

Kaz decided to just give key information to avoid being a distraction. "Two thousand feet, 42."

"Copy."

The Flight Director polled the room and heard no objections. All systems GO. Kaz relayed the vital bit of information.

"*Bulldog*, Houston, you're GO for landing."

"Copy, GO for landing." Chad could feel his heart pounding, even as he kept his fingers light on the controls.

At the SURGEON console, JW smiled. *That raised his heartbeat.*

"Five hundred feet, eighteen down." Just 500 feet up now, descending at 18 feet per second. Kaz spoke calmly, clearly.

"Copy."

"Two hundred fifty feet, eleven, 9 percent fuel remaining, all okay."

"Copy."

Svetlana was entranced by the practiced complexity of what was happening. She loved the wonderfully precise demands of the manual task. *I wish I were flying this!* She could see brown dust starting to blow in all directions below them, pushed away by the engine's down thrust. Through the hurtling bits, she caught sight of something silver ahead of them.

Chad's voice had a hint of triumph. "I have the rover in sight."

"Good to hear. A hundred feet, five."

The blowing dust was now streaming away below *Bulldog*, partially obscuring Lunokhod and the horizon. Chad snapped his focus inside the cockpit, eyes flicking across the instruments to keep control and hold the steady descent. He rapidly cross-checked outside, straining to see rocks through the dust storm, evaluating height and forward speed.

Kaz figured he had time for one last transmission. "Fifteen feet, one down, 6 percent fuel."

No response.

Fifteen long seconds ticked by.

Bam! The violence of the impact startled Svetlana. She'd been staring at the instruments, watching the artificial horizon and radar altitude, and was jolted by the sudden force up through her feet. She heard everything rattling in the ship, even through her helmet. She held her breath, waiting for alarms or for the vehicle to tip on a broken leg.

Nothing. Dead quiet. *Bulldog* sat solidly level. The astronaut was reaching and throwing switches. She leaned to look at his face through his visor. His mouth was curled in a smile, his eyes blazing.

"Houston, *Bulldog* is on the Moon."

THE

SEA OF

SERENITY

43

Simferopol, Soviet Ukraine

The group was clustered around Gabdul's workstation, all trying to get a good view of his small black-and-white monitor. The vista had been largely unchanged for months: the flat plain of the lava flow in Le Monnier crater, the occasional rock, small craters, the gray of the lunar dust.

Spot, drive, look, repeat. It had become a routine—the geologists seeing something, the drivers maneuvering close, and then the sensors gleaning what information they could. Excellent, methodical science, but not a spectacle everyone would gather excitedly to watch.

Today was different.

With a little luck, they were going to see a spaceship land. Even the cook and waitress from their small canteen were shyly observing from the back.

The group peppered Gabdul with questions.

"Where will we first see it?"

He didn't know for sure, but said likely they would spot it against the blackness of the lunar sky while it was still flying.

"How did you know which direction to point?"

He said he had made an educated guess, based on the trajectory information they'd sent him from Mission Control in Moscow. When the crowd heard that Gabdul had been talking directly with Moscow, there was a small hush of awe.

"What if it lands behind Lunokhod?"

"Well, then I'll turn around," Gabdul answered wryly.

"Why does it take so long to refresh your TV screen?"

"Because it's not really TV," he explained. "It's just still images, and it takes a while to send all the little ones and zeroes across the four hundred thousand kilometers from the Moon to their big dish, outside."

"When will we see it?"

Good question. Gabdul rechecked the clock and turned up the volume from their Apollo audio receiver. Right on cue, a voice crackled through the speaker on his desk. "Copy, GO for landing."

One of the geologists who spoke some English had been designated as the group interpreter. The voice from the Moon had been scratchy, but she understood the last word. "Skazali prizemlyayutsya!" They said they're landing!

A murmur went through the gathering, and they refocused on the monitor. Gabdul's hand shot out, pointing. "There!" His finger indicated a small blob of light that had appeared on the screen. Everyone leaned forward.

Gabdul mentally counted the 10 seconds until the screen refreshed. When it did, the blob had moved higher in the image, becoming marginally bigger. Each successive refresh made it clearer, until he could start to pick out the shape of the craft. He was closest to the screen, and leaned in.

"Looks like a fat spider," he said. They heard the radio voice say something else, and waited for the translator, who was struggling with the poor audio quality and the unfamiliar jargon.

"I think he said he has seen something." She repeated the English sounds in her head, grasping for the words. Suddenly it clicked. "The rover, the rover, that's us! The astronauts see Lunokhod!"

Wow, Gabdul marveled. *We're looking at each other on the Moon.*

The next image was fuzzy, the lunar lander less distinct against the black. The following image was even worse.

"What's happening?" the interpreter asked.

Gabdul shook his head. He'd feared this. "It's dust, blown at us by their engine." He pushed a button to send a command he'd prepared, and the next image was black.

He turned and looked at the faces, all now frowning at him. "I've closed the covers over our cameras to protect them from the sharp bits of flying dust. Lunokhod is tough, but I don't want our lenses to get scratched." Heads nodded. That made sense. "As soon as we hear they've landed, we'll look again."

The English voice kept repeating one word, and the geologist interpreted. "He's just saying 'Copy,' over and over."

There was a long pause, finally broken by a terse statement in English. The geologist spoke excitedly. "Gabdul, open the lens covers! They've landed on the Moon!"

Gabdul made a small, fervent wish as he sent the command. *I hope we're pointed the right way!*

The signal traveled from his console outside to the enormous dish, sped across the void to the Moon in just over a second and worked its way through Lunokhod's logic circuitry. Two small motors began spinning, and the circular lens covers slowly pivoted down, out of the way. The camera's photo receptors gathered the light and sent the digitized raster scan, line by line, back to his console in Simferopol. Once it was assembled, the new image blinked onto his screen.

Everyone in the room made a noise. Some praised God and a couple said "Look at that!" But most just exhaled in wonder.

Gabdul hadn't guessed perfectly, but on the right-hand side of the screen, where there had been nothing but a flat, monotonous plain, there now stood a spaceship, glittering metallically in the sunlight.

He peered closely at the static image on the screen. It was going to take a while for the Americans to safe their ship, open the hatch and climb outside. So he made a suggestion. "Let's take a smoke break and go look at the Moon!" The group laughed, but many took his advice to head outside. It was 8:20 on a fine Crimean night, and the Moon was near full. A great way for them to reflect on what had just happened.

But as Gabdul lit a cigarette, stepped outside and looked up, he was mulling a new problem. There had been far more dust than he'd expected, and he needed to check Lunokhod's systems for damage. More importantly, though, some of the dust might have landed on top of his rover, where the solar arrays gathered the power that kept it alive and the radiator allowed the internal heat to escape. If there was too much dust, the vehicle could both overheat and run out of power. He stared at the Moon for a few seconds, thinking of ways to clear the dust.

But first, they had to deal with the Americans. The astronauts would soon be climbing down the ladder and walking towards his rover.

Let them come. He took a long drag, the harsh tobacco raw in his throat, the moonlight on his face. *I'm ready.*

44

Mission Control, Houston

The celebration in Mission Control had been enthusiastic but brief. Raised fists, a small roar of relief and hurrahs after the pent-up tension, followed by a few handshakes. Then back to work: make sure *Bulldog* was healthy and get the crew fully dressed and ready to go outside. The real point of the mission, just begun.

Kaz picked up the console phone to call Washington, as directed. He heard two rings, and then the clunking noise of a handset being picked up.

"National Security Agency, General Phillips's office."

"Hi, Jan, Kaz Zemeckis here. Is the General available?"

"He sure is, Lieutenant Commander Zemeckis. Just a second."

A click, followed by Phillips's calm, warm voice.

"Kaz! Good news, I hope?"

"Yes, sir, they're safely on the Moon as of 12:17 Eastern Time, just getting into preparation for their moonwalk now. Best guess is Chad will head down the ladder in about three hours."

"How close did they get to the Soviet rover?"

"We're not sure of the exact distance yet, but Chad landed within sight."

"Excellent! Like Pete did on Apollo 12." In November 1969, just after Phillips had left NASA, the second manned lunar landing had touched down 538 feet from an American probe called Surveyor 3, and the crew had retrieved pieces of it during their spacewalks.

"Yes, sir, a good piece of flying."

"Kaz, I booked the meeting with the Security Council for 15:30. Does that timing sound about right?"

Kaz looked at the flight plan. "Should be good, sir. We'll get an out-the-window description from Chad soon, and that will help set priorities. And we have the Soviet call to the cosmonaut booked for 16:30, to congratulate her once she's standing on the surface."

"Sounds good. How about once you reset the priorities you call me with an update?"

"Will do, sir."

"And Kaz—well done."

It had been a long, unsettled day for Father Ilarion.

He'd missed the chanting of the bell ringer that usually woke him, but his eyes had opened by habit at five a.m., in time for morning prayers. He'd read from his liturgical text in his room until seven. It was nearing the end of the 40-day Lenten fast leading up to Palm Sunday; as always by now, his hunger felt deeply purifying.

He had forgotten about the time zones, though, and was surprised when Alexander arrived at his door to say it was actually nine, time to leave for Ivanteevsky Deanery, the Orthodox church he'd arranged for them to visit before they had to go to Mission Control that night.

The seminarians had quietly welcomed Father Ilarion for prayers, followed by time for reflection and then conversation over a meager lunch. Afterwards, Alexander had made their excuses. They'd walked back to their quarters and, at his interpreter's urging, the monk had tried unsuccessfully to nap in preparation for what would be a late night. Eventually he had risen to observe Vespers and Matins in his room, feeling somehow inadequate conducting the ritual alone, and so far from home.

As suppertime approached, Alexander again knocked on his door. It was time to go.

As they arrived at TsUP, Ilarion leaned against his car window, peering up while they drove the length of the massive, four-story stone-and-glass building and pulled to a stop at the columned entrance.

"Are we here?" There was wonder in his voice. "It's huge, Sascha!"

"Yes, we are here, Father."

The sign over the double doors read Glory to the Soviet Conquest of Space. Underneath it, a man wearing no coat was smoking. He spotted the car, flicked his cigarette to the side and strode across to open the back door.

"Welcome to Mission Control, Father Ilarion. We've been eagerly awaiting you."

The monk's eyes went wide as he followed the man down a long, broad corridor, looking at the portraits on the walls of Director Korolyov, of cosmonauts Gagarin, Tereshkova and Leonov, and a parade of color views of the Earth from high above. *Our world from the heavens,* he marveled.

They rounded a corner, where their escort waved them into a small room with chairs and a sofa set around a low table with food, the dark paneling harshly lit by flickering fluorescent ceiling bulbs.

"Please be comfortable. Someone will be here shortly to bring you to TsUP." He turned and exited, closing the door behind him.

"What time is it, Sascha?" Ilarion asked. He'd lost track again.

"It is nearly 8:30, Father, well past time for supper. I suggest we eat a little and observe Compline before they come for us."

The table was laden with bread, cheese, sliced meat, tomatoes, parsley and cucumbers. Alex prepared two small plates, handing one to the monk, and poured them each a glass of water.

"Sascha," the monk asked, "is my brother already on the Moon?"

Alexander checked his watch. "He should be landing very soon, Father. Perhaps we will be able to watch it."

A boyish smile spread across Ilarion's face. "I would like that very much." He set his plate down and took just a small sip of water. "In truth, I am too excited to eat."

He closed his eyes and calmed himself by quietly chanting a prayer. It was Friday of Great Lent, and he included the memorized verses of the Penitential Office. At the end, he offered a special thanks for the privilege of the day, and a wish for the health and success of his brother.

As the monk opened his eyes, there was a knock on the door. It opened abruptly. The two of them stood as a strong-looking man in a suit entered, wearing an air of unmistakable authority and urgency. He flicked his eyes dismissively past Alexander to rest on the hieromonk.

"Father Ilarion, I am Director Chelomei, Vladimir Nikolayevich. Thank you for traveling all this way. It is an honor to have you in Mission Control."

The monk bowed his head, his high kamilavka and veil magnifying the motion.

"I am glad to tell you that your brother is safely on the Moon."

Ilarion's heart fell that he would not see it, but he gave no sign.

"Soon you will have a chance to speak with him directly. Would you come along with me now?"

The monk nodded and followed Chelomei, with Alexander trailing. They walked down another long corridor, this one ending at a set of wooden doors, where Chelomei stopped, turned and spoke formally. "Welcome to the Center for Control of Soviet Manned Spaceflight." He turned the knob, pushed the door open and gestured for the monk to enter first. The black-robed figure said "Spasiba" quietly and stepped into the heart of the Soviet space program.

It was much bigger than he had expected. *Like a cathedral.* There were rows of consoles to his left, each manned despite the late hour, and a sweeping semicircle of observers' chairs to his right, where a handful of people were seated. Terse, sporadic English came through a loudspeaker. Chelomei led them to the viewing chairs and asked the monk to sit.

"Please be comfortable, Father. Very soon you will speak with your brother." He flicked his finger for the interpreter to follow him, turned and walked quickly towards the center console. Ilarion sat, his gaze probing the strangeness of his surroundings.

The front of the room was dominated by a large, dark screen, showing a map of the Earth with several digital timers above it. An inset TV screen showed a grainy image of what he guessed to be the Moon's surface. The rows of consoles below it glowed green, silhouetting the operators. He noticed Director Chelomei and Alexander, now standing in the middle of the row, talking intently. Chelomei gestured with his hands, one fist forming a ball as the fingertip of the other circled it. The interpreter nodded his head and walked back to Ilarion.

"Father, it's time to talk with your brother. Unfortunately, the radio link is limited, so he won't be able to respond. But he will definitely be able to hear you. Director Chelomei thinks that after his long and dangerous voyage, your voice will be a great comfort to him, giving him strength before he steps outside to walk on the Moon."

The monk's brow furrowed in disappointment. "He won't be able to talk to me?"

Alex shook his head gently. "The Moon is so far away, Father, and he is in an American spaceship, which complicates communication. This is a rare privilege, just barely technically possible." Alexander turned and pointed at the TV screen. "You can just see his ship there — that shiny metal spider on the lunar surface."

Ilarion peered closely at the distant glowing image with eyes weakened from decades of reading in low light, barely making out a glint of reflection standing on the horizon. Suddenly he felt uncertain as to why he had come all this way.

"Are you ready, Father?" Alexander said, interrupting his bleak thoughts. "It will be such a wonderful surprise!"

The monk took a breath, setting his shoulders under the cassock, and nodded. "I am ready."

I did it! The triumph that coursed through Chad felt like fire. Under all the layers of his spacesuit, he could feel that he had an erection. He turned to Svetlana. "We're here!"

She abruptly turned her head and looked outside, uncomfortable with the intensity of his stare. *This is not a nice man. But a very skilled pilot.* She reached down surreptitiously and felt for the angular metal shape she'd transferred to the suit's leg pocket, just in case.

The dust had settled around the ship far more quickly than she'd expected. *Must be because there's no air.* She bounced a little on the balls of her feet inside the roominess of the suit. The strangeness of the low gravity was surprisingly unfamiliar, especially after her weeks in weightlessness. She felt clumsy in it.

Her gaze went to Lunokhod, silhouetted against the blackness of the horizon, harshly shadowed in the blazing sunlight. Chad was looking that way too, and pointed. "Lunokhod!" He pronounced it properly, the guttural sound of the "kho" very familiar in her ears. *Who taught you to say that?*

She turned to the window again and noticed glinting on the Moon's surface. She realized it was crisscrossing tire tracks surrounding the silver rover and trailing off into the distance. *They've been busy here.*

Kaz's voice broke into her thoughts. "*Bulldog*, you'll be glad to hear we've polled the room, and you're Stay for T-1."

Each Mission Control technician had verified that their systems had survived the landing and that they were safe to stay on the Moon for the first orbit of *Pursuit*, high above their heads.

Michael's voice came from *Pursuit*. "Good to hear. Stay there a while! I finally just got the place to myself, stretching my legs a bit."

Svetlana listened as Chad talked with Houston, obviously verifying pressures and throwing switches. He reached back and unlatched something behind her, pulling a water gun on its hose into view. He inserted it through the adapter on the side of his helmet, turned the red valve and took a long drink. Pulling it out, he offered it to her, and she mimicked what he had done, grateful for the liquid, suddenly aware of how thirsty breathing the dry oxygen in the suit had made her. She traced the hose back and restowed it.

"Cenk yu," she said. Chad ignored her, focused on working procedures with Houston. She looked back outside.

Why had they landed so near Lunokhod? In the briefing, the interpreter had said there was going to be just one moonwalk, so landing here must serve the main purpose of the mission. But the astronaut's death and her being on board had been a huge modification to their original plans. So was this new plan somehow related to her being there? She'd already reasoned that even though she was unfamiliar with the American equipment, they wouldn't have risked sending Chad to the surface alone; if he fell or had suit problems, they needed someone to assist him. But the only thing they'd told her that she was going to do was to climb down the ladder, stand on the Moon, talk to Moscow and go back inside *Bulldog*. Typical window dressing! What were they really doing here?

Once she was down the ladder, she realized, no one could stop her from moving around. She'd definitely walk the distance to Lunokhod and have a detailed look. The Soviet engineers would appreciate her description of what the months on the Moon had done to it. She also wanted to figure out the reason for all the tracks. She'd look for what the rover was looking for.

Michael's voice came through her headset. "Hey, *Bulldog* and Houston, *Pursuit*'s about to go behind the Moon. I'll be back with you in forty-five minutes or so."

Kaz responded. "Copy, *Pursuit*, enjoy the solitude. See you at 101:19 mission time—that'll be 12:40, lunchtime here in Houston."

Michael clicked his mic twice in response.

Chelomei smiled at the sound. Almost time. As soon as the orbiting ship was blocked by the Moon, he'd be able to talk to the crew on the surface. He'd been thinking carefully about what to say and how best to use the monk. He looked up to see the interpreter and the black-robed figure making their way towards his console, and glanced at the TsUP clock. He decided to wait another five minutes, just to be sure. He raised an open hand for the pair to stay back, out of earshot.

In *Bulldog*, Chad heard Michael's call and thought about what that meant. He reached across and switched both him and Svetlana off hot mic. To respond, they'd need to push a transmit switch. He needed to be able to control what the cosmonaut said.

He checked the cabin pressure and began removing his gloves and helmet, gesturing for her to do the same. They'd need to eat, and then attach all the extra equipment to their suits before going outside. As he temp-stowed the gear, he went over the moonwalk plan in his head. *It's all on me.* This was why he'd loved flying single-seat fighters. Only his decisions mattered. His skills, his ideas, his actions. Every one of those nobodies in Houston—hell, in Moscow too—needed *him*. The power of it was exquisite. Only he had the whole picture, and everyone else had to ask him for what they wanted.

He looked at the cosmonaut as she lifted the helmet off her head. Especially her. *She's mine to control.*

They both heard the Russian voice simultaneously.

"Transmission test, transmission test, how do you hear me?" Chelomei paused briefly, and then said, "If you can hear me, call Houston for a comm check."

Svetlana's head whipped around to look at Chad.

He was looking directly at her, smiling oddly, as if he had anticipated her reaction. His eyes narrowed slightly, and he said one word to her. "Podozhdi!" The command for an underling to wait.

She was shocked. Had he just said a Russian word? She had to repeat it again in her head in order to believe it. He *had*, clearly, with no accent!

He held up his hand with a finger raised, staring at her intently—the clear signal to wait for him to do something.

Without breaking eye contact, he pushed the mic button on the control stick. "Houston, *Bulldog*, comm check."

Kaz answered by reflex. "Loud and clear, how us?"

Chad sneered, just a little, his eyes boring into hers. "Five by, thanks, just checking."

They waited. The voice spoke again in Russian.

"Thank you. Senior Lieutenant Gromova, if you can hear this transmission, cough twice."

Chad thought about it, then pointed at her and pushed the mic button.

Svetlana was confused, but coughed as requested, her mind reeling.

Chad released her mic and toggled his own. "Sorry, Houston, she's just coughing a bit in *Bulldog*'s dry air."

"Copy, Chad, let us know if it's a problem," Kaz responded. "SURGEON is standing by."

Chelomei was pleased—the astronaut was cooperating—but knew he had to keep it short. "Listen to me," he said. "You'll see we have parked Lunokhod in a very specific location. Just under the front of the rover, you'll find a good-sized stone. You will retrieve it without telling Houston, and stow it separately in your ship, so you know which one it is. Click your mic twice if you understand."

Chad pushed the mic button twice.

In Houston, Kaz heard the double click and a puzzled expression crossed his face. *Someone bumped the mic button again? What the hell?*

The Russian voice continued in Chad's and Svetlana's headsets. "We have your brother here, Major Miller. He is fine, but we hold him in our palm, like a dove."

Svetlana saw Chad's eyes narrow. *What the hell is going on?*

Chelomei waved for the cleric and interpreter to come closer. "Here is your brother," he said. He held the microphone up to the monk's mouth, pushed the button and nodded.

Ilarion was nervous, and Alexander quietly prompted him. "Speak to your brother, Father, he needs you."

Oddly, the monk felt like crying as he spoke. "Yuri? Yuri, they say you can hear me but cannot answer. That is okay." He felt the need to reassure his little brother as best he could.

Svetlana's eyes widened even further. *Yuri?* This new voice had called Chad by the name of Yuri. Was this American astronaut Russian?

"Yuri, I am so proud of you," the voice continued, full of emotion. "What you are doing is magnificent, and for all of mankind. You have taken great risks and traveled so far, and done our family honor, but also I will be so glad to see you safely back here on Earth."

Chelomei frowned slightly and made a spinning motion with one finger. Wrap it up.

The monk grew flustered. "Um, there was something I wanted to say to you, Yuri. Ah yes—you will need much strength to complete your voyage. Know that you have it from me, and more importantly, if our blessed mother were still alive, her pride would be pouring over you."

Alexander spoke softly. "Time to finish, Father."

"I bless you, and God is watching over you to make a safe return, my dear brother. Glory to the Father and to the Son and to the Holy Spirit, now and ever and forever. Amen."

Chelomei released the mic button and nodded at the interpreter, satisfied. That would do. He waved them back towards their seats, then pushed the mic button again. "You'll hear from us again officially via Houston while you're outside." He quickly reviewed whether he'd said all he wanted.

Enough. "Vsyo," he transmitted.

———

Chad was holding her gaze, his face unreadable.

She was incredulous. "Ti—ti gavorisch pa russki!" You—you speak Russian!

He gave no response, and his expression didn't change. He picked up his checklist, turned away and went back to working procedures.

Svetlana felt like she was falling. *What just happened?* She was sure the first voice she'd heard had been Director Chelomei's. How had he contacted them, and why couldn't they respond?

Was this astronaut a spy? If he was, then why were they threatening him with his brother?

Treat this like any emergency, she told herself. *I'm a test pilot, dammit! What do I know, and what should my actions be?*

She pictured how the comm system must work, imagining what her people must have built to intercept it. She glanced through the overhead window at the Earth to confirm that Russia was facing them—it was, just turning out of sight on the darkened side of the planet. She realized that they could listen to Moscow, but could not reply directly or the Americans would overhear them.

The small solution calmed her. She was gaining some control.

But how did Chad come to speak Russian? Had they taught him that in America? Not likely, given that he had a pious Russian brother who had called him Yuri.

He was still ignoring her, behaving as if nothing had happened, unclipping from his restraint cable and methodically retrieving items to get ready for the moonwalk. It was clear that he wasn't going to explain himself. That meant she had to find a path through this alone. Not giving away Chelomei's secrets, and scheming a way to do what he had just asked. Svetlana unclipped from her own restraint cable and looked around the unfamiliar landing ship, sizing up her options.

She was going to have to count on this astronaut. But she'd been right not to trust him.

———

Kaz took a sip of coffee. Years as a fighter test pilot had taught him to pay attention to the smallest, most insignificant breaks in any routine or expected course of action. Why had he heard a double click again? Michael was behind the Moon, so it wasn't him bumping the mic. It had to be coming from *Bulldog* on the surface. Could the cosmonaut be trying to get their attention? Did Soviets double-click? If it was Chad, why would he do that?

He squinted to moisten his eye; the air-conditioned air was so dry his eyelid was sticking. As he blinked to clear it, he looked up at the timer: two hours until hatch opening. The Security Council would meet shortly after that. He put down his cup and picked up the checklist. *Forget mic clicks for now. I need to be prepared.*

He glanced up as JW passed him, heading for the Flight Director console, and he stood to listen in. JW spoke quietly to the two of them. "A few minutes ago, for no reason I could see, both Chad's and Svetlana's heart rates spiked. Like something happened that surprised them both. Hers, especially—I saw a hundred and forty beats per minute. Yet per the timeline and after checking with other consoles, they were just standing there, doing a comm check with us, setting switches."

Gene took a deep pull on his cigarette, considering, and then stubbed it out in the full ashtray on his console. "Struggling to take their helmets off, maybe?"

JW shook his head. "We compared to previous flights, and it doesn't match. Plus, it was simultaneous. Like they both suddenly saw or heard something they weren't expecting." He paused. "We did hear the cosmonaut cough, but Chad called down about that."

Gene picked up his copy of the checklist, running his nicotine-stained finger down the timeline, finding nothing. He looked at Kaz. "Any ideas?"

"I wasn't going to mention it, but I also heard a double click from them around that time. I assumed one of them bumped the switch."

Gene paused, thinking. "How do their heart rates look now, Doc?"

"Hers is higher than it was, but acceptable. Chad's is back to normal."

"What do you recommend?"

"Nothing for now, FLIGHT. There's probably some simple answer. But it was out of the ordinary and I thought you should know."

JW looked at Kaz and raised his eyebrows. Kaz shrugged in agreement. Not serious enough to be alarming, and not enough info to respond in any way.

Gene decided. "Thanks, Doc. Keep watching them closely, especially the cosmonaut. Once they head outside, we need to be ready to order her back in if you don't like what you see. I don't want either of them anywhere near the cooling limits of the suit."

45

Bulldog

Having Luke's corpse in the way made their moonwalk suit-up awkward. As Chad retrieved the needed items, one by one, talking with Houston, it felt like he had to move the bulky, suited body every time. But at least, in one-sixth gravity, it was light.

Throughout, he was aware of Svetlana watching him, her face intense and wary, right beside him in the tiny space. He occasionally handed her an item and pantomimed what to do with it—which pocket it went into or how it mounted on her suit.

"Obyasni po russki!" she demanded. Explain in Russian!

He ignored her. She could figure it out, and no way was he admitting anything that gave her an advantage. *Control is everything.*

When he got to tool prep, he paused, considering. She'd seen Luke with the bolt cutters at Almaz, and she knew he'd landed *Bulldog* next to the Soviet rover on purpose. No doubt she'd already put two and two together, and might do something stupid. He decided to leave the cutters stowed until he figured out a way to get them outside without alerting her.

Chad meticulously checked their outsized backpacks. On the moon-walk all their life support would be contained in them, with no link to the mother ship. When he finished, he got her to assist him with donning his, and then he helped her with hers.

"Houston, we're putting the PLSSes on, and I'm about to start connecting the plumbing, if you can talk me through the procedures." He pronounced it "plisses"—the prosaically named Portable Life Support System.

"Will do, Chad. We're with you on page 2-6. Let's start with the O2 hoses." As Kaz read the checklist, Chad confirmed each connection and double-checked function.

The interpreter's voice came through in Russian. "Svetlana, how do you hear Houston?"

Chad pressed her mic button so she could reply. "I hear you well, how me?"

"Houston hears you well. Let us know if you have questions."

Hearing the Russian words finally broke Svetlana's composure. She grabbed Chad's shoulder and turned him so they were face to face. "This is stupid! Your brother said your name is Yuri! You speak Russian. Why are you pretending you don't?" Her Russian was rapid fire as she spit out the words.

Chad shrugged out from under her grip and squinted at her in apparent incomprehension. "What are you babbling about, toots?" He pointed to the US flag on her shoulder. "This is an American ship. A-mer-i-can." He pronounced each syllable. "Speak English!"

She exhaled in frustration. She was certain he'd said some Russian words to her and, more importantly, that he had understood Chelomei and the person Chelomei said was his brother. She took several deep breaths, calming herself, puzzling it out. Chad was ignoring it, but Chelomei must have something on him, and had chosen his moment carefully for leverage and so their interchange would stay a secret. Also, she realized, knowing that Chad spoke Russian might work to her advantage.

I'll play this game, she resolved. *For now.*

Chad was holding her helmet up, motioning that it was time to put it on. She guided it into place, the mechanism making a loud click as it locked into the suit's neck ring. Chad attached the visor assembly to it, and then donned his own. He handed gloves to her, and she put them on.

He moved switches on *Bulldog's* control panel and on the suits, and she felt cooling water flowing and heard the steady hiss of continuous communication, listening to the conversation between Chad and Houston in her helmet.

Chad grabbed her arm to check that her gloves were attached properly, and then reached for more switches. She felt air moving in the suit as it pressurized, and cleared her ears. *Feels just like our suits.*

Kaz's voice came into their headsets, verifying that the specialists in Houston who had been watching the suit data had verified no leaks. "Chad, both suits look tight at 3.8 psi delta."

Chad tugged on Svetlana's sleeve again and pointed to the pressure gauge on her wrist, nodding and holding up three fingers, then eight. "Roger, Kaz, both look steady here."

"*Bulldog*, you'll be glad to know you are GO for depress." Permission to vent the ship's oxygen out into the vacuum of space, in final preparation for the moonwalk.

"Copy, here it comes." Chad reached down between the two of them and rotated the hatch pressure handle to Open.

"*Bulldog*, we see pressure dropping. Rates look good."

Svetlana's suit was stiff, like a balloon. She wiggled her fingers, looking at them, marveling at the dexterity. *They have a better design.*

It took three minutes for the cabin pressure to go to zero. Chad tapped the gauge with his fingertip, watching the needle settle.

"Houston, I show nothing on the gauge. Opening the hatch now."

"Copy, *Bulldog*."

He turned the handle, pulled hard to overcome the tiny bit of remaining air pressure and rotated the hatch inwards, pushing Svetlana out of the way to get it fully open. Sunlight streamed in around their booted feet.

He stood back up and turned the cooling system on for both suits—a water sprayer that instantly evaporated into the nothingness, like sweat, taking away heat.

"Sublimator waters are open, Houston."

JW had been watching Chad's heart rate with all the extra activity. "FLIGHT, Chad's heart is up around one-forty. Suggest he take a short break."

Gene Kranz nodded, and Kaz spoke. "Chad, just hold a second while we instruct Svetlana." Two birds. He nodded for the interpreter.

"Svetlana, Houston. Chad is about to exit and set up preliminary gear. We want you to stay where you are until instructed. If you get too cold or hot, let us know. Eventually, we'll have you come down the ladder. The entire moonwalk will be five hours max. Do you understand?"

"Ponyala."

Svetlana had squeezed back against the dead body, trying to make room as Chad turned and got down on his hands and knees to back out. His voice was labored with the effort.

"Houston, I'm climbing out now."

Kaz looked across at JW, who gave him a thumbs-up. "Copy, Chad, the doc's okay with your heart rate. Let us know as you deploy the MESA." The Modular Equipment Stowage Assembly would pivot down from the exterior of the lander when released, opening access to needed tools and uncovering the video camera that would transmit live Apollo 18 images from the Moon's surface.

Chad answered. "Okay, Kaz. Pulling the D-ring now." A short pause, with just his breathing audible. "There she goes."

Gene Kranz spoke. "INCO, let's get that TV image up ASAP."

"In work, FLIGHT."

All eyes turned to the front screen as the blank video image suddenly resolved into a familiar scene, the grainy white of the ladder angling down from the dark LM to the gray lunar surface. The bulk of Chad's white-suited legs were visible, his feet on the rungs.

In their back room, Laura and the geology team all leaned close to their monitors to see this first video image. As she figured out exactly where they had landed and what was on the surrounding terrain, Laura felt a wave of exhilaration course through her. *All right! We're here!*

A white object suddenly arced down through the scene, followed by another, falling slowly.

"Houston, I've chucked the equipment bags out. Climbing down to the surface now."

"Copy, Chad, we're all watching you through the MESA camera."

Chad paused a moment to take a deep breath, reveling. They *were* all watching. Watching *him*! He squeezed hard on the rung, through his glove. Feeling it, exulting in the reality of it. He turned his head inside the helmet, looking around to absorb the moment. *I'm about to step onto the fucking Moon!*

He bounced slightly in the weak gravity, his feet feeling for the last rung, and hopped down onto the circular foot of the LM's landing leg. Letting go with one hand, he turned, got his balance and stepped out onto the surface.

"Houston, this blue-eyed American boy is standing on the Moon."

His lips curled in triumph. All it had taken was a lifetime of hard work and the strategic loosening of one nut.

In DC, all eyes around the table were staring at the television in the corner.

Nixon rasped, "What's he doing now?"

Sam Phillips, the National Security Council meeting's space expert after his years leading Apollo at NASA, answered. "Major Miller has set up the TV camera, and he's now doing a visual survey around the lander. Shortly he'll start a traverse to the Soviet rover. He'll gather as many rocks as possible along the way to bring back for the geologists to analyze." Best to give the boss context.

"And the woman cosmonaut is waiting inside?"

"Yes, sir, until we're ready for the call from Russia, then she'll climb down the ladder to the surface." He checked his watch. "That's in about an hour from now. Miller will get the US flag set up in the meantime, and make sure the Soviet rover isn't in the shot, so we can rebroadcast it later."

Kissinger's bassoon voice rumbled. "You should talk to Miller first, Mr. President, and separately, to clearly show American preeminence."

Bob Haldeman piped in, "That's the way we have it set up, sir."

Nixon nodded. "What do we have to decide here today?"

Sam Phillips was the one to reply. "We don't like the Soviets gaining any advantage in discoveries on the Moon, and this new rover of theirs is far more capable than any that NASA has landed. It could work for months or even years, surviving the cold of lunar nights with its polonium-210 internal heater. Once Miller has had a close look at what it's doing and taken detailed pictures, we think he should disable it in a way that allows deniability. That needs to be done off camera and without the cosmonaut seeing. It needs to look like it was disabled by the blast of the *Bulldog*'s engine, for instance, rather than by deliberate action."

He was looking into the eyes of each of the men around the table. "The Soviets are only in contact with their rover when their big antenna in Simferopol is facing the Moon, and that ends in about an hour. Miller has bolt cutters on board, and we have some other ideas that might work as well. But with this Council's approval, Mr. President, by the time Apollo 18 blasts off the Moon tomorrow, Lunokhod will be dying, or dead."

Nixon didn't move, waiting for any dissenting voices. Silence.

He lifted his head to take a long look at Phillips, and then he nodded. "If you take no risks, you win no victories. Do it."

Inside *Bulldog*, Svetlana was bending as far as the suit would allow so she could watch what Chad was doing outside through the window.

The voice from Houston had instructed her to wait, but Moscow had given clear instructions about retrieving a specific rock from Lunokhod.

She stared at the rover on the horizon. How long would it take to walk that far? Could she trust the American to do what Moscow had asked?

No.

She'd studied how he'd climbed down the ladder. The hatch was wide open. But how would Houston react to her leaving the lander? If she could stay out of sight of the camera, how would they even know?

A thought occurred to her, and she studied the switches and circuit breakers in the cockpit. Her English was rudimentary, but a far-thinking high school teacher had forced her to learn the alphabet. She silently thanked her now as she sounded out the printed names, hunting for two specific letters and hoping their engineers had kept the labeling simple.

"Chyort!" she muttered. So many! Why hadn't she paid closer attention to the switches he'd moved before going outside? She paused to picture exactly where his hands had moved.

She found a row labeled Comm and sounded it out. English was so confusing; was the "C" hard or soft? She tried saying both, and suddenly realized that it was probably short for "communications," a technical English word she knew. Excitedly, she checked each of the breakers' names in the sub-row below it.

And there it was, the last one on the right side. Exactly like she'd hoped.

TV.

"Televizor" in Russian. He *had* reached for that one. She rapidly checked the rest of the panels to be sure it was the only circuit breaker labeled that way. She looked back at it closely. It was a standard design, meaning she'd just have to squeeze it between her thumb and two forefingers and pull. It would pop out, unpowering the TV camera. Houston wouldn't see her coming down the ladder.

But when to do it?

She looked back out the window, not seeing him. *Blyad!* Had he already headed for Lunokhod?

She twisted further and spotted movement on the far left. Chad was still near, unstowing something beside one of the lander's legs. It had two dinner-plate-sized, fat rubber tires on it, and he was unfolding long, parallel handles out and locking them into place.

Tachka, she decided. A wheelbarrow. For carrying things like tools. And rocks. That meant he was almost ready.

She touched the gun in her pocket. So was she.

At his console in Simferopol, Gabdul moved his hand controller carefully. Director Chelomei in Moscow was watching Lunokhod's video feed, and had demanded the best view he could give him; Gabdul was precisely turning the rover so its cameras were facing the Apollo lander, but without damaging the Ugol rock underneath.

There! That ought to do it. He stopped and looked at the slowly refreshing black-and-white still image to see if he'd gotten it right.

The metallic glint of the NASA ship was centered in the frame. "Otlichna," he muttered in satisfaction. Perfect.

He leaned close to the screen. He could just make out a white blob by the legs of the lander. As each new image processed, the blob was in a different place. *Spacewalker*, he concluded. He watched several successive frames. The blob was slowly getting clearer and larger. One of the images caught a reflective glint off the helmet's reflective coating. *And now he's headed our way.*

Chelomei's harsh voice came through the squawk box.

"I see the astronaut. Are you ready?"

"Da, Glavni Director. We are ready." Gabdul rubbed his palms on his legs to wipe off the sweat.

He quickly double-checked his command selections, watching the spacewalker get bigger with each image.

Not spacewalker, he corrected himself wryly. *Moonwalker*. "Lunokhod" in Russian. *Same as us.*

———

"Houston, Chad here, you'll want to see this." His voice was breathy with physical exertion.

Kaz looked intently at the front screen, watching the white of Chad's spacesuit against the moonscape as he bulkily walked towards Lunokhod, hauling the small handcart behind him.

"See what, Chad?"

The figure had stopped and was pointing off to the right.

"There's a really dark spot flush with the surface over there. Maybe a couple hundred feet away, hard to tell. Want me to go have a closer look?"

Kaz ran through possible explanations and mission priorities in his head.

"Chad, are there any rover tracks near what you're seeing?"

"Nope. Pristine Moon dirt. I mean, regolith."

Kaz nodded. If the Soviets hadn't investigated it, they likely hadn't seen it. He glanced at the Flight Director for a decision.

Gene said, "CAPCOM, Lunokhod survey is priority for now. Geology can wait a few more minutes—the rocks aren't going anywhere. Tell him we'll have him swing by it on the way back."

When Kaz passed the word, Chad shrugged. He'd been trying out different ways to walk, balancing the stiff bulk of the suit with the strange lightness of one-sixth gravity. Like the moonwalkers before him, he settled on a two-footed loping, hopping motion.

Kaz pushed a button on his comm panel to talk to the geology back room. "Laura, I'm sure you heard what Chad said."

Her excitement came through his headset. "Sure did! We think we see a smudge where he pointed, but need to get a closer look to know for sure. Can Michael zoom in and see anything when he passes overhead in *Pursuit*?"

"Good idea. He's just back on our side of the Moon again now. I'll ask him."

Kaz reset his comm switches. "*Pursuit*, Houston, welcome back Earthside. How was the view around back?"

The delight in Michael's voice was palpable. "Kaz, you can tell Pink Floyd I have *Dark Side of the Moon* playing full blast on cassette up here!"

Kaz smiled. "I'm just glad I don't have to hear you singing along. Meanwhile, you probably overheard Chad, but we'd like you to look closely at the landing site with the sextant telescope. Let us know if you see anything worth investigating."

"Already on it, wilco."

Michael floated down to the Nav panel, carefully grabbing the small joystick with his fingertips to point the telescope.

Kaz had an idea. "Svetlana, Houston, how are you doing?" The State Department interpreter translated.

"Normalna." Fine.

Kaz nodded for the interpreter to describe to her where to look. Svetlana leaned towards the window and peered hard off to the right of Lunokhod as directed, squinting against the harsh contrast of the light.

"There are dusty rolling hills and lots of small rocks," she said. "The Sun is not too high, so the shadows are fairly long." *Be methodical!* She followed the line of Chad's new footprints and deliberately searched to the right.

"I see one odd shadow, like a low spot. Maybe a small crater."

The interpreter translated for the room, and Kaz nodded thoughtfully. "Copy, thanks."

Svetlana looked back at Chad. *Time to do something.*

Chelomei had been listening intently. *What are the Americans seeing?* He looked at the timer: 40 minutes until the big dish in Simferopol could no longer see the Moon and they lost direct comms. On the screen, the astronaut was almost at Lunokhod. He heard him speak.

"Houston, I'm approaching the rover and starting to take pictures."

Chad turned his whole body to point the chest-mounted Hasselblad motor-drive camera, reaching underneath to squeeze the pistol grip trigger.

Kaz watched the distant figure shuffling slowly around the silver rover, small on the screen. "Copy, Chad. Those photos will be of great interest to our intel folks here."

"Kaz, it looks a lot like we expected: an eight-wheeled silver bathtub with a solar array lid open, a bunch of instruments dangling on arms out front." Chad completed his circuit and looked closely. "Three cameras on the front, and looks like a few wide-angle camera lenses on the side and back." He glanced up at the Earth. "They're probably looking at me right now."

Chelomei listened through his interpreter and nodded. Would this astronaut comply? Had the threat of harming his brother been enough? *Get the rock, and don't say anything!*

On the screen at the front of Mission Control, the TV video from *Bulldog* suddenly went blank.

From long experience, Gene Kranz gave it 30 seconds, allowing for a possible handover between ground antennas. When it persisted, he asked. "INCO, why'd we lose video?"

"FLIGHT, we're checking. Looks like it lost power."

Gene visualized the circuitry in his head. "Any other systems down?"

INCO was listening through his headset to the sudden blare of technical chatter in his back room, trying to filter out relevant information. "Don't think so. Electrical current drop matches just the camera power-down."

Gene rubbed his chin, frowning. During Apollo 12, Al Bean had inadvertently pointed the camera at the Sun while setting it up, and burned out the internal sensor. Doing the rest of the moonwalks blind had been a nightmare.

But doable.

"Okay, let me know what our troubleshooting options are. CAPCOM, let the EVA crew know. Everybody watch their data closely to make sure we don't have any cascading anomalies."

Kaz summarized the info to Chad and had the interpreter tell Svetlana, noting that it might affect her media event later.

After a short pause, JW spoke. "FLIGHT, SURGEON, I do have one other thing, probably unrelated. A few minutes ago, we lost the cosmonaut's biomed data. We've seen that happen before on other flights, and I wasn't too confident she'd get her sensors applied properly."

Gene frowned. "TELMU, is there any way we have a common cause between those two systems?"

Bulldog's electrical specialist shook his head. "No, FLIGHT, they're totally separate. Must be coincidence."

Gene Kranz scowled. He hated coincidences.

Michael's voice crackled from lunar orbit. "Houston, *Pursuit*, I just finished the overhead pass and am ready with observations."

Kaz thought they could use some good news. "Go ahead, *Pursuit*."

"It was easy to spot the long, straight line of the rille though the scope, and Lunokhod's tire tracks catch the light differently, so they helped as well. Pointing the sextant, I could just make out *Bulldog* on the surface." There was distinct pride in his voice. It had been finicky work. Some of the other Command Module pilots hadn't been able to do it.

"Nice work. You've got eyes like a hawk!"

"I looked where I think Chad meant and saw a few shadows. But one of them looked blacker and more distinct. Sort of crescent-shaped."

"Copy. Where is it relative to the LM?"

Michael pictured the long rille valley and the speck of *Bulldog*. "About halfway to the rille, and a bit north. Maybe have Chad aim thirty degrees or so left of *Bulldog* when he's walking back."

"Thanks, Michael, excellent intel, wilco."

Chad retrieved a long set of tongs from the handcart. With the video camera down, Houston was no longer watching him.

Too easy!

He walked around in front of Lunokhod, bent down in front of the lobster-like camera eyes and waved. He was confident that the tiny antenna on top couldn't be giving Moscow real-time video; they'd just be seeing fuzzy stills. He held his free hand up long enough for them to get an image.

Keep them guessing.

The rock they were interested in was supposed to be under the front end. He crouched as far as the suit would let him and reached in with the tongs. He probed a few times, pushing into the gritty resistance of the abrasive soil, feeling around until there was a hard stop. When he bent to try to see what he was running into, Lunokhod suddenly moved. Chad spasmed back clumsily in surprise, dropping the tongs, as all eight wheels spun and the rover lurched backwards for a yard or so. Then it stopped.

Shit!

"FLIGHT, SURGEON, we just saw a spike in Chad's heart rate. Without video, we recommend a check-in with him."

Gene nodded at Kaz.

"Hey, Chad, Kaz here, how's it going?"

Chad felt his heart pounding in his chest and guessed why they'd called. He deliberately calmed his voice. "All fine here on the Moon, thanks, Kaz. Just dropped the damned tool and tripped as I was retrieving rocks."

"Copy, no sweat. Since we've lost video, the Lunar Geology back room requests that you narrate as you go so they can track where each sample came from."

"Wilco, starting now."

He dropped into the patter they'd practiced in the sim, keeping it going as he looked back at the rover to see what its move had revealed. "The soil around Lunokhod is fine-grained, and much darker where the tracks have churned it up . . ."

An angular black rock was now sitting clear of Lunokhod's nose, jutting up out of the disturbed powdery regolith.

He pivoted his whole torso, the stiffness of the suit making it hard to see straight down, and finally spotted where the tongs had fallen. Other astronauts had warned him that picking things up off the surface was hard, and he didn't want to fall over. He bent his knees as far as he could, blindly reaching, and grabbed the metal shaft just as he started to topple over frontwards. He let the pressure of the suit bounce him back up and took a couple of steps to regain his balance.

"Whooee, Houston, just getting my balance here."

"Copy, Chad." Kaz looked at the timeline. "We're right on track. Once you've gathered enough samples so we can figure out what Lunokhod's been looking at, we'll have you start back towards *Bulldog*."

"Roger that. I'm going to start gathering local rocks with the tongs now." He squeezed the handle with both hands to open the tongs all the way, swung it into place over the rock and released, letting the springs clamp down. Lifting carefully, he turned and released it into the handcart.

It didn't look like much. He picked it up, turning it in the sunlight, startled by how light it felt. Sunlight glinted off internal crystals, and it had a dark, layered appearance, somewhere between deep red and black.

He looked around for similar rocks, but saw none.

How did you get here? And why are the Russkies so interested in you?

He pulled a plastic sample bag out of the larger duffel, carefully slid the rock in and rolled and twisted the wire top to seal it. He'd brought two collection bags, to make sure he kept this rock separate. Only he'd know which bag contained what.

He grabbed a collection rake from the cart and started gathering more samples, once more describing what he was seeing.

In Moscow, Chelomei had been watching the slow-motion sequence unfold, one still image at a time. He'd yelled at the technician in Simferopol to back Lunokhod up, and was gratified to see the result.

"Otlichna!" His plan had worked! The stone had been retrieved and was sitting there in the cart now on the first leg of its long journey back to Earth.

He glanced at the clock, seeing with surprise that it was already past midnight. He yawned hugely, suddenly aware of his exhaustion.

Kvatit. Enough. He gave the order to send the monk and his interpreter back to the hotel, since the American astronaut was behaving.

He just had time for a quick rest in his office before the joint press event with NASA. He nodded at the flight director, and turned to leave, thinking ahead to his next steps.

Gabdul's voice stopped him, sounding tinny through the squawk box on the Moscow flight director console.

"We see the second astronaut climbing down the ladder now."

What? Chelomei whipped around to face the image on the monitor. In the distance, beyond the nearby American and his handcart, there was a distinct blob of white against the angular shape of the lander.

He urgently queried the flight director. "Are we still hearing the astronaut?"

"Da, Comrade Director." He turned the volume up on the sound of the male voice steadily speaking.

The interpreter clarified. "He's talking about the geology of the samples he's gathering."

"Did the astronaut tell Lieutenant Gromova to come outside? Has she said anything recently?" It was frustrating not to be hearing what Houston had transmitted to the crew.

A headshake. "Nyet, Director."

What is she up to? He watched as the still images showed her leave the ladder and start walking. Towards Lunokhod.

46

Le Monnier Crater

Svetlana moved her head carefully, looking around the blocky structure of the LM up into the blackness of the sky, gauging the turn of the Earth. The western edge of Russia was still visible; she figured Moscow could see and hear them for another hour or so.

Good.

By squirming inside the suit, she'd dislodged the stick-on sensor from her ribs to hide her heart rate, and she was glad she had, given that she'd staggered when she'd let go of the ladder. She hadn't walked in weeks, and the oversized suit made her balance even worse. She'd grabbed the ladder again and held on until the dizziness passed.

Carefully, she let go and moved away from the LM, taking small steps. *Like a toddler learning to walk. I even have a diaper on!*

She cautiously followed the single line of tracks and twin wheel marks towards Lunokhod, feeling the blistering heat of the Sun through the fabric of her suit. *Take it easy, Sveta,* she counseled herself. She hoped the constant chatter between Chad and Houston would mask any extra breathing noises from her.

She kept her eyes on Chad in the distance. He was holding a long tool, alternately digging and working at the handcart, paying attention to Lunokhod and the soil around it. *Has he retrieved the rock?* She was able to move faster as she adapted, mimicking the gait she'd watched him use to move across the surface, willing him to keep his back turned.

She moved with purpose. Moscow had given orders. She was there to make sure he carried them out.

"FLIGHT, we're seeing odd data from Svetlana's EMU." The puzzlement in TELMU's voice was reflected on his face as he turned to look across the consoles at Gene Kranz. "Without her heart rate it's hard to tell, but it looks like she's moving around or something, breathing more, using more oxygen." His voice tailed off.

Gene's response was crisp. "Anything out of limits?"

The specific question got him back on secure ground. "No, FLIGHT, the suit is fine, all well within norms."

Gene pictured her in the LM, alone. She should be just standing there. What was she up to?

"CAPCOM, have the interpreter check in with the cosmonaut."

Kaz gave quick instructions, waiting for a gap in Chad's geology reporting, and the Russian language request went up.

"Svetlana, Houston. How are you doing?"

Svetlana abruptly stopped walking. Hearing Russian out here, unexpectedly, it felt like she'd been caught.

Why are they asking? Maybe they were seeing something in her suit data and she just needed to give them a reason for it.

"Normalna. I've been moving my arms and legs around to keep from falling asleep."

Kaz and the interpreter glanced at TELMU, who shrugged and nodded his head.

"Copy, thanks. The event with Moscow Mission Control will be in about an hour."

She made herself sound bored. "Gatova, spasiba." *I'm ready, thanks.*

She'd kept her eye on Chad during the exchange, but he'd been preoccupied with lifting a new sample and was still facing away. She started moving again and picked up the pace.

To Chelomei, it sounded like Houston was somehow okay with the cosmonaut being outside. *Can they not see her?* He watched the Lunokhod camera image as she began moving again.

He checked one of the timers at the front of the room; the orbiting capsule would be on the Earth side of the Moon for another 30 minutes. If he called now, that astronaut, the *Pursuit* pilot, would hear. He did the math. There'd be a half hour or so after *Pursuit* went behind the Moon when he could call. That was an ace up his sleeve, to be played if he needed it.

Patience, he told himself. But he hadn't gotten this far by being a patient man.

"There are many small crystalline rocks in this sample, an admixture of basaltic and anorthositic, up to maybe an inch across, maximum. Color and morphology appear to confirm they are largely made of the same material as the regolith." Chad continued his description as he tipped the collector on the rake into a bag.

"Copy, Chad," Kaz said in a monotone.

No wonder, Chad thought. *Geology is fucking boring.*

As he sealed the sample bag, he paused to look around at where he was. He turned his head deliberately, left and then right, like a male lion. Top of the food chain. He peered out onto the flat, gray-brown terrain and the perfect blackness of the lunar sky above. No one else had ever been here, in all of history, to see this. The power of that, the realization that it was only *him*, felt like a hit of narcotic. Victory running through his veins.

He twisted his neck inside the helmet, turning to look at the Earth. Of all those losers, only *he* had made it here.

Then he saw movement.

Another moonwalker, 50 feet away, coming towards him.

What the? How did she get outside? He ran the recent conversation with Houston back in his mind. They thought she was still in *Bulldog!*

He took a breath and opened his mouth to challenge her, but stopped. Secrets were good.

He raised both hands waist-high, palms up. *What are you doing?*

She continued towards him, raising one finger to her visor. The sign for silence.

He reached up and rotated the gold visor off his face, squinting hard against the glare. She watched, and did the same. Now they could read each other's facial expressions.

She gestured with her chin at Lunokhod and pantomimed scooping something solid up with her hand. She raised her eyebrows.

He stared at her, his face impassive. *No reason to make it easy for her.*

She held his gaze for a moment, and then looked away towards the rover, her lips tight with frustration. She reached past him to grab the tongs from the handcart, and walked towards Lunokhod, trying to read the disturbed soil and tracks. His footprints were all over, but the underlying wheel tracks showed where it had recently driven forward and backed up again.

Why?

As she was watching, the rover lurched into motion. It rolled straight towards her, slowly, and then stopped. She glanced at Chad, who stood watching her.

They're signaling me, she decided. As she watched, a slender arm pivoted down, touching the lunar surface in a darker, hollowed-out area, as if it were pointing. After 10 seconds the arm rotated back up, and the rover retreated again.

Svetlana nodded. She moved closer and probed at the disturbed soil with the tongs, grasping and releasing, finding only loose dust.

He had the stone.

She turned to him and pointed at the handcart with the tongs, jerking her chin for him to clarify, looking hard into his eyes.

He smiled broadly, shrugged and stared back at her as he spoke.

"Houston, I've got a pretty good sampling of everything in this area. How about I head back to *Bulldog* and start setting up the flag for the Rooskie press event?" He emphasized and pronounced the word carefully; in America, Rooskie was a derogative, but when said with a rolled "R" and the right weight, it was the word for "Russian" in her language.

A frown flashed across her face. She'd heard it, amongst the incomprehensible English. *Perfect.*

"Copy, Chad, sounds good. On the way back we'd like you to check out that darker spot you saw. Our best guess is about thirty degrees left of *Bulldog*."

"Will do, just tying down the samples now."

Svetlana watched as he pulled the bungees across the bags and tools in the handcart, wondering what he had said. She'd clearly heard the Russian word, and he'd moved his head as he'd said it, to be sure she'd notice. What did he tell them? *Can't ask without giving myself away.*

He looked directly at her, reached up and rotated his gold visor back down over his face. He turned, grabbed the handle of the cart and started walking away.

She glanced at Lunokhod, motionless, still pointed at her. She walked around it, looking closely so she would be able to describe its status to Moscow when she got back. *Dusty, but all there.* Still holding the tongs, she turned and hustled clumsily after the astronaut.

Behind her, unobserved, Lunokhod's eight wheels began turning together. It picked up speed and followed them, like an oversized, lumbering pet chasing its master.

Or a wild animal tracking its prey.

"Houston, I'm keeping *Bulldog* at about one o'clock as I track back, but haven't seen anything yet." Chad was walking slowly; he didn't want any of the samples he'd gathered to bounce past the bungees and out of his cart. Especially the bag with the rock.

"That heading sounds about right, Chad." Kaz made a "V" with his hands, picturing what Chad was doing, remembering how long the traverse to Lunokhod had taken. "You should be coming up on it soon."

Laura was next to him at the console. He'd asked her to come sit in the front room to make it easier to discuss whatever geology Chad ran into, especially with the TV camera down.

"Okay, Houston, I'm seeing something now." Chad's voice tailed off.

Laura had both hands up on the console, her fists clenched in anticipation. As the seconds ticked by, her fingers slowly extended, palms up, and she turned to Kaz impatiently, eyes questioning.

He nodded and asked, "What are you seeing, Chad?"

"Uh, it's weird. Like a big sunken acne pockmark in the Moon. There's a downslope all around, and then what looks like a rocky round edge to it. Inside that I'm just seeing black. I think it's one of those holes the geologists were talking about."

A smile of triumph spread across Laura's face.

"Copy, Chad, that's the first one of those anybody's seen up close. Just hold position for a sec while we talk about it."

He stood up and gestured for Laura to do the same, turning to the flight director console.

Gene spoke: "What risks are we facing here, GEOLOGY?"

Laura fumbled for her mic switch, but then spoke confidently. "FLIGHT, from Chad's description, it sounds similar to the four holes we've got pictures of from lunar orbit. We hadn't spotted this specific one, but best guess is it's an old lava tube like we've studied in Hawaii, with a collapsed section where it's thin on top. It likely has sloping sides, not sure how steep."

Gene considered that. This could be one of the most important discoveries of the whole Apollo program. Access below the surface of the Moon, providing potential shelter from the temperature extremes and radiation on the exposed surface, might be a key to eventual lunar settlement. Also to understanding the geology of the Moon itself. But not enough to risk the crew. Especially with only one person outside. A trade-off, like everything in spaceflight. Purpose versus risk.

"What info would be most useful to you?"

Holy cow! Laura thought. Gene Kranz was asking her directly what to prioritize. She worked hard to keep her tone professional.

"Characteristics of the hole: size, surrounding debris differences, angles of repose, exposed bedrock. A look directly down inside would be the ultimate, to understand the interior lower wall structure—smooth or rough. If possible."

Gene put her on the spot. "How close would you walk to the edge?"

Laura swallowed, realizing that this was a pivotal moment in her life. All the years of study, the fieldwork, staring at photographs, writing endless grants and reports. All was in preparation for this.

"I recommend caution, FLIGHT. Nothing has disturbed that regolith in maybe a billion years. It's probably compacted and solid, but it could be ready for a landslide. Chad will be fine on the flat, but if it were me, I'd stay clear of where the slope gets at all steep."

Would I really? she wondered. Probably not. Geologists were explorers.

Gene nodded and looked at Kaz. "Let the crew know."

Close, but not too close, Chad summarized in his head. Typical. Everyone sitting in comfortable chairs, sipping coffee, congratulating themselves on their good judgment. Leaving the real risk to someone else.

To me.

He let go of the handcart and took a step forward, describing as he went, hyper-aware that everyone was hanging on his every word.

"Hard to judge distances, but the hole looks to be about fifty feet across and maybe fifteen feet below the surrounding plain. The slope steepens as it gets closer to the hole, interrupted by small ridgelines of bedrock sticking up. I'm going to walk along one of those outcroppings as they stay level closer to the edge."

"Okay, Chad, understood, but err on the side of caution. Where you are now is already giving us info we've never had before."

No shit. "I'm taking pictures as I go. The surface color is unchanged, and there's no perceptible difference in the soil surrounding the hole. Same mix of dust and stones."

He walked to his left, following a higher ridgeline that led towards the hole.

"Okay, I'm seeing deeper down into it now." He stretched in his suit, craning his neck. "I can see the far rim of the hole in the bedrock. The rim is thin—maybe a yard or so—and it's just black below."

Gene Kranz said, "Tell him that's far enough, CAPCOM."

Kaz transmitted, "Chad, hold there while we talk about it." He turned to Laura. "What do you think?"

"With the angle of the sunlight, he won't see the bottom unless he gets right to the edge." She left the implied decision to Kaz.

He held her gaze as he pushed the button. "Chad, once you're done taking photos, we'd like you to back away and head back to *Bulldog*. We'll have you come back to collect samples later if there's time."

Chad took a step closer, and then another, which brought him near enough to see the end of the harder rock that held up the narrow ridge he was on.

"Copy, Kaz."

He took another step, feeling a rush of exhilaration. This was the same as flying a jet close to the ground at high speed, away from where any prying eyes or radar could stop him. Feeling the danger of the trees and rocks whipping past, the risks all supremely controlled by him, and him alone. His skill. His decisions. He took another step.

Svetlana was watching, alarmed, and rapidly decided the risk of speaking was worth it. She'd known pilots like this, and they often crashed. She calculated that Houston would think she was watching out the windows of the lander.

"Ostorozhna!"

The female Russian voice cut through Chad's reverie. Still, he stayed where he was, defiantly, and decided to take one more step forward, to just a few yards from the edge. The ground was angling away from him now.

The translator clarified for the room. "She said, 'Be careful.'"

Kaz pictured her watching from the distance, seeing Chad doing something dangerous. He had no idea yet as to how Chad was going to achieve the new military aim of disabling Lunokhod discreetly with the cosmonaut there as a witness. Calmly, he instructed, "Chad, as you're walking back, please describe for the geologists what you saw."

Enough, Chad thought, his face breaking into a triumphant smile. *No one has ever done that!* He retraced his steps, turning when he had enough room. Ignoring Svetlana, he grabbed the cart's handle and started towards *Bulldog*. He said, "At my closest approach I could just see deep enough to catch sight of sunlight on the inner wall of the hole. It looked smooth and curved."

Svetlana followed him, shaking her head. When would he have stopped? *I'm on the Moon with a crazy man.* As she walked, she felt the reassuring weight of the pistol moving in her leg pocket.

Both of them were focused on the traverse back towards *Bulldog*, immersed in thought. Neither looked back to notice Lunokhod, starting and stopping with successive commands, moving in 10-second increments.

Following them.

In Simferopol, Gabdul glanced worriedly at the clock. Thirty minutes until they lost signal. It was helpful to have footprints to follow, as the team didn't have to analyze each image as it came down before sending another command to move. He just verified he was on track, adjusted direction, rolled forward for 10 seconds and then stopped. Repeat.

He wanted to get to whatever the astronauts had been looking at before the radio link dropped out. To give him time to think about it and maybe pass on a request to them while they were still on the Moon.

Part of the problem of building a tough, compact rover was that the topmost camera didn't stick up very high. The Moon was small enough that the horizon dropped away rapidly, and he couldn't see very far into the distance. It was like driving at night with the headlights on low beams, and it made him uncomfortable when he had to hurry.

But Chelomei had ordered him to do it. And this was what he had trained for. His quick responses had helped the astronaut find the Ugol rock, and he'd even moved the magnetometer to show the other astronaut where to dig around for any more fragments. Decisiveness and finesse.

He jammed the stick forward again, counting *raz, dva, tree* in his head, and on up to ten, and then released, waiting for the refreshed image.

This one showed something odd, though. Only one set of footprints now, and a low darkness beyond them. Better to move with more caution. He decided on five seconds forward, not ten. He eased ahead on the stick, counted carefully and released.

He glanced up at the clock. Twenty minutes. Get a suite of images, and some scientific samples. Then they'd have to wait until the Earth brought them around again.

Until moonrise in Simferopol.

47

Le Monnier Crater

"Chad, we need you to check on the power to the TV camera, and then get the flag set up for the joint event with Washington and Moscow."

"Copy, Kaz." Chad glanced at Svetlana, who'd just arrived beside him at the lander. "You want me to bring the cosmonaut down the ladder first to make more room up there?"

Kaz looked at Gene. "We talked about it, Chad, and we'd prefer her to come down the ladder at the start of the joint event. So please leave her inside for now."

Chad shrugged. *People playing games.* "Copy."

He pointed at Svetlana and swung his finger around and up the ladder, towards the cockpit of *Bulldog*. She couldn't already be on the surface when he got the TV camera working again.

The interpreter's voice came into Svetlana's headset from Houston. "Lieutenant Gromova, the astronaut will be coming back up into the lander now to check on the TV system, and we'll have you come down to the surface to speak with Director Chelomei in about ten minutes."

Ah, that's why he's pointing.

"Ponyala," she said. She walked past Chad to climb the ladder, crawling on her hands and knees through the hatch.

Chad walked around the camera on its tripod, checking for loose connections. "Houston, all looks normal with the camera itself. I'm headed up the ladder now."

Svetlana stood and turned inside *Bulldog*, raising her gold visor and looking at the pulled TV circuit breaker. *Best to show ignorance,* she decided. She shuffled back and pressed into the dead body, making way as Chad crawled in and stood up.

He ran his fingers across the panels, quickly narrowing in on the black-and-white stripes of the protruding breaker. He turned deliberately, raised his visor and looked accusingly at her. She met his gaze steadily.

"Houston, I see the TV breaker is out. Did you see any overcurrents? My guess is the cosmonaut bumped it or snagged it somehow, being clumsy in here."

Kaz had already confirmed with the electrical back room. "No, Chad, no abnormal signatures, so we agree with you. You have permission for a reset."

"Copy, on my mark, three, two, one, mark." He pushed with his thumb and felt it click back into place.

Instant response. "Chad, we're seeing current flow and camera boot-up signal. Should have good video by the time you get back outside. We're about ten minutes from the Washington-Moscow event, if you can get the flag in place, please."

Five o'clock in Washington was 1:00 a.m. in Moscow. The lateness of the hour and the America-centric nature of the event had dissuaded any politicians from traveling from the Kremlin to TsUP. They'd delegated the task to Chelomei, and to the long-serving Soviet ambassador in Washington, Anatoly Dobrynin.

That suited Dobrynin fine. The press blackout meant that only a sanitized version of events would be made public, and even that wouldn't be released until after splashdown. He'd talked at length via secure phone with Andropov, the KGB head, and had clear direction from Brezhnev. They would create a triumphant way to present this in future. For now, they just needed a few key images and video recordings from the Moon.

And the always necessary calm of diplomacy.

Waiting for Dobrynin in the Oval Office was Henry Kissinger. The two had worked back-channel issues on behalf of their bosses for years together, and today was no different—protect national interests, maintain their deep, respectful friendship and make Nixon and Brezhnev look good.

"Anatoly Fyodorovich," Kissinger rumbled, his warmth genuine. "It is a pleasure to see you, especially on such an historic occasion."

Nixon got up from behind his broad, polished desk to greet the ambassador.

Dobrynin bowed his head with respect. "Mr. President, Mr. Kissinger, it is an honor to be invited here today." He'd been the ambassador since the Cuban Missile Crisis, and his Russian-accented English was flawless. He shook both men's hands, and Nixon waved him to sit in the gold chair at the corner of his desk. Kissinger took his accustomed place at the other corner.

The Oval Office had a formal, masculine feel. Nixon had hated the pale, limpid drapes that his predecessor, Johnson, had favored, and had replaced them with thick gold brocade curtains that matched his new deep-blue carpeting. Seated again in his black leather chair, he was flanked by US and Presidential flags, with a bust of Lincoln and a large photo of his family on the window table behind him. He preferred a clean desk. All that was in front of him was a neat briefing book, a penholder, his daily calendar and a black phone. One of its small lower buttons was blinking.

As the men chatted comfortably, Haldeman came through a side door, nodded at Dobrynin and walked around behind Nixon. He pushed the blinking button and adjusted the volume on the small speaker box. He'd wheeled a television in earlier, and he turned it on, getting the feed linked through from NASA. The image showed an astronaut standing on the Moon, flanked by the lunar lander on one side and the Stars and Stripes on the other. Haldeman leaned close and spoke in Nixon's ear, pointing to some writing in the briefing book. Nixon nodded, and Haldeman stepped back.

Kaz's voice came through the squawk box. "White House and Moscow Mission Control, this is Houston. Stand by for the event."

Kissinger and Dobrynin shifted in their chairs to be able to see the TV screen.

In Moscow, Chelomei checked his watch.

"Apollo 18, Houston, voice check."

Chad was facing the camera, his gold visor up so his face was visible, squinting in the bright sunlight. "18 has you loud and clear, Houston."

Kaz looked at the script the White House had sent. Nixon first.

"Mr. President, the comm is yours."

Nixon checked his briefing book. "Major Miller, this is President Nixon, your Commander in Chief. I can't tell you how proud I am, as an American, to be speaking with you, there on the Moon. Especially with the colors of the US flag so clear and bright next to you."

Chad's voice was scratchy through all the connections. "Mr. President, I am honored by the privilege of speaking with you, sir."

Nixon continued. "Chad, I know this mission you are commanding has been arduous, and has involved regrettable loss of life. Such is the cost of voyaging into the unknown. The nation and I offer you both our condolences and our gratitude as you work in the name of scientific discovery, and of peace."

Haldeman had written the words in consultation with Kissinger, knowing the Soviets would be listening.

"I am very pleased that we have found a way to use space exploration not just for technical human understanding, but also now for international cooperation. The world needs symbols of how we can work together, and you and NASA are leading the way. I have some Soviet representatives on the line who are eagerly looking forward to speaking with one of their own, there with you." He double-checked his script. "On their behalf I invite you now to welcome Senior Lieutenant Gromova, a female cosmonaut, to descend from the American lander onto the surface of the Moon."

In Moscow, Chelomei had been waiting for this moment. He spoke urgently via the squawk box to Gabdul, poised at his console in Simferopol, 1,200 kilometers to the south. "Now!"

Gabdul slammed his control stick forward and held it. Not the time for caution.

In Houston, the interpreter next to Kaz called for Svetlana to exit the lander. Her white form came into view on the screen as she smoothly backed down the rungs. She turned and strode over to stand on the opposite side of Chad from the flag. She glanced at him and raised her visor to match.

Nixon nodded at Dobrynin, who quietly said, "Mr. President, as this is so important a day for my country, with your permission I'm going to speak to the cosmonaut in Russian, and then in English."

Perfect, Haldeman thought, watching Nixon nod. *No doubt as to who is in charge.*

Behind the astronauts, a silver shape was slowly entering camera range. Kaz spotted it and spoke rapidly. "FLIGHT, their rover's approaching *Bulldog*!"

Gene Kranz's jaw was thrust forward, his eyes narrow. "I see it, CAPCOM." The Soviets were doing this on purpose. His mind clicked through possible dangers and potential reactions.

Dobrynin turned towards the screen and raised his voice for the speakerphone.

"Major Svetlana Yevgenyevna Gromova, this is Ambassador Dobrynin. I bring you the greatest of congratulations and honors from General Secretary Leonid Brezhnev, supreme leader of the Soviet Union. Your sacrifices, skills and accomplishments are already legendary, and will be a permanent source of pride for all of history. We salute you—the first Soviet citizen to walk on the Moon."

Major? I just got promoted two ranks. She responded formally.

"Thank you, Ambassador. I am deeply honored and forever grateful to be the fortunate first Soviet to be here, in this rare place, today."

In Simferopol, Gabdul had been counting aloud. As he hit "treedsit-shest," thirty-six, he released the hand controller. At full speed the rover should have traveled 20 meters. He looked to the screen for the updated still image, and said a quick prayer.

Dobrynin was still speaking. "Secretary Brezhnev asked me specifically to say he is greatly looking forward to welcoming you to the Kremlin on your safe return."

"Thank you, Ambassador," Svetlana said once more.

Dobrynin turned to Nixon. Neither man had been paying enough attention to the TV screen to notice the silver vehicle in the background. Haldeman had, though. He strode up closer to the television, frowning.

The Ambassador noticed Haldeman, but he was used to staying on topic while underlings dealt with distractions. "Mr. President, our nation celebrates with you in this shared cooperation, as we lead the world in space exploration. The support team in Moscow would also like to say a few words to Major Gromova."

Lunokhod was now squarely in the center of the TV image.

There were several clicking sounds as the phone lines were patched through, and then Chelomei's voice came clearly through the static. The Houston interpreter translated quickly as they spoke.

"Cosmonaut Major Gromova, this is Director Chelomei in TsUP. We salute your bravery, our first human explorer of the Moon, a true Soviet pathfinder and example to us all."

"Thank you, Tovarisch Director."

Haldeman turned to face the president. "Sir, they've driven their rover into the picture." Disgust at having been taken advantage of was thick in his voice. The three men around the desk leaned closer to the screen to see.

Chelomei delivered his coup de grace. "With your historic landing at this Soviet discovery site, with Lunokhod, which has already been exploring for three months, directly behind you, your name will forever join the ranks of Gagarin, Tereshkova and Leonov. Pozdravlyayem!"

Chad whipped around to look, startled to see Lunokhod now just 15 feet away, centered behind them. Svetlana had turned as well, and nodded at the tactic. *Smart move.*

She spoke in response. "It is with great pride that I follow such heroes of the Soviet Union, and in the tracks of Lunokhod. I thank you and every member of the support team, Director Chelomei. It is a great honor to be here on behalf of you all."

There was a pause. Kaz sensed the uncertainty as to who would speak next and stepped in. "Mr. President, back to you, sir."

Haldeman stepped forward quickly and whispered in Nixon's ear.

The President decided to ignore the rover. People were what mattered, not machinery. "The United States adds their congratulations, Major Gromova, on your historic human achievement. Major Miller, I'd personally like to thank you for skilfully piloting your ship to the surface and bringing another nation to the new world of the Moon."

Leave no doubt as to who did what.

"America wishes you and your crew a successful completion of tasks on the surface and a safe return home to Earth. We'll see you soon here at the White House."

"Thank you, Mr. President," Chad responded. "I look forward to it."

Kaz counted to five in case anyone had last things to say. Radio silence.

"Thank you, Mr. President, Ambassador Dobrynin and Director Chelomei. Apollo 18, Houston adds their congratulations, and that concludes the event."

In the Oval Office, Kissinger shook Dobrynin's hand, saying, "I'm certain you would have told us if you'd known they were going to drive the rover into view, Anatoly Fyodorovich." The men had many battles left yet to fight together. Not worth magnifying this one.

Dobrynin recognized the opening and spoke smoothly but loudly enough for Nixon to hear as well. "Yes, my apologies for the overzealous driving of our rover team. Even though they stayed at a safe distance, it seems they wanted some of the spotlight." He nodded to the president as he moved towards the door. "Secretary Brezhnev and I thank you again for the historic opportunity."

Nixon nodded back, but did not offer to shake the Ambassador's hand. He truly detested surprises.

In Moscow, despite the long day and the late hour, Chelomei wore an uncharacteristic smile, the seldom-used muscles squeezing his tired eyes nearly closed. It had worked!

His rocket, his rover, his ingenuity and tenacity had shown the Americans—the entire world—the true extent of Soviet capability. He had put a cosmonaut on the Moon. And a woman, something the Americans had never done! Forever there, recorded next to Soviet technology the Americans couldn't match, for all to see. A triumphant day for the Soviet Union!

He watched as the timer clicked over, signaling the relentless turn of the Earth's face away from the Moon and the end of the day's communications through his giant antenna in the Crimea. He nodded at the flight director, thanking him, and turned, walking out of TsUP.

As his steps echoed in the long hallway back to his office, he focused his weary thoughts forward. Lunokhod had discovered something valuable on the Moon, and he, Vladimir Chelomei, had found a way to get the Americans to unknowingly carry it back to Earth.

Still many problems to overcome. But he had more ideas up his sleeve.

With the press event over, Al Shepard walked up to Kaz's console in Mission Control and spoke quietly. "Got a minute?" He tipped his head towards the exit.

Kaz temporarily handed over to the evening shift CAPCOM, who had arrived early. He followed the Chief Astronaut to an empty briefing room. Al came straight to the point.

"How well do you know Chad?"

Kaz shrugged. He'd been expecting this. "We met during Test Pilot School nearly a decade ago, and then crossed paths again during MOL selection and training. But he's not really my kind of guy, and we didn't socialize much."

Al nodded slowly. The creases were deeply shadowed down both sides of his mouth. "He ever tell you anything about his childhood?"

Kaz looked away and down, recalling what he knew. "Not much. He's a Wisconsin redneck farm boy, went to the State U, I think, ROTC directly into the Air Force, pretty standard. First time I met his folks was at the launch, and they seemed just what you'd expect. No brothers or sisters. Chad never married, and I've never met a girlfriend. Bit of a loner." Kaz paused for a moment, then said, "Now that you ask, Al, I don't really know him that well at all."

"Yeah, me neither." Al looked into Kaz's good eye. "You know if he speaks any other languages?"

"I don't think so. Chad's an all-American type. Very Wisconsin, not too . . . nuanced, if you know what I mean."

Al nodded again. "One other question—any idea about his finances?"

Kaz shook his head. "He never seemed to buy anything flashy, and he paid for the round when it was his turn. I never heard him talk about money." As liaison, Kaz had gathered the necessary legal paperwork from all three crewmembers. "The will that he turned in before flight was just the standard fill-in-the-blanks military form, dead simple. He left everything to his folks."

Kaz decided to ask a question back. "Is there anything you know that will affect how I should be thinking for the rest of the flight?"

Al chewed his inner lip. "It's partly why I didn't ask Gene or the doc to join us. Crew concerns are *mine* to protect and solve, and the last thing I want to do is raise a red flag that distracts everyone from the mission. But the sheriff's investigation has brought a few things to light about Chad. Nothing conclusive yet, but we may well need to let some other folks in on the information soon. For now, I want you to watch what's happening with Apollo 18 extra closely."

Kaz nodded, suddenly thinking about the double clicks on the radio.

As Al turned to head back to Mission Control, Kaz asked him to wait. The recent discovery on the Moon had made him think of something else, and he quickly outlined his plan.

Al blinked several times, considering, and then nodded decisively. "Good idea, Kaz. Just need to call Vice Chief Mo Weisner, get his blessing from the Joint Chiefs. I'll do that, and you talk to FLIGHT and the EVA team."

48

Le Monnier Crater

As Chad climbed *Bulldog's* ladder, moving the two bags of geology samples up into the cabin, the conversation with the White House was playing over and over in his head. The president of the United States had called him by his first name and invited him to the White House! *A long way from the Wisconsin farm. Even farther from Berlin.* So what if the Soviets had driven their rover into the shot. Having it nearby just gave him more opportunity to disable it, and then they could blame any damage on the rocket blast at liftoff. *Idiots.* The Russians had played right into his hands.

He put the rock he'd retrieved from under Lunokhod by itself in a bag normally used for in-cabin tools, clipped into place under the computer entry panel. No one but him knew it was there. Then he moved the two duffels to the racks in the back, transferring the samples into hard-sided vacuum-sealed sample containers. He wedged the bolt cutters inside one of the empty duffels, happy that they just fit. He zipped the bag closed, checked that the cosmonaut was clear below and chucked it out onto the surface.

Now for Luke, and the new plan.

Houston had offered some suggestions for getting the body down to the surface, but Chad had decided to keep it simple. In the lighter Soviet suit, Luke only weighed 30 pounds on the Moon. Like picking up a medium-sized dog. No sweat.

But he didn't want Houston to watch.

He shifted the body forward along the floor until his feet were sticking out through the hatch, then reached up and pulled the TV circuit breaker. He bent and pushed Luke through, tucking the arms in and watching as the body slipped over the edge and fell, guided somewhat by the ladder. He quickly climbed down himself, finding Luke doubled over in a heap at the base. Svetlana watched as he straightened the body out and then climbed the ladder again, pushing the breaker back in.

Gene Kranz frowned as the TV image dropped out again. He waited for the team to diagnose the problem and tell him about it, and was about to push the button to ask, when the camera signal came back. As the image reappeared, he could see two suited figures standing beside a large bag on the ground. It took him a few seconds to recognize it as Luke's body, in the Soviet suit.

"FLIGHT, INCO, we had another TV camera dropout, but you can see it's back now. All indications normal, no action recommended."

"Copy, INCO, glad it didn't happen during the event with the President."

Kaz, seated at the console, quietly guessed what had actually happened. In Chad's place, he wouldn't have wanted a video record of the body tumbling down the ladder either.

Surprised, Svetlana had watched the astronaut push the body in her old spacesuit through the hatch, and had stayed clear as it had tumbled in slow motion down the ladder. Maybe Americans were less prissy than she'd thought.

Chad was now beckoning her towards the body. She glanced up at the Earth; the Soviet Union had rotated out of view.

She was on her own. *Might as well help.*

She joined him, and together they reached underneath the body, lifting, shuffling sideways and centering it crossways, face up, on the handcart.

Chad tapped on Svetlana's suit and pointed to Luke's feet, dangling almost to the ground. He motioned her to grab them, and walked around to the handle. He lifted it in one hand, glanced back and started walking. Past Lunokhod.

Towards the hole. Where the Americans now wanted their dead astronaut buried.

Standing by the door of Mission Control, the Navy officer's dark-blue dress uniform stood out, the heavy brass buttons glinting in the fluorescent light. His escort waited until the Flight Director waved them in, and then walked him up to Kaz at the CAPCOM console.

"Commander Zemeckis, this is Navy Chaplain Lieutenant Parham, serving with the Galveston Coast Guard." Duty complete, the escort nodded, turned and retreated.

The chaplain smiled apologetically, holding his white flattop hat under his arm. "Lieutenant junior grade, actually, sir," pointing at the thick and thin bars with the stylized cross on his sleeve.

Kaz smiled an acknowledgment. "That's okay, I'm only a lieutenant commander. And call me Kaz. Thanks for coming on short notice. Did they brief you on what we're doing?"

Parham nodded. "I'm honored to assist." JW had rolled an extra chair over from the SURGEON console for him, and Kaz waved for the chaplain to sit, plugging in a headset for him.

Kaz looked at the clock and the TV image of the two suited figures receding into the distance. "We'll get started in a couple minutes. We'd like you to keep it short, please, but by the book."

The chaplain nodded again, pulling folded papers from his breast pocket and smoothing them on the console. "Understood."

"Houston, we're almost at the rim, will get set up." Chad's voice sounded labored in their headsets. Wheeling the suited body had been more cumbersome than he'd expected, and they'd had to stop a few times to recenter it on the cart.

"Copy, Chad, let us know when you're ready." INCO zoomed the TV camera in as far as it would go; they could just see the two small, toy-like figures moving against the horizon.

Chad set the handle down, letting the cart's two front legs stabilize the weight, balanced just at the point where the slope steepened towards the pit. He reached into one of the cart's stowage bins and retrieved a thick white bundle with two heavy locking hooks. He attached one to a fabric tether ring on the Russian suit's hip, and the other to the attachment bracket on the front of his own suit. Reaching under the body, he pulled out the flag and unrolled it, laying it across Luke's chest. He leaned left and right, looking at the slope and visualizing his actions.

"Houston, Luke's in position, and we're ready."

Kaz gestured to the chaplain and they stood together, the rest of Mission Control following suit. The comm loops went quiet.

Kaz pressed his mic button and spoke, his voice reaching into all back rooms, and to Chad and Svetlana on the Moon. The orbiting *Pursuit* ship had just reappeared from around the far side, and Michael was quiet and listening as well.

"All hands bury the dead." The traditional call for ships to stop engines, and to lower flags to half-mast.

Chaplain Parham took his cue and read from Scripture. "I am the resurrection and the life, saith the Lord: he that believeth in me, though he were dead, yet shall he live: and whosoever liveth and believeth in me shall never die."

He paused and looked up at the TV image of the lonely figures on the Moon. He'd decided to change the traditional prayer's words slightly.

"We therefore commit Captain Luke Hemming's body to the depths of space, to be turned into corruption, looking for the resurrection of the body, when the Universe shall give up her dead, and the life of worlds to come, through our Lord Jesus Christ. Who at his coming shall change our vile body, that it may be like his glorious body, according to the mighty working, whereby he is able to subdue all things to himself."

His quiet "Amen" was echoed by voices throughout Mission Control, and 240,000 miles away by Chad and Michael. Svetlana silently mouthed her own amen, thinking of her crewmate, Andrei Mitkov, his body all alone, orbiting the world next to Almaz.

Kaz spoke as if on parade. "Atten—shun." He paused to give the moment its significance, then said, "Chad, you can commit Luke's body to the deep."

Chad lifted the flag off the body, handed it to Svetlana and with a quick two-handed motion tipped the cart abruptly to push Luke towards the pit, careful to keep his tethered line clear. The body arced several feet through the vacuum and fell to the surface halfway to the rim, rolling to a stop. Chad followed his previous footsteps out towards the promontory, unclipping the line from his suit, holding it clear in both hands. He turned to get good leverage and gave a sharp upwards tug. The body lifted and tumbled several more feet down the slope and stopped just short of the edge.

Chad eyed the footing and the angles, and walked back to the cart. He took two tethers out of a pocket, clipped them together lengthwise and attached one end to himself. He turned and quickly clipped the other end to the metal loop on Svetlana's suit. He beckoned for her to follow and started walking back towards the edge.

She held her ground, jerking him to a stop. She raised her visor and shook her head vehemently no.

Chad grabbed the tether in both hands and yanked, pulling her off balance, making her stumble towards him. He followed his tracks, tugging her onward to keep her from getting her feet set. She deliberately took a large hopping step and landed with one foot forward, the other behind her for stability, and stopped moving.

How crazy is he? She shook her head at him again. *Bad enough that he falls into the pit, but to drag me too?*

Chad looked at her, and again at Luke, lying in the dirt just beyond his reach. He lunged towards her, both hands up as if to strike, and as she took a reflexive step back, he dug in a foot and reversed direction, hard. Even though they were light in the lunar gravity, mass was still mass. The tether between them pulled taut, and she stumbled two more steps towards the hole before she caught herself.

It was far enough. He bent and picked up the line to the body, wrapping it around the thickness of his left glove so it wouldn't slip. He braced his feet, stabilized by the tight tether to Svetlana.

He saw her glancing at the hook releases and began counting backwards in Russian to unnerve her. "Tree, dva, udeen, nul!" He twisted and pulled with all his strength.

Luke's body jerked up off the surface and flew the remaining short distance towards the hole's edge, bouncing once and landing in a sitting position right at the rim. The arms continued the motion, flailing towards the yawning darkness. Slowly the body overbalanced, toppling towards the pit, accelerating as it leaned. Suddenly it was gone, leaving a fresh dark streak in the dirt where it had disturbed an eternity of meteorite dust.

But Chad had misjudged his balance. As he'd heaved, one foot had slipped out from under him. He fell on his side and bounced twice down the slope. The bulk of his suit kicked up a small cloud of dust, and the regolith shifted with him, pushed downhill for the first time in millennia. A small one-man landslide, momentarily jerked to a stop by the countering pull of the linked tethers to Svetlana.

Out of sight over the rim, Luke's body accelerated down slowly, free-falling in the one-sixth gravity. On Earth, after one second, it would have already dropped 16 feet, well out of sight, but on the Moon it had gone less than 3. Chad's tug, combined with his fall down the slope, had put an extra 6 feet of slack in the line.

Newton's laws of motion were universal. In 1.5 seconds, the slack was fully taken up by Luke's falling body. The line, still wrapped around Chad's hand, snapped straight and pulled tight.

Chad was just sorting out how he was going to climb back up the slope when the yank on the line pulled his left arm straight. He opened and spun his hand wildly, relieved to see the line unravel and whip clear, accelerate down the slope and with a flip of the end, disappear from sight.

But the damage was done. The unexpected jolt had pulsed through the tether and jerked Svetlana forward, and now she was scrabbling to get her feet back under her in the bulky, ill-fitting suit.

In Houston, Kaz was staring intently, trying to figure out what was happening to the small figures on the screen. Luke was no longer on the cart, but one of the suits was out of sight. He'd heard someone — Chad? — saying what sounded like a countdown, but in Russian. With the minister standing next to him, he needed to be respectful. *But what the fuck is going on?*

"Durok!" Svetlana grunted. Idiot! She twisted and planted her left foot into the sloping dirt, leaning away hard to counter the tether's pull. Chad was on his back, arms and legs splayed to try to stabilize. The shards of dust, rock and lunar sand under him caught and held in their new position at the pit's rim.

Motion stopped.

Just beyond the edge, the body accelerated as it fell, the cord snaking, into the shadowed darkness. In absolute silence, with no air friction to slow it, the fall took 11 seconds. Luke's body landed near the center of the pile of rubble that had fallen when the roof of the hole had caved in; at impact, his lifeless form was going 40 miles per hour, straight down. It bounced high once, turning, and then landed forever on its back, the Yastreb suit's tough plastic visor unbroken. Luke's sightless eyes stared upwards towards the small skylight in the blackness, shining with the eternity of the stars.

Chad pushed carefully with his left hand, rolling himself uphill onto his side. He dug his right shoulder in and bent his knees as far as the suit would allow. It gave a bit of slack in the tether, and Svetlana eased back to hold the tension.

Moving cautiously, Chad swung his left arm over and got onto his hands and knees. He tipped his head back hard inside the helmet and was just able to see the taut tether leading away towards the cosmonaut. Experimenting, he moved his left leg and right arm forward, and found the leverage to pry himself slightly up the hill. With the extra pulling from Svetlana, it worked. He shifted his weight and moved the other arm/leg, repeating the process, gaining a few more inches. A clumsy sniper crawl wearing a pressure suit.

Frowning, Kaz ran out of patience. "Chad, Houston, how's it going?"

Straining, Chad spoke. "Doing okay, Houston, just tripped and fell. Luke is on his way." As he alligatored his way up the slope, Svetlana moved back, keeping the line taut.

Kaz nodded at the chaplain to give the final benediction, and bowed his head.

"O God, by whose mercy the faithful departed find rest, send your holy Angel to watch over this distant grave," the chaplain said. "Through Christ our Lord. Amen."

Ceremony complete, Kaz shook hands with Parham and thanked him. The chaplain turned to shake hands with Gene Kranz and the doctor, and carefully walked down the steps and out the door.

Kaz squinted again at the front screen, seeing one figure standing and the other rocking to get up off their hands and knees.

"Apollo 18, the final step is the folding of the flag. Per protocol request from the Joint Chiefs, we'll be asking you to bring it back with you to be given to Luke's parents."

Chad shifted forward onto his hands, and then abruptly moved his weight back, bouncing to his feet, staggering a couple steps as he regained his balance. Svetlana unclipped the tether from her suit and threw it dismissively towards him, then turned her back.

The flag was lying where she'd dropped it. Chad coiled and stowed the tethers, picked up the flag and held it high as he folded it so the TV camera could see.

No need for them to know what just happened.

"Houston, we lowered Luke's body carefully over the edge and into the deep. I've folded his flag and am stowing it now."

"Copy, Chad, thanks. Geology would like you both to retrieve as many samples from around the hole as possible, to verify their theories on how it formed. Please take multiple images too." Kaz turned to the interpreter, who repeated the plan for Svetlana.

"Roger, Houston, in work." Chad looked down at the camera mounted on his chest, glad to see it was still in place, and brushed the dirt off. He handed the cosmonaut a soil collection bag and a scoop, and started his narration.

"The soil around the hole looks quite similar to the surrounding terrain, with no visible ejecta or ridges indicating impact." He took the rake and starting filling a bag, turning and clicking pictures as he moved. Collecting the rocks reminded him of being a kid on the farm, picking the stones the winter's frost had brought to the surface and moving them to the fencerows. *Less back-breaking on the Moon, though.*

As he worked, he realized that after this was done, there was only one task remaining on the surface.

He had to admit the sudden tumble towards the pit had startled him. But he'd anticipated it might happen, hooking the linked tether to the woman just in case. His own ingenuity had saved the day, as usual. Houston hadn't had any real plan to get Luke's body into the pit; they'd all counted on him to solve it. And, as usual, he had.

He glanced at *Bulldog* and the Soviet rover, and then at the cosmonaut, filling a bag with her scoop. He looked up to the Earth—Russia had rotated out of sight—and glanced at his wristwatch, strapped around the bulk of his pressurized sleeve. *Still lots of time.*

Time for him to do what they'd really come for.

49

Le Monnier Crater

The Soviet engineers had built Lunokhod to survive the Moon's temperature extremes. All the important and sensitive gear was protected like vital organs, safely nestled within the pressurized, insulated magnesium-alloy body. During the glaring sunlight of lunar day, a small fan blew cooling air up under a flat radiator at the top. With the protective lid and solar array pivoted open, the excess heat was shed to space. At nightfall, the lid swung closed over the radiator to keep the heat within, like a flower closing its petals. Inside, a small lump of radioactive polonium-210 provided warmth, the way a hot-water bottle warmed a bed. Awaiting the dawn.

Engineers at the RAND Corporation in Santa Monica had prepared a summary of Lunokhod systems that the DoD had analyzed for vulnerabilities. As Chad walked back towards *Bulldog*, trailing the handcart laden with bagged samples, he weighed the options they'd given him for disabling it. But really, it was up to him to figure it out. With a damned female cosmonaut watching over his shoulder.

While she'd been collecting the samples near the hole, he'd taken the bolt cutters out of the bag and strapped them down out of sight. Now, eyeing Lunokhod, another idea for disabling it occurred to him.

He turned around and waved at the cosmonaut. When he got her attention, he pointed up the ladder into *Bulldog*. He then motioned with both hands as if he was lifting the bag of rocks.

Svetlana considered. Helping to collect samples had made sense, because it gave her practical scientific experience to bring back to the cosmonaut program. She also figured that if she helped, the Soviet Union would have some leverage to demand a share of the lunar rocks and dirt.

Now he was asking her to help get them up the ladder. She shrugged. *Might as well.* She climbed, turned and faced him, reaching down as far as she could. As he hoisted the bulging bag up, she lunged for the straps, caught one and lifted.

Heavy, even here. She swung it back and forth, higher and higher, like a pendulum, and gave a good heave to get it up onto the platform. Climbing up the rungs, she pushed the sliding bag through the hatch and turned to look back at the astronaut. He pointed for her to enter, and then at himself, indicating he would follow.

In Houston, Kaz spoke. "*Bulldog*, we see you transferring the samples. We have about an hour max left on the surface, and show you doing well to finish on time." He had the interpreter translate. Svetlana saw that Chad was climbing the ladder behind her, so she turned and crawled through the hatch.

She pushed the bag all the way to the back and stood, lifting it with both hands onto the raised platform. She felt the astronaut bump into her from behind, and moved all the way up beside the bag. He pointed to a hard-sided, suitcase-like container in the narrow space.

He spoke evenly. "Houston, can you have the interpreter tell the cosmonaut to transfer the samples into the case while I do final button-up outside?" Svetlana listened to the Russian instructions, looked at the confined working quarters and nodded her acceptance. It would also give her a quick chance to look for the Lunokhod rock. She picked up the bag and wedged it into place as Chad turned to exit.

On the front screen in Mission Control, for the third time, the TV image went blank.

Chad backed out and down the ladder and walked to the handcart, glancing up at *Bulldog*'s windows. He wheeled it a few feet around the corner, so he was out of sight in case she took time to watch him, and released the bungee holding the bolt cutters. He also grabbed the scoop tool. With one last glance up the ladder and at the unpowered TV camera, he loped quickly towards Lunokhod.

The recommendations from the military brass had been simple: don't cut any cable that might be carrying high voltage, but be sure to permanently kill the ability of the rover to function.

He decided to go with the simplest option first, the one he'd thought of while walking back to *Bulldog*. He bent and filled the scoop with the fine dust of the top surface layer and carefully poured it onto the flat of the rover's radiator. He was pleased to see how well it matched the color of the dust that had collected already, and added another scoopful, smoothing it evenly with his hand.

He took a pace back to survey his work. The thick layer of dust would stop the radiator from functioning properly, trapping the heat inside. With the Sun beating down and nowhere for the heat to go, the interior electronic components would cook. Hard to tell how fast, but a good first step. And when he turned the TV back on, nobody would be able to tell he'd done anything.

He stepped around the front of Lunokhod. There were thin, telescoping metal rods, like whiskers, slanting down from each of the four corners. *Too small for high-data transmission*, he reasoned, and left them alone. No sense dulling the bolt cutters on those.

He spotted several electronic devices, flush-mounted in multiple locations, and looked closely at each. He decided they were scientific sensors and discounted them as targets. *Looks like the intel was pretty accurate.*

Mounted high and clear on the front was a cone-shaped device, like a small silver Christmas tree. Beside it, pointing towards Earth, was a long, scalloped cylinder, resembling a kebab loaded with marsh-mallows. *Omni and high-gain communications antennas*, he recognized. He traced the wires leading to them, finding a location where he could slip the cutters under a protruding loop. He dropped the scoop and raised the bolt cutters, positioning his suited arms for leverage.

"Stop!" a voice loudly commanded. And then, "Smotri!" Look at me!

He turned. Standing between him and *Bulldog* was the cosmonaut. Glinting darkly in her hand was the distinctive angular black barrel of a snub-nosed pistol, pointed at him. The fatness of her gloved finger was wedged inside the guard, on the trigger.

"Nyet!" she said, pronouncing every letter.

His first thought was, *Where the hell did she get a pistol?*

His second was, *No way will she shoot me.* She didn't know how to fly *Bulldog*. To injure or kill him would be to sign her own death warrant. He raised his gold visor so she could see his face. Staring straight at her, he shook his head, a mocking smile spreading across his lips.

Kaz heard the urgent words from Svetlana and was puzzled when Chad didn't answer. The interpreter quickly translated what she'd said, but it didn't help him figure out what was going on. The lack of TV coverage didn't help. He gave it several seconds and then called.

"18, Houston, did you call?"

Svetlana took two paces forward, aimed carefully and pulled the trigger.

The Makarov Pistol was a proven Soviet design, standard military issue, and had been included in the Almaz return capsule's survival pack in case of off-target landings. It was modeled on the German Walther PP, but it was heavier, all steel, ruggedized with fewer moving parts for simplicity. As Svetlana pulled the trigger, the connecting rod released the spring-loaded hammer, driving the pointed firing pin hard into the center of the 9.27 mm cartridge loaded in the chamber. The impact ignited the mercury fulminate primer, sending a shower of sparks into the gunpowder, explosively burning it, the expanding gases pushing the round-nosed steel bullet up the short, rifled barrel. As it exited at the tip, the small, six-gram metal-jacketed projectile was traveling at just under 1,000 feet per second.

The explosion pushed the sliding bolt against a blowback spring, ejecting the empty casing and allowing the eight-round magazine inside the pistol's handle to push a fresh bullet up into the chamber. The heavy spring yanked the bolt forward, and the new round snicked home into place, ready for a second shot. Svetlana had trained on the firing range in Star City, and had squeezed her gloved fist tightly against the recoil. The gun kicked up, but by the time the new round was in the barrel, she was lowering it to aim again.

The small ejected empty steel casing arced high to Svetlana's right and behind her, glinting in the sunlight as it tumbled, finally raising a small cloud of dust as it hit the surface 120 feet away.

Chad saw the muzzle flash and instinctively jerked back. The bullet flashed past him, falling slowly in the light gravity with no air to slow it, eventually plowing a short furrow and creating a small new crater 1,300 feet behind him.

Svetlana had intended to miss. She wanted him to see that she was willing to shoot—to let him know that the pistol worked.

"Seriozna," she said, her voice flat. I'm serious.

JW spoke on the Mission Control internal loop. "FLIGHT, SURGEON, we just saw a big jump in Chad's heart rate."

Kaz nodded, and asked again, "18, did you call?"

Chad's thoughts were reeling. *Holy shit! That bullet barely missed!* He stayed still to reassure her, thinking fast, weighing the options. He couldn't tell Houston what was going on: there were too many secrets, and some of them the cosmonaut knew. He forced his voice to sound normal. "Hey, Houston, we're just working on something here. Disregard."

Kaz looked across at JW, who shrugged.

Svetlana waved twice with the pistol, gesturing for Chad to move away from Lunokhod, then aimed again at his head. She watched him step clear and decided it was time for her to take control.

Through the interpreter, she said, "Houston, this is Major Gromova. The lunar soil samples are stowed in their carrying case, and the astronaut and I are both back outside. How can I best help complete the moonwalk?" She beckoned with her free hand, pointing for Chad to hand her the bolt cutters.

Kaz turned to talk directly to Gene Kranz. "FLIGHT, I don't know if Chad disabled Lunokhod or not, and I'm still not sure how much English the cosmonaut understands."

Gene rubbed his hand over the back of his head, feeling the brush cut. "He should have had enough time while she was inside, and we need to keep deniability." He rubbed harder, then said, "He knows the priorities. Let's let him choose his moment."

Kaz nodded, and pushed his mic button. "Major Gromova, Houston, we copy, and will have tasks for you shortly." He held up a finger so the interpreter wouldn't translate what he said next. "Chad, just a reminder to complete mission priorities, and we're standing by with clean-up items when you're ready." *Innocuous enough.*

"Copy," Chad responded, watching the cosmonaut intently, trying to guess her mental state. She still had her gold visor down, which made the steady, aimed pistol seem more menacing. She gestured with her free hand again, more insistently.

Fine. There's still time.

He threw the cutters at her feet, warily, and walked past her. She bent awkwardly to pick them up, still aiming the pistol. As soon as she had them securely in hand, she reached down and slid the gun into her leg pocket.

Chad climbed the ladder to push the TV circuit breaker back in. "Houston, all priorities are complete, and I'm ready to start final cleanup."

She'll have to set those cutters down at some point. And she can't watch me the whole time.

Svolich! She shook her head, watching him climb the ladder. You bastard! Giving her a menial task while he went outside to damage Lunokhod—the arrogance!

She looked at the bolt cutters in her hand. Quickly she walked out of sight of the windows and dug in hard with her heel in an area of kicked-up soil to make a small trench. She dropped the cutters in and kicked loose dirt over top, stomping repeatedly across the area to camouflage it. She stepped back to look; just tracks in the dust, the same as those all around the lander. She glanced back at the ladder; Chad still hadn't descended.

She walked to the front of Lunokhod and bent to look closely at the area Chad had been studying. She traced the antenna wires carefully, seeing nothing disturbed or dangling. She stepped back and did one full circuit, checking the side power cables and wheels for damage, seeing none. He hadn't had that long; she'd hurried down the ladder when she'd spotted him by the rover, and had stopped him in the act.

She saw a scoop lying next to Lunokhod, and she grabbed it and walked back towards *Bulldog*, satisfied for now. But she'd have to remain vigilant. He'd try again, no doubt.

She weighed what she could do. Having watched him fly and land the LM, she was certain she couldn't operate it herself, even with verbal instruction from Houston. If he died, she died.

Was protecting Lunokhod worth her life? She was a soldier, and had sworn fealty to the Soviet Air Forces. Her childhood heroines, Lydia Litvyak and Yekaterina Budanova, both Great Patriotic War fighter aces, had died in battle. *How is this any different?* She looked around at the barren landscape and the low, rolling hills, the empty desolation. *But to die here?* They'd already retrieved the rock Moscow was interested in. Lunokhod had been exploring for three months already. *What would my death accomplish?*

He had come back outside and was stowing equipment. She scanned his spacesuit. Maybe she could damage his life-support backpack, which would force him to hurry inside the lander and connect to its umbilicals. Shooting the backpack might work, but it just as well might cut a vital line or rupture a pressure tank, or pass through and kill him instantly.

She looked up at the lander itself, seeking a vulnerability to exploit that would hasten their departure. *But what?* The legs and lower section had all been built just for landing and were here to stay; only the upper section would take off, and all its antennas and cables were far out of reach.

She thought back to the design of her own Yastreb spacesuit, which had an emergency oxygen tank to provide extra reserves in case the suit developed a leak. The American suit must have one too. Their engineers would have needed a solution to the same problem. But how to start a survivable leak in his suit? She looked at the scoop in her hand. Where could she find a sharp edge?

A Russian voice broke into her thoughts. "Major Gromova, Houston, we see you with the scoop and would like you to pass that to Major Miller to stow, please. And then we have some more actions, as requested, when you're ready."

"Ponyala, minutichkoo." Understood, just a minute.

He'd turned to face her, reaching a hand out for the scoop. She inspected the hoses on his chest as she passed it to him; they were a jumble of covered connectors. No way he'd let her get close enough to disconnect anything. She stepped back and told the interpreter to go ahead.

She was on the Moon with a man who had much to hide and who still had time to do damage.

5 8

Mission Control, Houston

Kaz rested his forehead in his left hand, his elbow propped on the console. He'd found that rubbing the outer edge of his left eye socket with the tip of his thumb helped ease the burning in his fake eye. He blinked several times to clear the grittiness; it had been a long day. They just needed to get the moonwalk cleaned up, the crew inside and the hatch closed. Then they could all take a break. Crew included.

He opened both eyes wide, like he was stretching them, and refocused, running his finger down the checklist items. There were only a few left.

"Chad, we just need you now to reposition the TV camera to a launch observation location, and then we should be good for the two of you to head inside."

"Copy, Kaz."

Chad turned, walked the length of the snaking white cable out to the TV camera and picked up its tripod. He backed up slowly until the cable was nearly taut, to give maximum clearance from the rocket blast. Looking down the lens at the LM and Lunokhod, he had a thought. He took several paces sideways, the cable dragging across the dust, ascribing an arc around *Bulldog*. He set the tripod down again and rechecked.

"Houston, that look okay to you?"

Kaz had been watching the camera bouncing wildly with the reposition. Now *Bulldog* was centered and Lunokhod was no longer in the frame, out of sight. No matter the suspicions swirling around Chad, the man was sharp.

"Looks good, 18, nice and square to watch your liftoff. Suggest one last look-around for any loose items, and then we think you're done on the surface."

"Wilco."

Chad started back. Svetlana was facing him by the base of the ladder. *Where did she hide the bolt cutters?* He'd looked everywhere during the close-out, even into the distance in case she'd thrown them. *Sneaky bitch!* It left him with only one option.

He turned abruptly, taking long, hopping strides towards Lunokhod. He'd looked at the angles; no way she could physically intercept him in time. And she wouldn't actually shoot him. It'd be sealing her own death warrant. Without him, she'd die badly, slowly suffocating as her oxygen ran out.

Svetlana didn't have much time to react. She took several fast steps towards Lunokhod to cut him off while he was still moving, and as he reached for Lunokhod, she braced herself with feet apart and carefully fired at the thickest part of the target. His intent was obvious, and she was a good shot; it was worth the risk.

The 9 mm bullet entered his life-support backpack from the left side. It went through the cloth covering and missed the aluminum frame entirely, penetrating the stainless-steel oxygen tank, rupturing it and instantly releasing the remaining 600 pounds per square inch into the vacuum of space with a brief burst of flame. The thin walls of the tank barely slowed the bullet, which tumbled on destructively through the plastic and wires of the power distribution bus, eventually slowing and stopping as it shattered into the multiple thick layers of the silver-zinc battery.

The force of the bullet and the explosively escaping oxygen pushed the backpack hard to the right, but Chad managed to correct the imbalance with his next stride, planting his right foot farther out, already slowing himself. He heard the warbling tone of a suit malfunction, and glanced down at the indicators on the top of the control unit on his chest; he saw he had low oxygen flow. *What the hell?*

First things first. He grabbed the rover's long, bulbous antenna in his right hand and the low, conical one in his left, and squeezed them together, like he was doing a chest press in the gym. He felt them both give way, the antennas and their mounting structures bending. He kept squeezing until they were pointed at each other, nearly touching. *Enough!*

In Houston, Kaz could only see *Bulldog*. Chad had headed out of frame to the right, and then he'd seen Svetlana move quickly in the same direction. Towards Lunokhod.

A voice broke urgently into the Mission Control loops. "FLIGHT, there are problems with Miller's suit. Looked like there was a sudden drop of tank pressure, and then we lost all signal. No data at all from it now."

Gene Kranz's jaw thrust forward. This was serious, especially with no visual on the crew. "CAPCOM, let's get a voice check ASAP."

Kaz pushed his mic button. "18, we're seeing a data dropout from Chad's suit. Comm check."

The tone had stopped sounding in Chad's headset, and he glanced at the pressure gauge on his right wrist; it showed only 3.4 psi, almost into the danger section. He turned towards the lander and saw Svetlana holding the pistol, and realized what had happened. *The slut shot me!* He mentally surveyed his body to see if he was injured. *No pain.*

"Easy, toots," he said, raising both hands, but he didn't hear his voice in his headset. He realized he couldn't hear his breathing either. His comms had died. He looked closely down at the control unit; his oxygen tank pressure was zero. *Shit!* He needed to open the emergency tanks on the top of his backpack before he breathed the last of the oxygen in his helmet. The steps were instinctive: he raised the lever on the control unit on the right side of his chest and slammed it into emergency position, and quickly reached across his body over his left rib cage and popped open the red purge valve. That let waste air escape, allowing the emergency oxygen to flow into his helmet, flushing the carbon dioxide buildup from his exhaled breath. He now had 30 minutes to get plugged into the lander's oxygen system. Less, if the suit itself was leaking. He started moving towards *Bulldog*.

Kaz pointed at the interpreter to repeat his comm check in Russian, and was relieved to hear Svetlana's voice in reply. "I hear you fine, Houston." She sounded angry.

"We hear you fine also. Chad, how do you copy?"

No response.

Kaz worked through the interpreter. "Major Gromova, we've lost comm with Major Miller. Can you apprise us of his status?"

Svetlana was at the front of Lunokhod, surveying the damage. *Dermo!* Shit! She hadn't protected the rover and she'd done unknown harm to the only person who could get them off this rock.

She glanced back at him. Maybe he was okay. "He's moving towards the lander, but I don't hear him saying anything."

Kaz assessed possibilities. Had Chad somehow damaged his suit while sabotaging Lunokhod? She must have seen what he was doing. Had she caused the suit problem? How best to handle it?

"Thank you, Major Gromova. We'd like you both to end the moonwalk now and return to the Lunar Lander for ingress. We need to get him plugged into the ship's systems to restore comms."

"Ponyala," she said, grunting as she grabbed the long antenna and heaved it back, trying to restore its original shape. The metal of its support mount twisted, and she pulled and looked up to align it with

Earth. She bent the smaller antenna as well, until it was near vertical. *Hopefully enough!*

She turned and saw that Miller was almost back at the lander. She glanced at the distant TV camera, pocketed the gun and loped after him.

There was an audible sigh of relief in Mission Control as Chad came into view. *Maybe just a data dropout*, Kaz thought. They watched as he went straight to the base of the ladder and began climbing, Svetlana following. The moving images were blurred, but they could see the white of Chad's suit disappearing as he crawled through the hatch. The cosmonaut was on the ladder, following.

Chad's anger roared in his ears. *You goddamned whore!* He got up off his hands and knees, turned inside *Bulldog*, reached down and closed and locked the hatch.

As soon as he could get oxygen flowing into *Bulldog*, the climbing cabin pressure would push against the wide, square surface of the hatch, holding it even more firmly in place. She could turn the handle on the outside, but no matter how hard she pushed against the pressure, soon she wouldn't be able to budge it.

Svetlana was trapped outside.

Her helmeted head was just clearing the top of the ladder when she saw the hatch swing closed. *Nyet!* She pulled hard on the railings with both hands and pivoted her body up onto the small porch, reaching to push the hatch back open, but it was already securely in place.

She leaned back to try to look up through the windows, but the space was too confined. *Would he actually leave me out here?*

She studied the bare metal face of the hatch. On the left there was a semicircle of gold foil and on the right a larger brown semicircle of bare fiberglass. There was writing across the center of the hatch, with what looked like instructions. *Instructions mean options. Think, girl!*

By the right half circle there were two orange lines painted like clock positions and words in block capitals. She puzzled out the English letters: Lock and Unlock. *Must be otkrit and zakrit*, open and close. There had to be an external control. She scrabbled at a rectangle inset into the fiberglass, and a Velcroed cover peeled off, revealing a metal handle. It was pivoted down, aligned with Lock. She grabbed it and twisted, but it didn't move.

She leaned hard forward and worked her fingers behind it until it was securely in her palm, and pivoted with her whole upper body, pulling with all her strength. It released, turning through the short arc, and with a push the hatch swung away from her. *I'm in!*

Chad was reaching up to turn the oxygen control rotary switch when he felt the opening hatch bump into his legs. He looked down in irritation. *Fuck!* He urgently needed to solve his suit problem.

He stepped clear so she could open the hatch all the way, and he grabbed and yanked on her backpack to get her through faster. Moving around her as she got to her feet, he bent and relatched the hatch closed, reached up to his right and pushed the Cabin Repress circuit breaker in. An unseen valve clicked open, and oxygen from *Bulldog's* tanks started flowing.

"FLIGHT, they've started cabin repress." The calm voice of the Systems Officer belied the release of tension in the room. The small interior size of *Bulldog* meant the crew would have breathable atmosphere in just over a minute, and could take off their helmets.

Chad watched as the cabin pressure climbed. When it hit 2.5 psi, he moved the lever on his suit to Off, and as it stabilized at 4.3, he started taking off his gloves.

Watching from the back of the cabin, Svetlana warily copied his actions. Had he really just tried to kill her? Or was closing the hatch his way of showing her who was boss? Her hands ached after the hours fighting the pressure in the ill-fitting gloves, and it was a relief to get them off and stow them in her left leg pocket.

He was hooking his suit up to the ship's hoses, his hands moving confidently as he bypassed the failed systems of his damaged backpack. Turning, he beckoned her closer, pointing at her hoses, reaching out.

They'd both raised their gold visors, and she watched his face as he worked. It was curiously expressionless, giving her no hint of what he was thinking.

He turned and threw some panel switches, and suddenly she could hear him breathing again.

"Houston, *Bulldog*, we're back inside, hooked up to the ship." He stared at her. "Not sure what happened with my suit comms, but we got everything done outside and are putting things away in here now. Both of us in good shape, ready for the rest period before we head up to dock with *Pursuit*."

Kaz nodded and then summarized, waiting as each sentence got translated. "The team here congratulates the two of you and thanks you for your teamwork during your historic moonwalk. The plan now is for a well-deserved eight hours sleep, with liftoff to redock tomorrow at 11:54 Houston time. Major Gromova, we have an interpreter here at all times, so call if you have any questions."

Svetlana looked at the watch on her suit, adding the nine hours for Moscow. "Ponyala, spaciba bolshoi." Copy, thanks very much.

She was planning ahead as she watched the astronaut taking off his helmet, ticking off the key items in her mind. Find the rock he'd taken from Lunokhod. Get launched, dock, fire the engine to head home and make it through re-entry. And somehow get herself and the rock back to Russia.

Transit time back to Earth would be three days—lots of opportunity to sort out a plan.

For now, though, she was locked inside this small place with a man she couldn't trust. A man she'd fired her gun at twice, and who'd latched the door with her outside.

First step was to survive this night, on the surface of the Moon.

51

Bulldog

"Help me," Chad said. He pointed at the buckles on the backpack straps. He'd wedged himself into the aft of the cabin, the weight of the backpack supported on the engine cover.

She looked at the attachments, reached in and popped them free. He stepped clear, flipped the backpack around and peeled back the thermal covering to survey the damage the bullet had caused.

A small neat hole had been punched on the left side where the round had entered the oxygen tank. On the opposing side, the metal had torn outwards with the escaping pressure, leaving an oval opening and sharp edges. Broken bits of plastic fell from the shattered circuit board and battery casing, tumbling slowly to the floor of the LM.

He raised his gaze to meet Svetlana's, shaking his head slightly.

"Bad girl."

He stuffed the backpack down beside the engine mount and turned to release the clips on hers, stowing it as well. He moved to the front of the cabin and connected black tubing to a connector on his suit. He had a condom-like cuff on his penis, and his urine had been collecting in a bag inside the suit all day. He turned a valve, and it was sucked out by partial vacuum into a LM storage tank.

He knew Svetlana was wearing a diaper under her suit. He looked at her as his urine transferred. "You can just keep pissing yourself," he said.

She replied rapidly in her native tongue. "I know you speak Russian. Why are you prattling on to me in English? It's stupid!"

He made an exaggerated face of not understanding. "Russia didn't get you to the Moon, toots. America did." He pointed to himself. "I did."

Svetlana exhaled loudly, watching as he turned to organize the stowage. He handed her a food packet and squirted water into his mouth from the dispensing gun. She realized she was hungry and stood chewing on the dried food as he unpacked the hammocks, bumping her out of the way, clipping them into place for the night.

The sample container where she'd stowed the bags of rocks and dust had been empty when she'd started; the Lunokhod rock hadn't been in it. There was a second hard-sided case on the aft shelf; it must be in there. She decided to just ask.

"Where did you stow the rock that Russia asked for?"

He ignored her.

"I know they have your brother in Moscow. And the Americans don't know about him, or the rock. Or that you speak Russian. Or that Moscow is talking to us secretly."

He kept his back to her.

"Stop!" she commanded in English, loudly. He turned and looked at her, his eyebrows exaggeratedly up. She continued in Russian. "You need me to keep your secrets. To get that rock to Russia, where it belongs." She suddenly realized the leverage she had, and the extra danger it put her in.

He nodded and replied, in English, "That puts you in a tough spot, doesn't it, sweet cheeks. You need me to get you home, and I'm the only one who actually has the whole picture."

A small smile curled the corners of his lips as he leaned his face towards hers and said one word, distinctly, in Russian. "Ostorozhna."

Be careful.

The unrelenting sunlight was shining directly on the metal hull of Lunokhod, parked next to *Bulldog* on the Moon's surface, and reflecting up off the ground around it on all sides. If there had been a thermometer touching the rover's exposed magnesium-alloy skin, it would have read 242 degrees Fahrenheit. The metal was conducting that heat through to the inside, where the energy from the lump of polonium and the quiescent electronics added to it. The small ventilation fan was earnestly doing its best, pulling the nitrogen air past all the warm surfaces and blowing it hopefully up to the radiator to cool.

Like a blanket, though, the layer of dirt that Chad had spread on the radiator's surface was holding the heat in. The bottom of the radiator was starting to get warm to the touch. Instead of cold air flowing back down from the top, with each passing minute the return air was getting hotter. A cycle feeding on itself, where even the small heat from the fan motor was making things worse.

Yet most of its systems were still asleep, patiently waiting for the big antenna on the far side of the Earth to rotate back into view. As soon as it did, small timers would go off, the high-gain antenna would move to point exactly to the planned angles, and Lunokhod would come fully to life, everything on, awaiting its next command.

As soon as that happened, the problem was going to get rapidly worse, turning the rover into a forced-air oven on the Moon, baking all its delicate circuits to death. Unless the team in Simferopol could recognize the problem and figure out a way to solve it.

A race with a thermometer.

Kaz was beat. He'd driven right past the U-Joint, headed for home and a much-needed night on his own.

He pulled the fridge door open and opted for what he saw; bacon, eggs, toast and beer. The sound and smell of the bacon starting to fry in the pan set his mouth watering; his first gulp of cold beer from the bottle cut through it perfectly. He broke two eggs in next to the bacon and pushed two slices of bread down in the toaster.

He looked out the window absently as he waited for the toast to pop, reviewing the day. It had been an unprecedented one, but the crew was safe and Luke's body had been buried with honor. He raised his beer before taking another swig and toasted him. *Here's to you, buddy.* He picked up the frying pan and swirled it slightly, freeing the still-runny eggs from sticking, then set it back down. He realized he felt deeply uneasy, the inner voice he'd learned to listen to as a pilot, the one that paid attention to subtleties and tried to make patterns out of the seeming randomness sending off various alarms.

What have I missed? He took another pull on the beer, deliberately letting his mind relax.

The recurring double clicks popped into his head. If that happened again, he was going to pounce on it and worry it until it was solved.

But the obvious major problem was Chad. Could he really have done such a wicked thing? How was it possible that he'd made it this far, with all the hoops he'd had to jump through, and still kept himself so secret? And why would he kill Tom? The only reason he could come up with was that Chad had been desperate to get on this mission. How did that even make sense? It wasn't as if the whole program was over. There'd still have been chances for an astronaut as technically gifted as Chad to get to space.

The toast popped as he tilted the bottle up and drained the last of the beer; he got the butter and another bottle out of the fridge. As he slid the bacon and eggs onto a plate, he realized how hungry he was, and ate rapidly until he was mopping up the last of the egg with the second piece of toast. He slid the plate and cutlery into open slots in the dishwasher and took the remaining half beer into the living room.

He picked up the Gretsch, letting his hands play whatever chords they chose as he looked out into the darkness. He recognized a couple of sad songs and exhaled, deeply, twice, feeling the exhaustion.

The last of the beer suddenly lost its appeal, and he set it down, put the guitar back into its stand and took himself to bed.

52

Simferopol, Soviet Ukraine

Sitting at his console in Simferopol, waiting for moonrise, Gabdul allowed himself to feel proud. It had been his idea to drive Lunokhod in a max-speed dash across the lunar dust to get close to the American lander. He'd pictured how the iconic photo would look: the first cosmonaut descending the ladder to the Moon, with Lunokhod posed heroically in the background. The established presence of Soviet technology as a perfect counterpoint to the American ship newly on the surface; a seasoned Russian explorer there to greet it. He just wished someone had thought to paint a large red hammer and sickle on the side of the rover.

Outside his operations building, the huge dish antenna was tipped up on its edge, pointed at the exact place on the southeastern horizon where the Moon was about to appear. As the three-quarter crescent wavered into view through the Earth's atmosphere, the first set of commands pulsed out through the amplifiers, bounced off the huge parabolic dish and raced to the Moon. Just 1.35 seconds later, the faint signal washed over Lunokhod's receiving antennas.

The long, bulbous high-gain receiving antenna missed it completely. Even with Svetlana's attempt to bend it back, the tightly focused receptor was no longer pointing in the right direction. But the smaller omni antenna turned out to be sturdier. It dutifully collected and passed on the commands from Earth, and Lunokhod came to life, the mechanical beast readying for its day's work.

Sitting at her console behind Gabdul, the antenna operator frowned. There was no systems signal coming back from the steerable high-gain antenna. It had been working perfectly the day before. She sent a test command for it to go through a search cycle, but nothing. Without the high-gain, they could only get limited, low-rate data back.

Beside her, the specialist engineer felt growing alarm as well. As the new data populated in the systems table on his screen, he saw that the temperatures were far higher than they should have been, with a couple already approaching limits. Both technicians spoke at the same time, summarizing what they were seeing.

Gabdul listened, his concern increasing. How could they have lost the high-gain and thermal control at the same time? Had his bouncing race across the surface broken something? The team rapidly pulled out schematic drawings, hunting for a common link. More importantly, looking for a solution. The internal temperatures were climbing alarmingly.

The systems engineer, looking closely at the data, recognized the pattern, but it made no sense. "It's as if the solar panel is closed over the radiator—we're getting near-zero cooling. But we're getting power from the array, which shows open, so that's not it." He looked at Gabdul. "Maybe the Americans already blasted off and covered us in dust?"

"They're not supposed to take off for a few more hours," Gabdul said, then asked the question that worried him. "Could our high-speed run or their moonwalking have kicked up enough dust to cause this?"

"Unlikely, but possible." The tech studied his data. "But if we don't do something soon, we're going to start losing systems."

Gabdul stared at his TV monitor. The small omni antenna had a very low data rate, and images were going to process very slowly. Whatever he did, it was going to have to be mostly blind. He made a decision and quickly briefed the team. He got reluctant nods from everyone; his proposed course of action was risky, but worth it, given the reality of what was happening.

Gabdul put his hand on the controller and began.

Chad kept his eyes closed after he woke up, listening for a minute to the reassuring mechanical sounds of the LM—the fans and pumps that were cycling the life-support systems, keeping him alive in this little bubble of air on the Moon. *Like I'm in a womb, listening to my mother's heartbeat.*

As he'd slept in the hammock, comfortably slung in the low gravity, he'd been dreaming of his mother, a familiar dream that he both longed for and hated. Oleg, his brother, pushing to do something, his mother in faded colors, her voice conveying more of an emotion than actual words. The three of them had been in a room somewhere in Berlin, Oleg demanding, their mother quietly urging caution. Even now, as he opened his eyes, he could feel the soothing effect of her loving voice. And the jagged unfairness of losing her.

And Oleg. What had happened to the tough, decisive older brother he remembered and dreamed of? The war and loss had somehow changed him, made him soft, turned him into this monk, Father Ilarion. Who was now being threatened by the Russians, and used as a lever against him.

He glanced at his watch. Time to get up.

He rolled onto his shoulder and reached to peel back the covering on his triangular window, letting harsh sunlight blast into the cabin. He leaned to look at the nearby horizon. *Strangest place I've ever woken up.* He glanced at the cosmonaut, crosswise below him, blinking in the bright light. *And with a woman, no less. Though not one I'd pick.*

Movement outside caught his eye. Lunokhod was rolling forward. As he watched, it abruptly stopped, as if they'd slammed on the brakes. It reversed, then immediately halted again. A small cloud of dust shook loose and fell.

He snorted. *Clever Russians.* Somehow they still had comms with their machine and were trying to shake the dirt off the radiator, like a cow shaking off flies. He watched it change direction jerkily a few more times, but very little dust was coming off now. *Driving all those motors will be heating it up even faster.* He was satisfied that he'd done his job and more. Hell, he'd gotten shot in the process.

So many secrets now. A fistful of cards held tight against his chest. And three days' ride home to decide how to play them.

He rolled out of the hammock, stretching against the suit as he stood. Yesterday's work had left bruises on his knees, shoulders and back, and his body protested the movement. But he didn't feel much different than he had as a teenager, the day after a wrestling tournament. Pain was just a reminder of victory.

"FLIGHT, Chad's awake." JW had been watching his console data for the change of heartbeat.

"Copy, SURGEON. CAPCOM, let's get them into the checklist ASAP, and headed towards launch."

Kaz nodded. "Good morning, *Bulldog*, we trust you had a good sleep, and when you're ready, we'd like an IMU Power-Up, on page 7-9 of the Surface book."

Chad acknowledged and threw the switches. *Time for me to do what I'm best at. Time to fly this thing.*

In Moscow, Chelomei had heard Miller's voice and waited impatiently for the orbiting vessel to disappear behind the Moon so the other astronaut—Esdale—wouldn't hear him. As soon as the TsUP flight director nodded, he pressed his mic button.

"Major Miller, listen to me carefully. I have a plan for your splashdown when you return to Earth." He quickly explained the key points of what he had set up with his contacts at the KGB and the Kremlin.

Chad had ceased moving, holding perfectly still, listening, rapidly weighing Chelomei's plan. Svetlana was watching him, listening as well.

Chelomei said, "I need you to be ready and make it happen. If you do not, we will reveal to your masters where all the money you thought your brother was sending you actually came from." He paused to let that new threat sink in, and then said, "If you understand, Major Miller, use the word 'Russia' in your next call to Houston."

All these years, you've been using my brother as a means to compromise me? Anger roared through him. *You asshole!* He pounded his clenched, gloved fists on the flat of the instrument panel.

I need to win this! He wrestled his thoughts back under control, his mind clicking into overdrive; yes, there was still a way to come out on top. In fact, this new demand gave him even more power over the course of events. He looked at the cosmonaut, warily staring back at him.

"Houston," Chad said, "it's been great here on the Moon, Russia and America working together like never before."

Kaz looked up, frowning. *Odd thing for Chad to say.* "Copy, Chad."

On the other side of the world, Chelomei smiled.

Svetlana stood on Chad's right in the cockpit, watching him go through the pages of checklist steps before launch, listening to the technical chatter with Houston. She pictured what the geometry would look like for them to blast off, rendezvous and dock. They'd offered translation, but she'd declined it as unnecessary. Better to just watch, listen and beware. She glanced at her watch—still over an hour to go.

She'd slept poorly, fully expecting that Chad would try to take the gun from her during the night. When she'd finally dozed off, she'd been clutching the pistol inside her leg pocket. But when he'd opened the window cover, waking her up, the hard metal was still there under her hand. It was an important win; once they docked, she'd have the other astronaut, Mikhail, always present as a witness, which would decrease the constant threat. Just three more days and nights to go.

Chad looked sharp and well rested, as if he'd had an untroubled sleep. Even with what Chelomei had said. *Psychopath*, she decided.

During a lull in the chatter with Houston, a Russian voice broke in. Chelomei again, from Moscow.

"Major Miller, we know you can hear this, no need to respond. We think your normal procedures have you opening the hatch once more to jettison unneeded items. When that happens, we need one of you to walk quickly to Lunokhod and brush the dust off the radiator. We just got word that it's overheating. This is critical."

Svetlana saw that Chad's hands stopped moving while Chelomei spoke, but his expression didn't change.

Dust on the radiator! She leaned to get a clear view of the rover. So that's why it had been moving around! But how had anything gotten on the upper surface? She thought back to her close inspection for damage. Had there been dust on top?

Chyort! She couldn't remember! *Did he put it there?*

She turned and looked at the pile of items on the floor behind them: a couple of duffle bags full of trash and their two backpacks. It made sense to throw them out so their engine didn't have to lift useless weight off the Moon. But neither of them could go outside now. Their hoses were plugged into the ship.

The astronaut hadn't reacted to Chelomei's demand and was back talking to Houston in English as if it had never happened. She looked again at Lunokhod in the distance, visualizing what it would be like at liftoff. She spoke quickly, before Chad shut off her mic.

"Houston, will our launch blast blow dust onto Lunokhod?"

Chad's arm shot out and flicked off the transmit switch, his face a mask of fury. "Don't you talk!" he yelled. She saw a spray of spit fog the lower part of his visor. But he'd been too slow.

The interpreter answered, translating what Kaz told him. "Major Gromova, the analysts here have looked at it, and they think the local blast from the upper stage motor will be mostly horizontal near Lunokhod, so should pose no dust threat."

Excellent, she thought, defiantly looking into Chad's eyes. Their launch would blow dust off the rover. *If Chelomei and his team read between the lines, they'll move it even closer!*

Chad was reaching to re-enable voice transmission when they heard Chelomei again.

"Thank you, Major Gromova, we understand. And if—"

The Russian voice cut off abruptly as Chad shut off all external communications. He spoke on intercom, his eyes blazing at Svetlana. "You try that again, I'll kill you!" His hand came up fast and punched her helmet, and her head banged into a handrail. She focused quickly to see if the plastic visor had broken, but saw only a new deep scratch on the outer surface.

"Ponyala?" he demanded.

She eyed him warily. "Da."

He turned back and threw the comm switches. "The cosmonaut's nodding, Houston, sorry for the interruption. I'm ready when you are for the depress and trash jettison."

She got out of his way as he opened the hatch and pushed the items out, watching through the windows to see if Moscow had understood her. With satisfaction, she saw that the rover was still moving in short bursts, each pulse getting it closer to the LM.

She smiled tightly.

There was no doubt that he was in charge. But she'd won another battle.

By design, *Bulldog* had just one chance to leave the Moon, a solitary rocket engine to lift the upper half clear of its heavy landing legs, get it going fast enough to catch up with *Pursuit* in orbit and dock.

Many things had to happen perfectly, in sequence. If any one of them failed, Chad and Svetlana would stay on the surface forever. Or perhaps worse, crash back into it. Either way, Michael would be flying his ship back to Earth alone.

It began with two bangs, as battery power ignited explosive charges. The larger of them shattered threaded nuts and drove a guillotine that severed all mechanical connections with the landing section. They were free. The smaller one then opened valves, letting high-pressure helium rush through small tubes connected to the propellant tanks. The helium squeezed the volatile liquids down into the engine, where they mixed and instantly exploded.

With a shower of sparks the engine fired, pushing *Bulldog* up and away from the surface of the Moon.

"I see pitch-over, Houston." Chad's voice was calm as 16 small steering thrusters pulsed, turning *Bulldog* from the pure vertical liftoff to aim towards *Pursuit*.

On Earth, Kaz was watching the data closely on his console monitor, listening to the technical confirmation on the comm loops. "You have good thrust, *Bulldog*."

The sudden ignition of the motor had pushed Svetlana down into the floor with double her weight. *Like standing on Earth again.*

She leaned forward, looking down through her window to try to see what effect the rocket blast had had on Lunokhod, but couldn't tell. Within seconds the bottom half of the lander had disappeared from sight and they were accelerating towards rendezvous.

Chad was running his finger along a checklist table that showed altitude, attitude and climb speed, double-checking the steering computer. "*Bulldog*'s on track, Houston." The radio filled with static.

Kaz called *Pursuit*. "Michael, looks like our signal's getting messed up by their exhaust plume, as expected. Please relay that all numbers look good."

Michael had been staring at the Moon's surface, camera in hand, hoping to see the liftoff. "Will do, Kaz. I don't see them yet." He repeated Kaz's message to Chad.

Chad was watching his instruments. "Thanks, Michael, I have a solid radar lock on you. Guidance looks good. Engine shutdown time looks as planned at 7:18."

"I'm looking forward to the company! It's been quiet up here. Nice view, though."

"Copy that." Chad looked at the timeline. "We'll be docked in a couple of hours."

"I'll make some fresh coffee."

Ignoring the chatter, Svetlana was looking at the strange battered roughness of the Moon's surface falling away below them. As they accelerated towards the sunset, the shadows got longer, exaggerating the jagged peaks and smooth craters beneath her. *I'm like a fly over a skull*, she thought, trying to imprint the image into her memory. She twisted and looked up at Earth, the improbable blue orb suspended as if by magic in the blackness.

Her spaceflight was ending. She'd launched expecting to be on Almaz for months, yet now she'd be back in three days. A sudden pang of loss for her crewmate, Andrei, rushed through her. To command that spaceflight had been his life's dream.

She glanced at Chad, his eyes focused on the engine parameters and navigation instruments.

One thing at a time. First, they needed to get docked.

53

Moscow

*

Father Ilarion was troubled. His expectations for speaking with and honoring his brother, Yuri, had been so high, yet the day had been so strange. They'd gotten back to their quarters very late, and as he wearily rose for Matins, he had much to think on. And pray over.

Alexander was quieter than normal when he brought him breakfast. Ilarion asked if they would speak with Yuri again, and the interpreter said he didn't know, but that they needed to spend a few more days in Moscow, depending on how the space mission went.

"But why, Sascha?"

Alexander looked at the cleric. His kind face was creased with uncertainty, his discomfort with the disruption of his normal life evident in the deep cleft between his eyebrows. He decided the best course was to reassure.

"We have traveled so far to be here, Father. Director Chelomei thinks your presence could be very important for Yuri if he experiences any troubles during the remainder of the flight. He has requested that we stay for the sake of the mission."

Ilarion's face cleared. If he could help, he had purpose. Meanwhile, he could keep Yuri and his crewmates' success foremost in his prayers. He nodded slowly as he picked up the dry toast.

Bowing slightly, Alexander excused himself and stepped into the corridor, closing the door. There he stood up straight and took a deep breath. Chelomei had made it plain that he still needed the lever of threat against the cleric to get the American astronaut to do what was required.

He decided he needed to talk to his handler at Lubyanka to update him on the importance of *his* influence on what was happening on the Moon, and for the American's return. This was his chance to be recognized by the KGB for his work. His longtime loyalty and cleverness.

Alexander liked Father Ilarion. He hoped nothing bad would happen to him here. But this was his chance.

"Okay, Michael, I'm stopped, a hundred feet away. You're cleared to give *Pursuit* a spin."

"Copy, Chad, in work."

Michael had watched as *Bulldog* approached, a metallic insect rising from the surface of the Moon. He moved *Pursuit*'s hand controller to the side, gently rolling the ship like it was on a slow-motion barbecue spit. That would give Chad a chance to inspect the exterior for any micrometeorite damage before they fired the engine and headed across open space back towards Earth.

Svetlana watched *Pursuit* turn in front of them: the pointed, wide cone of the capsule at the front, the squatty silver cylinder of the main body, and the fat brown curve of the engine's exhaust nozzle at the rear. *Strannaya reeba*. What a strange fish.

"Looks clean as a whistle, Michael. Just hold her there, and I'll come in and dock."

"Good to hear." Michael nulled rates and re-engaged the autopilot to hold attitude. "You're cleared in."

Chad smiled as he began moving *Bulldog*'s controls. There was no one anywhere doing what he was doing now—docking his spaceship in orbit around the Moon. He pushed forward, closing the gap between the two vehicles.

Svetlana watched, appreciating the astronaut's ability, deeply disliking the man. She evaluated as he corrected the small misalignments, predicting his inputs, comparing them to what she would do.

On the outside of *Bulldog*, above her head, there was a cone-shaped indentation. Sticking out of *Pursuit* was an extended probe on a tripod; Chad was staring at a visual target to align the two. She heard Mikhail on the radio and recognized the words for numbers.

"Twenty-five feet, Chad."

"Copy."

"Twenty feet, rates look good."

"Agreed."

Pursuit grew in the LM's window like a flower blossoming as they neared.

"Ten feet, good alignment."

"Roger."

A pause as Chad made a last few inputs. Svetlana listened for the sound of metal on metal, hearing the scrape and thunk as they docked.

"Contact and capture!" Michael said. "Nice flying, Commander!"

"Thanks." It had been perfect. Chad safed the control system as he listened to the probe retraction mechanism pull the two ships together.

The specialists in Mission Control had all been watching closely, but Kaz had stayed radio silent, letting the crew do their work to get docked, one of the last major critical events.

"Congratulations, Apollo 18," he said. "Glad to see you reunited. If you look below you, you're just passing overhead your landing site at Le Monnier Crater. To let you know, we're planning to put a request in to the International Astronomical Union to name that local valley Hemming Rille, in honor of Luke." It had been Laura's idea, and Kaz had thought it fitting.

"Copy, Houston," Michael said. "He was a good man."

There was a moment's silence.

"Now let's get the hatch open and start heading for home."

Michael had cleaned house for their arrival. He'd gathered all the unneeded items and trash into one large transfer bag to leave in *Bulldog*, and had opened up *Pursuit*'s lower lockers, ready to receive the all-important lunar rock and soil samples for return to Earth. The stowage was below the seats, to keep the added weight in a secure place for the high forces they'd face while re-entering Earth's atmosphere, and for stable floating in the ocean after splashdown.

In contrast, *Bulldog* was filthy, everything coated with the gritty lunar dust they'd brought in on their suits. Weightlessness was making it worse, as movement filled the cabin with the tiny, sharp, floating shards of countless meteorite impacts.

Previous crews had identified a need to clean the dust off items before transferring them out of the LM, and NASA engineers had rigged up a portable vacuum cleaner using a suit hose, fan and filter. Chad plugged it in, dragged it on its power cable through into *Bulldog* and held it out it to Svetlana.

"Here's where you turn it on, toots." He pointed to the silver switch on its side, and then at the walls and floor of *Bulldog*. "Now get cleaning."

He wants me to vacuum?

Instantly irritated, she crossed her arms. But she needed a reason to be in the LM, to watch every item being transferred. She realized that this would give her an excuse.

"Spasiba," she said, with a small nod, and reached out to take it. *Play his game.* She turned it on and the motor whirred tinnily to life.

Chad smirked. "Make sure you get into all the corners."

He turned and yelled down the tunnel. "Michael, you ready for transfer items?" A muffled voice called back affirmative, and he began collecting suit hardware, cameras and vacuum-sealed sample boxes to float through the hatch to *Pursuit*. Prior to transferring each one, he held it up for Svetlana to once-over with the vacuum.

"Look at us, a model of international cooperation," he said over the noise.

She ignored him, concentrating on the task. From the size of the hole in front of Lunokhod, the rock had not been big. She was certain the astronaut would have stowed it separately from the other samples. As she vacuumed, she considered possibilities. She now had the pistol tucked into the waistband of her underwear; maybe he'd done something similar with the rock? She looked at the white flight suit he'd put on; no obvious bulges. Their moonwalking suits were still bundled bulkily under bungees at the back of the LM; he'd have to pull them out for transfer, as they'd need to wear them again for re-entry.

In between cleaning transfer items, she vacuumed the cabin itself to keep the floating dust to a minimum. *Where else might he have put it?* The main stowage area was in the back; the front of the cockpit was spartan and functional. She looked along the edges of the instrument panel for any recesses, and her eyes settled on a small white bag clipped below the data entry panel. *Is that big enough? It's here somewhere, and he's going to try to bring it into the other ship without my knowing.* She just needed to be patient. And observant.

"Houston, *Pursuit,* I show us in LM jettison attitude: Roll 014, Pitch 038 and Yaw 344."

Kaz glanced to confirm the data on his console screen. "Looks good, Michael, you're GO for Pyro Arm. We show separation in thirty seconds."

Michael threw the switch and kept his hands floating near the controls. As soon as the pyrotechnic charges fired, the bit of air pressure they'd left in the tunnel would help to push *Bulldog* away, like a gust of wind on a sail. To be safe, he'd also fire *Pursuit's* thrusters to get clear.

The digital timer hit zero, and there was a metallic bang as the docking mechanism and tunnel released.

"*Bulldog's* away, Houston." Michael pulled back smoothly on the controller, hearing his maneuvering thrusters fire, watching through the window as the LM slowly receded. He released the knob, satisfied.

"Copy, *Pursuit*." Kaz left a small pause. "She was a good ship."

Chad was at his window, watching *Bulldog* against the blackness. "Sure was, Houston. You drive her gentle now."

The specialists in Mission Control were uplinking commands, ready to fire the small thrusters on *Bulldog* to steer it deliberately towards a controlled crash into the Moon. The force of the impact would echo through the solid rock and be picked up by seismic sensors installed during previous Apollo missions, mapping the shape of the inner mantle and core of the Moon.

Svetlana watched the two men as they stared out the windows, *They're so different*. She smiled wryly to herself. *Like black and white*.

She had vacuumed the spacesuits as Chad held them out for transfer, but had felt nothing in his suit's pockets. He'd sent her out of the LM before he finished collecting the last items, and had brought them all in one larger transfer bag, stowing it in a locker under the headrest of the left seat. *The rock has to be in there*.

She heard the voice from Houston again.

"*Pursuit*, when you're ready, I've got your coming-home PAD to read up to you."

Both men pulled themselves reluctantly from the window and peeled checklists off of Velcro, grabbing their floating tethered pencils.

Pursuit was Michael's ship, but Chad wanted to re-establish who was in command now that *Bulldog* was no longer attached. He was the one to respond. "Go ahead, Houston, *Pursuit* is ready to copy."

Kaz took a breath. "Okay, it's TEI-74, SPS G&N, weight 35768, plus 0.57, plus 0.88 . . ." As he carefully voiced the data, he pictured what each word meant, making sure it made sense to him. A mistake of even one digit or decimal place could be fatal. *Pursuit* was going to orbit back around behind the Moon, and, out of communication with Earth, the crew was going to point the ship in exactly the right direction for the big engine to fire. At precisely the right moment it would ignite and burn for 141 seconds; without the weight of the LM, that's all it would take to escape the Moon's gravity. By the time *Pursuit* reappeared, it would already be arcing high above the lunar surface, racing home.

He finished calling up the numbers. "Standing by for the readback, over."

Chad motioned with his chin at Michael to respond, and floated back to look out the window. *Bulldog* was rapidly becoming too small to see, soon to be just another memory, another vehicle that he had piloted well. Another event in his past.

He glanced up at the Earth. The past didn't matter. His future was three days away.

He felt a surge of confidence course through him. He just had to play his cards right. And he had a winning hand.

EARTHBOUND

54

Pursuit

Michael was looking forward out the windows at the Earth as *Pursuit* slowly turned in the sunlight. Svetlana was dozing, loosely strapped to her couch.

"Hey, Boss."

"What?" Chad looked up from the emergency entry procedures he was reading. The pages were pale red, highlighting their criticality.

"Did you ever think that since we fired *Pursuit*'s engine for the Trans-Earth Injection, we've really just been falling? Like a rock dropped from an enormous height, accelerating as Earth's gravity sucks us in, closer and closer?" There was awe in his voice.

Chad looked at him. "Nope."

Michael shrugged. "I just think it's cool."

Chad went back to his checklist. *Really? That's what he's thinking about?*

Kaz's voice crackled in his headset. "*Pursuit*, I've got your mid-course numbers when you're ready."

The huge antennas at Goldstone had been precisely tracking the spaceship, calculating exactly where it would enter the Earth's atmosphere; now the engineers in Houston wanted a small engine firing to adjust the trajectory a tiny bit.

Chad peeled Michael's headset off the console and held it out to him. "Houston's calling with mid-course data."

Michael grabbed a checklist and pushed the mic button. "Go ahead, Houston." Kaz read up the information, and Michael eased himself into the center seat to type in the data.

Kaz continued. "While I've got you, Michael, we'd like an updated stowage inventory so the guys here can finalize your center of mass for entry."

Michael stopped typing to respond. "Copy, Kaz, I'll get at it after the correction burn." Boring task, but an important one. Their capsule was going to hit the top of the Earth's atmosphere going just under 25,000 miles per hour, and had to fly itself through the thickening air, using friction to slow down. The only way to steer was to have the center of mass offset a foot or two so the capsule flew slightly crooked; that gave it a little bit of lift. By rolling the capsule left and right, the autopilot would be able to control where that lift was pointed and how fast they fell, which would determine how much g they pulled and where exactly they would splash down. If the computers failed, there was a backup system to manually roll the ship using just time and g-load. But it was all dependent on knowing where the crew had stowed the added weight of the moonrocks.

After the burn was complete, Michael dug around under the seats, opening lockers one by one. He was being methodical. The flight home was long. There was no sense rushing.

"Okay, Kaz, in locker A2 we've got"—he pulled the items out individually—"two sample return boxes and several bags." He hooked his toes under footloops to brace his body, and swung the first box left and right, estimating the mass by how much it resisted his motion and twisted his upper body. "My guess is the furthest forward-stowed box weighs fifty or sixty pounds." Not exact, but the best he could do.

The scientists were also interested in the characteristics of what the crew was bringing home. Per their request, Michael unclipped a thick silver tube from its bracket on a side panel, and twisted the upper section to turn it on. It resembled a foot-long flashlight, but in fact was a radiation-survey meter. He held the protruding rounded end close to the sample box and peered closely at the device's dial.

"Houston, the Geiger counter shows just background radiation levels." He checked each sample as he went, confirming what he'd been briefed to expect. The Moon's surface had been absorbing cosmic rays for billions of years, and they'd anticipated that it would have slightly elevated readings compared to Earth.

Svetlana saw that Michael's hands were full with multiple boxes and the sensor, and floated over.

"Pomotch?" she asked. Can I help? She snagged a bag that was floating free and held it for him to check for radioactivity.

Michael looked up in happy surprise. "Thanks!" Inventory was easier with two.

Feigning disinterest, Chad kept his head tilted towards his checklist while closely watching what they were doing out of the corner of his eye. He didn't want to highlight where he'd hidden the rock, and was confident that Michael's inventory would miss it. But he had a plan, just in case.

In Moscow, Chelomei was listening to the transmissions to Houston with rising concern. Their intelligence hadn't included the fact that the Americans had a portable radiation detector on board. He'd deliberately not told Miller and Gromova that the rock was radioactive when he'd ordered them to retrieve it, knowing they might overreact to having it inside their ship; now there was sudden, grave risk that the third crew-member, Esdale, would discover it and tell Houston.

His options were limited. If he transmitted a warning, Esdale would hear his voice—unacceptable. And even if he did, what could he say?

He pictured the sequence of possible events at splashdown, evaluating the different American actions if they knew it was on board. Slowly, his worry subsided. Their plan was robust enough.

Al Shepard walked down two levels from his management console in the rear of Mission Control and grabbed an empty seat between CAPCOM and SURGEON. He waved Kaz and JW closer.

"You two ready to go to Hawaii tomorrow?"

They nodded. "What time's the C-141 leave?" JW asked.

"Wheels up at six a.m. I'll be at Ellington by five thirty."

"Ouch," Kaz said.

Al nodded. "Yeah, I hear you. I'm planning to mostly sleep en route, plus we get four extra hours with the time difference. We'll land at Hickam around ten a.m. local, and then a Navy helo will take us out to the *New Orleans*."

"Any surprise passengers coming from DC?" Kaz asked.

"Yeah. The Soviets are insisting they need a rep at splashdown to greet the cosmonaut, so they're sending an attaché from their consular staff." Al rolled his eyes. "I promised the Joint Chiefs we'll take good care of him, but Bob Carius, the skipper of the *New Orleans*, is gonna be just thrilled to have a spy on board."

JW frowned. "Any change to normal recovery ops as a result?"

"Nah, we'll do it by the book, Doc. As Crew Surgeon you'll be on the prime helo with the Navy divers and med techs as usual. Kaz and I will stay on the ship with the attaché, getting ready to grip and grin with the crew for the *Stars and Stripes* cameras. The *New Orleans* will bring us back into Pearl Harbor, and then we'll all fly back here Tuesday, including the attaché and the cosmonaut." He rubbed the side of his face, grimacing like he had a headache. "We still have to inform Luke's family, and then the media, and sort out military protocols to honor Luke, plus how to debrief lessons learned from the cosmonaut herself. But we still have a few days to set all that up."

JW smiled. "That's why they pay you the big bucks, Admiral."

"Yeah, right," Al said. "This'll be the last Moon mission, and the end of my time at NASA. A chance to go make some real money after thirty-two years with the government."

He tipped his head at Kaz and said, "Could you excuse us a minute, Doc?" JW nodded and wheeled his chair back over to his console.

Al moved closer to Kaz, speaking quietly below the hum of the room. "I wanted to update you on what Sheriff Heard's found. Stuff the Air Force should have caught a long time ago. You might know that Chad was adopted, a war orphan from Germany, raised by the ex-soldier who brought him out, on their family farm in Wisconsin. But at some point, sheriff's not sure when, it seems Chad was contacted by a surviving brother in East Berlin. Russian-born, it turns out, and a monk with the Orthodox Church there. He's been sending him money for years. And judging by Chad's bank accounts and the cash at his house, quite a bit more money recently."

He paused and looked at Kaz. "You ever play poker with Chad?"

Kaz shook his head. "No, I'm not a gambler."

"Yeah, me neither. But Chad's been playing some, locally, back room stuff. Quite a bit of money changes hands, apparently. Makes him vulnerable."

Kaz said nothing, thinking about what that meant.

"Bottom line, though, Heard has found no clear evidence tying Chad to the helo crash, or of him being involved in anything illegal. But several people are going to want to talk to him when he gets back. Including the Defense Intelligence Agency."

Kaz looked around the room, his eye pausing briefly on Gene Kranz. "Anyone here know this?"

"No. I need us to focus on getting Chad and the crew safely into the Pacific and then back here. The wheels of justice can wait until then."

55

Pacific Ocean

The radio signal began on the muddy banks of the springtime-swollen Amur River, just across from the eastern Soviet military-industrial city of Khabarovsk. The message had been coded for transmission at the Red Banner Pacific Fleet Intelligence Center just downriver, and now the pulsing electricity was traveling up 30 connected antenna towers, each nearly 800 feet tall. Like an entire orchestra of bass fiddles, the antennas throbbed deeply in unison, each vibrating, sending a low-frequency signal out into the surrounding air.

Very low.

The radio waves flowed out through the atmosphere, reflecting off the surrounding flatlands of the Amur River delta and 100 miles up to the electrically charged ionosphere, where their long wavelength bounced back down again. Trapped between the earth and sky, the Very Low Frequency signal followed the curve of the horizon across Sakhalin Island and the Sea of Okhotsk, and out over the Pacific Ocean.

Coded information, headed out to sea.

Most ships' antennas were far too short to pick up the signal and missed it as it passed by. But 50 feet below the water's surface, more than 6,000 kilometers away, a long trailing wire received it loud and clear. The electrical impulse passed through the deployed underwater antenna and into the ship, all the way forward to the communications chief's station. When he saw his yellow message light come on and the VLF needle jumping on the small screen, he turned to watch as the printer chugged to life, slowly tapping out the long, decoded message onto the thin roll of paper. He scanned the Cyrillic letters as they appeared.

New orders. He sighed. The Captain would not be pleased. They were already past due returning to their home port in Vladivostok, and a quick scan of the densely worded message looked like it would add at least another week at sea, maybe two.

But it was definitely not his job to scrutinize messages for Captain Serdyukov. He waited until the printer stopped, then carefully tore the paper off the machine just under End of Message and clipped it inside a folder marked Captain's Eyes Only. Locking the radio room hatch door, he turned up the narrow corridor towards the central post, in search of the captain of the nuclear-powered submarine K-252.

It was a Nalim-type sub, what the American Navy called Yankee class, 420 feet long, with a crew of 114 men, nuclear-powered, armed with 16 R-21 vertically launched ballistic missiles and 18 Type 53-65M wake-homing torpedoes. K-252 was a new ship; she'd been built two years previously just down the Amur River from Khabarovsk, and this was her second extended Pacific deployment. Captain Vasily Antonovich Serdyukov had commanded both.

As he was most hours of the day and night, Captain Serdyukov was seated in his brown leather swivel command chair, surrounded on all sides by the flat yellow panels of gauges and levers that gave him insight into and control over all systems of the sub. At the moment, they were moving quietly under the Pacific at 16 knots, 400 miles northeast of Hawaii, headed west. Towards home.

The comms chief stopped behind Serdyukov's right shoulder, checking if the Captain was busy, or perhaps dozing. The leather seat had a padded headrest for the relentless hours of work, and it was a mistake to waken Serdyukov if he was grabbing a nap during a quiet moment. He leaned forward to see if the Captain's eyes were closed.

They were. He looked closer at the face—the droopy eyelids, long nose and protruding chin of a tall man. Unusual in the submarine service, where the high hatches and low ceilings banged heads and knees mercilessly.

He decided the message's importance required him to clear his throat. The Captain's eyes instantly opened, flicking immediately across the gauges and digital readouts.

"Da, Pavel?" Captain Serdyukov's voice was deep.

The comms chief started in surprise. *How did he know it was me?* He stepped forward and handed over the message folder, nodded and returned immediately to his post, not wanting to be there when the Captain read the bad news.

Serdyukov opened the folder, scanned the message and then read it again, methodically. He leaned his head back to think. *This is a surprise.* The months of ballistic missile patrol up and down the American and Canadian coast had been successful, but also uneventful and monotonous. His ship had done well, but in essence, nothing had happened. Communications with the outside world had been rare, and the crew had turned inwards, busy with work and, in their highly regulated off-hours, making their own entertainment within the very limited confines of the ship. Except through the periscope, they hadn't seen another vessel, or any other people, since they'd left port. Food stores were getting low, and it was becoming increasingly harder to give the crew something to look forward to in the repetitive days. Arrival at home had been the next anticipated event.

He pictured what this message was going to mean for the ship. He would need to task his men to do things they had only practiced in drills and training exercises. Doing something very different, and with definite risk and potential consequences. Something clandestine and important. A smile curled his lips. The very essence of a submariner's purpose.

He reread the last lines of the message, which said further details would be sent shortly. But for now they had a specific destination, rough timing and expected actions. He began making a mental list of the skill sets of his men and the exercises they'd need to practice over the coming days. This was a chance for K-252 to distinguish herself as an outstanding ship of the Pacific Fleet, and for his crew to return to port with something to their credit besides bland reports of quiet patrols.

Captain Serdyukov was realistic; this had been his second command tour on the same boat. He knew there wouldn't be a third, and he was still only a captain of second rank. Successfully doing what the message described would go a long way to getting him promoted to full captain, able to wear the single thick bar and three stars on his shoulder that told everyone he was on his way to becoming an admiral. He nodded to himself. They needed to get this right.

He called the navigator over and gave him the updated coordinates. He watched as the information was typed into the inertial nav system, and felt the change of motion as the sub began to turn.

He'd have to brief his executive officer and the four department heads, and find some surface time for the specialist crewmen to practice operations. Their new orders were going to require patience, pinpoint accuracy and swift action.

He needed to get his men ready.

The sheltered harbors of the Hawaiian island of Oahu are a natural wonder. The inlets and bays reach deep inland, giving the islanders access to fresh water flowing down the steep slopes of the Ko'olau Range and protection from the ocean's storms. Food is abundant on the lush surrounding land, and under the bays' clear, still waters are pearl-producing oysters. Since before written history, Pacific sailors had found sanctuary in what the ancient Hawaiians called Wai Momi, the Waters of Pearl.

The harbor's entrance had been dredged and widened as ships got bigger, and the USS *New Orleans*, a flat-topped amphibious assault ship, required at least 30 feet of depth. As she exited Pearl Harbor and cleared Hammer Point, headed out to sea, she came left to exactly 154 degrees to stay in the center of the 1,000-foot-wide channel. Captain Bob Carius, standing by the forward windows of the conning tower, was relieved to see the depth sounder fall away rapidly, from 50 to 100, and then to over 1,000 feet as they cleared the island's shore. The brief stay at Pearl had been pleasant for the crew after a nine-month cruise, helping with Philippine flood relief and de-mining the coastal waters of North Vietnam as the last American combat troops were finally leaving. But he was looking forward to the tasking they'd received.

The *New Orleans* was sailing to recover the Apollo 18 crew.

Captain Carius wasn't sure what the post-Vietnam era was going to mean for the Pacific Fleet, but the *New Orleans* had acquitted herself well, and helping to bring the Apollo astronauts home was a definite feather in their cap. He'd even heard that Al Shepard, the first American in space and a Navy Rear Admiral, was going to be aboard to see the splashdown.

They passed the red and green harbor entrance buoys, and he relaxed, walking around the bridge, looking out at his ship. Most of the 700 crewmen had come up onto the large, flat deck as they'd left port, and he'd had the Apollo rescue helicopters proudly positioned on the bow to let everyone know where they were going. The maintainers had made sure that the Sikorsky SH-3A Sea Kings were freshly painted bright white, and the crews of Helicopter Sea Combat Squadron SIX had been practicing recovery procedures for several weeks.

They'd been waiting at Pearl for the exact location of the splashdown, and now NASA had given the Navy the coordinates: 300 miles north and a bit west of Oahu. An easy sail out, a little over a day to do final preparations on station, and they'd be ready.

Fun, really. Deploy the helos as soon as the capsule was under parachute, drop divers into the water next to it at splashdown, attach the flotation ring and help the crew into the rescue raft, hoist them aboard the *New Orleans* and welcome them back to Earth.

Unless something went wrong. He'd gotten a detailed briefing while in port, and he'd been running over his crew's readiness for multiple scenarios. There'd been storms in Apollo 11's planned landing area, and the rescue ship had to steam full-speed to meet the capsule hundreds of miles downrange. The Apollo 12 capsule had hit a wave hard at splashdown and an internal camera had broken loose; it hit an astronaut in the head, knocking him out. The ship's doctor had to give him six stitches. Apollo 15 had vented caustic hypergolic fuel that had melted parachute lines, collapsing one of its three canopies. And several capsules had landed upside down in the water, and the crew needed to quickly inflate emergency flotation balls to right them. From the briefing it was clear that Apollo 18 had had its share of serious trouble already, but he was confident that his ship and crew could deliver. They'd proven themselves on this cruise, in both war and peacetime, and they still had a couple of days for final polish. No matter what NASA threw at them, they'd be ready.

Carius leaned forward and looked up at the blue Hawaiian sky. This one should be a piece of cake.

Under the hot Sun on the surface of the Moon, Lunokhod was dying. Like a child with an uncontrollable fever, it was slowly shutting down internally, less and less capable to survive its own rising body heat.

Gabdul had worked frantically to try to save it just before the Apollo craft had lifted off. He'd alternated between driving and braking as violently as he could, trying to dislodge the layer of dust on the radiator, all while moving as close to the lander as possible, hoping its rocket blast might scour the flat surface clean. The team had talked quickly about the risk of debris damage, but it didn't matter. If they couldn't clear the dust, their mission was over.

They'd sent commands to close the camera covers just before liftoff, squinting their rover's eyes against the sandblast. But the light upper stage had left the surface so fast that it had blown only a little of the sand off; the rate of heating had slowed, but it hadn't stopped.

Gabdul had announced one last idea hurriedly, and had clicked the eyes back open while mashing the hand controller to full speed. His team had mapped a small, steep-sided crater a couple hundred meters away that they'd steered around on the way to the landing site. Now he was driving directly at it.

"I need the best timing countdown you can give me. Start at ten!" he urgently told his navigator. They needed to guess exactly right as they watched the new images slowly process, blurred with the bouncing motion, delayed by the enormous distance.

The navigator did his best, using every clue he could gather: forward speed readout, their nav map, the heading data and the latest looks at the lunar surface on the screen.

"Ten!" he said decisively. Then "Nine!"

He'd play the cadence right to the last, based on everything he saw. He said eight, seven and six quickly, and then five, four and three in an even rhythm. He could feel his heart racing, knowing this was all or nothing, based on too much guesswork.

"Dva . . . raz! Now, Gabdul, brake!"

Gabdul reversed hard, held it for two seconds and released his hand completely, listening to the small springs make a quick thocking sound as the hand controller returned itself to center. All eyes were glued to the screen.

His plan had been to bound over the edge at full speed and then lurch to a stop, driving the eight wheels backwards, encouraging the sand to slide off the top as Lunokhod came to rest on a steep angle.

The image resolved itself, drawing line by line from top to bottom on the monitor. All they could see was a screenful of lunar regolith, no horizon visible.

"We're in!" Gabdul turned to look at the rover's attitude sensor—a bit tipped left, but steeply nose-down. He read the number aloud, triumphant: "Thirty-five degrees!" That was basically the physical limit for a slope of loose regolith. They couldn't have done it any better. No one knew if they'd be able to drive out, but they'd done all they could.

Gabdul turned to the vehicle systems operator and asked the question on behalf of everyone. "Are we still getting hotter?"

The internal temperature readout was steady for many seconds. Longer than they'd seen during the race across the surface. Hopes rose. Then it clicked up by a tenth of a degree. And then another. And, as they all watched, by yet another.

It hadn't worked. The jolt hadn't shifted enough of the blanket of dust.

After three months of exploration, thousands of images and data points, and discovery of concentrated radioactivity on the Moon, the mission was over.

Lunokhod was in its grave.

Outside their building, the huge antenna that had brought the team the bad news pivoted, almost imperceptibly, its focused commands and patient listening circuits searching for a new signal. As soon as it found it, the self-tracking mechanism locked on and began following, steering precisely. The processors analyzed the timing and frequency shifts of the signals, and started doing the math. As it continued to track, the accuracy got better and better, until it had a solution threshold that could be trusted.

A second computer took that information and ran it through equations that included the mass and exact positions of the Moon and the spinning Earth, and used models of the friction that the atmosphere and shock waves would cause. It added the known characteristics of how previous missions had steered themselves, and how much g they had pulled as they descended.

In less than two minutes it had a result, and automatically transmitted it to the flight dynamics officer at his console in TsUP in
Moscow. He looked at the screen with its table of flickering numbers,
watching them update and become even more accurate with each
passing second.

He leaned back and turned, waving to get the attention of the flight
director. They now knew exactly where Apollo 18 was going to splash
down.

56

Hickam Air Force Base, Hawaii

Kaz stretched and yawned as he stepped out of the dark interior of the C-141 transport plane, blinking at the bright Hawaiian sunshine, looking around the ramp and spotting the white Sea King helicopter waiting for them. He'd slept, but his lower back was aching; Air Force seats were built for troop transport, not comfort. As he stiffly walked down the airstairs, he could feel the heat reflecting up off the tarmac, his shirt starting to stick to him in the humid ocean air. Behind him, JW was noisily descending. A seaman met them at the bottom and took their hand luggage to transfer to the helo.

Al Shepard had gotten off first and was already taking the salute from the Sea King crew. Behind Al, waiting his turn, was the Soviet attaché, tall in a dark suit. In Houston, he'd introduced himself briefly as Roman Stepanov, his English good but thickly accented. He'd kept to himself during the flight, reading papers from his briefcase and dozing like the rest of them, even though each of the three Americans had moved to an empty seat in the Soviet's row during the flight to make conversation. Kaz had held out his hand across the seats. "Hi, I'm Kaz

Zemeckis, crew liaison. Been working in Mission Control throughout the flight." Stepanov, broad-shouldered and fit, had returned the handshake with a firm, dry grip and said, "Hello." The remaining hair on his prematurely bald head was neatly trimmed, his thick eyebrows were arched, and his small ears were a poor match for his large, hooked nose. His pale-gray eyes and thin mouth were expressionless. A thoughtful face.

"So did they brief you on what to expect during splashdown?"

"Yes." Stepanov held up a sheaf of papers on NASA letterhead.

A pause.

Kaz tried a different tack. "Been to Hawaii before?"

"No." Not unfriendly, just a clear vibe that he'd been doing something worthwhile and was politely waiting for Kaz to leave so he could get back to it. Like an interrupted professor.

"Okay, well, let me know if I can help."

The Russian had nodded and thanked him.

Not a chatterbox.

Kaz and the doctor climbed up into the helicopter and took their seats, opposite Al and the Russian, on the simple green webbing on metal frames that ran the length of the crew cabin. The crew chief gave them a short briefing on emergencies and handed them uninflated life jackets and earplugs as the five big rotor blades started turning above their heads.

The attaché listened attentively, then comfortably donned the safety equipment and did up the heavy shoulder and waist straps unaided.

Not Stepanov's first rodeo.

The Sea King lurched up off the pavement, pivoted in place, tipped forward and accelerated out to sea.

Chad looked out the window of *Pursuit*. The Moon behind him had shrunk to the size of a dime against the blackness. Ahead, what had been a thumbnail-sized marble, blue with white and green-brown highlights, was growing and resolving itself rapidly into the easily recognizable coastlines and country shapes of Earth; it felt like he was walking towards a lit globe on a darkened shelf.

He'd steered the ship to skim exactly against the side of that ball, where it would just brush the upper tendrils of the atmosphere. The ultimate high-stakes billiards shot: miss wide and they'd carom off into space with not enough oxygen to last until they could make it back. Hit with just a bit too much angle and the ship would dig in, disintegrating into flames under the violent deceleration.

He smiled at his reflection, repeating in the multilayered glass. He'd done everything perfectly. Been up for every challenge they'd thrown at him. And with the final test still coming, he was ready.

He glanced at Michael and Svetlana, thinking about the incomplete picture they each held in their heads, shaping their predictable choices and actions. He looked at Earth again, his smile growing wider. The Soviets thought they were directing what was going on—that they could control him! The Americans had arrogantly set the mission's parameters, yet needed someone who could actually do it.

I was chosen for this!

His life, from childhood until this exact moment, was like a movie script where he'd been the inevitable action hero.

Action hero. The words echoed in his head. He hadn't thought of himself that way before. But that's who he was. It was perfect. At every turn he'd taken the right action, moved forward, left the others behind—before they even knew what was happening.

And he was about to do it again. He had a plan that would achieve all the goals, and then some. He'd used this return trip, these two days when everyone else had just dozed and twiddled their thumbs, to dig into the details and come up with the right actions. His crew would be helpless to stop him.

He half closed his eyes and pictured it, his hands subtly performing the motions as if he were a conductor directing an orchestra. Reach here, move that, see this, say those words. A symphony of his own making, the ship responding, his actions setting the course of history.

A small thought popped into his reverie, unbidden. His smile faded and he frowned, picturing what it meant. He walked through the plan, seeing how it would unfold with this unwanted input, clicking through if/then statements, churning the wheel, checking the readout, then changing assumptions and rerunning it. Repeating until he had a way to make it work. As he saw the solution, his smile returned.

He checked his watch—enough time before tomorrow's main event.

One last look at himself in the window, the growing brightness of Earth highlighting his face, the endless darkness behind.

Action hero.

First nights on ships always kept Kaz awake. He wasn't sure why. Maybe it was the new sounds, the different motions of this particular hull in the water, the hardness of the thin Navy-issue mattress on the berth. From experience he knew it would be better the second night, and after a few days he'd sleep soundly. But for now, he was restless in the darkness of his small cabin aboard the USS *New Orleans*. He opened his eyes wide. *Weird*, he thought, not for the first time. An inner room on a ship with watertight closed hatches made for total darkness. He could feel that his eyelids were open, but his eye could see absolutely nothing.

A good place to think.

The sheriff hadn't found any proof that Chad had sabotaged Tom's helo, but the other information was troubling. Why had Chad never admitted to anyone that he was born into a Russian family, or that he'd retained enough of the language to stay in touch with this newly uncovered brother of his?

Kaz had learned that sometimes, to solve a problem, you had to take it back to basics and repicture it as if it were an exam question on a page. He tried phrasing it that way to himself.

A lander with two crew, American and Russian, is on the Moon. Above them, a spaceship with an American aboard is orbiting every 2 hours. Earth is a quarter million miles away, turning every 24 hours. Mission Control is in Houston, but has satellite dishes spaced around the globe to talk continuously to the crew. Once in a while, Houston hears the crew click their mic twice. Why?

Kaz blinked several times and turned his head against the hard pillow. He could feel the stiff crispness of the pillowcase, no doubt high-temp-washed and rough-pressed by a seaman somewhere in the industrial bowels of the ship.

Nothing.

He tried another entry point. Why had the Soviets sent a KGB officer? The way the guy was so quiet and calculating and the muscular bulk under the lousy suit were giveaways. Why wouldn't they send a political, maybe the deputy ambassador, someone who they could publicly identify in the PR pictures so they could wave the Soviet flag in everyone's face? He recalled Stepanov's face—this guy wasn't here for protocol. So what *was* he here for?

The cosmonaut was supposed to still be on Almaz, dutifully orbiting and photographing secret things around the planet, dropping film to Earth in canisters. No one had planned on her being part of this mission. So Stepanov was part of the reaction on their part, another attempt to turn the situation to their advantage. But what did they have control over, and what leverage could they use?

He stretched out on his back and scrunched the pillow under his neck for support. The berth was just long enough that the top of his head and his feet didn't touch the bulkheads. He closed his eyes and exhaled to relax.

His eyes snapped open in the darkness. *Could that be it?*

He tried to remember the exact timing, reviewing when he'd been on shift, mapping it out. He realized that it fit.

Christ!

The Soviets had been talking to the crew.

And the crew had responded.

57

Re-entry

Chad glanced at his small computer screen: 36,165 feet per second. He did the math. *Holy crap! I'm flying seven miles every second. Thirty-two times the speed of sound. Take THAT, Chuck Yeager!*

He leaned forward in his seat to look across at Michael, strapped in beside him, and the cosmonaut on the far right. "Get ready for the finest seven minutes of your life, kids."

The three of them had re-donned their spacesuits. NASA had learned that a Soviet crew of three had perished when re-entry vibrations and g-loads caused a cabin leak, and had added the safety measure for Apollo 18.

Pursuit was 75 miles high, just beginning to touch the outer atmosphere. Chad punched in the program code to check landing location, and compared it to the latitude and longitude Houston had given them. Identical. They were headed to an empty spot in the ocean, just a couple miles short of the USS *New Orleans*.

On the outside of the capsule, bad things were starting to happen. *Pursuit* was slamming into the rarefied air molecules with so much energy that it was ripping electrons free and tearing at its belly shield, burning off the outer layer. The mix of ionized gases clung to *Pursuit's* skin in a sheath of blowtorch flames; an electric plasma field, glowing yellow and orange and red, enveloped the ship in a hypersonic fireball.

"My God, look at that!" Michael was watching the flames lick and dance across the windows, the shadows flickering inside the capsule. "We're flying through a blast furnace!"

Svetlana let the chatter wash over her, probing how her body felt in anticipation of what was about to happen. She'd studied re-entry in detail at Star City, and had practiced repeatedly in the centrifuge trainer; to pass her cosmonaut flight qualification, she'd had to take over from the ship's computers and fly the simulated capsule by hand, all the way down to parachute opening. On an early training run she'd misjudged it, dug in too deeply and failed, pulling 14 g—beyond the limits of the simulator, barely survivable in real life. She knew how thin the margins were.

She looked at the horizon line in the overhead windows, judging their entry angle; it made sense to her. They were coming in belly first, slightly tipped up and rolled to the right, the computer ready to play the roll angle to control the g force. She nodded. *Just like I'd do it.*

Chad watched his entry monitoring panel, the large black arrow showing roll angle, the small digital readouts showing g and distance to go. He ran his thumb down the checklist and warned, "Here it comes!"

The sudden onslaught of force was vicious. In just 15 seconds the g slammed from zero to seven times their normal weight, pinning their heads hard back inside their helmets, forcing their arms down onto their chests, crushing them into their seats.

Svetlana could feel the skin of her face being pulled backwards, the strained tautness across her cheeks, her eyes watering to try to fight the brutality.

Michael gasped. "Hhhard to breathe!" he grunted. Pulling oxygen into his lungs felt like weight-lifting; he had to deliberately force his chest to expand, pushing his ribs forward.

Yet as soon as it was there it was gone, backing off to just 3 g as the capsule pulled out of its initial steep dive, settling into a shallower angle, racing and falling through the air. Chad knew the profile. "A couple minutes here, then we'll peak again."

They were on their own. The communications failure they'd had after launch had returned as soon as they'd jettisoned the lower Service Module, as expected. And even if the radios had been working, the glowing plasma field was blocking the antennas.

Pursuit was a fireball, plummeting earthward with the first step complete, now rolling precisely in readiness for the second g-spike.

Ever since the Apollo craft's launch day, the *Cosmonaut Yuri Gagarin* communications relay ship had been steaming northwards across the Pacific to be in position to observe splashdown. She was now just over the horizon from the USS *New Orleans*, her huge twin tracking antennas pointed along the expected entry trajectory. As the capsule emerged from the heavy g-load, still 170,000 feet up and racing towards the waiting ships, the *Gagarin's* systems found it and locked on.

The antenna operator said, "We have it, Captain. Exactly on track."

The Captain nodded and pointed at his communications officer. "Let them know." The lieutenant typed rapidly, and the coded message left the ship, relaying up through distant satellites and back down on the other side of the world to TsUp in Moscow. There, the flight director waved for Chelomei's attention and pointed to his screen.

Chelomei read the text and nodded. *Pa paryadkeh.* So far, so good.

A hundred miles to the northeast of the *Gagarin*, Kaz was on the bridge of the *New Orleans*, standing beside Al Shepard and the attaché, Stepanov. He checked his watch and glanced at the timings in his notebook, providing a running commentary for Captain Carius. "They're six hundred miles out now, sir, with the second g-spike to go, expecting drogue chute opening in just under six minutes."

Carius nodded. "And how long until splashdown?"

"The drogue will pull out the three main parachutes, and then they'll be under those for another five minutes, so into the water in about ten minutes." With no radio communication, Kaz was just guessing, using predicted times. The New Orleans would receive the capsule's homing beacon as soon as the deploying parachutes triggered it. Then they'd know for sure.

Carius turned to his executive officer. "XO, what's 501's status?"

"She cleared the deck ten minutes ago with our team and the NASA doc on board, and is on station." The XO pointed forward and left of the bow, where the white of the Sea King helicopter was just visible above the blue horizon. Carius raised his binoculars and could make out the large 501 painted on her tail.

"The helo crew's reporting pretty choppy seas, Boss, five-foot swells."

Shepard gave a low whistle. "That's worse than it was for my crew, Bob. More like what they saw on Apollo 12." He grimaced. "Poor suckers're gonna puke."

Bob Carius smiled. "That's what you get when you fly Air Force astronauts, Admiral."

The Captain had one more question. "XO, we seeing anyone else in the area?"

The XO deliberately didn't look at Stepanov, who'd been listening, stone-faced. "We've got the Soviet comm relay ship, the Gagarin, just over a hundred miles out along the entry track. Normal enough, and to be expected with a cosmonaut on board this time." He didn't mention what the captain already knew: they'd deployed several sonobuoys but had heard no sounds of any submarine activity. No sub had ever shadowed a previous splashdown, but the New Orleans was an anti-sub ship, and the XO was just being thorough.

Carius smiled. "So apart from maybe needing some sick bags, I think the good ship New Orleans is ready to pipe aboard three new crewmembers."

———

Chad watched the g-meter carefully for the critical moment. He had to time this just right: early enough to have the desired effect, but too late for Michael to diagnose what was happening and take countering action. He could feel the capsule lofting slightly under him, the force letting up slightly prior to falling into thicker air and starting the second g-load.

Now!

He reached out with his left hand and flicked the switch to take spacecraft control away from the guidance computer. He was holding the hand controller in his right, and he rocked it hard sideways, towards his leg, commanding a turn. Small thrusters on the hull fired in response, and the capsule began to spin up to the left, like a slow-turning top.

Michael was alarmed. "What are you seeing?"

Chad put incredulity into his voice. "Did you miss it? Our beta was building rapidly! I've taken over for now, getting ready to go to Program 66 for ballistic."   ⸴

Michael stared at the displays. *Our sideslip built up? Shit! How did I miss that?* He flipped the page in his checklist to the backup ballistic procedures. "Okay, I'm with you, Chad, on 2-6." He quickly thought about it. "With bad beta, though, I recommend against program ballistic, and that puts us in the starred block for manual EMS."

As Chad had expected, Michael was reacting just like they'd trained. "Copy, but let's try Program 66, to give the computer another chance. If no joy, I'll just take over manually again."

Michael weighed the odds. "Okay, agreed. I'm watching."

Chad released the hand controller and steadied his arm under the g-load as his finger poked at the small keyboard. Michael confirmed— "I see P66"—and Chad pushed the Proceed button. Their eyes locked onto the Entry Monitoring Systems panel.

Michael rapidly thought ahead. The ship was slowly rolling now, no longer generating continuous lift along its flight path; it had gone from flying under control like an airplane to just falling, arcing downwards like a thrown baseball.

"Hold on!" he shouted, and waved a hand near Svetlana to make sure she realized there was a serious problem. They were about to fall steeper into the thicker air and endure a lot more g than planned. As they fell faster, that air was going to slow their forward speed even more as well. There was nothing he could do.

Pursuit was going to land short.

At Kaena Point, on a high, windy ridge at the western tip of Oahu, an Air Force domed radar tracking antenna detected the subtle change in *Pursuit*'s motion. The data was automatically sent via undersea cable to Mission Control in Houston, appearing as numbers on the screen at the re-entry Guidance Officer's console.

"FLIGHT, GUIDO, the capsule's off trajectory." He watched for several seconds, listening to the rapid analysis in his headset from the experts in his back room. "We think it's gone to ballistic mode."

Damn! Gene Krantz thought. The weather briefer had talked about the rough sea state, and this meant the crew would be in the water longer than planned. "Copy, GUIDO, let me know when you have an updated splashdown location." He turned to his communications officer. "INCO, let's get the *New Orleans* that info ASAP."

Ninety seconds later the teletype machine began clacking in the communications cabin of the *New Orleans*. The Petty Officer tore off the page while reading it and hustled to hand it to the XO. He silently read it and handed it to the Captain, who frowned.

"This is from your boys in Houston," he said to the small group. "The capsule has gone into something called a backup ballistic mode, and is going to land short, apparently." He turned to the helmsman and handed him the paper. "Make for those new coordinates, full speed."

"How far short?" Kaz asked, evaluating causes for the unexpected change, already guessing the answer.

"About a hundred miles. We'll be there in four hours. The helo will take about an hour or so." He thought quickly. "XO, I don't think they'll have enough fuel now. Bring them aboard for a hot pit."

The Captain turned to Al Shepard. "Admiral, this just escalated. The new splashdown site is way too near that Soviet ship. I'm going to send two helos so we can have a few extra personnel on-site until the *New Orleans* can get there. Who from your team do you want to go?"

"The doc, of course, and Kaz. We'll need somebody on scene familiar with crew ops."

Stepanov spoke for the first time that morning. "I must go too."

The XO immediately shook his head and looked straight at the captain. "No way, Boss. We've already got all the skills we need, and Kaz is Navy-familiar. I don't need an embassy bureaucrat getting in the way." He glanced at Stepanov. "No offense."

Stepanov's expression said he took none. He spoke calmly. "Major Gromova doesn't speak English, and might be injured because of this new situation. There is no question. I must go also."

The Captain looked at his XO. "He's got a point, and our orders are clear that we provide full support to the cosmonaut. Put him on the same helo as Kaz, keep him out of trouble."

The XO started to speak, thought better of it and nodded. "Aye aye, sir." He nodded at the two men and headed rapidly towards the ladder leading down to the deck. "You come with me. We'll get you outfitted fast and on your way. We've got a lost space capsule to catch."

Kaz looked around inside the Sea King as it throbbed noisily, powering nose-low through the air at max speed towards the southwest. He was relieved that this wasn't a typical Apollo recovery crew, with safety divers and medicos. Filling the seats around Stepanov and himself were six large men, all wearing coveralls and heavy boots, each cradling an MP5 submachine gun on a shoulder strap, with a Colt M1911 pistol clipped on their webbed belt. The XO had decided that with the Soviet ship nearby there was potential for military action, and these men were the masters-at-arms of the *New Orleans*—the cross-trained sailors responsible for law enforcement at sea.

Sitting to Kaz's left was a black-haired man with a wide black mustache, the senior rate in the group. He'd shouted instructions as they'd hurried aboard the helo, and Kaz leaned close now to make himself heard through the earplugs, above the din.

"I'm Lieutenant Commander Kaz Zameckis, detailed with NASA. What briefing did your team get?"

"Petty Officer First Class Colombo, sir. We didn't get much of a briefing; the XO said the Apollo capsule has two astronauts and a cosmonaut aboard, be nearby for a show of force and take action only if needed." He looked at his men. "We had some pretty hairy times up the Vietnam coast and in the P.I., and have been training together this whole cruise. We're ready if something happens."

Kaz nodded. "Some of you may have to go into the water."

"Yep, we've got gear." He pointed at several large duffel bags inside the aft loading ramp. "I'll get the guys dressed when we're closer. No use overheating for now."

Kaz leaned farther, talking directly into the man's ear so he wouldn't be overheard. "If the XO didn't tell you, the guy with me is a Soviet attaché, likely military. Need to keep an eye on him."

Colombo nodded without looking and said, "My men can handle it."

Kaz sat back, satisfied. Stepanov was sitting motionless, staring straight ahead. Kaz thought back: the Russian had shown no surprise when they'd learned the capsule was landing short. Then again, he hadn't yet shown any emotion. *Did he somehow expect it?* Kaz had spent another full hour of the night in his bunk thinking through possibilities before finally falling asleep, and had briefed Al Shepard over breakfast. They'd agreed direct crew communication from Moscow might have been possible; this event only heightened the concern.

He turned back to the mustached Colombo.

"I'd like a gun as well."

Colombo turned and spoke into Kaz's ear. "We have extra in the bag. I'll get you one at a good moment."

58

Splashdown Zone

The g-load came on even more suddenly this time, like a skipping stone badly thrown into a pond; instead of skimming into the water at an angle, *Pursuit* was falling, nearly vertical, into the rapidly thickening air below. Michael called out the readings on the digital display, grunting more and more as the weight increased.

"There's five. Now six." He strained to take a quick breath. "Seven, eight . . . there's nine!" The flames on the other side of the glass deepened to an intense yellow, the cockpit glowing like it was on fire. On *Pursuit*'s belly, the three-inch-thick protective plate of fiberglass and epoxy resin took the brunt of it, burning off and vaporizing in the 5,000-degree, friction-driven heat. Through the windows the three of them watched the roiling sheets of flame and continuous sparks of burnt resin whipping past.

And then they were through. The crushing force disappeared like someone had just lifted it off them, and the windows filled with the blue of the sky. The capsule was now simply a skydiver plummeting straight down at 250 miles an hour, 5 miles above the Pacific, waiting for her parachute to open.

Bang! The noise of small explosives came through their helmets as a metal cover blew off the top of *Pursuit* and two small drogue chutes mortared out behind it. The beyond-hurricane-force wind caught the fabric and snapped the unreefing chutes fully open, yanking the lines taut, pushing the crew hard down into their seats.

A brief new normal now, a momentary calm, as they fell in a 120-mile-per-hour vertical dive, waiting for the final event.

At 11,000 feet a small pressure sensor sent the command to cut the drogue lines and explosively fire three small parachutes; they caught the air and dragged out the big main chutes, which blossomed and filled the sky above their heads with red and white.

Michael raised two gloved fists, relief clear in his voice. "I see three good chutes!"

"Slava Bogu," Sveltana said quietly. Thank God.

On the top of *Pursuit*, a small VHF antenna pivoted clear and began transmitting the good news, a triumphant beacon signal for the rescue forces to home in. But the two helicopters were still beyond the horizon, 70 miles away, and missed it.

On the bridge of the *Gagarin*, the signal came clearly through the loudspeakers. The radio operator had been tracking the re-entry and quickly narrowed in on the exact location: "Bearing 037, Captain, range twelve kilometers." All heads turned to scan the bright sky, the Captain raising powerful binoculars to his eyes. "Vizhu," he said with satisfaction. I see it.

He turned back to the radio operator and nodded once. "Let them know."

The impact with the water was violent; *Pursuit*'s broad, flat underside made for a resounding belly flop, like squarely driving into a wall at 22 miles per hour.

"Christ!" Michael swore. "What a car crash!"

Pursuit plunged deeply, the salt water curling up around her in an enveloping wave. Then, like a cork, she bobbed immediately back up and tipped, yanked sideways by the parachutes caught in the wind.

The Apollo designers had recognized from the beginning that the capsule could function as a boat, but not very well. Ideally it would float upright, with the crew lying in their seats; they named that orientation Stable One. But in testing they'd also identified that the capsule could easily float inverted. They called that Stable Two.

Pursuit came to rest in the water upside down, swaying in the heavy waves. The crew hung in their straps as checklists fell to the top of the cockpit, banging against the metal of the tunnel hatch.

"Stable Two!" Michael called.

Chad threw the switches to cut the parachute lines. "Yeah, I see that. I'll get the float bags." He pushed in several circuit breakers and listened as two small compressors spun into life, pumping air into three inflatable bags attached to the top of *Pursuit*. They were designed to give the capsule added flotation and flip it upright.

What the engineers hadn't considered was the relentless effect of truly heavy seas. Waves kept breaking over the exposed flat bottom of *Pursuit*, flooding the compressor air inlets, overloading the built-in drains. The bags filled too slowly, getting pulled back and forth with each wave, the forces prying them against their mountings.

Perhaps if they'd filled fast enough the design would have worked and popped *Pursuit* up to Stable One. But the partially filled and still floppy bags were worked mercilessly back and forth by the powerful surges. Stressed to the limit, first the center bag tore, followed within seconds by the other two. The compressors kept running, futilely pumping air into the water next to the flapping remnants of the bags, the stream of bubbles rising around the sloped sides of the ship, popping on the surface between the waves.

Pursuit was going to stay upside down. And her rescue divers were still sitting in their Sea King helicopter, 65 miles away.

———

"Shit! This is taking too long." Chad's anger grew as he looked at the timer and then through the dark of the underwater windows, trying to spot the yellow of the filling bags. He double-checked his switches: no mistake.

"Yeah, the bags aren't working," Michael said. "And with the ballistic entry, help's gonna be a while getting here. I'm thinking we should get outside by ourselves." They were swaying left and right as the capsule rocked in the waves, their heads hanging down and their arms and legs dangling back and forth. After a week of weightlessness, he felt dizzy and disoriented, and had already had a twinge of nausea.

Fuck! Chad thought. *I flew this perfectly, and the stupid engineers can't design three balloons that work?* The motion was getting to him as well, and he shook his head to clear it. "Okay, I'm starting into unaided egress. I'll get the hatch and the raft, and you take care of her." He disconnected his suit hoses and comm line and twisted around to drag the survival raft kit out of its locker, dropping it down by the hatch. The motion made his head spin, and he blinked hard until things stabilized. He released his harness buckle and immediately flipped down towards the hatch, landing hard on his hands and knees. The air in the cockpit was getting warm and humid, and his visor was fogging, his body banging left and right with the wave motion. As he reached to open the hatch, he felt the first surge of nausea, and swallowed hard. Just as the hatch popped free and water rushed in around its edge seals, Chad vomited. Focused projectile vomiting, filling his visor in front of his face, splashing back into his nose and eyes, the gastric acid blinding him.

"Fuck!" he yelled, the "k" ending in a wet, retching cough and a second spasm. He grabbed blindly for his neck ring and released it, yanking the fouled helmet off his head, rubbing his eyes clear. He rotated the hatch out of the way, grabbed the survival kit, took a breath and rocked forward through the hatch, headfirst into the black water.

Behind him, Michael was vomiting as well. He'd peeled his helmet off when he'd felt it coming, and was using it as a bucket to throw up

into while disconnecting himself and Svetlana. As soon as he saw Chad
go out the hatch, he released his harness and reached up to release hers.

Svetlana still had her helmet on, and watched as Michael waved
her urgently towards the water-filled hatch. *Weak Americans! Why are*
both these men sick? She'd trained for emergency water egress in an
inverted capsule in the Black Sea, and moved easily, grabbing the sides
of the hatch with both hands, and thrusting herself through, feet-first.
Behind her, Michael had one last look around, grabbed his survival kit,
took a deep breath and pushed himself into the hatch.

All three of them were in the sea.

As Chad floated rapidly up, bareheaded, the tight rubber seal around
his neck kept the water out of his spacesuit. Clutching the bulky survival
kit tightly under his left arm, he pushed repeatedly with his right to fend
off the sloping side of the capsule.

His lungs were screaming as he burst into the sunshine; instinctively
he gulped for a huge breath just as a wave hit, slapping him in the face
with a five-foot-high wall of water, smashing him into *Pursuit's* hard,
curved edge. He raised his hands to protect his head, and the survival
kit bounced out of his grasp, skittering across the belly of the capsule.

Shit! He coughed and retched up seawater, blinking his eyes against
the saltiness, scrabbling for a handhold on the smooth, wet underside
of the capsule. His gloved fingers blindly found a bolt hole and he
pulled hard, sliding himself towards the floating kit. The next wave
picked him up and slammed him again into *Pursuit*, the impact making him gasp. He swam clumsily through the surging water, kicking
inside the stiffness of the suit, trying to focus and time it right. Just as a
third wave hit, he reached hard with his right hand and felt his fingers
close around the survival kit's handle. The crashing water tumbled
them both clear of the capsule as he fumbled at the long zipper to
open the bag and deploy the raft.

Svetlana's helmeted head bobbed up behind him, and she looked
around, assessing, treading water hard to stay clear of the capsule. The

trapped oxygen inside her suit would only be good for a few more breaths, and soon she'd have to take off her helmet. She spotted Chad 10 meters away and started swimming hard towards him, letting each wave push her as she stroked and kicked. She watched as he reached inside an oblong bag and pulled; a yellow raft started inflating, rapidly filling, unfolding itself into a long rectangle. Chad was pulling on its handles as it reached full-size, twisting and timing the waves to try to yank it under himself, and finally he flopped facedown into the center.

She kicked hard and found a strap trailing in the water. As soon as the next wave rolled past she grabbed the raft with both hands and pulled herself up and in, landing on top of Chad's legs. Both of them flailed to get on their backs in the center, to stabilize and not capsize in the heaving seas.

As Michael's bare head burst to the surface, he spun, spotted them and started side-stroking hard, his elbow crooked through the end strap of his kit bag. But the raft was floating on the surface, the wind blowing it along the foaming tops of the waves. Michael stole glances each time he crested the top of a wave, gauging his progress, and realized he was losing the race; the kit was dragging him down. "Hey!" he yelled as loudly as he could, trying to get their attention above the noise of the wind and water.

Svetlana was getting dizzy with the buildup of carbon dioxide in her suit. As she popped off her helmet, she heard Michael's voice. She raised her head over the bulbous side of the raft and spotted him splashing towards them, 10 meters away.

"Morskoy yakor?" she shouted at Chad. Is there a sea anchor? He looked at her uncomprehendingly, dazed with the nausea and his repeated hard impacts with *Pursuit*. *Useless!* She probed under him, searching for a bundle on a thick strap that had been in every raft she'd ever trained on. When she found it, she tore the package open and hurled it overboard, letting the jellyfish-shaped cloth anchor unfurl and start dragging. Immediately she felt a tug and then the entire raft pivoted, stabilizing and slowing against the wind and the waves.

She propped herself up on an elbow again to see Michael, and spotted him struggling, seemingly farther away. "Syudah!" she yelled twice, as loudly as she could. Over here! She waved her hand high, back and forth.

Christ, I'm not going to make it! Michael thought. Every time he'd caught a glimpse of the raft it was getting away from him. He decided to let go of his kit just as he heard the female voice scream, and changed his mind, keeping the strap inside his elbow. He strained again to look, and saw a hand waving. Kicking harder, he pulled as strongly as he could with his free arm, cupping his gloved hand to get the most out of every stroke. He stole another glance and the raft seemed slightly closer.

He heard her voice yelling again—"Da, Da!"—and kept pulling, timing his strokes with each wave, clumsily trying to bodysurf with the kit in between crests. He thought her calls were getting louder, and craned his head up, relieved to see the raft just 10 feet away. "Syudah!" she shouted again, with one of her arms over the side, reaching for him. He gave a final maximum-effort stroke and found her hand, their gloved fingers locking together. She reached over the edge with her other hand and grabbed the kit as he twisted to find a handrail. Kicking and heaving with the last of his strength, with Svetlana pulling on the back of his neck ring, he got his upper torso onto the inflated curve of the raft, and with one final kick, tumbled in against Chad and Svetlana.

A jumble of bodies crammed into a pitching three-man raft, being blown steadily away from their spacecraft towards the open, empty, wind-swept Pacific.

Michael spoke first, in heaving breaths, to Svetlana. "Thank you! How do you say it? Spasiba?"

"Nyeh za shto," she responded. It was nothing. She handed him the kit, anticipating what was inside.

Michael took a breath to gather himself. He unzipped the package, pulling out two heavy, army-green metal blocks. He held them up to her. "Radio!"

Svetlana nodded. "Znayoo." I know.

Michael twisted his wrist rings to release his gloves from the sleeves of the suit, and peeled the heavy wet fabric off his hands. He tucked them into his leg pockets, and with bare fingers slid the cylindrical battery into the radio, twisted the cap into place and clicked the thumb-wheel to turn it on. Immediately there was an audible hiss of static, and he screwed on the whip antenna. He knew from training that they were now transmitting an emergency beacon signal, and that by push-ing the button on the side, they could talk.

"Give me that," Chad said. "I'll call in the helos." He held out his hand.

Michael looked at him across the length of the raft, paused for a second and then shrugged. "You're the boss." He leaned forward, hand-ing it over. Svetlana, watching the exchange, understood what had just happened. *Tipeechny*. Typical.

Chad held the radio up to his ear and pushed the button. "Rescue Forces, this is the Apollo 18 crew. We've exited the spacecraft and are secure in the raft." He looked back at *Pursuit* in the distance as the waves bobbed them up and down, and up at the Sun. "We've been blown about a hundred yards downwind, to the northeast, and are continuing to drift, with sea anchor deployed. Crew is fine, and so is the cosmo-naut." He released the button and turned the thumbwheel up until he could clearly hear the static, waiting for a response.

There was none.

He was bringing the radio to his mouth to transmit again, when he saw the sea begin erupting between them and *Pursuit*. Michael and Svetlana had been watching his face as he talked; when they saw his change of expression, they whipped around to look.

It seemed like the waves were calming somehow, and then as if they were parting. The dark water went suddenly clear in the sunlight, weirdly distorting up and over some unseen shape, the waves turning white as they broke alongside it.

Emerging from the depths, the broad, jet-black hull of an enormous submarine crested out of the water. All three of them looked back along its length to the upthrust conning tower, its diving planes protruding out like stubby wings. There were no markings on the glistening black hull; it was like a monstrous metal whale, unexpectedly there beside them.

A head appeared over the edge of the conning tower, and a megaphone appeared. They heard a brief squeal and then a male voice hailed them in Russian, the sound distinct above the wind and the waves.

"Major Gromova, welcome back to Earth. We are launching a rescue boat. Stand by to be brought aboard."

"Holy shit!" Michael yelled. "Chad, I don't know what he just said, but we need Navy helo support ASAP!" As they watched, a hatch pivoted open on the submarine's forward deck, and men started climbing out onto the wet flat surface.

Chad nodded, his mind racing. He pushed the button again on the radio. "Rescue Forces, this is the Apollo 18 crew. A submarine has surfaced and they're taking the cosmonaut. Need assistance immediately."

Twenty-five miles away, the Sea King flight engineer hurried back from the cockpit, stopping in front of Kaz.

"Commander, we just got contact with the Apollo crew." He tilted his head towards the cockpit. "You're the senior officer, and the pilot needs you on the radio now, sir." He looked at Colombo. "You too, PO."

They followed him to the cockpit, where he handed Kaz headphones and showed him where the transmit button was. Colombo donned a second pair to listen.

"Apollo 18, Apollo 18, Kaz here, how do you read me?" Kaz spoke loudly above the helo's noise, holding one earphone tight against his head.

Chad's voice came back, crackling with static. "Kaz! We're in the raft, and there's a Commie submarine here! They're launching a boat to come take the cosmonaut."

Shit! Kaz turned and yelled to the pilot. "How long to get there?"

"We're twenty-four miles out—nine minutes."

Kaz pushed the mic button. "Copy, Chad, we'll be there in nine minutes. Two helos, one with . . ." He stopped himself, realizing that the Russian sub would be listening to their communications. He looked out the side window at the other chopper and turned to the flight engineer. "Is that helo on this freq?"

A nod.

"Helo 501, get Dr. McKinley on the radio." As he waited, Kaz talked urgently with the pilot and flight engineer, briefing possible options.

JW's voice was in the headsets. "Dr. McKinley's listening."

Kaz updated him on the situation and what he wanted them to do.

JW's voice was crisp. "Copy, Kaz, I'll let this crew know."

All eyes strained forward, trying to spot the splashdown site. The flight engineer tapped the pilot's shoulder, pointing slightly left. "There it is!"

Low in the water, barely visible on the horizon, the long black shape of the submarine glinted in the sunlight, its conning tower jutting squarely up. Just visible was the splash of yellow of the raft. Kaz talked hurriedly with Colombo, who went back to brief his men.

In the raft, Chad held the radio out to Michael. "You direct them in."

Michael took it, puzzled, as Chad grabbed the open survival kit and dragged it forward. Kaz's voice rattled loudly in Michael's hand. "We're seven minutes out. Sitrep."

Michael looked across at the sub. "They have a black Zodiac on deck, and it looks like two frogmen are getting in to head this way." He squinted, trying to see detail. "Looks like they're armed, Kaz!"

As Michael was speaking, Chad turned away from Svetlana, his suit blocking her view. He dug into the survival kit bag, found what he was looking for and slid it into his leg pocket. As he turned, she spoke to him in Russian.

"Where is it?"

He looked at her. "What?"

She spoke rapid-fire. "I know you understand me! Stop being an idiot. The stone! Where is Lunokhod's stone?"

Chad frowned, shaking his head. "Don't understand you, toots." He glanced at Michael. "Any idea what she wants?"

Michael shrugged. "Beats me." He looked across at the Soviet Zodiac, now in the water. "How do you want to handle this?"

They heard the outboard motor sputter to life and saw a white curl start under the Zodiac's bow. Chad yelled, "If that helo doesn't get here in time, then there's not much we can do. She belongs to them, and they came all this way to get her."

Svetlana looked back and forth at the two men, and then at the Zodiac. Time to act. She reached down, unzipped her leg pocket, pulled out the pistol and pointed it at Chad.

"We are out of time. Give me the stone. Now!"

Michael stared, incredulous, and pushed the transmit button on the radio as he yelled, "Chad, she's got a gun!"

"I see that." Chad's voice was calm as he looked directly at her, shaking his head slowly. "Whatever you want, girly, I don't have it." He pointed across the prow of the sub at *Pursuit*. "Did you forget something in the spaceship?" He pointed again. "Makeup, or something common?" He accented the last word.

Svetlana frowned. *Did he just say "kahmen"?* The Russian word for stone. She snorted in frustration and shouted at him again. "Stop playing games! Is the stone inside the capsule?"

Chad nodded yes. "That's right, toots, you keep babbling. Your cavalry's almost here to rescue you."

Michael felt paralyzed. *Where the fuck did she get a gun? And what does she want?* He kept his thumb on the mic button, holding it down.

The outboard motor whine of the submarine's inflatable Zodiac was loud now, pulsing as it neared, rising and falling with the waves. Svetlana kept the pistol trained on Chad as the boat pulled alongside. The large, wet-suited submariner in the bow looked at the scene in the raft and turned laughing to his only crewmate. In Russian he said, "Looks like she doesn't need our help." His smile was broad as they reached and grabbed for the handles on the raft. "Major Gromova, we're here to rescue you."

She unleashed a torrent of Russian at him. His smile disappeared. He looked back at the capsule in the distance, and then at the sky to the northeast. He reached down with his free hand and lifted a Kalashnikov submachine gun, cradling it, waving it urgently at Michael and Chad. He spoke in thickly accented English. "Get een!"

Michael looked to Chad, who raised his palms. The Soviet reached across and took the radio, handing it to the helmsman by the motor, then grabbed Michael's arm and tumbled him onto the Zodiac's plank floor.

Svetlana was still pointing her pistol, and she ordered Chad in Russian: "You next." Chad shrugged and climbed across, the sailor grabbing him by his suit's neck ring and pushing him into place next to Michael.

Svetlana pocketed her pistol, stood to haul in the sea anchor line with both hands and passed the end to the Russian. Timing it carefully with the surging waves, she stepped neatly between the boats. The helmsman revved the outboard, and with the raft now trailing, steered hard towards the bow of the submarine and the capsule beyond.

Thinking about what Svetlana had shouted at him, the lead sailor put his face close to Chad's, his large, black-suited body menacing. "Vere is it?"

Michael was watching. *Where is what? What's going on?*

Chad had a strange smile on his face. *Excellent! This one speaks English! That'll make it simple!* He glanced at Michael. "I think they want some of our moonrocks." He turned and looked into the sailor's face. "Never had any of their own, and now I guess they think they deserve some." He looked up at the Navy helicopters, just visible in the distance. "But it looks like we're gonna capture the flag, Ivan. What are you going to do about it?"

This is going to work, just like I figured! The Soviets could have their precious cosmonaftka back, but the US would get the real prize. And all because of him.

The slap was sudden and totally unexpected, making the impact feel worse; the sailor's full-handed blow rocked Chad's head violently to the side. The sailor spoke again, his accent thick. "I ask once more. Vere is the radioactivni kahmen—the radioactive stone?"

"Hey, you can't do that!" Michael protested. The sailor twisted and shoved him violently towards the bow, and the helmsman raised his Kalashnikov to hold him there. Chad was shaking his head slowly, his hand going to the spreading red mark on his cheek.

Svetlana looked sharply at the submariner. "Did you say the stone is radioactive?"

He nodded. "That's what Moscow told us."

She growled in frustration. *Idiots! Why didn't they tell me!*

She moved rapidly towards Chad and frisked his suit, probing forcefully for a distinctive rounded shape. She turned to the sailor. "Not there. It must still be in the capsule." She looked across at the helicopters, and down at the scuba tanks strapped to the floor next to her. *There's still time!* She spoke quickly, and the sailor began rapidly assembling and donning equipment.

She turned back to Chad. "If you don't answer right now, he's going to hit you again and then force you underwater to show him. Where did you hide the stone?"

Chad was still blinking to clear his head, and Michael answered for him. "He doesn't understand Russian, Svetlana! Leave him alone!"

She yelled at him. "Molchi!" Be silent! She turned back to Chad. "Last chance!"

He stared at her, dazed and defiant.

"Bah!" she said in frustration, and turned to the sailor. "He's yours. And hurry, before the Americans can get into the water!"

The two crewmen forced straps over Chad's arms, tightened the waist belt and mashed the rubber regulator against his lips. Chad kept his teeth closed, and the lead sailor shrugged. *He'll want to breathe eventually.* He pulled a long, sharp knife from his leg holster and reached in by Chad's neck, puncturing the airtight rubber seal, and then the two men lifted Chad up and threw him into the sea. The submariner had on his tank and flippers; he pulled on a mask, sat on the inflated edge and neatly pivoted over the side. Grabbing Chad by the neck ring, he dragged him underwater and started swimming hard, descending towards the inverted capsule.

JW's voice crackled into Kaz's ear. "Kaz, did you copy that?"

The voices had faded in and out during the long transmission from the Apollo 18 crew. "I heard something, Doc, but couldn't make it out."

"I think I heard Michael say something about a gun!"

Kaz nodded. "Yeah, it's no surprise that the Soviets are armed. We're ready here too."

"Copy." JW paused. "Be safe."

"Wilco."

Kaz took a final look out the forward windows of the Sea King. The pilot had slowed, approaching the situation cautiously. Behind him, Kaz heard the big side cargo door sliding open, and could feel the buffeting air from the rotors. He leaned forward to the pilot. "All set?"

The pilot nodded, focusing on positioning where they'd briefed. Kaz moved aft and yelled to Colombo, "The crew's all in the Soviet Zodiac now, and they're headed towards the capsule. Your men ready?" He glanced at the wet-suited figures, all standing, holding on to the overhead straps with one hand, their weapons with the other.

"Yep, all set." A large block was on the floor by the open door. The helo's flight engineer leaned out the side, talking on headset with the pilot, guiding him into position. As the Sea King slowed and then settled its belly into the water, he kicked the block out and tugged on its line. It released a large raft, which began rapidly inflating.

Kaz felt a tap on his shoulder and turned to see Stepanov standing next to him, shouting above the noise. "Commander Zemeckis, I need to be in that raft to assist my countrywoman."

Kaz shook his head. "No way."

Stepanov was intent. "Think. You will need translation."

Kaz quickly pictured what was likely to happen. *Shit, he's right, and the Captain had insisted.* He looked at the size of the Navy men. *Worth the risk.* He nodded reluctantly and held up an open hand. *Wait.*

Colombo was loading his team and their gear into the six-sided raft as it bounced up and down in the rough seas. He turned to Kaz, who indicated Stepanov and yelled "Translator!" and pointed out the door. Colombo shrugged and guided the Russian into waiting hands in the raft.

"You're next, sir!" he shouted. Kaz felt in his leg pocket for the Navy-issue Colt pistol the PO had given him, and stepped out into the raft, dropping to the floor for stability. Colombo followed immediately. The noise from the helicopter increased as its blades dug in and lifted it, dripping, out of the water. The downwash covered them with spray as the pilot maneuvered clear.

The first crewman into the raft had attached lines to *Pursuit*, and they pitched and heaved in the waves next to it.

Step one, Kaz thought. *Capsule upside down, but secured.* He turned to look downwind. The Zodiac had stopped 50 feet away, holding position using the little outboard, the yellow raft trailing, the sub in the distance. But something was wrong. He looked closely, frowning, counting: There weren't enough white and black suits! Where did the others go? *Shit!* What had he missed while they were boarding their raft?

He turned to Colombo. "I need to get inside the capsule. Now!"

With no mask on, Chad was blinded by the salt water. His lungs were starting to burn, demanding air, and he reached down and back, grabbing the scuba tank hose. He thrust the regulator into his mouth, exhaled sharply to clear the water out and then took a welcome deep breath, hearing the familiar ringing sound of compressed air feeding from the tank on his back.

He let himself be pulled along. *Might as well let this Russian tire himself out, doing all the work.* He patted down his suited leg, feeling for what he'd put into the pocket. *Good. Still there.*

With the cut rubber neck seal, water was flowing into his suit, bubbles working their way up past his face, making him heavy in the water. *Need to be careful. The bottom of this pool is a long way down.*

The sailor stopped pulling. Blinking his eyes, Chad could make out the shape of *Pursuit* silhouetted against the light from the surface. He felt strong hands pushing him, and suddenly his head was through the hatch and into the air still trapped inside the capsule. He spit out the regulator and raised himself up into the familiar cockpit.

Didn't think I'd be back here so soon.

He felt bumping from behind and squirmed himself to the side as the sailor emerged through the hatch, pulling off his mask. He reached down towards his fins, and when his hand came back up it was holding his long, curved diving knife. He held it close to Chad's face.

"Vere is the stone?"

Chad turned and pointed above the Russian. "In a bag up there, behind the R2 panel." When the sailor turned to look, Chad opened his pocket and slid his hand inside.

"Vere? You show me!"

"I will," Chad said. His hand arced up fast, clenching the machete he'd taken from the survival kit. With all his strength he twisted and slashed, aiming just below the Russian's chin into the exposed softness of his neck.

The submariner's instant, primal reaction was to lash back at the sudden pain and shock of being wounded. Taking Chad by surprise, he drove his diving knife hard forward, a spasm driven by a surge of adrenaline. The tip plunged through the layers of the white spacesuit, past the liquid cooling garment and deep into the flesh, muscle and gut of Chad's belly.

Blood spurted from both men's wounds and they fell back, stunned. Each did a fast internal assessment. *Is this it? Am I fatally hurt?* And then, *How will I know?* Chad's hands went slack and the machete fell, clattering onto the metal below.

In that brief frozen moment, bubbles appeared in the water at the hatch. A head came up through the surface, and when Svetlana raised her mask, she stared in disbelief. Blood was spurting from the severed artery in the sailor's neck, around the fist he had pushed into it, trying to staunch the flow. Chad was lying back on the instrument panel, his hands clutching at the handle of a knife buried in his stomach.

"You morons!" she screamed.

She pulled herself up next to the sailor and slapped his fumbling hand away, reaching in to see if she could apply direct pressure to stop the bleeding, but immediately saw there was no use. The cut was wide and deep; there were foaming pink bubbles and exposed meat and tendons where the knife had sliced through his trachea and jugular. Each gush of blood as his heart pumped was weaker. His eyes were wide, looking at her in disbelief. He tried to speak, but was unable, his air whistling out through the mortal wound.

She twisted in the small space to look at Chad, who was staring down with a concerned expression at the knife in his guts.

"How badly are you hurt?"

He looked up at her, saying nothing. The body of the sailor spasmed and slumped.

"Where is the stone?" she hissed.

Chad looked back down at the knife handle, puzzled, ignoring her.

After the two men had left the Zodiac she'd realized there was a better way to search for the stone. She spun now and reached up along the side of the instrument panel over her head, feeling for the tool Michael had used. Her fingers closed around the metal cylinder, and she pulled it down, twisting and turning it on. She looked at the dial of the Geiger counter, hearing it begin to click. She rapidly started moving from locker to locker, throwing open doors and reaching in, listening for a reaction.

She stopped as a better thought struck her. She turned and looked at Chad, who lay motionless, his eyes following her as she moved towards him. She touched the rounded end of the tube to the fabric of his suit, starting by his feet and moving up his legs, swinging it left and right.

As she passed his knees she heard extra clicks. Sweeping up his thighs the clicking increased, the noise becoming a continuous chatter. She kept going, up his torso, but the sound decreased, so she moved it back down until she got maximum signal.

The bastard had hidden the stone in his crotch. He looked at her, his skin ashen, and managed to smile. "Right by the family jewels."

How to get it out? The spacesuit's long zipper was in the back, clumsy to get at, and time was short.

She looked at the knife in his belly. It sickened her to think of pulling it out. *But how did he cut the sailor? There must be a second knife!* She glanced around below Chad and spotted the machete.

She pulled the cloth of Chad's suit taut and hurriedly began cutting. She hacked through the white outer cloth and the layers of metal-coated plastic. Her fingers dug in, making an opening as she sliced into the airtight rubberized nylon.

Chad tried to push her away. She grabbed the knife handle sticking out of his belly with her other hand, and twisted. He screamed, and she kept cutting.

The innermost layer was the toughest, with hundreds of plastic cooling tubes sewn into a tight mesh against his skin, but once she cut a small hole in the woven fabric it parted, and she was through. She saw fresh blood; she'd cut his upper leg. *No matter.*

She reached into the slit with both hands, opening it as wide as she could, and then slid one hand between his legs. She felt the cloth of a bag with a hardness inside it, and worked her fingers underneath, prying it out. Like extracting the head of a newborn, she squeezed it through the layers, and with a final yank, the bag came clear. She grabbed the Geiger counter and held it close to the blood-smeared surface; the clicking went crazy.

As she turned to stuff the bag into a leg pocket, Chad grabbed onto the neck ring of her spacesuit. "Dye minyeh!" His voice was strained, but his Russian was clear. "Give it to me!" In his free hand he held the machete she'd set down while extracting the bag.

She reached for the knife in his belly, but he slashed at her hand, cutting across her knuckles. "No, no, toots," he gasped. "I'm planning to live through this." He beckoned with his free hand and repeated his demand. "Dye minyeh!"

She twisted away from him in the confined space, reaching deeper into the leg pocket. Turning back, she raised the pistol and pointed it at him. "Nyet!"

A voice spoke loudly from below them. "Don't move!"

Kaz climbed into the cockpit, his pistol rock-steady, aiming at Svetlana's head.

59

Pursuit

"Well, isn't this a pretty little Mexican standoff," Chad grunted. "Or should I say Russian?" He smiled at his own joke, and grimaced.

Keeping his gun on Svetlana, Kaz flicked his gaze around the cockpit, taking in the bloodied wet-suited body and the knife in Chad's belly.

"You okay, Chad?"

"Never better, buddy." His voice was raspy.

"I know you speak Russian. Ask her what she wants."

"I do *what*, Kaz? How would I know how to speak Russian?"

Svetlana kept her gun trained on Chad, listening to the men.

"Chad, it's no longer a secret. We know you've been in contact with your brother in East Berlin for years, and that you've been communicating with the Soviets, even while you were on the Moon. Dammit, you speak Russian. Ask her!"

Chad's voice was slurring now. "I don't need to ask her anything, Kaz. She's already got what she wants. She just stuffed it into her pocket!"

Svetlana pivoted fast and fired point blank at Kaz; as he saw her move he squeezed his trigger. The two shots sounded in rapid succession, the noise deafening in the small space. Her bullet had spun Kaz, a sudden slam on his left side. She pushed forward past him, straightened her body and fell through the open hatch into the water.

He looked down, fearing the worst, seeing blood on his left upper arm. No pain yet. *Fuck!*

Colombo's head popped up through the hatch. "I just saw someone in a spacesuit swim out, and I heard shots! You okay, Commander?" He looked around the capsule, his eyes widening. "Holy shit!"

"Yeah, I just got dinged. But Chad needs a doctor ASAP, and I need to stop the cosmonaut. Go topside and call the other helo for medical help, now!"

"Aye aye, sir." Colombo disappeared.

Kaz looked at Chad, speaking rapidly. "We haven't got the proof yet, but we know you're guilty of Tom's helo sabotage, and that you've been taking money from the Soviets. Time to get your story straight, Chad. It's not going to be pretty."

He clumsily pulled his mask back on one-handed, shoved his regulator into his mouth and slid down through the hatch.

Guilty! Is that what Kaz said?

The word echoed in Chad's head, and he moaned. He wasn't guilty! He was a hero! He alone had found what the damned Russians wanted and had been bringing it back to the good guys. He looked at the bloody body on the other side of the cockpit. *Shit, I was stabbed defending it.*

He looked down at the handle of the knife protruding from his belly. A wave of pain surged through him, a burning agony like the center of his body was on fire. As it subsided he reached into the hole the cosmonaut had cut in his suit, then pulled his hand out, wiggling his wet fingers, looking at the dripping red of fresh blood. Realizing what it meant. Realizing what Kaz had said about sabotage and money, and what would happen to him now that they knew.

Get my story straight! He closed his eyes against another wave of pain, and everything went searingly, blindingly white in his head. It took longer to pass.

I'm an action hero! He visualized the words, like they were floating in front of him on the cover of a comic book. He nodded, a smile curling his lips. *I need to keep it that way.*

Time to take one more action.

He reached up and unlatched the locker near his head, pulling out the strap that was attached to one of the vacuum-sealed containers of moon-rocks. He clipped the free end to the ring on his suit, then reached up again. The pain of pulling the heavy box out made him scream. He worked it past the edge, the agony a cascading roar in his head, until the box over-balanced, tumbling and banging violently past him, towards the hatch.

The tether yanked tight, hauling him after the box. The handle of the knife banged on metal as he was pulled through the hatch into the water; he shouted with the added pain, emptying his lungs. The weight dragged him clear of *Pursuit*, the white of his suit and red of his blood catching the fading light as he fell straight down into the blackness of the deep.

As consciousness faded, Chad reached up with his fingertips, feeling through the heavy cloth around his neck, finding the small, comforting lump of the silver pendant against his chest. His final thought before the world went black was of the gentle, loving smile of his mother.

In the raft beside the inverted capsule, the Soviet attaché had been watching and listening. He'd kicked his shoes off and worked his way around next to the jumble of diving equipment. As Colombo burst to the surface yelling urgently for a radio, Stepanov took advantage of the confusion. With all eyes turned away, he smoothly grabbed a tank, mask and fins, and rolled over the side. Easily donning the equipment under-water, he cleared his mask and looked around. Spotting what he was looking for, he pulled his switchblade from his pocket, flicked it open and swam hard in pursuit.

Kaz was kicking his fins as urgently as he could, pulling with his good arm, holding the pistol in his other hand, breathing heavily through the regulator. The salt water stung sharply in his wound. He'd glanced up to see the capsule and raft against the light, getting his bearings, and hoped he had the direction towards the Zodiac right. *She'll have done the same thing,* he reasoned. He strained his eyes forward, trying to spot her motion ahead of him.

How could my bullet have missed? She was right there! But she'd moved sideways as they shot, so it was possible. He hoped he'd at least winged her. Slowed her down.

He saw a flash of white ahead of him, and then another, and could see he was gaining on her. They'd chosen the same depth, about 15 feet down, just deep enough to not be easily seen from the surface. Both of them were swimming hard, but the bulk of her suit was slowing her. He listened to his labored breathing, the air squealing through the scuba valves as his lungs demanded continuous deep breaths, each stroke getting him nearer.

Kaz felt a sudden hard pull on his leg from behind, a strong hand grabbing and holding his calf. *What the fuck?* He spun in the water and recognized the gleaming bald head of Stepanov. One of his hands was gripping Kaz's leg, and the other was holding something that glinted in the watery light.

Kaz jackknifed hard, twisting and kicking violently, trying to free his leg from the attaché's grasp. Stepanov's arm arced towards Kaz's belly, a long, silver knife held firmly in his fist, the motion slowed by the resistance of the water. Kaz had to get inside the knife's trajectory; he grabbed Stepanov's shoulder strap and pulled violently, the pain searing in his arm. As their upper bodies slammed into each other, the knife curved in behind him and clanged hard into his tank.

Stepanov's grunt was audible through his mouthpiece. He released Kaz's thrashing leg and grabbed his webbed waist belt, stabilizing and then twisting his upper body. With the improved leverage, the knife once more came slashing through the water. Kaz was bashing at Stepanov's head with the pistol, knocking his mask off, but it had no effect. The slicing blade was going to make contact. Out of options, Kaz turned the pistol's hard metal nose against Stepanov's head and pulled the trigger.

The explosion blew the water out the end of the barrel in an intense high-speed blast wave that rocked the attaché's head sideways, away from the muzzle. But the 45-caliber bullet behind the wave was still going near normal exit speed, and it slammed into his skull at 750 feet per second, tearing through bone and brain. Stepanov's body went instantly limp, and the knife fell from his fingers, down into the abyss.

Kaz's heart was pounding. *Holy Christ!* He pushed Stepanov away and turned to look for the cosmonaut, spotting the white of her suit. She'd turned and was looking back at him. *Must have heard the gunshot*, he realized. Hoping he wasn't too late, he swam hard towards her.

He stopped far enough away to be mindful of the pistol in her hand, and held his up as well. Bullets didn't travel far underwater, but surfacing would be a different game. A hard game to win.

He saw that Svetlana was now fumbling with her leg pocket. *Shit!* he yelled, the word unrecognizable through his mouthpiece. He thrust forward, kicking and pulling to swim below the cosmonaut, diving deeper, looking up. As he watched, she let go of something white and then started swimming hard for the surface.

The object was falling fast. He swam as hard as he could, willing himself to intercept it, dropping the pistol and pulling the water with both hands, ignoring the pain in his arm. His lungs couldn't draw enough air out of the tank, and he was seeing red as the heavy object fell past his depth. He gave one last pulsing heave with his arms and legs, stretched out to his maximum reach, and grabbed for it, feeling his fingers close on a cloth bag, heavy with weight.

Dazed with the effort and pain, Kaz just floated, suspended, inhaling deeply. As he regained his breath, he carefully squeezed the bulky bag into his coverall leg pocket with his good hand, listening to the distinctive underwater whine of an outboard motor above. Looking straight up, he could see Svetlana splashing at the surface. And coming in fast from his right, the pointed black silhouette of the Zodiac.

He kicked hard, blowing excess air from his lungs as he ascended, watching as the boat coasted to a stop. Looking up, he saw the white-suited figure disappear out of the water and then oddly reappear, splayed and splashing, as if thrown back in. Just as he breached the surface, he heard the motor crank back up to full speed, and saw the boat turn abruptly and speed away.

Kaz swam through the waves towards the person in the water and was unsurprised to see that it was Michael, his suit over-buoyant, spread-eagling him faceup on the roiling surface. Kaz looked towards the sound of the Zodiac and spotted it pounding away through the crests towards the submarine.

"Michael, you okay?" His voice sounded odd to him, the words taken away by the wind.

"I'm fine, Kaz. So good to see you—that was nuts!"

Kaz's arm was screaming with pain in the motion of the waves. Holding on to the buoyancy of Michael's suit, he felt a surge of dizziness, dimming his vision. He heard the sound of a helicopter, and then some loud splashes next to him.

"Geez, Kaz, I leave you alone for ten minutes and look what happens!" JW was next to him in the water, supporting him, sliding a life jacket over his good arm. Two Navy divers were next to Michael. The Sea King dropped more divers and a raft; experienced hands grabbed Kaz under the arms and lifted him cleanly in, propping him against the inflated side, next to Michael. JW appeared beside him with scissors, neatly cutting off the sleeve of his coveralls at the shoulder and frowning at the bullet hole through his bicep.

He soaked the wound liberally with disinfectant, the added pain clearing Kaz's head, and quickly wrapped it in gauze and bandage and pulled it into a sling. He looked critically at his work. "That'll do for now."

Kaz fumbled for his leg pocket with his good hand, trying to pull out the white bag.

"Let me do that!" JW scolded. He worked it free and held it up, the weight swinging with the boat's motion.

"What's in there?" Michael asked.

"A good question," Kaz said. "Open it, Doc."

JW slid the zipper open, looked inside and glanced quizzically at Kaz. Frowning, he carefully reached in and pulled out a Soviet pistol by the tip of the barrel.

"Where did you find this?"

Kaz blinked twice, then scrambled to sit tall to see over the edge of the raft, turning to look at the submarine. The Zodiac was already stowed, and there were a few submariners working to close the forward hatch, the big boat beginning to move forward. A smaller, white-suited figure was standing facing him. She saluted suddenly, waved once and disappeared into the submarine.

Kaz watched for several long seconds after she'd gone, then raised his fingertips to the corner of his good eyebrow. He held them there for a moment, then lifted his hand and waved back.

60

Galveston Beach, Texas

"Hold my hand?"

It was evening, and the sun was just disappearing, the rich red light reflecting off the crests of the low, curling waves. Kaz had driven them out past the western edge of Galveston, beyond the lights, to where there was nothing but tall grass dunes, the flat of the coarse brown sand, and the endless Gulf of Mexico to the south. Small, stiff-legged birds hurried along the waterline, hunting for one last morsel before dark.

Laura slipped her hand into his, and they walked on the hard sand in silence, enjoying the quiet. Thankful for it.

Kaz looked up, and stopped. The Moon had waned to a delicate, thin arc, a sliver catching the sunlight. In the darkening sky he could barely make out the ghostly shadows of the flooded lava plains, and squinted to try to see the small circle of Mare Serenitatis. Luke's resting place.

Laura followed his gaze. "How did it go this morning?"

Kaz sighed. "I hate funerals," he said. "Arlington Cemetery is such a sad, beautiful place. But it was nice for the families. The Vice President came, and Sam Phillips. Michael gave a good speech at the graveside to honor his crewmates." Kaz looked bleakly at Laura. "Luke's parents just sat there in their seats, trying to understand what had happened to their boy. Admiral Weisner presented them with Luke's medals, including the Navy Cross." He paused. "Posthumous."

He could see tears welling in Laura's eyes. "Chad's folks were sitting beside them. Such nice people. So proud to be honoring their son, but forever sad that it had to be at Arlington." He started walking again. The military had decided to honor both men there, near where the other fallen astronauts had been buried. He and Al Shepard had reluctantly agreed.

"Much media there?" Laura asked.

Kaz shook his head. "No, none of the details of what happened have been released yet, and they asked to keep it just for family. They're calling the deaths 'classified under investigation' for now. As soon as Nixon and Brezhnev have a chance to meet, they'll make a formal announcement about Svetlana on the Moon, and find a way to spin it all so both sides look good." He shook his head. "So the two of *them* look good."

He glanced at Laura. "Have you had a look at the container of moon-rocks that made it back yet?"

She nodded, excitement creeping into her voice. "Sure have. We got the samples that were near Lunokhod, and mostly it's what we expected to see. But there were two small fragments that were a total surprise. A whole different type of morphology, like they were both broken off of one larger piece. And incredibly, when we checked closely, they're highly radioactive!" She shook her head. "As soon as we found that out, the military took charge, and everything's hush-hush until they decide what to do with the information."

Kaz kept walking, staring to the west, thinking. A small smile on his face.

Laura asked the question that everyone in the Lunar Receiving Lab had wanted to know. "Think this discovery will mean there'll be another Moon mission?"

Kaz nodded slowly. "Yes, I expect so. Maybe not another Apollo, but having a potential power source on the Moon will be too hard for the DoD to pass up. And with Lunokhod having originally found it, the Soviets will be hustling for a better look as well." He smiled at her. "Should be a bonanza for lunar geologists."

The last glow of the sunset was fading, and stars were starting to appear. Laura looked across at Kaz's sling as they turned to retrace their steps.

"How's the arm?"

"Healing fine. Clean in and out." He lifted his elbow, and grimaced slightly. "Still hurts a bit, but JW says I should have the sling off in a few days."

Laura shook her head. "Whenever they let you, you'll have to tell me everything that happened at splashdown."

"I will," he promised.

They were walking east now, and Laura suddenly raised her arm, pointing just above the horizon. "Look, Kaz! Mars!" The wavering light of the distant planet shone redly in the darkness. "From what the Mariner orbiters have been showing us, that'll be a *real* geologists' bonanza. And NASA's building a Mars lander they're calling Viking, to be there in a couple years!"

"But by then you'll be too busy training as a Space Shuttle astronaut," he reminded her.

"I sure hope so." She looked closely at him in the near-darkness, the distant lights of Galveston on his face. "What are *your* plans, mister?" She'd been thinking about it, but asked the question lightly.

"Funny you should ask. Sam Phillips talked to me this morning about a new project starting up out west, in Nevada. And he and NASA want me to stay here to support any future Moon flights and Skylab." He smiled, looking squarely at her. "Lots of good reasons to be here."

As they walked, the events of the morning rolled back into Kaz's head, like a newsreel. He quietly described it to her. "After the bugler played 'Taps,' the Blue Angels did the flypast. Six F-4 Phantoms, my old jet, tight in formation, low across the graveyard.

"Just as they passed overhead, one of the wingmen pulled hard up and away to honor Luke and Chad, leaving a hole in the formation for the missing man." He shook his head. "It breaks my heart every time."

He glanced back up at the Moon. The funeral had made him think of a small orphan boy, alone and afraid long ago. And an aging monk on the other side of the Berlin Wall, trying to make sense of it all.

He squeezed Laura's hand tightly and led them up off the beach, two joined figures in the darkness under the endless, star-filled sky.

AUTHOR'S NOTE

The Reality Behind The Apollo Murders

As I suggested at the outset of this novel, many of the characters, events and things in *The Apollo Murders* are real. Their inclusion made writing the book great fun, and a complex challenge. Here's a quick summary, to save you googling.

REAL CHARACTERS

Andropov, Yuri. Chairman of the KGB, went on to be General Secretary/ leader of the Soviet Union

Bean, Al. Apollo 12 and Skylab astronaut, painter

Carius, Bob. Captain of the USS *New Orleans*

Chauvin, C.A. "Skip." NASA Apollo Spacecraft Test Conductor at Kennedy Space Center

Chelomei, Vladimir. Chief Designer and Director of spacecraft factory OKB-52 for the Proton rocket and Almaz

Dobrynin, Anatoly. Soviet Ambassador to the US, 1962–86

Haldeman, Bob. White House Chief of Staff, 1969–73

Heard, Jack. Harris County Sheriff, 1973–1984

Kissinger, Henry. US National Security Advisor, 1969–75

Kraft, Chris. Manned Spacecraft Center Director, 1972-82

Kranz, Gene. Flight Director, NASA, 1962–94

Latypov, Gabdulkhai "Gabdul." Soviet Air Forces Senior Lieutenant, Lunokhod driver

Nixon, Richard. US President, 1969–74

Phillips, Sam. USAF General, Apollo Program Director, 1964–69, National Security Agency Director, 1972–73

Schlesinger, James. Central Intelligence Agency Director, 1973

Serdyukov, Vasily. Captain of the Soviet submarine K-252

Shepard, Al. USN Admiral, test pilot, first American astronaut

Slayton, Deke. NASA Director of Flight Crew Operations, astronaut

Weisner, Maurice "Mo." USN Admiral, Vice Chief of Naval Operations, 1972–73

ALMAZ SPACE STATION The Soviet spy space station in the story was real, including the fact that it was armed with a Kartech R-23 machine gun. It launched, unmanned, on 3 April 1973, but was fatally damaged after two weeks by an explosion, and depressurized into a trail of debris before a crew could be launched to dock with it. Its orbit decayed until it burned up in the atmosphere on 28 May 1973. A subsequent Almaz station was also armed with the R-23 gun, which was fired once in a successful test.

APOLLO 18 The US originally planned to launch Apollo 18 and 19, and built most of the hardware, including the rockets, for both missions. President Nixon canceled them both due to budgetary and other pressures after the near-disaster of Apollo 13.

AREA 51 A secret center for stealth technology development and testing captured Soviet fighter aircraft in Nevada.

FEMALE COSMONAUTS The first woman in space was Valentina Tereshkova, who flew solo on Vostok 6 for nearly three days in 1963.

The next was Svetlana Savitskaya, a test pilot and 1970 world aerobatic champion. She flew in space twice in the early 1980s, including doing a spacewalk, and eventually retired from the Russian Air Force with the rank of major.

LUNOKHOD The Soviets landed several unmanned probes on the Moon. The Lunokhod rover in the story is real. It touched down in the Sea of Serenity on 15 January 1973, exploring and sending back extensive data. It accidentally brushed a crater wall on 9 May 1973, knocking moondust onto its radiator. It overheated and died two days later.

MANNED ORBITAL LABORATORY The US had a military spy space station program, and selected and trained test pilots for it, but it never flew, and was canceled in June 1969. Several of the MOL astronauts flew as part of the NASA astronaut corps. One of them would have been Major Robert H. Lawrence Jr., the first African-American astronaut, if he had not been killed in a USAF flying accident in 1967.

POLLY RANCH A real suburban Houston community based around a private runway, with houses and hangars combined. Several astronauts have lived there.

RADIOACTIVITY ON THE MOON The geology of the Moon as we understand it makes anything beyond low-level radioactive rock highly unlikely. Mars, though, with its immense Olympus Mons volcano and water processes, could well have concentrated radioactivity; we have found nearly 300 Martian meteorites on Earth, so some have very likely landed on the Moon.

RUSSIAN ORTHODOX CHURCH AND SPYING The KGB recruited translators inside the church in the 1970s in an attempt to entrap people of interest by maneuvering them into compromising situations.

SVETLANA'S PISTOL The Makarov Pistol was the Soviet Union's standard military and police sidearm for decades, and it was carried in the survival kit of their space capsules. In 1986 cosmonauts were issued a specially designed triple-barreled pistol called the TP-82 instead, with two 40-gauge shot and one 5.45 mm bullet. That's the weapon I trained with as a Soyuz pilot.

THE U-JOINT Fort Terry's Universal Joint was a favorite hangout during the Apollo era. During the Space Shuttle years, it became the Outpost. I spent many an evening there, and my picture joined the hundreds on the walls. It closed in 2009, and the building burned to the ground in 2010. I don't know where the swinging doors ended up.

TSUP MOSCOW MISSION CONTROL Soviet Mission Control, known by its acronym TsUP (ЦУП), is located in the Moscow suburb of Korolyov (Kaliningrad at the time of this book). It has been in operation since 1960, with an adjunct NASA office therein to support joint missions. I worked there multiple times.

YASTREB SPACEWALKING SUIT The suit that Svetlana and Andrei wore outside was real, developed at the time of the Almaz program. It was only used in space once, in 1969.

REFUGEE CHILD ADOPTIONS IN THE UNITED STATES Eleanor Roosevelt helped form USCOM, the United States Committee for the Care of European Children, which in conjunction with the Displaced Persons Act brought nearly 5,000 children orphaned in the Second World War to America.

ACKNOWLEDGMENTS

Writing this book took a daunting amount of research, often demanding expertise I'll never have. I want and need to thank each of these friends for their insights, help, ideas and corrections, and for earnestly trying to set me straight.

Shannon Abbott—schedule
Syd Burrows—the original one-eyed fighter pilot
Lindy Elkins-Tanton—planetary scientist
Paul Fjeld—artist and Apollo sage
David Forster—Polly Rancher
Tim Gregory—cosmochemist
Kata Hadfield—beloved daughter and trusted reader
Kristin Hadfield—beloved daughter and trusted reader
Walter Heneghan—helicopter pilot
Cheryl-Ann Horrocks—trusted reader
Alla Jiguirej—Star City oracle
Heather MacDonald—assistant
Mildred McElya—longtime Polly Rancher and
        Astronaut Office secretary
Leland Melvin—astronaut
Aaron Murphy—finance
Destin Sandlin—explainer of things
Rusty Schweickart—Apollo astronaut

Alex Shifrin—trusted reader
Judy Tanenbaum—trusted reader
Anatoly Zak—Russian Space Web

Most of all, enormous thanks and hugs to Jon Butler for the idea and the confidence, Rick Broadhead for his endless patience and attention to detail, and Anne Collins for her tenacity of clear purpose and enduring, unflagging support.